Ignis:
The Central Fire

Ignis:
The Central Fire

by
Comte Didier de Chousy

translated and annotated by
Brian Stableford

A Black Coat Press Book

ISBN 978-1-934543-88-7. First Printing October 2009. Published by Black Coat Press, an imprint of Hollywood Com-
ics.com, LLC, P.O. Box 17270, Encino, CA 91416.

Introduction

Ignis was initially published anonymously, in Paris in 1883, by Berger-Levrault & Cie. Three more editions appeared; the third and fourth editions, issued in 1884, bore the signature "Le Cte Didier de Chousy" and boasted that the book was an "Ouvrage couronné par l'Académie française" [work honored by the Académie Française], although there is no independent evidence of any such accolade. There are a few differences between the 397pp. first edition and the 395pp. fourth edition, mostly consisting of the addition or subtraction of entire paragraphs.

The identity of the "Comte de Chousy" remains something of a mystery, the only surviving evidence of the existence of such an individual being associated with two letters bearing that signature. The first of them, dated July 25 1872, was sent to the writer Charles Cros, asking to see him in order to discuss a publication project. No further details are contained in the letter, so we can only guess as to what the project might have entailed, but the likelihood is that the self-styled Comte had already begun work on *Ignis* and was in search of advice as to its prospects of publication when it was finished. Cros was unable to attend the meeting, but the correspondence did not end there; one further reference to it is preserved in the Cros family archives. The only tangible consequence appears to have been that Cros dedicated a poem, "Sultanerie" (initially published in *L'Hydropathe* in 1879) to "Le Comte de Chousy." The annotators of the 1964 edition of Cros' *Oeuvres complètes*, Louis Forestier and Pascal Pia, say that Chousy made a financial contribution to assist the publication of Cros' first collection of poems, *Le Coffret de Santal* [The Sandalwood Box] (1873), but there is no mention of any such contribution in Forestier's 1969 biography of Cros, so it is unclear what evidence there is to support the claim.

Cros would have been a reasonable choice for the author of a satirical scientific romance to contact about such advice because he was one of the few people, even in a time long before the gulf between "the two cultures" grew so wide as to seem unbridgeable, who divided his efforts between science and literature. In 1872, he was at the beginning of his career in both respects, but he had published two scientific pamphlets in 1869—one on a pioneering method of color photography and the other on possible methods for communication with other planets—and he was rapidly acquiring a reputation as a poet on the basis of periodical publications.

He was later to achieve a peculiar sort of fame after sending a letter to the Académie des Sciences in April 1877 describing a device he called the paleophone, which was very similar to the one that Thomas Edison patented a few months later as the phonograph. Although most of his poetry and dramatic work has no speculative content, Cros did publish a number of short stories whose originality and imaginative scope suggested that he might have became one of the most important precursors of French scientific romance had he not died prematurely, at the age of 46, in 1888. One of those stories, "Une drame interastral" [An Interstellar Drama], appeared in *La Renaissance littéraire et artistique* in August 1872, shortly after the meeting requested in the letter from the author of *Ignis*; if, as is quite possible, the story had previous been read aloud at a literary salon, the author of *Ignis* might have been aware of it before publication and it might have prompted his letter.

The second letter bearing the Comte de Chousy's signature was a note addressed to the Comte de Villiers de l'Isle-Adam thanking him for *L'Eve future* (1887; tr. as *Tomorrow's Eve*), of which Villiers had presumably sent him a complimentary copy. If so, it presumably signifies that Villiers had read *Ignis* and was aware of its relationship to his own novel—both texts feature humanoid machines. Whether the two men were more closely acquainted is difficult to tell, but Villiers and Charles Cros were good friends and occasional collaborators, and it might well have been Cros who initiated the link between the two Comtes. No other contemporary record survives

6

of "le Comte de Chousy," which might well have been a pseudonym, but the previous history of the title is easy enough to determine.

The title Comte de Chouzy (with a "z"), derived from the town of Chouzy-sur-Cisse, belonged in the days of the *Ancien Régime* to the Mesnard family. Its most famous holder was Didier-François-René Mesnard, Comte de Chouzy (1729-1794), who was a member of Louis XVI's inner circle of courtiers and also a member of the Académie des Sciences, in his capacity as a pioneer of economic science. His close association with the King was, however, his downfall; he and most of his immediate family fell prey to the Terror and were guillotined, including his son and heir apparent, Jean-Didier Mesnard de Chouzy (1757-1794). The title did not die with him, however; after the Restoration, Albert-Didier Mesnard, Comte de Chouzy served as a *gentilhomme de chambre* to Charles X. Albert's wife, Louise, bore him three children, but all of them were female, so he produced no direct heir to the title.

What became of the title of Comte de Chouzy thereafter is unclear, but it was by no means unknown for titles that had effectively become extinct to be picked up by anyone who fancied that he might have a claim to it, with or without official sanction. Villiers de l'Isle-Adam's grandfather had been a humble Villiers until he took it into his head to adopt the extinct title of the Villiers de l'Isle-Adams who had distinguished themselves in days of yore, and his descendants' pride in the title was all the more fervent for it. When another Villiers, who had never heard of the writer, decided to adopt what he considered to be an extinct title for himself, the two of them got into a frightful quarrel, and spent months on end in the national archives trying to find evidence of a firm genealogical link before agreeing that their entitlement was essentially equal (zero, on both sides) and that further dispute was unnecessary.

Given that "Chousy" was an established alternative spelling of Chouzy, and that the surname Mesnard had a bourgeois equivalent in Ménard (when Nicolas Rétif wanted to imply that he was an aristocrat, he changed the spelling of his name to Restif as well as adding the suffix "de la Bretonne," after a field that his father had once farmed), it is not entirely unlikely that a man named Ménard might have thought the seemingly redundant title of "Comte de Chousy" a plum ripe for picking in the latter half of the 19th century, especially if his fore-names included Didier, which the Mesnards had employed with insistent regularity.

It is, alas, not possible to take this chain of conjecture any further, but it might be worth observing that several of the present-day Didier Ménards with an internet presence are scientists of one sort or another, and the one thing of which we can be quite certain regarding the author of *Ignis* was that he was a scientist whose literary activity was a sideline, intent on using narrative as an instrument for the dramatization and dis-cussion of scientific ideas. The science in *Ignis* is not good science, by modern standards, but it reflects the science of its own day well enough—especially its central controversies. It is difficult to be certain as to what kind of scientist the author might have been, but the likelihood is that he was a pragmatic scientist rather than a theorist, perhaps a mining engineer. It is worth noting that *Ignis*' publisher, Berger-Levrault & Cie., was at the time a virtual specialist in scientific texts, and that *Ignis* was something of a departure from its normal policy. (It seems likely that the author financed its publication himself, and that its three reprintings resulted from his ordering more copies rather than from any success in the marketplace.)

Despite its four editions, *Ignis* attracted little notice at the time of its publication—far less than *L'Eve future*—but it did prompt Alfred Jarry, when he read it at a later date, to pro-duce a short article "Sur quelque romans scientifiques" [On Some Scientific Romances] for *La Plume* in 1903. Jarry couples *Ignis* with *L'Ève future* as significant predecessors of an interesting nascent genre (to which he had just made his own contribution with *Le Surmâle*), but seems to have been particularly delighted with the former:

"Among the more recent precursors of Wells it is necessary to cite not only Villiers de l'Isle Adam, whose extraordinary Hadaly has been resuscitated—has she not?—in our music halls, in the name of the *autovierge*,[1] but the author of *Ignis*, who remained anonymous until the third edition, in 1884,
in which it was abruptly revealed that the work was crowned
by the Académie Française and that the author's name is Didier de Chousy. The subject of *Ignis* is the industrial exploitation of the central fire, a project that an inventor discussed
further during the exposition of 1900. But what is entirely
remarkable about *Ignis*, and proves once more that writers of
scientific fiction are harbingers, is the depiction of the revolt
of machines that have become intelligent, of steam-humans, of
atmophytes—the automobile was not invented then."

Jarry's recommendation was enthusiastically seconded
by Pierre Versins in his *Encyclopédie de l'Utopie et de la
science-fiction* (1972), who describes the book as "un chef-
d'oeuvre" [a masterpiece] and "une merveilleuse satire de la
science" [a marvelous satire of science] and provides a long
account of its plot, heavily elaborated with quotes demonstra-
tive of its "humour splendide" [splendid humor]. This essay
helped to establish the novel's reputation as an important precursor of modern science fiction, and prompted its reprinting
by Slatkine.

Versins, not unnaturally, links the themes of *Ignis* to
those of Jules Verne, implying—probably correctly—that its
author must have drawn some inspiration from *Voyage au
centre de la Terre* (1864; rev. 1867; tr. as *Journey to the Centre of the Earth*) and *De la Terre à la Lune* (1865; tr. as *From
the Earth to the Moon*), and perhaps also from *Hector Servadac* (1877; tr. as *Off on a Comet*) and *Les Cinq cent millions
de la Bégum* (1888; tr. as *The Begum's Fortune*). Indeed, it is
possible to read *Ignis* as a satire on Verne's science fiction as
well as, or even rather than, science—which would put it into

---

[1] The "autovierge" was an automaton recently exhibited at the
Moulin Rouge.

9

the same literary category as Albert Robida's *Voyages très extraordinaire de Saturnin Farandoul* (1879; Black Coat Press tr. as *The Adventures of Saturnin Farandoul*)—but the primary inspiration for *Ignis* certainly came from recent actual events and contemporary scientific controversies, and his satire is aimed squarely at the real world rather than any fictional response to it.

The first satirical target to be receive a strong whiff of grapeshot in *Ignis* is not science *per se* but the capitalistic financing of large-scale technological projects. Several such projects are mentioned in the course of the plot, including the drilling of a railway tunnel through Mont Cenis in the Alps and various attempts to construct a Channel Tunnel between the coasts of England and France, but the most immediate inspiration for the first phase of the story was undoubtedly the exploits of Ferdinand de Lesseps (1805-1894), who had began his project to excavate a Suez Canal, according to plans drawn up by two French engineers, in 1854.

With the active support of Napoléon III and the Empress Eugénie, a campaign for public subscription was launched in a blaze of publicity, which raised a capital of 200 million francs, and the Compagnie universelle du canal maritime de Suez was formed in 1858. The project was eventually completed in 1869. De Lesseps was appointed a member of the Académie des Science in 1873, and subsequently lent his support a project to create an inland sea in the Sahara, as well as chairing a conference called in 1879 to draw up plans for the Panama Canal, work on which began in 1882 (although it was not to be completed for many years). The novel's account of the launch of the Central Fire Company is an evident echo of the hullabaloo occasioned by the Suez Canal Company.

The target for which the author of *Ignis* reserved his heavy ammunition, however, was the controversy raised by mid-19th century advances in geology and paleontology, which had already prompted major rows between devout men and freethinkers as to the age of the Earth and the duration of its human occupancy.

In the early years of the century, the great pioneer of comparative anatomy, Georges Cuvier (1769-1832) had produced an account of natural history that retained faith in the account of human history contained in *Genesis*, while conceding that the six days of creation mentioned therein must be metaphorical, and that the Earth must have endured for tens of thousands of years before humankind's appearance, but this view had been challenged by his most prestigious successor, Etienne Geoffroy Saint-Hilaire (1772-1844), a proto-evolutionist who would not concede that humankind was a special case and contended that human species must have existed long before the 6000-year period covered by Biblical chronology.

This controversy raged throughout the century, becoming hotter as further evidence emerged by degrees and evolutionary theory made unsteady headway, especially after the publication of Charles Darwin's *Origin of Species* in 1859. The author of *Ignis* throws himself into the controversy with a fine fervor, and the fact that he lined up on what was subsequently established as the wrong side should not be allowed to detract from the significance of his work as a precursor of modern speculative fiction.

Although the direct influence of *Ignis* on subsequent literary works is slight, the story does anticipate numerous themes and motifs that were to crop up in later works and contribute significant threads to modern science fiction. Foremost among them is the one pointed out by Jarry—the mechanical humans that are among the most striking early depictions of what subsequently became known as robots—but there are also fanciful digressions into such subjects as biological engineering, Utopian city planning, the possibility of brain control by means of electrical stimulation and the potential exhaustion of fossil fuels.

The author's handling of all these themes is blithely absurdist, in the tradition of Cyrano de Bergerac and Jonathan Swift, but—as is usual in such satire—the scathing humor is underlain by serious issues. The sharp parody of parliamentary democracy featured in connection with the revolt of the At-mophytes, although quite irrelevant to the plot, still has considerable bite today, easily appreciated in an era when parliamentary discussions are televised. The many digressions within the narrative make it something of a patchwork, but that is not entirely to its disadvantage.

Given that the plot of *Ignis* contains a climactic twist that is rather startling, in spite of its careful precorroboration, it would be unfair to give too much away in advance, so I shall postpone some of my comments of the novel's principal themes to an afterword, where a more detailed discussion of their propriety will not spoil any surprises. Suffice it to say here that, although the literary quality of some individual passages is undermined the author's obvious inexperience in writing fiction, and the plot is rambling, Jarry and Versins were right to call attention to the striking boldness of the novel's imagery and the highly original nature of some of its conjectures. *Ignis* is, as Versins contends, a masterpiece of sorts, and thoroughly deserves this belated translation, which will help to increase modern readers' insights into the roots of scientific romance and science fiction.

This translation has been made from a photocopy of the fourth edition, kindly supplied by Jean-Pierre Moumon, but I have compared that text carefully with the London Library's copy of the first edition and have supplied some of extra text featured in the first edition but omitted from the fourth in the form of footnotes, although the longest excision—a labyrinthine calculation sprawling over two pages whose conclusion was presumably wrong, since the final figures are amended—did not seem to me to be sufficiently interesting to reproduce in full; I have also footnoted one item of text added to the fourth edition that is not to be found in the first. It is perhaps surprising that the author did not take the opportunity to correct any of the several obvious misprints in the text while making these alterations.

Ignis poses several unusual challenges to the translator, particularly on account of the author's unusual syntax—which takes a cavalier attitude to the conventional requirement for sentences to contain verbs and is so productive of exceedingly long sentences that the text even takes time out to issue a rueful boast to that effect at one point—but I have met them as best I can.

I have made considerable efforts to preserve the flavor of the text, but I have taken slightly freer advantage than usual of the translator's prerogative to adjust grammar and syntax in the interests of preserving the narrative flow in the destination language. I have maintained almost all of the author's frequent tense-shifts, even though I suspect that a few of them might have arisen from forgetfulness rather than strategy. I was unable to reproduce the many puns in the original text, but I have added explanatory footnotes to a few for whose sake the author made the most strenuous effort; I can only apologize for the inevitable losses, in the confidence that the rest of the humor survives more-or-less intact.

The translation is, I fear, somewhat footnote-heavy, but I felt obliged to reproduce all of the author's own footnotes and thought it necessary to explain many other references to scientific, historical and philosophical matters that must have seemed rather esoteric in 1883, let alone today. In the interests of economy, I have left numerous references that are of no particular significance to the story unfootnoted, in order to concentrate on those of greater relevance.

I have not commented at all on the author's mathematical calculations, although some of them are highly suspect, but I have occasionally corrected figures that were obviously misprinted. I have also corrected a few misprinted names without comment, and have unified the usage of one forename that is given in two different versions in the printed text (Tom/William Barnett—I have preferred the latter).

The internal chronology of the novel is woefully inconsistent, containing numerous anachronisms, which appear to have resulted from the insertion before the publication of the first edition of substantial new material into a story whose original draft was probably written in snatches between 1864 and 1877. I have used footnotes to clarify the chronology as best I can.

Brian Stableford

IGNIS

Ignis unique latet; naturam amplectitur omnem
Cuncta, parit, renovat, dividit, unit, alit.[2]

Preface

Industrial and scientific enterprise, with which the following work is concerned, leaves in its wake the greatest ac-
complishments: drilling through mountains, the piercing of
isthmuses and other famous gigantic endeavors.

The success of this enterprise is so considerable, and its
results so fruitful, that the entire human race is making its fortune and, having become rich and happy, released from economic, social and political problems, has no more left to do
but live in the midst of the Edenic luxury of the new world it
has created. Is not this dream, to some extent, the reality of the
future?

It seems to be in conformity with the schemes of nature
that, before the Earth turns into the Moon and its inhabitants
perish, human beings will fertilize every furrow, gather all
growth and exhaust every well, just as the agriculturalist does
not abandon his field until the harvest is complete.

Now, the *central terrestrial fire*, the object of this study,
is a source of energy, heat, wealth and of immense protean
power, almost inexhaustible but so far unexploited. Attention
has been drawn to it, however; curiosity has been directed

---

[2] This couplet can be found in versions of Voltaire's *Diction-
naire philosophique* [Philosophical Dictionary] (1764) that
contain an entry on *Feu* [Fire] (not all of them do); it is Voltaire's own composition. It translates, approximately, as "Fire
is found everywhere and envelops all of nature, comprising,
begetting, rendering, dividing, unifying, separating."

toward it; and, at this very moment, some ingenious French engineer is drawing up the initial plans for the superb conquest and calculating with compasses and set-squares the routes opened up by the novelist.

Here, as in other works in which scientific truth has been combined with fable, the reader must expect severe tests: he will be projected into space, precipitated into the abyss, dragged from catastrophe to cataclysm, but by other routes, toward a different end and in a different spirit.[3]

---

[3] The first edition has some extra text concluding this preface: "For this book is, or at least has tried to be, as much a satire as a story. To mock chemistry, geology, philosophy, physics or mathematics is an immense audacity, and those grand dames of science would have a facile reply, if they deigned to make one. They would say that, like the fox in the fable, I find grapes hanging too high up to be sour, and that, in turning around the tree of science, I am mutilating its trunk and lacerating its branches for want of being able to gather its fruits— and what is worse for me is that they would be telling the truth."

PART ONE

Chapter One
In Which the Reader is Requested to Dress Up
(Black Suit and Gold-Rimmed Spectacles)

I beg you to accept my excuses for such a request, Sir, but we are in England, where etiquette is rigorous and one can only talk to someone after being formally introduced—and the meeting of the shareholders of the Central Fire Company, which will be taking place shortly, seems to me to provide a invaluable opportunity to introduce you to its founders.

I want a good impression to be created on both sides, in order to establish the basis of a mutual esteem and a cordial relationship, and so that my readers will be immediately recognized as readers of distinction in the elite society into which I am taking them. Would you, therefore, Sir and Madam, dress up before embarking on the following chapter and maintain, so to speak, a proper appearance for its duration. Nothing excessive, mind—no white cravat or bright straw-colored gloves, no horn-rimmed spectacles to make the eyes suggestive of oysters; elegance of dress consists, above all, of appropriateness to circumstance and environment. Everyone knows that Monsieur de Buffon, who put on his best suit to describe a horse, remained in his pullover to talk about a pig.[4]

---

[4] Georges-Louis Leclerc, Comte de Buffon (1707-1788) published 35 volumes of his comprehensive account of *Histoire naturelle* [Natural History] during his lifetime; nine more were added posthumously by other hands. The pomposity of his style became legendary, and the joking remark that he "put on formal dress" in order to write, save for occasional lapses, was very widely quoted—an obvious inspiration for this entire chapter.

These explanations will, I hope, suffice for you not to retain any resentment with regard to this necessity; you might even be grateful to me for having warned you. My God! I shall not give anyone away, but if I wanted to, I could name readers, even respectable ones, who could be caught reading in extremely negligent attitudes and costumes: the reader in the short and skimpy dressing-gown who curls up gracelessly with his feet on his hot-water bottle and his head under his lampshade, warming himself at both ends with the minimum of expense; the apoplectic reader who reads with his head low down and his feet on the mantelpiece, hoping, by means of this ruse, to deceive the circulation of the blood and make it rise up to his feet; the apathetic reader who reads for health reasons, as he eats vegetables; the ancient reader in his second childhood, who spells the words out aloud, confusing the lines with his magnifying-glass, failing to understand any of them, and shaking his head as he deplores the obscurity of contemporary authors; the summer reader cradled in his hammock after the fashion of Lamartine; the Sunday reader who takes a stroll in Romainville in a volume by Paul de Kock; the reader in the open street—a dangerous variety, which ought to be exterminated—who is recognizable, even at rest, by his tilted spectacles, keeping one eye on the road and the other on his book, a hat battered by collisions, and an umbrella with a handle carved into a paper-knife—which is the ultimate foppery on the austere turf of fashionable savants (the paper-knife! an implement for cutting books—what a fecund element of psychological diagnosis! an ivory knife, as big as a Turkish saber, which one brandishes over a book, and which makes its pages shudder like leaves); the reader without a knife, whose moistens the edge with his tongue and separates it by absorption; the passionate reader, who turns the page immediately, at any price, cutting it with his hand, his toothbrush or his shoehorn in such a way that the edges of the volume are torn and thus made ragged, reminiscent while being read of a paper poodle.

Female readers, especially blondes, gently cut the pages with the filed fingernails of their index fingers; brunettes, true to their own ideas, arm themselves defensively against the book with double-pointed hair-grips, very well-adapted for gouging out the author's eyes. But God forbid that I should put off female readers—who, not having, like male readers, to hide their innate ugliness and the disgrace of their species, are very welcome in any costume they might care to adopt, whether it emerges from the hands of the couturier or from the hands of the Creator.

Chapter Two
The Meeting of the Shareholders of the General Company for Lighting and Heating by Means of the Earth's Central Fire

The assembled shareholders representing more than four fifths of the society's capital, the meeting is declared constitutional. Lord Hotairwell, the founder, is nominated as president, Mr. Edward Burton as secretary. Viscount Powell and Mr. Stopman take their places at the table in the capacity of assessors.

The president takes the floor, expressing himself in the following terms:

"Gentlemen, in our meeting on April 20, you commissioned the engineers James Archibold and William Hatchitt, in collaboration with Samuel Penkenton, professor at the Geological Institute, to present a report to you on the three following questions:

"Firstly, does the Earth's central fire exist?

"Secondly, is its exploitation within the scope of human beings?

"Thirdly, what would be the costs and benefits of that exploitation?

"These gentlemen have completed their enquiry, and solicit the honor of acquainting you with the result. In consequence, I give the floor to Dr. Samuel Penkenton.

Professor Samuel Penkenton's Report
"Gentlemen,

"In an epoch whose distance Buffon estimates at 74,047 years[5] and others at a billion years, about which it is more

---

[5] In addition to his natural history, Buffon also produced an account of *Les Epoques de la nature* (1778), which attempted a history of the Earth, in which he discarded Archbishop Us-

exact not to be precise, a cloud escaped from the Sun and came, spinning, to occupy a place in the ether indicated to it by a great invisible finger.

"This cloud was the future Earth, and the ante-prehistoric times commenced.

"Isolated in the cold immensity, the still-flamboyant nebula was gradually extinguished. A crust wrinkled its face; the embers of its combustion veiled its flames, like an unpolished globe eclipsing a lamp; the solar light, stifled beneath its cinders, became the central terrestrial fire.

"The existence of the central fire, the surviving remnant, in the bosom of the globe, of its original flame, is attested by the most ancient peoples, who, emerging shortly after that nucleus had disappeared, walked upon its ashes while they were still arm, and almost glimpsed it.

"These races elevated their belief in the Earthly fire to the rank of dogma, and consecrated it as the King of mysterious and infernal empires. Moses celebrated the fire that burned in the depths of Sheol and scorched the roots of mountains. Plato and Aristotle testified to its existence. Pythagoras indicated its limits. Herodotus explained that it required nine days to descend thereto, and the geometer Dionysiodorus evaluated its distance, with remarkable precision, at 42,000 stadia.[6]

---

sher's estimate that the Creation occurred in 4004 B.C. in favor of this new calculation, based on the rate at which iron cools.

[6] This calculation, cited by Pliny the Elder, was an estimate of the Earth's radius rather than the depth of its hot core. The Greek *stadium* was about 607 standard English feet, so 42,000 stadia was approximately 4828 miles. The estimate proved to be a little on the high side, but was not discreditable, given the limited means available to Dionysiodorus, who was attempting to confirm an earlier calculation made by Eratosthenes, on the basis of shadows cast by the Sun in two North African cities.

"Science has confirmed these testimonies; going back as far as the Creation, our scientists, integrating the testimony of *Genesis*, Newton and Laplace into sublime visions, have discovered the great work of cosmic molecules combing in space, condensing in clouds, rolling up into spheres to become worlds. Cuvier, Arago and Saussure, scrutinizing our planet from its depths to its summits, have felt the warmth of the central fire and have measured it, always increasing the further they descended toward its nucleus.[7]

"The terrestrial fire advertises itself, furthermore, by means of earthquakes and volcanoes; by mean of vents, geysers and thermal springs; by mean of the oscillations of the ground which, for a century, have elevated the coats of Chile and Norway and raised up the temple of Serapis[8]: the tempestuous surf of that ocean of flames, the respiration of a giant oppressed beneath his armor.

---

[7] The author inserts a footnote at this point, attributed to Dr. Penkenton: "From observations made by Gensanne, Saussure and Humboldt, it follows that the progression of the heat the further one advances into the terrestrial depths is one degree per 30 to 35 meters." The first person to whom he refers is presumably the mineralogist Etienne Gensanne, who published an *Histoire naturelle de la Province de Languedoc* in 1776. Horace de Saussure (1749-1799) was a famous Swiss geologist, while Alexandre von Humboldt (1769-1859) was the author of *Kosmos* (1845-58), a heroic attempt to describe the universe then describable by science. The other writers to which the main body of the speech refers in this context are the naturalist Georges Cuvier (1769-1832) and Dominique-François Arago (1786-1853).

[8] There was, of course, more than one temple built to the syncretic Greek/Egyptian deity Serapis, but the most famous—and the one renowned for its elevation—was in Alexandria; it was not, however, destroyed by the earthquake that shook that city and destroyed the famous Pharos, but by Christian rioters.

"In the face of such evidence, gentlemen, what further proof is needed? The central fire exists, and I, Samuel Penkenton, delegated by you to verify its existence, in agreement with the immense majority of my colleagues, declare it certified.

"Signed: Samuel ב א Penkenton, geologist."

After the reading of this report, warmly welcomed by the assembly, a member asks for the floor in order to raise an objection. The chairman makes the observation that discussion will be more profitable when the meeting is party to all the facts of the matter; in consequence, he invites the engineers, James Archibold and William Hatchitt, to read the report of their work.

Report of Messrs. James Archibold and William Hatchitt
"Gentlemen,

"As you know, the enterprise that we were commissioned to investigate, from the viewpoint of its means of execution, its benefits and its expenses, has as its goal:

"Firstly, to establish a communication between the surface of the Earth and its reservoir of heat, known as the Central Fire, by means of a well of the appropriate depth.

"Secondly, to construct a model city, on an entirely new plan, adapted to the similarly novel civilization that will derive its source from this well. This city will be named *Industria*, and will accommodate 25,000 inhabitants. The well, three leagues in depth and 45 feet in diameter, should furnish on a daily basis, in the form of steam, warm air or electricity, one million horse-power (203,000 calories)—which is the equivalent, for each inhabitant, of having 40 horses dedicated to his service and trained by mechanical science to every employment of domesticity or industry.

"Thirdly, to exploit the monopoly that the Central Fire Company has acquired by its patents, in making itself the entrepreneur of geothermal wells that others will want to excavate according to its example, as well as canalizations, conduits, tubes, pipes and nozzles, district reservoirs, neighborhood cisterns, steam-tanks for railway stations and any other central fire depots that it might be deemed useful to establish.

"The benefits of such an enterprise would take an extremely long time to enumerate, being as enormous as their source, and being indistinguishable in their duration with the very duration of this planet and its humankind. So, the immediate fear is that the obstacles and expenses will be proportionate to them. Fortunately, that is not the case; the expense is modest, and the difficulties are very easily overcome.

"Our globe, gentlemen, is nothing but an earthenware vase, whose 40-kilometer thick walls are filled with 1060.5 billion cubic meters of vapor or liquid fire, and it is merely a matter of contriving an escape-valve in this boiler, of drilling a hole that wall—an operation that is carried out every day in our workshops, with the difference that our boilers are made of copper and iron, while the terrestrial crust is made of clay, and that we are only proposing to drill a hole through a part of its thickness.

"Having convinced ourselves, gentlemen, of the feasibility of reaching the central fire, the duty remained of investigating whether digging a well was the best method, for other, very seductive, routes offer themselves to us, it must be admitted, wide open and seemingly more economical: the route of volcanoes, those outlets of the central fire to which it would apparently be sufficient to fit a tap or a lid in order to capture and distribute their heat, even if it were necessary to carry out a certain amount of preliminary work to regularize and increase the debit—a new and very interesting kind of work to which your commission would devote itself with pleasure.

"England and Ireland, however, only possess extinct volcanoes, effaced from the surface, which would require great expense in order to recover the seams of their flame, which disappeared so long ago. On the other hand, was there any chance of finding a volcano somewhere else, in good condition, for sale? Your commission asked itself that question, and transported its gaze successively to the most esteemed craters.

"Firstly, it was necessary to discount a few examples that were very energetic, but of an inconvenient nature, or were too far away: Iceland, especially, where scraping the soil with a spade brings forth fire and hot water, but which is too remote; Cotopaxi, in America, which produces mostly carbon dioxide and would be particularly appropriate to the manufacture of soda-water; Papandayang, in Java, a volcano of great power, but inapplicable to industry, since it would be limited to one eruption every 100 years.

"Returning to Europe, our attention was directed to Stromboli, a good volcano, whose activity has been persistent for 20 centuries, commended by Homer for the beauty of its flames and classified by him among the lighthouses of the Mediterranean, but situated in a sheer landscape, on a sea whose amphibious isles emerge or sink unexpectedly, like the isle of Giulia, which, since 1831, has spent 44 years underwater.[9]

"With Vesuvius, which is exhibiting a praiseworthy activity at present, but is subject to periods of idleness that last between six and eight years, the Central Fire Company, appealing to its collaborators, would be obliged to submit to stoppages, or to embark upon expensive modifications to the bosom of its crater. In addition, the aptitudes of Vesuvius are less suited to its being a producer of fire and motive force than

---

[9] The island in question, which emerged off the coast of Sicily as a result of a volcanic eruption in July 1831, became the subject of rival claims to sovereignty; the British, who got in first, named it Graham Island, while the French named it Giulia and the Spanish Ferdinandea; the question became moot when it sank again in December. It has not extended above the surface since then, although the row might, in principle, flare up again if it were ever to emerge again. The citation of a 44 year interval suggests that this part of the narrative is notionally set in 1875, but later dates cited in the text imply that this scene must actually be set in 1860. 1875 might, therefore, be the year in which this chapter was initially written.

a volcano of leisure- and day-trips. Although it ruined Herculaneum and Pompeii, it enriches Portici and Naples by the spoils of the foreigners it attracts, and those cities would no more consent to sell their volcano than the Alps would part with their glaciers or the Pyrenees their waterfalls.

"Etna, to which we finally directed out study, presents a remarkable combination of qualities, but it has its faults. We doubt that the violence of its crater would permit it to support a lid—and how could we block, seal and secure the fissures of a mountain under pressure, 30 leagues in circumference and 3315 meters in altitude, obliging us to make the illogical effort of climbing up into the clouds in order to descend into the subterranean depths?

"The profound examination of these various means led us to abandon them, and to choose, in preference to the rapid path followed by Empedocles,[10] a surer route: a well that would lead us to the goal one step at a time, but at the certain velocity of one degree of temperature per 32 meters, requiring an excavation of 12,000 meters to obtain the 203,000 calories corresponding to the proposed million horse-power.

Estimates for a Geothermal Well 15 meters in diameter and 12,000 meters in depth, with a city of 25,000 inhabitants.

Excavation, extraction, ordering and transportation of 2,124,000 cubic meters,

@ £2 8s.[11] each...................................£5,097,600

---

[10] The pre-Socratic philosopher Empedocles was reported by Diogenes Laertius to have committed suicide by jumping into Mount Etna; various motives were suggested by later promulgators of the legend.

[11] All the sums in these accounts are given in francs in the original, but as they pertain to an English company I have translated them into sterling, at the rate of equivalence given by the author (25 francs to the pound). I have, however, left measurements of volume, length, etc. in the metric system as

Metallic structure, 120,000 tonnes of iron
@ £28 each...................……………..……….£3,360,000
Concrete and masonry, 700,000 cubic meters
@ £1 4s. each………………………………......£840,000
Piping for motive force, 6,250,000 cubic meters
@ 8s. each…..….....................£2,500,000
(Building land) Purchase of 10,000 hectares
@ 4s. per meter………………………….......£20,000,000
Construction of a model city of 25,000 inhabitants, with gardens, squares, surrounding countryside and subterranean industrial city………………………………………...£4,000,000
Interest on capital during the construction of the well
(£35,797,600 at 5% for 8 years…..……..….£14,319,000
Costs of issues and publicity, gratifications, remissions, commissions, tips and bribes to newspapers and bankers..……………………..……………….……………£912,800
Total expenditure…………………………..£50,294,400

Annual Income

Benefits accruing from continuous operation:
1. Rent of buildings constructed by the Company; 10% of the corresponding capital…….....………………….…£400,000
2. Lease of motive force at a rate of 2 francs per horsepower per day, rather than 3.50 (present price)……………………………………..……………£29,200,000
Total income………………………………£29,600,000

"Which is 58% of the committed capital.

To which benefits will be added the rights of exploitation of the Company's patents, and the gains accruing from the general enterprise of all the geothermal wells.

---

the conversion would have been awkward and the old imperial system has now been abandoned.

We are ready, gentlemen, to discuss before you, in specific detail, the figures that we have just had the honor of submitting to you.

"Signed: William Hatchitt and James Archibold, Engineers."

The reading of this report is followed by a profound discussion, involving Messrs. Stopman, William Barnett, Viscount Powell, James Archibold, William Hatchitt and various members of the assembly.

Mr. Greatboy having asked to pose a question, the president gives him the floor. The honorable member, while rendering full justice to the conscientious studies of the eminent engineers, expresses the fear that they have forgotten one thing. James Archibold and William Hatchitt protest forcefully, and affirm that never, in human memory has an engineer graduated from the Polytechnic forgotten anything. They deem the allegation regrettable, and summon Mr. Greatboy to explain.

Mr. Greatboy explains. He fears that the geothermal wells might be overextended, by reason of their great advantages, and the central fire excessively exploited and prematurely exhausted. Before conclusively committing his capital, the honorable shareholder desires that the engineers should guarantee a minimum duration for the central fire—99 years for example, that being equal to the duration of the Society.

James Archibold and William Hazlitt reply that Mr. Greatboy has made a mistake in attacking the precise point that they have studied most closely, not only as engineers charged with the interests of the Company but also as honest men desirous that the contemporary generation should not squander a resource as important as the central fire, the indivisible patrimony of all humankind, and that a share of it might be reserved for their descendants. Mr. Greatboy can be reassured; the provision of the central fire is adequate to the greatest eventualities. Assuming, as a reasonable estimate, the creation of one million-horse-power well per 100,000 inhabitants of the planet, they would be sufficient, according to the most precise calculations, not merely for 99 years but for 2,153,300,000 centuries. It would, furthermore, be the prerogative of the concessionary Company to moderate the extension.

Mr. Greatboy replies that he is glad to have posed a question whose response surpasses all his hopes. He declares himself satisfied, and thanks the engineers.

As no one else in the audience asks for the floor, the president rises and makes the following speech:

"Gentlemen,

"After the reports that you have just heard, so illuminating and fact-filled, supported by such figures, and after this discussion, which has dissipated the final shadows, what doubts can remain? What objections can possibly be raised?

"The Earth exists; the geologist Dr. Penkenton leaves no doubt in that regard. The central fire survives in its bosom, and its conquest is open our efforts. Through a thin pellicle, from beyond the wall of earth that separates us, this fire extends to us its arms of flame; and through 300 active mouths, by means the thunderous voice of all its eruptions and quakes, it cries out to the man who has not yet heard it: 'I am the soul and the genius of the Earth, its light, its heat, its limitless force, as eternal as your humanity. I am a terrible, ill-chained monster; a demon who stirs my fires beneath your continents and precipitates them thereon at my whim! But I can, if you wish, love you and serve you like the slaves of antiquity, turning the grindstones of your mills and the machinery of your factories, inflating the sails of your ships, animating your railway locomotives with my fiery breath and providing you with warmth when they day comes when the last remnants of your forests and coal-mines have been burned in your furnaces.'

"That is what the central fire says! Let us make haste to reply. Let us open a wide breach in the prison that confines us; let us capture, in its entrails, this source that is more productive the deeper it is; let us dig to abyssal depths the foundations of a new city, the walls of which will rise up all the high-

29

er, as great trees stand on powerful roots: a British Jerusalem, sited on the edge of a river of light, radiant with incomparable brightness! Who can measure the height of its towers, the feet of which rest on the ancient nebula and the summits of which are veiled by cloud? A metropolis of the future! The seed-germ of cities that will grow and flourish on the fertile soil of the fatherland; which will graft themselves to one another and henceforth be only one city; which will make England, reconnected to the continent by the hand that it will reach out to them beneath the Channel, into a factory occupying an entire nation, pouring out its produce and its profits upon the world, through its tunnel-funnel."

When the applause that greeted this eloquent speech had calmed down, the president proposed to put to the vote:

Firstly, the conclusions of the reports of Professor Penkenton and the engineers.

Secondly, the resolution to constitute definitively a Society for Lighting and Heating by means of the Central Fire, with a capital of 50 million pounds sterling, divided into two and a half million 20-pound shares.

Thirdly, the election of a committee, which, under the chairmanship of the founder, Lord Hotairwell, would immediately take the measures necessary for the accumulation of social capital by means of public subscription.

These resolutions are carried by acclamation.

James Archibold, William Hatchitt, Samuel Penkenton and Edward Burton are added to Lord Hotairwell as members of the issuing committee, and the assembly, having completed the agenda of the meeting, breaks up after the minutes were signed and dated by the members of the abovementioned committee.

Furnished with these powers, the delegated administrators set to work, initially occupying themselves, by the usual means, with gathering the support of the newspapers. The latter immediately begin explaining the business, simply, without emphasis and without any optimistic slant—on the contrary, analyzing it minutely, scrutinizing it severely, examining it from so many sides and turning it through so many angles, that its creators sometimes have difficulty recognizing it, and that the favorable conclusions, resulting from so stern an examination, profoundly excite the public,

Other means of publicity were by no means neglected: printed or handwritten circulars, private and confidential; posters in every format, some stupefying the eye by their gigantic dimensions and others, scarcely readable, luring by the attraction of mystery.

Satisfied with the initial results, but ceaselessly striving to do better, the administrative committee printed several million advertisements of the same size and form as sticks of sealing-wax, which were distributed during the night in such abundance that London, on awakening, was horrified to find itself covered with such pustules—but the eruption continued all day: passers-by, carriages, dogs, horses, doors and walls—everything possessed of a body and every living being showing a face, received the Company's stamp. The population became annoyed, and one gentleman, speckled like a tiger by the bill-posters, launched a lawsuit. The administrators gladly took advantage of that means of judiciary publicity. Found guilty by the initial judges, they dragged their adversary through all the courts, finally being sentenced to pay costs of £420, a sum much inferior to the profitable noise generated by the case.

Without going into more detail, suffice it to say that for three months no Englishman could go out or stay at home without being reminded of the Central Fire Company at every moment, in the most various respects. Public interest was, therefore, extremely excited; its good opinion reached its height, and there never was a more psychologically propitious moment for opening counters to a crowd avid to subscribe. By virtue of an error that one would not have expected of such men, however, no counters opened; the date of issue remained vaguely indicated; silence—an inexplicable apathy—succeeded all this noise so completely that it even became impossible to interview an administrator or to obtain any information.

Was information sought regarding Lord Hotairwell, the founder and kingpin of the enterprise? His secretary would tell you that he had gone to Scotland, leaving all his affairs in abeyance, summoned by a migration of snipe. Snipe are birds that determine the time of their own migration, to which it is necessary to submit if one wishes to hunt them, so Lord Hotairwell was excused to some extent, while criticism was heaped on the carelessness of men of the world who hurl themselves into business, throwing forth fire and flame, only to sputter out like a firework. Astonishment knew no bounds, however, when further research revealed that the Company's chief engineer, James Archibold, whose health had never suffered a dent, was taking the waters at Brighton, and that his right arm, William Hatchitt, having obtained a leave of absence, was visiting the works of the Channel Tunnel and seemed unready to come out again.

It is true that the chief geologist, Samuel Penkenton, had not left London, and a few people had tried to interrogate him—but Penkenton, adopting his most fossilized manner, without appearing to understand, had replied incoherently in a language that was dead before the Deluge. Now, as little was known about this bizarre and irascible scientist, who was always armed with a massive walking-stick, no one dared persist when he was disinclined to reply. In truth, a Company had to have lost its head to absent itself at such a moment, leaving such a man as its only representative.

These annoying occurrences and lack of regard for the public caused as much resentment as surprise in London and throughout England. To excite a nation, to make it withdraw its funds and hold its capital ready, to lure it so ardently, only to withdraw the bait and leave it there, open-mouthed, was too much of a mockery. Thus, the most disobliging rumors were not long in taking flight. It was said that the subscription had been secretly bought up before issue: the money-changer Goldlove, in syndication with the banker Shylockston, had bought the business in order to sell it on with a high mark-up—and, as usual, sincere subscribers and small investors would be sacrificed.

Everyone was looking for a card up the sleeve; no one could believe in such artlessness. Everyone kept his money on him, at all costs, so that he would be ready to subscribe, and watched his neighbor, suspecting him of being in on it: a population of aspirant shareholders, launched in pursuit of its escaped social status—a sterile pursuit, whose lack of success sharpened its resentment and wrath on a daily basis. Meetings were held and resolutions passed. The police feared riots, and it is certain that violence would have been committed if there had been anyone to subject to it. As has been said, however, Professor Penkenton, the only administrator present, was little known to the public and unready, by reason of his bad temper, to play the role of victim.

Although, therefore, the initial actions of the administrators had served the Company well, in making it known and attracting popular favor to it, one could say that their artlessness and negligence had multiplied this good result tenfold. The enthusiasm of the public had turned to rage, but their negligence would be largely repaired if they were able turn it to their advantage.

On the night of August 7, at about 11:45 p.m., the inhabitants of London were given an urgent warning. A fire had broken out on the far side of Regent's Park, and its flames, doubtless alimented by chemical products, were projecting the sparks of fireworks and dangerous rockets over the City.

The fire brigade, immediately alerted, was launched at top speed from its Watling Street headquarters, led at a distance of three engine-lengths by its commander, Captain Shaw. Carried forward at a furious gallop by four fine half-thoroughbreds, while steam rose from their flanks under the driver's whips, the engines, guided by helmeted men armed with lances, were reminiscent of ancient war-chariots. They plowed through the streets like a storm, cleaving through the crowd that cheered them and urged them to greater rapidity with shouts—for the anxiety was extreme; a fire as intense as was implied by the glare it produced spelled the ruination of the whole of Camden Town, and half the city adjacent to that district might similarly fall prey to the disaster.

What relief there was, therefore, what enthusiasm, what clamors of gratitude and what a thunderous clapping of 200,000 hands, when the fire, acquiring a new violence and its flames rose up to a terrible height, spelled out these words in scintillating letters against the darkness:

CENTRAL FIRE COMPANY
TOMORROW!! NINE O'CLOCK!

The next day, at daybreak, the population of London, having not gone to bed, was up and about, and the Central Fire Company was awaiting its firm tread in 60 office-kiosks set up during the night, each one provided with a cashier lying in ambush behind his grille, ready to open as the appointed hour struck.

Long before 9 a.m., enormous queues wound around these offices: feverish, nervous, fretful tails tangled up in reptilian knots, making alliances or lashing out, so that one tail lost the kiosk that served as its head, while another head acquired several tails. Soon, though, in the ever-increasing flow, all these queues disappeared, like waves in the Ocean, and nothing could any longer be distinguished on the stormy sea but the kiosks projecting from the swell, sometimes floating above it and sometimes drowned by it—but without the work of subscription suffering thereby, as the elite cashiers, porpoises playing amid the waves, never relented for an instant.

At 10 a.m., the tide was such that the Government took fright and put measures in place. Police reinforcements were requested from neighboring towns, but could not be sent, in view of the fact that those towns found themselves, at the same hour, prey to the same fever, and that the police, preoccupied with subscription themselves, were much more intent on getting through the crowd than containing it.

British common sense sufficed to preserve order, and such a great tumult only resulted in a few trivial accidents.

Kiosk number 36B, established at the entrance to Hyde Park, could not resist the pressure of its clientele and sank beneath the popular wave, leaving nothing behind but debris, and kiosk number 42, situated at the western extremity of Kensington Gardens, was found that evening in Victoria Park—without its resident employee, hard at work, having noticed the displacement. The surge of the human tide had driven it aground, like a boat deceived by the sea and drawn away without its master being aware of it.

The subscription was overwritten to such a degree that only a few privileged individuals received fragmentary entitlements: an admirable success due, on the one hand, to the skill of the founders and, on the other, to the enterprise itself, of which the ever-pragmatic English had immediately taken the measure.

How could it have been otherwise? What fears could even the most timorous have entertained? The existence of the central fire not being in doubt, the risks were reduced to the greater of lesser expenditure of effort and money—details without importance in a business in which the profits might multiply the capital 100 times over, and in which the capital had two billion centuries to be amortized. So the subscribers were, in the main, serious capitalists, family men eager to add such a safe share to their portfolios, offering a large dividend and capable of multiplying in value enormously: an industrial and territorial investment of the first order, guaranteed to be the first mortgage on a portion of the globe evidently free of previous claims.

Chapter Three
The Inaugural Celebration of the General Company
for Lighting and Heating by Means
of the Earth's Central Fire

If a vigorous reader would care to lend me a little assistance, the two of us can lift up the roof of the dining-room of the Mansion House as easily as one lifts the lid of a soup-tureen, and everyone may enjoy the magnificent sight offered by that hall and its immense table, rimmed by its 400 guests.

If you would like to look in this direction, I shall have the honor of introducing to you, first of all, to the chubby little man seated to the right of the Chairman. This is William Barnett, horse-merchant and Lord Mayor of London, who, having remained obscure and thin until the age of 60 but forced thereafter, to fatten himself up in order to become Lord Mayor, finds himself somewhat oppressed within his rind, and often makes a gesture as if to unbutton his skin. His intelligence has, however, remained agile within is heavier body, and although William Barnett is not as sensitive to poetry as his predecessor in the year 1770, who offered Chatterton a position as his valet,[12] he is a great connoisseur of business, as is proven by the great part he plays in it. It is thanks to his benevolence that the Society of the Central Fire has been able to use the Mansion House for its banquet.

To the Chairman's left, you can see Sir Richard Wallson, a sincere demophile and cosmopolitan philanthropist , as rich as it is necessary to be when the heart is ever-generous, the hand ever-open, to whom these words of Bossuet's might be

---

[12] The Lord Mayor of London who offered slight relief to the poet Thomas Chatterton was William Beckford, the father of the more famous namesake who wrote *Vathek*.

applied: "His wealth is a public fountain, which rises up to spread out."[13]

We have already recognized the engineer James Archibold sitting next to Sir Richard Wallson, and there is no need to name Captain Shaw, who, by pushing two plates aside, has improvised a place next to the engineer. By virtue of an inconceivable error, Captain Shaw, the commander of the London firemen, has not been invited, but, chancing to be passing by the Mansion House and hearing mention of the Central Fire, he has come in, scenting a fire, and has found a table set at which his old friend Archibold has made him sit down—the illustrious engineer Archibold, that is, whose name, already attached to all the Herculean labors of the century, will acquire an incomparable glory in the enterprise of the central fire.

James Archibold is a cool, balanced and positive man, whose technical knowledge is equally extensive in breadth and depth, whose intelligence is both presbyopic and myopic, seeing clearly at both long and short range, as skillful in analysis as in synthesis: a reflective and attentive mind that knows how to listen, and is still listening when one is no longer talking. You might believe that sound did not pass between him at 300 meters per second, so slow are his replies to arrive, but they finally arrive so complete, so lucid, and so well-chewed in every part, that the listener recovers the time he has lost in waiting by virtue of the ease with which he digests it.

He is authoritarian and absolute in the government of others and himself, never letting a muscle twitch or a nerve tremble without the authorization of the central power, transmitted in an orderly fashion by the competent organs, never authorizing those organs to start operation without motive, and only providing for their needs in proportion to their expenditure. A handsome and efficient machine of a man! Not one of

---

[13] The famous Churchman Jacques-Bénigne Bossuet (1627-1704) gave several famous funeral orations; this quotation is presumably taken from one of them, but I have not been able to identify which one.

those high-pressure, high-speed locomotives that drink space and get drunk, passing through stations without crying "look out!" and stopping exhausted, breathless, coughing up scrap metal, having used up in a day organs tempered for a lifetime, but a stationary, low-pressure machine, variable in output according to the task, operating at a regular 90 piston-strokes per minute, solid in every part, a trifle massive but so strictly equilibrated, so normal in action, that he might equally well be applied to operating the shafts that move the paddle-wheels of the *Leviathan*.

His physique comprises a summarily squared-off torso supported by a dorsal spine in a single piece, like all English spines, and supported by a pair of legs of sufficient length for someone who, not liking to trot or gallop, is content to march through life at a steady pace.

Place on this body a cubic head whose squarely-designed profile presents a strict economy of contours and whose skull is internally divided into two parts: the workshop and the store-room. The workshop, situated at the front, highly-placed beneath the ceiling, well-lit by two windows, receives the raw materials, the minerals of thought, the brute ideas still in their wrapping, which are passed into the crucible, forged, laminated, isolated or soldered together. The store-room, situated at the rear, encloses the fabricated products, the acquired knowledge ready for use, arranged in the bunkers of the memory in an orderly and symmetrical manner, offering visitors a magnificent display of human sciences.[14]

It is understandable how precious, from the viewpoint of the Central Fire Company, such a combination of capacities was, and how the adhesion of such a man had sufficed to dissipate all the doubts as to the value of an enterprise of which he was the engineer—seconded by the little man that you see sitting on the other side of the table, whose agile hands are clearing his plate so actively, whose movements are so lively

---

[14] This paragraph does not appear in the first edition.

and whose physiognomy is so expressive, immediately revealing his high intelligence.

This dwarf is, in fact, no less than the kingpin of all the
great drilling operations of the day. He has cleaved, penetrated, transported, fragmented and drained seas, continents
and mountains; I have described William Hatchitt!

William Hatchitt! Mining engineer, geotrupe,[15] a specialist in the penetration of isthmuses and tunnels of every sort,
drilling mines or artesian wells, a collaborator in all the mining operations of the last 20 years, and so absorbed therein
during that period that he hardly ever emerged therefrom—
with the result that the engineer's great renown extended much
further below ground than above it. The man was a mole, and
his external traces gave only a slight idea of his labors underground, where he was confined by a love of obscurity and a
horror of broad daylight, from which his sight suffered as
much as his modesty.

As is well-known, it was the engineer Hatchitt who organized the piercing of Mount Cenis[16] and put an end to un-
certainty regarding the internal make-up of that geological
gibbosity by forcible penetration. As thin and supple as a
blade, as insinuating as a drill-bit, snaking around irregulari-
ties, adapting himself to fissures, his body following his head,
or preceding it, he slid from fault to fault into the very heart of
the mountain, and came out again through a chink on the other
side, having mapped the massif as he passed through it. It was
he who directed the Italian crew during the 160 months that
the operation lasted, with neither respite nor sleep, without
ever coming to the surface to breathe, always at the fore-
front—to the point at which the workers, who adored him,
debated as to whether it was the engineer's head or the points

---

[15] A geotrupe is a member of a family of earth-boring scarab
beetles.
[16] The construction of the Mont Cenis railway tunnel, between
1857 and 1871, was actually directed by Germain Sommeiller.

of their pick-axes that had first appeared in France at the moment when the barrier between the two nations fell.

The piercing of the Gotthard languished until the day when an appeal went out to William Hatchitt.[17] He arrived, and the rock crumbed before him. Since his departure, it seems to have recovered its tenacity.[18] But these hypodermic

---

[17] The Gotthard railway tunnel was begun as soon as the Mont Cenis tunnel was complete, in 1871; it was opened in 1882 but suffered various misfortunes; its original director, Louis Favre suffered a heart attack in the tunnel and died, and 200 workers were killed in various accidents, at one point occasioning a strike that was broken up by the Swiss Army

[18] The author inserts a long footnote here: "Perhaps you will be curious to know the opinion of this engineer regarding the question of the linking of England and the continent, so much discussed at present. William Hatchitt regarded as puerile the means proposed by his colleagues Thomé de Gamond, Vérard de Sainte-Anne and Dupuy de Lôme, and would admit neither tunnels, nor bridges, nor boat-trains; he would construct an isthmus. Having measured the strait of the Pas-de-Calais and the volume of the Scottish mountains, he had recognized that the latter, heaped up in the former, would form a flat expanse of land which, extending as far as England, would endow it with a fertile plain akin to its productive lands, and unite it with the continent as intimately as in the epoch when the North Sea and the Channel did not yet exist, and the Thames continued its course through prehistoric Europe.

"Whether the earthworks were carried out with spades and wheelbarrows, or whether the southern part of the mountains could be made to slide in one piece, as the city of Oran is said to side on its bed of clay, the expense would, however, have been considerable, and the engineer was forced to revert to a more modest plan: a concrete jetty joining Boulogne to Folkestone, seven leagues long and a kilometre wide, equipped with a lock-gate for the passage of ships; an embankment created by human hands with two sides and two

scratches, as he called his great works, were only beginnings in his eyes. The man's obsession was excavation. In contrast to the aeronaut, the mountaineer of the clouds who lightens himself in order to climb, Hatchitt would have liked to become as heavy as mercury, in order to hollow out the ground by his weight. He would have dismembered the globe had he been allowed to do it, and if it is true, as Pliny reports, that the inhabitants of the Balearic islands were imperiled by an invasion of rabbits, to the point of appealing for the help of a Roman legion, one may believe that a legion of rabbits as strong as

---

ends, breaking, on one side, the great Atlantic tides and transforming the waves of the strait into dormant waters, inscribing in its side walls a port made to measure for the ships of the future, having the shores of England and France for its quays and the North Sea for its sea-lane.

"The expense would still have been enormous, but Mr. Hatchitt covered the risks by promising, on his honor and with dedication, to carry out the work under contract and to complete it within 50 year. Even so, and although very tempted, the capitalists hesitated, objecting that, given the speed at which scientific progress is advancing, railways, ships, bridges, jetties and roads would soon be replaced by improved means, and that by the time their dike was delivered it could be left on their hands. Discussions opened on this basis ten years ago between Mr. Hatchitt and his shareholders are continuing sporadically today."

J. A. Thomé de Gamond (1807-1876) pioneered discussion of a Channel Tunnel in 1830 and carried out geological and hydrological surveys. Vérard de Sainte-Anne proposed building a railway bridge in 1870, the same year in which the famous naval architect Henri Dupuy de Lôme (1816-1855) proposed a fleet of ferries fitted with rails so that trains could drive on at one side and drive off at the other. Companies intending to build channel tunnels were founded in 1875 and 1882, but soon failed.

Hatchitt would have made that land into a skimmer or a warren.

He is small-framed, with the face of a proboscidian, long and conical, like the snout of a boar shadowing a toothbrush moustache, with a mushroom-like pallor, the cranium bald and the sinciput so pointed that one could have made a hole by pressing that head into the ground, and swiveling on his legs as on a capstan. Agile and restless, like most little men, he expresses his thoughts two-thirds in gesture as opposed to one third in words: sometimes the swift gestures of a dog scratching itself, sometimes the gyratory movements of a drill for hollowing out thoughts. He is no less tenacious than ardent, proceeding toward his goal like a screw fixing itself in a hole. While he was biting into the terrestrial core at one point, one could have sectioned him from one shoulder-blade to the other, and from the occiput to the caudal vertebra, without making him let go.

Extremely irascible and intolerant in argument, but otherwise very affable, he delights in uniting men by means of ideas, like continents by tunnels, and is extremely obliging and polite, to the point of saying "bless you" to a passer-by who sneezes. He has an iron constitution, although he is subject to eye trouble when he emerges from underground, and also to choking fits. His chest, designed to breathe parsimoniously, suffocates in the open air, for, just as one becomes habituated to eating very little, and anything at all, Hatchitt the engineer has been constrained, underground, to breathe very little, and anything at all. The first gas that came along, the slightest miasma of previously-exhaled carbon dioxide, were sufficient for him; at the very most, in exceptional cases, he dissolved a little solidified air—pastilles of which he always had in his pocket—on his tongue.

Hazard, which commits stupidities more often than not, had placed next to William Hatchitt at the table the one person for whom he lacked benevolence: Dr. Samuel Penkenton. Penkenton was a giant whose dimensions alarmed Hatchitt; bitter, but essentially inoffensive, arguments often arose between the two men, like quarrels between a little dog and an elephant.

"There is scant merit," the little engineer sometimes said, while considering the doctor's enormous stature, "in being big and strong, as you are, in the open air—a medium without resistance. Only the man or animal who moves underground has the right to call himself strong. Hollow out a burrow with an elephant, or hollow it out yourself, try like a mole to dig tunnels a kilometer long and gallop along them at the speed of a horse! You'll chip your teeth and wear out your trunk in vain, because you have neither the skill lot the power of that little creature. Give a mole the statue of a pachyderm and it would turn the world upside down; but if you were reduced to the size of a mole, what good would you be?"

Dr. Samuel ב א Penkenton, who had never revealed the meaning of the bizarre signs that served him as middle initials,[19] was the Professor of Natural History at the British Museum, but the naturalist doubled as a geologist, and the essence of Penkenton was in his duplication. Knowing the past as if he had lived it, and prehistoric events as if he had seen them happen, treating the most remotest individuals as old acquaintances, he was less a scientist than a spectator who had seen everything that he taught, or a scientist so deeply incrusted in his science that he could no longer distinguish his own substance therefrom: a seed of madness that every geolo-

---

[19] In representing these symbols I have followed the example of the original typesetter in using the Hebrew letters *beth* and *aleph* (ב and א), although it will subsequently be revealed that they belong to an earlier language, which presumably left no written relics. It is only fair to warn the reader—although the original text does not—that the two symbols do not have the same phonetic values as *beth* and *aleph*. It seems probable that the typesetter simply chose two symbols bearing a superficial resemblance to those the author had improvised in his manuscript.

gist's head conceals—except that in this huge head, the seed was huge.

Penkenton had even more nostalgia for the past than love, and was homesick, yearning to return to it. Depressed by living in a time that was not his own, which was not to his taste, into which he had come by mistake, he detached himself from it, and sat pensively on its bank, watching its life go by like a river weary of its flow, desirous of returning to its source. He was blasé about everything, even science and the terrestrial globe that he had scratched in every direction—on which his body was forcibly retained but from which his soul was often absent, doubtless searching for another world, a portal to escape from this one, or a ladder into the past.

Penkenton's structure and proportions, like the tendencies of his mind, belonged to another era; they were architectural rather than human. The man might have been constructed by the Pelasgians, or even perhaps more anciently, and carved in broad sweeps from a block of granite. His Titan's head and his broad face, without being handsome, had something of the majesty of sphinxes: type-specimens of primitive humankind, creations retaining the most immediate imprint of the creator. Like that of a sphinx, Penkenton's head diminished toward the occiput; his face was only a façade that extended cavernously; that human face had the skull of a wolf. There was no capillary growth on that that strange skull; on his parchment-cheeks there were a few stray hairs, like the morbid vegetation of volcanic terrain and collapsed summits. A stiff cravat—a high collar, a false collar or a halter—connected the head to the body, like a stone frieze consolidating a tower.

Penkenton had a fortune, consisting in his collections, certain items of which were priceless. They included the shoulder of a fossil sheep (*Ovis prisca*)[20], still fitted to its forelimb, with near-purulent hair and tendons—which is the ideal

---

[20] *Ovis prisca* is a fictitious hybrid derived from elements of *Ovis musimon* (the mouflon) and *Capra prisca* (a species of goat).

state of freshness for a fossil; the hindquarters of the Trojan Horse, reduced to dust by the effect of age, contained in a two-hectoliter sack, in which the vulgar saw nothing but sawdust, but in which scientists and horsemen clearly discerned equestrian dust; and a highly accurate drawing of Noah's Ark, engraved with a pointed flint on the bone of a halitherium[21] and discovered by Dr. Penkenton himself in the Asiatic floodplain, on the southern face of Mount Ararat—an inestimable engraving, the object of controversies so lively and so jealous that the scientist Mr. Bryce did not hesitate to climb the 17,120 feet of Mount Ararat to see whether, as the Armenians assured him, the ark was still there and to be able, if it was, to check the resemblance of the drawing and the model.[22]

In addition to these treasures and many others, Penkenton had another wellspring of fortune in the publication in progress—in Athens, by the firm of Leonidas the younger and Pelopidas junior[23]—of his Syrian Dictionary in glagolitic characters, in a new edition placed within the range of men of the world by means of a glossary in Coptic and Hebrew.

The doctor had no family. A few people thought that he had had a brother who had died tragically a long time ago, but it was no good questioning Penkenton on that subject any

---

[21] An Eocene Sirenian (i.e. a sea-cow).

[22] The English explorer James Bryce reported in 1876 that he had found a four-foot length of hand-tooled wood on Mount Ararat at an elevation of 13,000 feet.

[23] It is possible that the Leonidas the author has in mind in improvising the name of this fictitious Athenian publishing company is the one who tutored Alexander the Great, but the coupling of the name with that of Pelopidas, an ill-fated Theban general, is more suggestive of the Spartan king who was killed while holding back the Persians at Thermopylae. The glagolitic alphabet was that of the ancient Slavs; the "Syrian" to which the text refers here is the hypothetical source-language of the group of languages that includes Aramaic and Hebrew.

more than it was to touch his cane, if one could give that name to an enormous knotty branch of unknown species, which had bizarre signs engraved in its bark by hatchet-strokes. That staff seemed to be riveted to his hand; the man and the cane were never apart. Each leaning on the other, they carried the burdens of the day, and during the night, the doctor's clenched hands hugged the rugged body of his companion to his breast. Touching his cane and mentioning his brother were equally offensive to the doctor; he became furious, brandishing his staff, and a bloody lighting-flash streaked his gaze with a gleam that one never forgot once one had been subjected to it—but it was only a flash; his hand, scarcely lifted, sank down tremulously, as if afraid of itself; he mumbled excuses and fell back into his melancholy.

Since Penkenton had become interested in the enterprise of the central fire, he had improved, becoming less black in his mood and more expansive; he had been gripped, in respect of that business, by an enthusiasm foreign to his nature, and it dispelled all his cares—which was welcome, for, if the man was eccentric, the scientist was indisputable. No one appreciated that more than the founder of the Company, who was an eminent geologist himself—except that, while the morose doctor turned his back on his own time and buried himself in his science, Lord Hotairwell, ardent and enthusiastic, rode the road to the future off the bridle, and his scientific returns to the past were merely a springboard to launch himself forwards.

Chapter Four
The Acme of Patriotism;
or, The Man Who Would Move an Island

His Honor Lord George Hotairwell, whom we saw at the outset of this enterprise, was tall in stature—a stature that surpassed the crowd and made him imposing without being amazing, like fairground giants or Dr. Penkenton. His face, very handsome in the upper part, perhaps left something to be desired in the inferior, animal part, which was provided only with what was strictly necessary. His head was nothing but a cranium, a forehead and eyes: eyes steeped, at rest, in a phosphorescence whose gleam, suddenly illuminating, sprang forth from the orbit like the overflow of devouring fire that escapes through the windows of a burning house. The forehead was enormous, sometimes as smooth as a marble statue and sometimes striated by little waves of quivering thought, oozing out. On seeing that forehead, one sensed that Lord Hotairwell must suffer from intellectual plethora, as others are inconvenienced in the blood, and that if it were not for taking flight into wide-open spaces and the expenditure of great efforts, he would have needed the thick walls of a padded cell to tame that head. Let us add that his cranium would have delighted phrenologists by the amplitude of its protrusions, especially those of wonder (organ 18 in Gall's classification) and idealism (organ 19), both so protuberant that they were reminiscent not so much of phrenological eminences as stumps over which one might tumble.

A former captain in the Horse-Guards and a member of the Upper Chamber, Lord Hotairwell was also a scientist of rare merit; his knowledge acquired less by study than by a marvelous intuition of all the questions of the day. His was a keen mind, taking in all the aspects of an enterprise at a glance, broadening its field, fertilizing its soil, and sewing crop-seeds by the handful. Passionate in his endeavors, acting as leader and slave, capitalist and workman, he sacrificed to success both treasures of genius and prodigies of labor, almost always seeing his capital and his efforts sunk by some unexpected shipwreck.

Were these continual failures due to an irritation of fortune directed against a man incessantly harnessed to his wheel? Or did that great mind find its own ruination in the excess of its activity? Perhaps there were fissures in that volcanic brain through which imagination, passing by surprise, momentarily troubled lofty and rigorous reason. This poet of industry needed a severe associate, a mentor with an icy brain, a human calculator to bridle the man of ideas.

Curious about everything, this starveling of science, who might have been represented by the algebraic symbol *?X*—interrogation before the unknown—was naturally drawn to become a geologist: a geologist as enthusiastic and progressive as Samuel Penkenton was reactionary and morose. The two were linked by a friendship that was maintained in an acrimonious state by the dissimilarity of their character and by scientific discussions of such violence that on more than one occasion during their quarrels, the doctor's staff, raised above his associate's head, had encountered Lord Hotairwell's revolver, already aimed to respond.

With regard to the birth of the Earth, its exodus from nothingness, its Neptunian or Plutonic metamorphoses,[24] and the arcana and archives of its prehistoric past, Lord Hotairwell had taken account of all the publications, discovered all the secrets and scrutinized all the sources, and had gone back even further. Like a hunter retracing a track to discover his quarry's lair, following the track of humankind back through the ages,

---

[24] These terms refer to a geological controversy between those scientists who thought that the primary force shaping the Earth's geological history had been the solvent and sedimentary effects of water (Neptunians) and those who thought that the volcanic effects of fire had been more significant (Plutonians).

he had gone back through all the geological phases and all the phases of genesis as far as the nebula that as the planet's embryo, and he had convinced himself that antediluvian man—the fossil of Moulin-Quignon,[25] Miocene man himself—was actually modern, the son of fathers even more ancient. He affirmed, and furnished proofs, that at the time when the Earth was no more than an incandescent ball floating in the ether, there were already humans living upon it, incandescent and vaporous themselves, adapted to the physical conditions of their globe.

On studying the maps of the Earth before the creation, drawn by Lord Hotairwell with an exactitude that would not have disgraced the geologist-geographers of the secondary and tertiary epochs, one becomes convinced, in fact, that the terrestrial cloud that escaped the Sun was already configured into seas and continents, populated by plants and animals as nebulous and flamboyant as itself. The oceans, in a vaporous state, covered four fifths of the globe, as they do today, bordered by flaming lands of various colors, according to the materials burning in their entrails. There were neither days nor nights on that luminous globe, no weight for that matter refined by superheating, no distance for those weightless bodies, and no opacities limiting gazes. Eyesight plunged from one pole to the other, through the diaphanous mass, following the course of marine monsters in their abysses, or the flights of comet-birds streaking the azure of the skies.

Why did that Earth-Sun descend to the state of a planet of condensed gas? Lord Hotairwell presumed that this fall must have been the punishment of an original sin—far anterior, of course, to that of Adam—which must have been com-

---

[25] Moulin-Quignon is a quarry near Abbeville where the pioneering paleontologist Jacques Boucher de Perthes (1788-1868) found a human jawbone in 1863. The author will return to the crucial significance of this particular item of evidence within the controversies he is addressing, and I shall add some further comments in the afterword.

mitted in the Sun, following which that star would have purged itself of a portion of itself, chasing it from the solar paradise and condemning it to death by freezing in the Siberias of space. The Earth is, therefore, nothing but a morbid secretion of the Sun, and humankind a gas fallen from grace.

Gaseous humankind on the nebulous Earth; the solid humankind of the present day; and the humankind to come, having become gaseous again by resorption into the Sun: these were the three sections of the work entitled *Man before the Earth and the Earth Before Genesis*, which Lord Hotairell had recently published, and in which he caused science to take such a great stride that the most agile of men became breathless following him, and the scientific world did not know what to think. The passionate discussions that book evoked, and the treasures of erudition that were expended, on all sides, to the profit of questions genuinely devoid of practical interest, are well-known. Lord Hotairwell was crushed beneath the weight of his heterodoxies, condemned by a council of geologists who, by chance, had listened and heard, and among whom Dr. Samuel Parkinson distinguished himself by his violence.

Lord Hotairwell, without considering himself defeated, went in search of new documents, while reflecting that he had something to hand better than arguments and proofs, since a remnant of the original nebula still persisted at the center of the globe under the name of the Central Fire, within which gaseous humankind might survive. He thought, with reason, that it would be an immortal glory for a geologist to disinter that humankind, and an unanswerable argument for his thesis. From then on, the idea of the conquest of the terrestrial fire began to develop within him—but diplomatic complications arising at that time, which preoccupied his patriotism, distracted him from it temporarily.

Offended by the attitude of Europe to his country, Lord Hotairwell went to the Upper Chamber one day and there put forward a famous motion, with so much passion, eloquence and technical knowledge, that no one ever knew whether, in the orator's mind, the project was anything more than a threat or whether he really had the means to carry it out. It was a matter, by means of mine-workings whose plans had been provided by the engineer William Hatchitt, of detaching England from its terrestrial pivot and making it a free-floating island, like the isles of Lake Superior in Canada, which had broken off from Rice's Point during a storm and had ended up running aground in Wisconsin.

When this preliminary operation was completed, Great Britain would raise anchor and say farewell to the hemisphere that had given birth to it. Its armored ships, its steamers and the horsepower that moved in their flanks, and its speedy sailing-ships would take it in tow, and the royal Amphitrite, guiding her docile flock, would advance over the sea. It would set a northward course, with Scotland in the bow and the Lizard at the tiller, cross the passes of the North Sea by means of skillful maneuvers, and then, steering to port between Ireland and Iceland, move into the Atlantic.[26]

Searching for the wide spaces and deep water necessary to its draught of water, it would pass through the open sea within sight of the coasts of France, which would send sad adieux to its old neighbor, a faithful friend in happy days. It would go past Spain and the coast of Africa, allowing itself to be borne by the arm of the Gulf Steam that runs from the Azores to Cape Verde, grazing, at low steam, the Canaries, which might be drowned by its wake, keeping watch to starboard on the Sargasso Sea, that octopus-meadow with tentacles of wrack and kelp.

One can imagine the delicacy of piloting of a vessel like England, measuring 700 kilometers from stem to stern and

---

[26] Although I have shifted it into a conditional tense, because none of this actually happens in the context of the story, the author relates it in the past tense, suggesting that it might have originated as a separate short story that was transplanted into the novel. Several other digressions from the main plot might also have been cannibalized from independent works, adding to the patchwork quality of the narrative.

300 amidships, so the greatest precautions would be taken. Night and day, the First Lord of the Admiralty would stand a watch on the highest summit of the Grampian mountains, the ship's bridge. It was from there that he supervised the tugs, by means of electric wires assembled in his hands like a sheaf of reins guiding racehorses. Progress would be slow, one eye kept on a Siemens bathometer, which measures depth by the intensity of terrestrial gravity,[27] skirting the Atlantic thalweg—a dark valley 15 kilometers deep still in the process of being hollowed out, which connects with the thalwegs of the Indian and Pacific Oceans in the gulfs of the pole—half way up the slope.

Having passed Cap Verde, about to cross the equator, the maritime convoy—leaving the arm of the Gulf Steam, which turns back toward Mexico—would pass Saint Helena at sea; then, doubling the Cape of Good Hope, England, with all sails deployed, hoisting the flag of her Queen-Empress, would penetrate the Indian Ocean and labor the waters of her Asiatic empire,

At this unexpected spectacle, the sight of the large island, their sister and their sovereign, the continental shore-dwellers would tremble with excitement and shudder with delight. From the tip of the Cape to the coasts of Australia, Java and Ceylon, from Bombay to Aden, all her vassal peoples would hurry to the beaches. In India, as soon as the news arrived, the Kshatriyas, agile warriors, the younger sons of Brahma, would launch themselves forward first, tightening their hempen loincloths in order to run faster. The Brahmins, so knowledgeable and wise, issued from the very head of Brahma, would close the books of the Vedas in haste and abandon their temples, without even serving the god his clarified butter. The Sudras would quit their trades, and also the workers of Madras, Puli-

---

[27] The bathometer, invented by William Siemens in 1861, measured the depth of sea by measuring tiny variations in gravitational attraction at the surface, caused by the fact that water is less dense than rock.

cat, Masulipatam, who make cotton cloth, as well as those of Patna and Surat, who weave gold-embroidered silks and carpets. It is only the 30,000 weavers of the distant valley of Kashmir who would not leave their work, along with the Vaisyas who would not leave their counters, the heretic Pariahs whose uncleanness is not washed away by the Ganges, and the Poulias, who are more abject still, who cannot be relieved of their accursed solitude for a single day.[28]

India entire would flock to the shore, in an indescribable tumult, in all the confusion of its races, his castes and its languages, singing a magnificent hosanna to the glorious suzeraine descended from the Occident: an immense human dust, chased by the same wind toward the same horizon; advancing still and crushing beneath their carts the superb rajahs guiding tigers four-in-hand, in gold harness lighter than the monsoon rains.

A similar ardor would be manifest in all the English lands bathed by the Indian Ocean: in Australia, where the aborigines, stupid Papuan negroes, would climb to the tops of baobabs, trying to see and despairing of understanding, while convicts sob on their knees on the shore, on seeing their exile ended by the arrival of the fatherland. As far away as Van Diemen's Land, the old queen Lalla Rookh[29] would quit Hobart, curious to see, before dying, those who had widowed her of five kings and her people. Coming from even further away the Malays, hardy canoeists, pirates with brick-colored complexions, more perfidious than the waves on which their skiffs play, would hoist sails like flotillas of insects before the great navigatrice.

---

[28] "Poulias" was a name used in various accounts of the Raj to designate slaves of the Malabar coast

[29] "Lalla Rookh"—borrowed from Thomas Moore's famous poem of 1817—was a nickname casually conferred on Truganini (1812-1876), "the last of the Tasmanians," by the genocidal settlers who exterminated her people.

From the bosom of this delirious crowd, crowded like and on the beaches, enormous acclamations would rise up in sonorous gusts, polyglot and cacophonous, proffered by all those voices in all those tongues, accompanied by the musical instruments of all those peoples. Hottentots from the Cape and kaffirs from Natal would show their delight by imitating the trumpeting of their elephants, echoing it on darabukka drums and canouns, five-string tambouras and Kordofan lyres, to which a chorus would respond from other shores of seashell tabors and gongs, kaffir violins, kamanjas and negro-skin tambourines, so renowned for the softness of their sounds.

Meanwhile, in order to savor her triumph, Great Britain, having furled her sails and moderated her propellers and paddles wheels, would progress at low speed over that shallow sea strewn with coral reefs. She would pass eastwards of Madagascar, the Mascarenes and the Seychelles and drop anchor in the vicinity of the 20th parallel, in the confines of the Sea of Oman, her prow turned toward India like the eye the master upon the slave, blocking access to the Mediterranean with its poop at the Gulf of Aden, lying in the Sun like her symbol the leopard, her claws posed on the austral globe, her tail unfurling over Europe via Suez, Egypt, Malta and Gibraltar.

As soon as the long and difficult anchorage maneuvers were complete and the Britannic Isle was moored at its new latitude, a great silence would fall upon the shores and the waves. Then the artillery of Woolwich, Chatham, Plymouth, the cannons of monitors and armored ships would blast away like a battery of volcanoes; England would render her salute to Asia. Then the 100,000 seamen of the crew covering the yardarms and the 20 million passengers crowning the hilltops would sing the national anthem, *God save the Queen, Empress of India*, in one immense hurrah; and the populations assembled on the shores would repeat it in chorus; and the sea, welcoming that sonorous tempest, would propagate it over its waves, roar it in its abysses, and murmur it tenderly on its beaches: *God save the Queen, Empress of India*!

The expenses of transporting Great Britain to Asia would have been considerable, but inferior to the benefits. What profit, in fact, and what security would England gain by annexing herself in this fashion to her colonies, living in the midst of its interests, in the bosom of its Hindu family! On the other hand, what a relief it would be to the European equilibrium, to the political equilibrium! As for the terrestrial equilibrium, Hatchitt, with his vast knowledge of such things, had guaranteed that it would not be affected.

Ireland, despite the urgent entreaties that Lord Hotairwell had made to her, had not shown herself desirous of following her big sister to Asia, preferring to continue its relations with her from afar, and to serve her as a colony and pied-à-terre in Europe.

The diplomatic annoyances that had given birth to this idea came to an end, as we know. In exchange for the isle of Cyprus,[30] which was given to her, England rendered her affection to Europe, and Lord Hotairwell, recovering his freedom of spirit, immediately returned to the conquest of the central fire—which, during this interval, had ripened various sorts of fruits in his mind.

To the first, purely scientific project, he had grafted an industrial concept—the utilization of that fire for lighting and heating—which was favorably welcomed by everyone: by the

---

[30] This reference must be to the events of June 1878, when the British were allowed to occupy Cyprus by the Anglo-Turkish agreement; the resignation of the prime minister, Lord Derby, in January 1878 after the cabinet voted to send a fleet to Constantinople to help settle "the Eastern question" had generated an outburst of jingoistic fervor in England—presumably the one that motivated Hotairwell to make his absurd proposal. This date is, however, completely at odds with all the other chronological indications given in the novel, suggesting that this cannibalized section must have been written after the first draft of *Ignis* and added to the version submitted to the publisher as an afterthought.

public, which loves novelty, by the experts, who had weighed it up immediately, and by his numerous friends, happy to see him turn his hand to such a fine business proposition. A few pushed enthusiasm so far as to see a prognostication of success in the founder's very name, the name of Hotairwell,[31] which did indeed indicate a singular kind of affinity between the man and the enterprise.

If the public looked avidly at the lucrative side of the affair, however, without worrying much about the scientific point of view, Lord Hotairwell himself had both goals in view, and promised himself that he would attain them both by first drilling to a depth of 12,000 meters, which would give the shareholders the promised heat and energy, and then continuing, to the profit of science, as far as the incandescent nucleus.

Despite this elaborate description, the portrait of the founder of the Central Fire Company would be incomplete if one did not introduce the reader to his dog, a poodle named Mirk, which was as attached to his master as Penkenton was to his cane.

Finally, the list of the principal guests at the Mansion House will be complete when I have cited my own name, the modest name of Edward Burton, well-known in London as that of a businessman who had given sufficient proof of his honesty and ability in the conduct of his affairs for the Central Fire Company to have invited him to join it in the capacity of managing director.

---

[31] The author inserts a footnote here to explain the meaning of "Hot-air well" to his French readers.

Chapter Five
A Three-League Well

On the Atlantic shore of northern Ireland, in the west of the county of Donegal, in the province of Ulster, there is a poor expanse of land, uncultivated and uncultivable, with no other vegetation than fir-trees and various kinds of heather: the accursed infants of Flora, trees that have become herbaceous by virtue of rickets, which can be cut with a scythe like a lawn.

A wretched Sun, its rays fringed with hoar-frost, sometimes illuminates this country, which is more often plunged in an opaque, stinking and insipid fog, oozing dropsy and fever, as if the Eskimos of Greenland, which faces it, had already breathed it out. If, by some misfortune, this fog dissipates, depriving this shivering land of its mist, the cold becomes intense; its viscous atmosphere crystallizes in needles of ice, which score the unfortunate inhabitants with their points. The latter, famished and emaciated, wander over the soil that does not want to nourish them, lamentable and grotesque in their ulster coats, whose disheveled skirts are inflated by the wind like sails, as ragged as street-singers, as ridiculous as beggars in suits, and as proud as bards descended from the race of Ossian. A few wolves, fortunate escapees from the proscriptions of Cromwell, are added to this human fauna: wolves misshapen by hunger, domesticated by misery, clad in hides too large for them, which form sack-like overcoats over their thin bodies, only too happy to have entered the service of such masters as dogs.

This misfortunate territory is 80 kilometers long by 40 wide, bordered along its length by the sea and by the little river Whitewater, which runs parallel to the coast from Oldtown to Weststand. The Great Central Irish Railway leads there, or at least approaches it, as far as Poor Farm Station,

57

where the locomotives stop, whinnying and shying away like oxen that have just scented bad pasturage.

Such is the terrain that Lord Hotairwell, in his great wisdom, has chosen for his enterprise, reckoning that a trial, in order to be decisive, must be carried out in the worst conditions, that the country that is most suitable for progress is the one that has everything to do, and that the civilizing might of the central fire will be demonstrated superabundantly on the day when it has created a city in this desert, fertilized this soil and rendered this climate hospitable.

When we penetrate into the yards of the geothermal well, six years have passed since the work began, and the excavation, which is due to attain 12,000 meters in eight years, has so far only extended for 2000. Even so, the totality of the social capital has been spent, although the expected call for funds will be warmly welcomed by the shareholders, full of faith and hope. The engineers too remain full of confidence, in themselves and in the project, which, these circumstances apart, is following an extremely favorable course.

The Great Central Irish Line, which formerly terminated at Poor Farm, now extends as far as the edge of the shaft, to the great satisfaction of the Company, which benefits from the transport of all the materials necessary for the construction of the shaft and its city.

What one can see on the horizon, when one has passed over the embankment that descends into the plain of Industria City, is the enormous periphery of a flattened cupola, the roof of a hall similar, save for its gigantic proportions, to the circular sheds in which locomotives are housed. The shaft opens in the middle of this hangar, with a tangle of rails radiating from it or converging upon it, bearing the wagons containing raw materials or rubble. A sufficiently accurate idea of the external appearance of this gulf by imagining one of the fountains in the Jardin des Tuileries as deep as five times the length of the Champs-Elysées, or 67 times the height of the Arc de Triomphe, or 75,000 times the height of William Hatchitt. Then, by leaning over the edge, with all the precaution than such an abyss inspires, one may take in the whole of the subterranean workshops.

The geothermal well presents an opening whose section has been extended to 15 meters; its current depth, as indicated by the bathometer fixed at the rim, is 2100 meters—which, following the progression of one degree per 33 meters, indicates a temperature of 73 degrees. The excavation is carried out by hand, 30 workmen to each crew. Fifteen picks alternating with 15 spades clear in a circular fashion: a living Archimedean screw digging into the soil, slowly but inexorably.

As the excavation progresses, a steel lining descends and dresses the wall. This lining is superimposed on itself in fractions two meters in height, which a crane places, one by one, on the positioned sections, joined to one another and unified to the point at which, when the well is finished, if its circumference were cleared, a column of steel would be obtained three times as wide and 200 times as high as the Colonne Vendôme, which might serve as a pedestal for 20 dozen Napoleons.

Before adopting this system, the engineers had investigated the question of whether the well's metallic lining should be integral and responsible for supporting itself along its entire length, or whether it should be established in sections supported by brackets and underpinned. William Hatchitt had warmly recommended this means and had proven, according to the evidence, the impossibility of a self-supporting tube 12,000 meters long and weighing 120 million kilograms, whose inferior parts would be crushed by its own weight. James Archibold, however—a committed supporter of an integral lining—had established by means of the same evidence the inanity of Hatchitt's calculations and demonstrated that the molecular dilatation of the metal, which had to be assumed to be proportional to temperature, and consequently to depth and the burden of weight, would oppose itself with proportional efficacy to the crushing force. The latter opinion had prevailed, by reason of its technical merit, and also its hierarchical merit, since it was that of the chief engineer.

For the other items of equipment, such as the bucket-elevators, the winches, the skips and the chains, which would not have been able to extend to such depths without breaking, the distance had been divided into ten sections or stages, supported on ledges in the metal wall and serving as supports and relays for all the apparatus of movement and traction, and tubes and wires of every sort, as well as a 15 horse-power locomotive on each stage, answering to the needs of the station.

It is extremely difficult to describe the appearance of this abyssal building-site, full to the brim with noisy activity and silences as profound as itself, thick intervals of darkness and sparks cutting through that darkness: sparsely-distributed errant electric lights, like captive will-o'-the-wisps or caged bird-lights bumping into the walls of their prison in their flight.

All these comparisons are apt, but they are all impotent to describe what an eye applied to the orifice would see, peering into an inferno in which demonic armies stir, armed with spades, picks and pincers, torturing the bosom of old Cybele! A crater hollowed out by human hands! A gargantualesque mouth drinking creatures and objects, vomiting fumes and vapors, gusts of darkness and waves of light that spring forth and overflow the rim in sparkling steams: a swirling, tumultuous swarm of mad machines and men plunging down or disinterring themselves; skips charged with debris slowly climbing their vertical path, tipping over, emptying themselves and falling back at a crazy speed; rapid elevators carrying relays of workmen; atmospheric tubes from which bustling overseers launch themselves like jack-in-a-boxes.

Is it necessary to mention the poodle Mirk, Lord Hotairwell's dog? He is a trusted employee carrying messages between the surface and the depths, heading straight into the gulf, hurtling down a tube, sliding along a wire, holding on as best he can and falling any old how, on his back, his belly or the Hatchitt's head—the latter having a horror of the baying commissionaire.

The more one looks into this hole as profound as the heavens, similarly full of stars and shadows, the further the vision is multiplied. After the large items come the small ones; after the stars, the cosmic dust; after the corpulent machines, the little vertical locomobiles standing on their ledges like bottles on a plank; the zigzagging ladders spanning the depths; the electric wires creeping and clinging like lianas, insinuating themselves like ivy—the climbing flora of metallurgy. It has the apparent disorder of an ant-hill; a circulation so active in a narrow space that it seems that everything must eventually be reduced by collisions into the same dust, equalized by friction.

In Paris in winter, on the Boulevard Montmartre, when night falls and the movement of the pedestrians and vehicles attains its apogee, the people coming and going bump into one another, the carriages become entangled and the horses stumble; a passer-by breaks an arm, a fiacre breaks a shaft—but the quantity of those damaged is infinitesimal compared with the great number who follow their route safe and sound, almost all arriving at their destinations, and all achieving their destiny. By the same token, the disorder in the well—this vertical boulevard encumbered by an intense circulation and an eternal night—is only apparent, and the men and the things slide in their grooves and follow their correct paths. It could not be otherwise for a track whose line-managers are the engineers James Archibold and William Hatchitt, the former on watch at the orifice, the latter remaining in the depths in his suspended office, trellised like a cage to facilitate his surveillance.

Hatchitt had taken up residence underground in a conclusive manner, only emerging on days when there were committee-meetings, or to take care of matters of great urgency. He had installed himself there in modest comfort, sufficient to his tastes. Horticulture was the preferred distraction of his leisure-time, and he obtained great success therein, due to his intelligent care and the exceptionally favorable circumstances in the well, which offer him a complete series of perpendicular climates, a graduated scale of all temperatures, from that of Ireland at the orifice to that of the torrid zone in the depths. It

61

was, according to Hatchitt's own expression, a marvelous underground hothouse.

Having little space at his disposal and only able to cultivate on stairs or on the flat ground of the ledges, William Hatchitt applied himself especially to the culture of orchids, those plants that live anywhere, without humus, on a hurdle, on a wall or wedged in a crack: interloper creatures—"animals with roots", as Linnaeus says—more alive than certain animals, hybrids of Fauna and Flora, flower-birds and insect-butterflies provided with roots that are feet and leaves that are wings.

For the absent Sun of his garden Hatchitt substituted electric light, adapted and assorted to the temperaments of his seedlings. Everyone knows the magnificent results of animal and vegetable culture that have been attained by the application of isolated rays of light, and what economies of time science has procured for nature by such means. There is no need to recall how Monsieur Béclard, placing flies' eggs in violet light, obtained larvae three times as fine as those hatched in sunlight, three times as fast; how tadpoles that are anemic in white light, and others mortally afflicted in green light, came back to life and turned into frogs as soon as they were placed in blue; and how finally, little sows afflicted with threadworms, almost killed by those parasites, became vigorous and edible as soon as their owner, General Pleasonton of Philadelphia, placed them in a more favorable light.[32]

With the support of these facts and others, which demonstrate that red light is as much of a tonic to plants as violet

---

[32] The physiologist Jules-Auguste Béclard (1817-1887) published his findings on the effects of blue, violet and ultraviolet light on animal growth in 1858. Augustus James Pleasonton, the scion of a famous American military family, born in 1808, began his own experiments shortly afterwards but the key paper reporting his results was not published until 1876, which is anachronistic within the context of the story; contemporary French readers would have been aware of the "blue glass craze" prompted by the publicity given to Pleasonton's work.

light is to animals, Hatchitt nourished his cultures on red and violet rays—the latter being, as everyone knows, very abundant in electric light—and he obtained results that were prodigious, but which were, in the mind of the intensive gardener, only a beginning.

Judging, like his compatriot, Mr. Huxley, that the difference between plants and animals is less a difference of kind than one of degree,[33] Hatchitt had no doubt that, by means of the apt selection and progress of lighting, one would not only be able to achieve prompt hatchings, increased growth and improvements of species, but further advances in degree: transformisms[34] and rapid evolutions of plants toward the animal.

Hatchitt directed his cultures toward this goal, with so much success that on some days, brave as he was, the sight of his flowers frightened him. It might have been his troubled eyesight, an effect of shade or electric light, but several times,

---

[33] Thomas Henry Huxley (1825-1895) made this remark in a classic lecture on "Yeast" (1871) subsequently reprinted in his *Collected Essays*; again, its citation here is slightly anachronistic.

[34] I have transcribed *transformismes* directly into English rather than substituting "transformationsm," because "transformism" was the name given to a particular kind of evolutionism, which argued that species changed into new species over time; it was particularly characteristic of the thesis outlined in the Chevalier de Lamarck's *Philosophie zoologique* (1809), which argued that all living creatures are equipped with an innate evolutionary impulse—which Henri Bergson subsequently named *élan vital*—that is perpetually driving them to progressive improvement. Although the thesis was overtaken and displaced by the Darwinian theory of natural selection, it retained a strong influence in French thought throughout the 19th century—this passage, though calculatedly absurd, is fairly typical of French literary accounts of evolution in this period.

walking among his flower-beds, he had discovered among his plants evident signs of intellectual culture, pronounced symptoms of animal activity, nervous contractions and marks of authentic sensibility, embryonic gestures and sketches of physiognomy. Certain flowers swooned at his approach, or turned toward him as if toward their Sun; pansies stared at him languorously with their golden eyes. Others, meanwhile, appearing to hate him, bristled their velvet cilia and fled his touch all along their stems. Bengal roses sharpened their claws like tigers, and snapdragons made as if to bite him. One day, a Venus fly-trap (*Dionaea discipula*) tried to seize him, and every day, clouds of pollen, as aggressive as insects, took flight to deposit on his lips their virginal perfume and the taste of kisses.

In the presence of this progress, which gave cause for reflection, Hatchitt had extinguished the violet in his electric lamps, and no longer entered his garden without taking precautions.

Hatchitt's health held up admirably underground, and he reckoned personally that his faculties were expanded there. Having become something of a materialist in his perpetual dealings with matter, he solidified the soul and the body beyond the measure that philosophers and physiologists have marked so exactly, and claimed to have more intelligence at the bottom of a well than at the summit of a mountain, and more below ground than above it. He argued, in support of his thesis, that the electrical charge of the atmosphere diminishes on high mountains, to the point of no longer being sufficient to dynamize the cerebral circumvolutions that generate, digest, secrete, solidify and excrete thought. At an altitude of 10,000 meters, he contended, the weight of the atmosphere is considerably reduced, and water boils before getting hot; similarly, at that height, thought melts and evaporates before being in possession of its expansive force and heat.

An instrument of his invention, the psychometer, permitted Hatchitt to measure this mental depression, and the experiments that he had carried out on his head by means of the apparatus had led him to the conclusion that if, departing from the bottom of a shaft where his brain-power measured +80%, he climbed breathlessly to a peak in the Himalayas, his intelligence, on arriving there, would have descended to -10%—which is to say, below the mean level of human stupidity. He obtained further evidence from the stupefaction that tourists experience on arriving at the summit of Mont Blanc, which persists in some cases when they come back.

Accustomed to living so profoundly, seal-level—the planet's ground floor—was Hatchitt's sixth floor; he got vertigo there. His intelligence weakened, and in order to increase it again he had to go back down into the shaft, where he soon recovered what he called his *esprit du bas de l'escalier.*[35] He anticipated, therefore, that his faculties would increase further in descending more deeply, and that, if he reached the nucleus of the globe, he would certainly be an engineer of genius.

On this basis, Hatchitt recommended a sojourn in the well to feeble-minded individuals and, more generally, to all anemics and rheumatics, who would find there, at the temperatures that would be reached in the geothermal gulf, climatic conditions superior to the warmest places in the South of France, variable according to the ledges, and getting better every day by virtue of the excavation.

At the exit from the well, the visitor's eye is initially attracted to the marvelous machines that aliment the life and movement of the workplace, in the depths and at the surface: the enormous generators, the flanks of which snore like constricted chests; the breathing apparatus—the air-pumps that fill the lungs of the diggers at long-distance; the Pictet devices,

---

[35] This pun does not translate; *esprit de l'escalier* ["staircase wit"], in English as in French, signifies the tendency everyone has only to think of clever rejoinders once the moment appropriate to their use has passed, but *esprit* signifies "mind" as well as "wit," so Hatchitt is referring to his "foot-of the-staircase mind."

which solidify oxygen;[36] the cranes that overhang the orifice and furnish the sections of the lining—giants of iron and bronze, shaped according to their destiny.

If one then passes through the western door of the hall, a couple of 100 paces further on one runs into a conical mountain, which presents, on that flat plain, the violent relief of a lump of sugar on a tabletop: an artificial mountain, created day by day by the rubble of the well, rising up as it is hollowed out, and serving to support and surround the pipe that serves as a ventilation shaft—the chimney of the central fire.

In the surrounding countryside, the future city extends, formed into plots of land for sale and streets to be built. The founders, having arrived first and had the choice of neighborhoods, have mostly taken up residence in the vicinity of the works. The chief engineer, James Archibold, shares with me, Edward Burton, a modest chalet at number 1, Burton Street. Professor Samuel Penkenton, disdainful of comfort, who is used to inhabiting the caves of primitive humankind for pleasure, has ordered the construction, in an outlying district, of a sort of sentry-box, extremely tall and thin, more a wooden overcoat than a house, comprising a very high ground floor—by reason of the tallness of its inhabitant, and a loft forming a

---

[36] This clarifies an earlier reference to Hatchitt taking air in tablet form. Raoul Pictet (1846-1929) notified the Académie Française in 1877 that he had succeeded in liquefying oxygen. Louis Cailletet (1832-1913) succeeded in doing so almost simultaneously by a different method. The author of *Ignis* was not the only speculator who imagined that the feat might be taken a stage further; Georges le Faure and Henry de Graffigny supplied their space-travelers with solid oxygen reserves—also making reference to Pictet—in *Les Aventures Extraordinaire d'un Savant Russe* (Black Coat Press tr. as *The Extraordinary Adventures of a Russian Scientist*), whose first volume appeared a few years later than *Ignis*. Yet again, the reference is anachronistic with respect to the dates specifically cited in the story.

guest-room, in which Hatchitt sometimes stays when he has occasion to decamp from the well. Such nights are devoted to scientific discussions, which almost always degenerate into matters of personality—quarrels so violent that the neighbors, if there were any, would often see Hatchitt hurled into the street by an enormous hand, still arguing and refusing to give an inch.

Lord Hotairwell, determined to set an example and to entertain guests as soon as the city has inhabitants, has had a very fine house built in Hotairwell Square, in which he has obligingly provided a room for board-meetings: a vast room, sternly functional in appearance, furnished with a conference table equipped with telephone and telegraphic receivers connected to the subterranean workshop, and also with tetroscopes, mirroring at a distance—a channeled mirage reflecting the absent spectacle, which permits the administrators to follow the slightest details of the work, even during meetings, and to discuss them with a competence unfamiliar to administrations that do not possess tetroscopes and who cannot see very far.[37] Other similar instruments of lesser dimension, in the form of hand-mirrors or globes, scattered here and there, facilitate an incessant surveillance and make it impossible for Hatchitt to absent himself or to slow down without his superiors being immediately informed.

At the depth attained in January 1867, the heat caused the diggers to suffer considerably, but the anticipatory measures taken to combat it were increasingly brought into play, like troops deploying parallel to those of the enemy. The consecutive duration of work was reduced to two hours, alternated with three hours rest, and the skips were functioning unrelentingly, loading and unloading relays of workers. The latter

---

[37] The word "tetroscope" produces no hits on Google that refer to 19th century sources other than *Ignis*, and I cannot identify any prior origin of the term; interestingly, however, Google does bring up references to a 2008 invention with that name, which does exactly what the author of *Ignis* describes.

worked under showers, dressed in sponge-cloth gowns impregnated with water, the evaporation of which—caused by the ambient heat—refreshed them, like vases exposed to the Sun wrapped in moist cloths. The cutaneous sweat that also cools by virtue of latent heat, naturally activated in such a warm environment, was carefully replenished by abundant drinks.

Thus clad, the workmen looked like awkward specters, devoured beneath their rags by the sort of fire that fumes before bursting into flame. The side-walls of the well, similarly dressed in constantly-moistened spongy materials, exhaled enormous clouds of mist, contributing to the thickness of the atmosphere. One might have thought it a London crossroads fallen into a gulf, along with its beggars, its thieves, its fog, its mud, and even its rain—for, if the air currents happen to relent, the ventilators lacking energy, all these vapors condense into hot rains falling back into dirty pools. Then the unfortunate diggers, their heads beneath the hot water, their bodies in a Turkish bath and their feet on the central fire, breathing nothing but miasmas and seeing nothing but darkness, could have believed themselves to be men who had arrived by mistake before the sixth day of Creation on a dark and red-hot Earth, prey to diluvian downpours, only fit for habitation by zoophytes and mollusks.

Their life was, however, sustained in that exceedingly inappropriate environment, and Archibold had not even authorized free distributions of Pictet oxygen as yet. The supplements of breathable air taken from the workplace canteen were paid for in cash or deducted from salary. By way of compensation, the service providing ice from Greenland was fully functional, bringing the workers considerable relief.

This importation of ice had gone through various phases in its establishment. To begin with, following Archibold's orders, the Company's agent in Greenland had cut small icebergs in the shape of a ship from the circumpolar ice-sheet and equipped them with a tiller and enough sail to run them aground on the coast of Ireland. Several shipwrecks having taken place, however, and recruitment of crews for these ice-boats—one of which, after straying into the Gulf Stream, had melted completely—being difficult, the Company had adopted a more practical system of equipping solid steamers to hunt icebergs, capturing strays or detaching them from the arctic sheet.

Hatchitt, it was said, was perfectly resistant to the fatigues of his life, simultaneously so sedentary and so active, and had made no other concession to the heat than to don his summer clothes. On the other hand, he suffered from the cold and caught a chill every time he came up to the surface—which he rarely did, always enveloped in furs. His stature permitted him to squeeze into compressed air tubes of small diameter, in which his body formed a piston, and he got around in this fashion with great rapidity. Besides, in order to guard against accidents, he usually carried on his person a little ladder made of aluminum, a very light metal: a sort of stilt, which supplemented his height and facilitated his relationships with things or people, providing an attachment or allowing him to reach Dr. Penkenton's ear.

Because Hatchitt had come up only a short time before, his colleagues were surprised to see him emerge unexpectedly from his tube on the morning of June 23. He seemed to be worried, and did not respond with his usual promptness to the affectionate handshakes that were lavished on him.

"My workers are going on strike," he said, briefly. "They say that it's too hot."

"Pooh!" said Penkenton.

"They have some cause for complaint," I opined, being unable to look into the well without breaking out in a sweat.

"You're right, Mr. Burton," Hatchitt agreed, "and it's easy for the doctor to talk, as someone who lounges around in the temperate climate of superficial England and almost never goes down below."

"I reckoned on them keeping going until it reached 100 degrees," Archibold put in.

"And do you know what you're going to do when they reach 100 degrees?" asked Hatchitt.

"Of course—the matter's in hand."

"So much the better! Their demands have increased."

"What are they, Mr. Hatchitt?"

"They want an hour's rest per half-hour of work; they want their rest to be counted as work, and an increased hourly rate; and finally, they demand breathable air for free."

"They're mad!" said Archibold. "Giving them air for nothing would cost me sixpence a liter! If they can't afford it, let them hold their breath! Do they expect to breathe as much as rich people?"

"I've told them that; they understand it perfectly well, but they've objected that they're not doing ordinary work."

"That's true," agreed Lord Hotairwell.

"They also say that the well wasn't as deep when they started, and even Tom Foster, who is very devoted to us, is of that opinion."

"That's true too," said the ever-impartial Lord Hotairwell.

"I forgot to say," Hatchitt continued, "that they also demand that their ration of pale ale, which is 20 liters per man per day, should be raised to 50 liters."

"That's at least ten liters more than their skin can transpire. An ordinary human skin—I don't mean the skins of Penkenton, Hatchitt and Burton, which are too large, too small or too thick, but an average human skin, two millimeters thick, pierced by sweat glands a twentieth of a millimeter in diameter and offering a normal surface area of 12 square feet, folds and wrinkles includes, allowing a deduction for fingernails and toenails—never contrives, even in the most favorable conditions, to exude more than three liters of sweat per hour. That's 30 liters per ten-hour day, which is 20 liters less than the quantity of beer they're asking for. Thus, if they drink 50 liters, they'll be drinking to excess; they'll become hydropic, cachexic and rachitic[38]—so I shan't give them their 50 liters. In fact, I won't give them any."

"As you wish," said Hatchitt, "but we must deliberate and make a decision urgently, for they're waiting down below."

"Ask them to come up," replied the chief engineer, "for I've deliberated, and decided that I'll sack them."

"You're stopping the work, then?" said Hatchitt, nettled.

"No, Mr. Hatchitt. I shan't stop the work for an instant."

"Not an instant," confirmed the doctor, who seemed to be in on the secret.

"You're presumably proposing to dig yourselves?" asked William Hatchitt. "You'll do well—that the best way of utilizing Penkenton, who is big and strong and doesn't do anything."

"We haven't come to that yet," the engineer replied, simultaneously giving a blast on his whistle.

A foreman presented himself and received his orders. A few minutes later, a door in the hall slid back on its rollers and gave passage to two hermetically-sealed wagons, which came closer, pushed by hand.

"Have they eaten today?" asked Archibold.

"Not yet," replied the employee.

"Open them carefully, then."

They were opened, and two solidly-barred menagerie cages appeared behind the removed panels, each filled with about 30 large black creatures, nude and hairy, which set about celebrating the advent of daylight in their dwelling with animal cries, bestial laughter, panther-like leaps and ape-like gestures, with their hands or claws extending toward their hosts, to seize or clutch them: a swarming confusion of savage

---

[38] Hydropsia, usually abbreviated to dropsy, is an abnormal accumulation of fluid in the body; cachexia is a condition of general ill-health provoked by a chronic condition; rachitis is an inflammation of the spine, most commonly caused by rickets.

acrobats with their limbs entangled, welded into a single body with neither form nor limit.

"What's that?" asked Hatchitt, disgustedly.

"It's your new work crew," replied the chief engineer.

"Are they great apes of some kind?"

"Apes, Mr. Hatchitt!" said Archibold. "What are you saying? They're superb specimens of humanity!" As he attempted to feel a limb, which immediately kicked out at him, he added: "What torsos and calves!"

"And the calf," added the doctor, fixing his eyes on Hatchitt's meager tibias, "constitutes one of the most significant differences between man and ape."

"They seem ferocious!" observed Hatchitt.

"They have nice faces!" I said, at hazard, with the intention of encouraging him.

"Do you think so, Mr. Burton?" the little engineer yelped, ironically.

"Don't judge these brave individuals by their appearance," Archibold resumed. "Remember that they're weary from a long voyage, and perhaps intimidated by this introduction immediately upon arrival."

"Where do these apes come from?" Hatchitt asked.

"One of the hottest countries in Africa, Mr. Hatchitt. One can't find men more accustomed to heat, and it's a veritable godsend that the doctor has found…"

"Yes," Penkenton put in, seizing the conversational initiative by force, as was his custom, "these natives of Cololo, as I've noticed in my trips to Africa, are a simple and industrious people, a little less ferocious than neighboring tribes. Accustomed to enormous heat, they'll scarcely be tested by that of the well, and I expressed the opinion to Mr. Archibold a long time ago that these workers are the only ones who can complete it."

"So it's you that has had this fine idea?" Hatchitt sniggered. "My sincere compliments."

"I accept them with pleasure," the doctor replied, "for I'm convinced that these men will give you full satisfaction.

The only delicate issue is getting them out of their cages without them getting irritated and without them escaping, for once they're in the well, they'll have to stay here, and will then be your concern. I advise you, however, to exercise all your vigilance on them, for they can climb like monkeys, and they'll scarcely be down below than they'll come back up." Graciously, the doctor added: "I have no need to tell you how to direct workers, and I'm convinced that the great agility of these, transformed by you into useful work, will yield quite surprising results."

"These savages must cost a great deal," said Hatchitt—who, according to his habit, had not been listening to Penkenton. "It would be better to negotiate with our workers."

"They cost less than you think," said Archibold.

"How much did you pay for them?"

"160 pounds the lot, freight and delivery included—that's not much!"

"160 pounds a day?"

"No, Mr. Hatchitt, a single payment of 160 pounds, since I've bought them."

"You've bought them! But England prohibits the trading of negroes."

"On the surface, Mr. Hatchitt, but underneath…oh, when they come out of the well, they'll be free—but they won't, of course, be free to come out."

"You'll feed them, though—slaves are always fed."

"No, I shan't feed them, since they're not slaves. Taking their particular situation into consideration, however, I'll advance them their nourishment and debit their current accounts. Anyway, their alimentation is very simple: a few dates, and a watermelon on Sundays, that's all. I shall, in any case, give you the pleasure of seeing them eat."

Archibold took some dates from a basket and hurled a volley of them into the cages, which filled with a joyful racket and chewing noises, such as one might hear at a collective banquet held by the director of the Jardin de Plantes for all his animals. Only one thing troubled the charm of this spectacle, which was the fear that the bars of the dining-room might give way to the petulance of the guests.

"See!" said the chief engineer. "What good humor, and what zest!"

"The humor of a pack of hyenas," replied Hatchitt. "What do you expect me to do with this crew of ferocious beasts?"

"I assure you," said Penkenton, "that they're gentler than they seem; the proof is that, in their own country, they're left at liberty."

"That doesn't change the fact that they're ferocious enough for anyone obliged to attach himself to them," replied Hatchitt, furiously.

"Then don't forget," Archibold put in, "That Pot'alo is there to command them, under your orders."

"Who's Pot'alo? An overseer?"

"A king, Mr. Hatchitt, a king! The king of these people, who sold himself to us at a premium."

"An abdicated king," sneered Hatchitt. "A bad lot."

"No, a king who carries himself very well."

"Where is he? I can't see one that looks any better than the others?"

"He's not with the others," replied Archibold. "One doesn't place a king in the regimen of a subject; that would be contrary to etiquette. His majesty travels in a first-class cage."

The engineer having opened a trap-door at the back of one of the wagons, a negro's head appeared, gracious and respectful. He made as if to come out, but Archibold swiftly reclosed the panel.

"You're not letting him come out?" said Hatchitt, astonished. "He's as ferocious as the others, then?"

"I don't think so, but it's more prudent. He might try to escape, even though he's a very meek character, and since these gentlemen won't take up their posts until tomorrow, it's best not to disturb them."

The following day, at the appointed hour—not without reluctance on Hatchitt's part—the 48 negroes, under the guidance of the king, were ranged in a silent and orderly manner around the well, spades and pick-axes on their shoulders. When the engineer appeared the silence became more profound, the alignment and attitudes more correct. When he came closer there was the sort of quiver of love and dread in the ranks that runs through an army at the sight of its commander-in-chief. Commander Pot'alo stood in front of his men, stern and dignified, brandishing his ironwood cane in his royal hand—a scepter appropriate to his new role.

Received with a courtesy and honors that he had no right to expect, Hatchitt found himself almost tongue-tied, and did not quite know how to conduct himself in the face of such correct savages and a prince who retained, in slavery, a majesty superior to that which he had had on his throne. Hatchitt rubbed his eyes, drew himself up to his full height, and touched himself to make sure that he was not black and naked himself, a negro general or a savage major making a tour of inspection.

In the meantime, Archibold took inventory of the men, marking them up as he did so with a piece of chalk. "I beg you to observe," he said to Hatchitt, "that instead of delivering 48 negroes, I'm giving you 52, without being able to explain the excess."

"They must have given you 13 to the dozen," Hatchitt replied, his good humor having returned. To the amazement of the two engineers, this joke, understood and appreciated by the savages, caused them to start and burst out laughing. The king, who had trouble containing himself, hastily reprimanded them by means of a few blows with his scepter.

Having added his signature to the official register of the workmen, and provided a receipt for 52 negroes, Hatchitt turned to his men and showed them the well. They broke ranks, and there was a confused movement caused by the haste of the troop to see their leader at closer range and to express their naïve affection for him by touching him curiously, sniffing him respectfully, seeking to judge his character by his odor, as animals and savages do whose perception is more intimately linked to material contacts.

Hatchitt could not any longer have a shadow of doubt as to their disposition, and even less as to their obedience, for, when he had repeated his gesture inviting them to go into the well, the entire company, the king included, made as if to hurl themselves into it. These poor folk knew nothing of the means of descent that civilization has invented, and the engineer hardly had time to hold them back in order to make them enter the skips one by one. When they were all seated therein, and after a final exchange of civilities, Hatchitt embarked himself in his rapid-transit tube, in order to supervise the arrival, as he had presided over the departure.

More anxious deep down than we wanted to appear, we were extremely glad abut that the relationship had commenced so well; nevertheless, we remained on the lookout all day, often asking the engineer for news.

The latter only came back eight hours later to spend a few minutes on the surface. He was delighted. "These blacks," he said, "are excellent savages; they work like negroes, breathe quite easily, and their frizzy hair, which absorbs water, keeps their heads cool. I'll make good workmen of them, and perhaps render them white. Is it the influences of cave-life that's making them go pale, like lettuces? They already seem less black.

"If these negroes become white," said Penkenton "They'll acquire an intrinsic added value, which will permit their resale at a profit."

"No," Archibold replied, firmly. "I promised that they'd be free when they came out of the well, and if they come out white, I'll make them a gift of their added value."

Chapter Six
A Walk in the Forest

A few months later, on a fine June morning,[39] we found ourselves reunited around the excavation, which had been passing through friable layers for several days, at an extremely satisfactory speed of nine meters per 24 hours. Lord Hotairwell listened pensively to the regular hammering of the fine tools, and the sounds of the rock-drill, whose muffled echo rose dully out of the well. A few paces away from him, Dr. Samuel Penkenton was rummaging through the rubble spilled out by the skips—which must have been full of geological treasures, for the doctor, not knowing which of his discoveries to attend to, was running from one to another like a child with an embarrassment of toys.

Near the well, Archibold, who had just telephoned a question to the subterranean worksite, was waiting to hear the reply. Suddenly, from the funnel applied to his ear, there emerged a cry so loud that the engineer thrust the telephone away, as if a slap in the face had emerged therefrom instead of a sound. "Stop! Hoist away!" cried the same strident voice, supported by a ringing bell that dislocated the apparatus.

As swift as lightning, Archibold executed the requested maneuver. A serious accident had evidently just occurred, and it seemed to be a long time before the wagonettes brushed the surface, bringing forth the workers.

Were the men safe and sound? Were they even men? One would not have been able to say so, on seeing those negro heads, bristling and livid, their eyes haggard.

"For God's sake, Tom, what's happened?" demanded Lord Hotairwell of the foreman, who seemed to have retained more self-composure.

---

[39] The author seems to have lost track of time slightly; the last scene also took place in June.

""What's happened, Milord," the man replied, not without effort, "is that in another second we'd have been burned."

"Burned?" said Lord Hotairwell.

"Yes, burned by the central fire."

"By the central fire? That's impossible.

"By the central fire, whose fumes tried to choke us."

"You're not serious, Tom," said Archibold in his turn.

"Mr. Archibold," the foreman replied, "do you think that these savages are play-acting? One would think, on seeing them, that it's more like they're feigning life."

The negroes, huddled together for mutual support, looked at Tom Foster, shaking their heads like dolls with springs for necks, in a sign of assent or imbecility."

"Even so, Tom," Lord Hotairwell continued "it's absolutely impossible that you've encountered the central fire at this depth; the scientists place it 20 times further down—not to mention that, if you had got close to that fire, the temperature of which is enormous…."

"195,000 degrees," Archibold specified.

"…Nothing would remain of you, at this moment—not even a pinch of ash, just a mere bubble of vapor."

"Not to mention, too," Archibold put in, having looked at the thermometer, "that under the influence of such heat, that instrument would have shattered into little pieces. It's all impossible." By way of conclusion, the engineer buttoned his overcoat, as was his habit, as if to enclose himself within his conviction.

"Mr. Archibold," Foster replied, "the central fire is there, since it has burned us, and the scientists think it's elsewhere because they haven't been there, or because they went there by another route. The thermometer hasn't climbed because it hasn't had long enough to indicate the heat that you mention, and because it has no reason to climb, since the central fire isn't hot."

"The central fire isn't hot?" I cried.

"No, Mr. Burton; it wouldn't boil a kettle. The central fire is a cold fire, a sad fire, which is nothing but smoke, which doesn't flame and which extinguishes others—for it has put out our lanterns—but which, of course, burns the eyes and the throat like a true fire."

"In any case," said Archibold, "how did the accident happen?"

"We'd been working for an hour in rock that had a funny feel to it, in a mixture of sand, gravel, rubble, pieces of tree-bark and other bits of wood that resembled timbers—more like a demolition-site than an earthwork. There were branches and tree-trunks so thick that it was necessary to saw them up to load them into the skips, and when the disaster happened, we were picking out way through undergrowth, in a wood. It was the wood that the central fire heated up, for it was at that moment that its smoke gushed over us to choke us, and the bottom of the well fell into a hole."

"The bottom of the well collapsed?" said the engineer. "That's very serious."

"Only half of it," said Foster. "Otherwise we'd all have perished."

"Nevertheless, it's serious, for the lining is now without support and might collapse. It's necessary to verify this as quickly as possible."

Archibold, followed by Lord Hotwairell, got ready to go down.

"Don't go down there, gentlemen!" cried Foster. "Don't get yourselves killed for a fire that's nothing but smoke—a smoke that isn't smoke, since it's invisible—and seal the well securely, in case that fire takes it into its head to follow us…but not before telling William Hatchitt to come back up."

"William Hatchitt!" cried Lord Hotairwell and Archibold, in a stupor. "We forgot about him! And you, Tom Foster, have abandoned him!"

"Pardon me, Milord, but I found it impossible to persuade Mr. Hatchitt to come back."

"We must bring him back by force," said Archibold.

"That's what I tried to do. Three times I had him put in the skip, but he wriggled out like an eel from a bucket. When I had gone, he shouted to me to tell you not to worry about him, that he would come up later, but that he was going to go down first."

"Go down where? Into that gulf? The fool must have been asphyxiated."

"No, Mr. Archibold, for he called out to us again, telling us to tell you that he wouldn't be asphyxiated—and he's quite capable of it. Mr. Hatchitt has a strong temperament, and he played with that vapor with his nose, as if it were the smoke from a cigarette."

They were no longer listening to Foster; the chief engineer was giving orders in all haste. The most urgent was to send air to Hatchitt and to evacuate the mephitic gas by forcing it up to the surface. To that end, the ventilators and pumps were started, and operated at maximum speed.

"Encountering the central fire at this feeble depth," said Lord Hotairwell, who was busy about the apparatus, feverish and impatient, "can have no other explanation than meeting the chimney of a not-quite-extinct volcano."

"The nature of the terrain falsifies that hypothesis," the engineer replied. Pointing to Penkenton—who was more intricately entangled than Abraham's kid in a pile of dusty brushwood with which he had been struggling for some time—he added: "Just look at the doctor."

Never had any pit-sawyer whose saw had been stopped by sweat presented a stranger face. "You see me emerging from a forest into which I was trying to restore a little order," the doctor said to his colleagues, as they drew closer. "Here are a few trees already arranged." Penkenton pointed to the largest section of an oak picked out of the debris and carefully reconstructed: the forks of the trunk juxtaposed with their branches, and, on the latter, whole series of decreasing branches, each extreme tip of which was only lacking its foliage.

"Look at this oak, Gentlemen. Save for the mahogany color that mummified trees and humans acquire over time, wouldn't you think it an oak from Hyde Park, stripped by winter? Winter has been long for this tree; it has lasted centuries, and also for this vine, and ancestor of the ones that England once cultivated, whose wine wasn't bad—a touch bitter and hard to conserve, like all weak wines, but healthy and with an honest bouquet." Penkenton clicked his tongue like a wine-taster as he concluded: "You're laughing, Mr. Burton; you don't believe it—but Bentham, in his history of Ely,[40] will tell you, as I do, that the county of Gloucester was renowned for its *crus*, and that Windsor Park was a smallholding esteemed by the Romans. It's true that, in that era, the climate of England was warmer, for the Sun is going out…slowly."

"One degree per 57,000 centuries, which is 1/30,000th of a degree since the Roman Empire," James Archibold specified.

"Yes, so it was not only the Sun that was responsible for the cooling of England and other countries, but also deforestation. The people of long ago did not conserve forests, not understanding that they are as necessary to a plant as hair and fur are to an animal."

Penkenton returned to his work before his loquacity had permitted him to learn about the recent accident, adding: "At any rate, this is a fine day for geology, and for the Central Fire Company, which will make a fortune if it perseveres on this course of discovery; as for me, if my capital were to bring me no further return than this debris, I would consider myself the most fortunate of shareholders. We are only at the beginning, for these specimens demonstrate that we are entering a fossil forest swallowed up by a cataclysm. We're entering through the branches, but we shall descend to the trunks and the roots."

"Mr. Archibold! Milord! Mr. Burton!" cried Tom Foster's voice at that moment. "The central fire's arriving! It's coming out of the pumps! It's extinguished my lantern again!"

No flame or incandescence of any sort was visible, but Archibold, having presented his face to the orifice of a

---

[40] Jeremy Bentham's *History of Ely Cathedral* was published in 1771.

pump—as Foster had—began choking and was seized by a violent fit of coughing.

"That gas," said the engineer, "is carbon dioxide, which extinguishes life as rapidly as it snuffs out a lantern, and there's reason to fear the worst for Hatchitt."

The activity of the pumps was increased; the pipes roared like organ-pipes under the pressure of the air compressed by their sides, but so much mephitic gas gushed forth in enormous gusts, amassing at ground level in the hall by virtue of its density, that it seemed probable that they were dealing with one of those inexhaustible natural reservoirs, like Cotopaxi, which releases more carbon dioxide in a day than the lungs of 20 million human beings, or the sinister valley of Tungguranga.

The atmosphere was calm; no air-current dispersed this mounting tide, the level of which could be measured with a torch. The flame, flickering as it approached, went out in the waves, which were rising like a liquid: a redoubtable invasion; an inundation that might constrain them to leave the hall, under the threat of death, deserting the equipment and losing any hope of saving Hatchitt.

Unnerved by the anguish and the inebriating emanations, Lord Hotairwell and Penkenton—who, having finally shut up and learned of the catastrophe, had run into the room—raised invisible tempests in the colorless waves by stamping their feet.

"If this goes on," cried the doctor, "this gas will have drowned us within an hour—for I declare that I shan't give way to it."

The doctor was the man who had the greatest height advantage over his adversary, which had only reached his knees when it was already up to his colleagues' waists. His head, perched at the altitude of his huge body, would be unsubmerged long after his companions had been swallowed up.

"As for me," said Lord Hotairwell, pausing beside the well, "I prefer to die trying to rejoin William Hatchitt."

Archibold stopped him as he stepped over the edge. "My lord," said the chief engineer, "I'm in charge here, and no one will go down without my order. I think that the attempt will soon be possible, but at this moment, you wouldn't get ten meters into the well without being asphyxiated."

Archibold presented a light to the valve of the pumps, which flickered and went out. He repeated the experiment at various intervals, and after some 20 minutes, he made a sign to his colleagues that the moment had come to descend. Lord Hotairwell and I got into a skip with him. Penkenton, by reason of his size, placed himself on his own in another, the load of which was made up by rescue equipment.

The winch skidded, grating, and the wagonettes began to slide down, alongside the heavy lining that was no longer supported by anything, and which would have collapsed into the abyss if lateral pressure had not retained it.

With his hand on the button, Archibold stood ready to check the progress at the first sign of danger, but nothing abnormal seemed to occur, and we had gone more than 1,500 meters when strident cry—a sort of whinnying or a wild and mighty sneeze—struck our ears, coming from the depths.

"What could be making that noise?" I asked, in amazement.

"William Hatchitt, perhaps!" cried Lord Hotairwell. And, leaning over the rim of the skip, he called Hatchitt's name.

Lord Hotairwell's voice, naturally powerful and echoed by the metallic walls, took on the intensity of a roll of thunder, but it elicited no reply.

"Hatchitt is lost!" murmured Lord Hotairwell, with the bitterness of a hope deceived.

At that moment, we arrived at the bottom of the well—or, rather, the bottom of the lining, the well no longer having a bottom.

Things were as Tom Foster had described them. Half of the terrain inscribed within the walls had crumbled into a gulf—and might not the rest, devoid of any sure support, give way beneath our feet? Lord Hotairwell set foot upon it, and we followed him—and the loaded skips were set back up to the surface, leaving us cast away on that reef.

William Hatchitt was not there; no sound could be heard. Without losing a moment, Archibold made arrangements for the exploration of the precipice.

"What's that?" asked Penkenton, who had just bumped into something reminiscent of the tail of an animal coiled around a stone, whose end, excited by the impact of the doctor's foot, began to quiver.

"An animal at this depth!" said Lord Hotairwell. "It can only be a living fossil!"

The animal belonging to that tail could, indeed, only be of antediluvian nature and size, given the length of the appendage wound several times around the rock and then extending into the abyss, where its body was swinging.

"It's a monkey," said Penkenton, leaning over the black hole. "Only monkeys suspend themselves like that when they're idle."

"A primitive monkey," confirmed Lord Hotairwell. "A *Mesopithecus* saved from the Deluge in this cavern."[41]

"Which is still alive!" I marveled.

"As you can see, since it's moving."

"Is that possible?"

"Why not?" replied Lord Hotairwell. "At Blois, in France, a large Tertiary toad was found alive inside a block of stone."[42]

---

[41] The best-known fossil of the primate *Mesopithecus* was the "Turin specimen" reported in 1839; the species was not, however, equipped with a prehensile tail.

[42] The affair of the Blois toad, allegedly discovered well-diggers in June 1851 inside a lump of flint, occasioned considerable controversy when an investigative commission delegated by the skeptical Académie des Science failed to find any evidence of fraud.

"If this creature has been imprisoned for so many centuries, it must be famished and ferocious," I remarked, judiciously, "and we have no weapons."

"Who could have expected to need weapons at the bottom of a well?"

"Or to find game in a fossil forest," added Penkenton.

"Might the doctor not attempt to knock the creature out with a stone thrown with all his strength?" said Archibold.

"Oh!" said Lord Hotairwell. "It would be a pity to kill it! It would be so precious, conserved alive! Not to mention that the doctor, who lacks skill, might miss it and kill Hatchitt if he's at the bottom of the hole."

"I could swiftly untie its tail," Penkenton proposed. "The creature would fall into the gulf, and we'd be rid of it."

"Rid of it here," said Lord Hotairwell, "only to find it again down below indisposed. It's necessary to kill its cleanly or capture it, and I vote for the second option. Why assume in advance that the animal is an enemy? If it's the first monkey, it's the first man, and perhaps by demonstrating our regard, approaching it with filial respect…."

"Doctor," said Archibold, who did not like discussion to get in the way of action, it's a matter of deploying your muscular strength. Get hold of that tail and hoist the animal up slowly, in order that we can lend you a strong hand at the moment when it gains a foothold. The four of us will be able to hold on to it or strangle it."

Reluctantly, the doctor grasped the knotted caudal apparatus, which was bald and sticky, and, having unrolled it without encountering ay resistance, set about hauling it up, while the creature, climbing after its tail with surprising agility and without leaving time to seize it as it passed by, hurled itself into Penkenton's arms. The later, in surprise, let go completely—but it did not let go of him.

"God bless you, Doctor!" cried the animal, reiterating the terrible sneeze that they had already heard.

The tail was a rope, and the creature was Hatchitt—who covered Penkenton, not yet recovered from his surprise and disgust, with kisses.

"My dear Hatchitt!" cried Lord Hotairwell, annoyed by the loss of a fossil ape but very happy to recover a friend. "My dear Hatchitt, what a pleasure it is to see you again!"

"Are you well?" I said, exchanging a warm handshake with Hatchitt.

"Perfectly," the engineer replied, after snorting with the force of a sperm-whale. "Perfectly, although a trifle congested—but that's nothing; it's the coryza of the abyss, which is unknown on the surface, and which I attribute, without reproach, to the atrocious current of air in which you have placed me. Between the gas that vomited from the gulf and the air spat out by your pumps, I was shaken like a cork in a whirlpool, and I was obliged to engage in a serious struggle in order not to be sucked into the pipes. So I tried to get out; I attached myself, but I wasn't able to get down—my rope got tangled, and I waited for you."

"That's very good of you," said Lord Hotairwell, "but why didn't you reply when I called out to you?"

"Because I didn't hear you."

"We heard your sneezes clearly.

"You heard me, Mr. Burton, because sound is more agile in going up than in coming down; an aeronaut can hear a dog barking on the ground from a great height."

"2000 meters," Archibold confirmed.

"While at a meager altitude...."

"150 meters," said the chief engineer.

"...One can't hear a dog barking in a balloon," Hatchitt continue. "But let's not waste time; now that you're here, I can get down without difficulty. Penkenton will be able to support my weight."

Hatchitt, who had remained tied to one end of his rope, graciously presented the other end to the doctor.

"Wouldn't it be better if I were to go down myself?" Penkenton objected, dying to precede his colleague.

"That's quite impossible," replied the latter, who would have leapt into the gulf rather than let the doctor get ahead of him. "Your weight forbids it. It would take a crane to support you, and there isn't one here."

"With ladders," Lord Hotairwell observed, "We could all go down at the same time."

"No, no!" Hatchitt retorted, holding on to the doctor's coat-tails as the latter tried to go in search of ladders. "We mustn't risk ourselves all together. Before going down, let's do what mariners do and throw down a sounding-line to investigate the depth."

"Right, let's lower a plumb-line," Penkenton agreed, well-disposed to any expedient that would delay his colleague.

"And the plumb-bob is me," Hatchitt went on. "Would you are to hold on to the end of this rope, Doctor, and let me go down?"

While Penkenton, who had run out of objections, grudgingly took the end of the rope, Hatchitt, having noticed a ball of fat in a corner, used for greasing tools, anointed himself with it abundantly.

"Why are you doing that?" Archibold asked him.

"I'm a sounding-device, and I'm treating myself accordingly, making myself sticky like Brooke's sound—one of the best—in order to bring back specimens of the bottom automatically, even if I faint or drown.[43] Come on, Doctor—deploy your capstan."

Penkenton, resigned, spread his legs over the void, one foot remaining on firm ground while the other was braced against a projection in the side-wall. Holding Hatchitt at the

---

[43] The sounding apparatus designed in 1853 by John Mercer Brooke was used on an extensive expedition to measure the depth of the world's oceans undertaken by H. M. S. *Challenger* and also by William Thomson (later Lord Kelvin) to take the preparatory soundings for laying the first transatlantic cable.

end of his cable, he resembled the Colossus of Rhodes in the process of catching a sailor with a fishing-line.

The rope slid through the doctor's hands, who measured it out in fathoms. When he had counted 12, he had to knot a new length—a delicate operation for his large and clumsy hands, all the more so because the impatient Hatchitt started performing trapeze exercises, producing shocks that the doctor received in his jaw, having been obliged to grip the rope in his teeth in order to tie the knot.

When ten more fathoms had been paid out, Hatchitt's shrill voice cried: "Land!"

The doctor immediately moored the rope.

"On what have you touched down?" asked Archibold.

No response was forthcoming.

"He didn't hear you," I said.

"I'll make him hear me," said the doctor, "but I'll have to make him listen first." Shaking the rope as if it were a dog's leash, he roared in his trombone-like voice: "On what have you touched down?"

"On a pile of leaves on a sandy path," was the swift reply.

Five steel ladders, bolted to one another, having been sent forth, the four explorers, with Davy lamps on their foreheads, like specters with luminous heads, plunged slowly into the darkness. They followed one another at intervals, making sure of their footholds on the fragile stairway—which, the inverse of Jacob's ladder, supported its crest on the Earth and its foot in the unknown.

This second part of the journey was similarly effectuated without any accident. On the final step they found Hatchitt, obligingly standing there to steady the ladder—and also because, Penkenton having given him too little rope, he had not been able to untie himself and was still suspended, only touching the ground with his toes.

"Why didn't you loosen the rope?" cried the furious little engineer, ceasing to maintain the ladder once the doctor was alone thereon.

"To keep you from getting lost," Penkenton replied.

"No! To prevent me from exploring this cavern before you! It's an outrage!"

Penkenton made no reply, but came down with large strides, at the risk of breaking the ladder, which was swaying like a seesaw under his weight.

The electric lamps, which Archibold immediately switched on, then lit up a strange spectacle. They were in a circle of rocks whose walls disappeared beneath a trellis of tree-trunks and branches: a tangle of trees of all sorts of species and sizes, some standing vertically, extending all the way to the vault, others extended horizontally, struck down and crushed, others compressed perpendicularly by the enormous weight that had oppressed them. It was all mixed up and tangled: the disorder of a forest gripped by a furious madness, which had gone to war against itself, in trunk-to-trunk and branch-to-branch combat, blinding its foliage and falling, without conceding victory, interlaced in its debris; a prodigious heap of demolition-materials, of sand and stones, colossal unopened timbers, pieces in an enormous game of spillikins precipitated pell-mell by the hand of a giant in that somber valley.

Such was the scene that offered itself to the gaze and stupefied the spectators, Penkenton excepted. He was radiant, blooming, transfigured; his granite face had become flesh, having suddenly acquired muscles and nerves capable of quivering. That dead man, in penetrating this place, had come back to life; that mummy, returned to his own time, had taken off his bandages and reknotted the thread of his life; and if any surprise revealed itself in his face, it was that of a traveler who, returning to his homeland after a long absence, is astonished that people and things have changed. The expression is ephemeral, however, and the traveler does prompt justice to the metamorphoses; he soon finds the young faces beneath the wrinkles, the paternal house beneath the ivy, and the pathway under the foliage.

Thus, the doctor naturally took the head of the troop, like a host showing of his house and his forest. Without hesitation, he led us to the foot of a maple-tree that formed the center of a crossroads, and there, leaning against the tree, speaking in a low and emotional voice, abruptly and jerkily, he said:

"In coming into this place, we—you, and me even more so—have been rejuvenated by a great many centuries, traveling back in time toward its sources, penetrating its most intimate arcana. This tenebrous abyss has known the surface of the world's most ancient ages; these trees grew in the first sunlight, and the first humans sat in their shade. They followed these pathways, the humans contemporary with the mastodon, the megaceros, and the bear *Ursus speleus*, which sank, like them, beneath the waters of the Deluge. We are treading in the zone of the great ossuary of the Pliocene earth that supported our first steps: the final phase of the long periods of Genesis, which were days for the Creator and dawns for the Earth.

"It is to the convulsions of those first ages that the formation of this cavern is due. It is similar in some respects to the Irish caves of Shandon and Cappoquin,[44] but differs from them in its origins; it is not, like them, a fissure enlarged by erosion, but a portion of the Earth swallowed up in an abyss that has closed over it: the stage of a theater disappeared into the cellars.

"Look at those trees broken by their fall, but still attacked to the clods of earth in which they grew, as brown as lignite, but not mineralized like coal, nor crushed in similar fashion by heavy geological strata: forests and countries buried alive, fallen into lethargy without dying, trees stripped of their leaves, desiccated of their sap, but wearing the burden of

---

[44] The Shandon caves north of Dungarvan were a particularly rich source of fossils of the kinds named in the previous paragraph, most notably the so-called "Irish elk" (*Megaceros*) and the cave-bear (*Ursus speleus*). The Cappoquin caves, near Waterford, were less productive.

ages without weakening, like those old men in whom time has scythed away the hair, atrophied the flesh and ossified the wrinkles, reducing them to skeletons with souls, offering no purchase to corruption or to death."

Chapter Seven
Pulvis in Pulverem…

Several paths departed from the crossroads to which Penkenton had led us, one of which we embarked upon, after Archibold had fixed an electric lamp in place to serve as a reference-point and guide our return.

One might have thought that a whirlwind or a runaway locomotive had hollowed out this path through the forest, to see the broken and twisted trees piled up on its edges by the storm, or dragged in its wake, barring the passages that it had opened by parting the branches and maneuvering between the trunks. We advanced with extreme precaution, gliding through the darkness like shadows, holding our breath, as if it were capable of breaking these phantoms and spreading the dust. Under the empire of that ambient death, we spoke in hushed tones, as one does near graves, sometimes pausing and redoubling the silence in order to catch the noises and discover the secrets of that enchanted land.

For some minutes, Dr. Penkenton, who was marching in front, seemed to have been prey to a singular agitation. Sometimes, leaning over the ground like a hunter following a trail, he stopped, absorbed in some incomprehensible contemplation. Then he resumed his course, stopped again and got down on one knee or lay on the ground in order to see better.

Suddenly, getting to his feet, raising himself up to his full height and doffing his hate respectfully, he exclaimed, a strident tone: "Man!!! Here is Man!!!"

These words, assuredly the first that had resonated here since times proximal to Genesis, awoke the echoes of the abyss with a start, which replied: "Man! Man…!"

"Yes," the doctor continued, drowning out that noise with his metallic voice, "a man! An antediluvian man! A man who witnessed the Deluge! *Ecce Homo testis diluvi!* Here is his undeniable trace, the imprints of his bare foot, profound, fleeing—for he was fleeing, this man! He was fleeing, tracked by his implacable hunter, by the nature that assailed him on every side, with these trees that were collapsing upon his head, these rocks that were pursuing him as they tumbled, by the earth itself, which was trying to swallow him."

Penkenton paused, and then continued, as emotional and exuding as much sweat as the actor of that flight: "And what completed these horrors was that the unfortunate was not alone, that he had two lives to defend against all these accumulating deaths. Look, next to the large and strong footprint of the man, there is a smaller footprint—a woman's foot. Here, there imprints overlap; further on, the prints of the smaller foot disappear, which shows that our man was alternately dragging or carrying his companion. What horrible drama was played out here? Who knows whether it is still going on? A little while ago, amid the noise of the echoes, didn't it seem to you, as it did to me, that you heard human voices? Voices calling for help? Ah, if there were still time!"

The doctor fell silent, in order to listen. "Let's not delay," he resumed, almost immediately. "Let's follow this track hastily. Let's attempt to save these humans, these shadows, perhaps still fleeing through the pathways of their sepulcher, unable either to escape or to die!"

We listened to Penkenton in bewilderment. Already so strange, had he gone completely mad? As for him, he was already moving on; he had set off on that human trail like a hunter of chamois. Even a chamois could not have surpassed the agility that surged within that huge body, which bounded over obstacles, pushed through thickets and insinuated itself through narrow defiles, taking no account of and refusing to be slowed down by the trees with which he collided, which shook under the impact.

Hesitating to follow him, in fear of getting lost, but not wanting to lose him, since he knew the way, we soon found ourselves running flat out after him, each of us as fast as he could go. We were all outstripped by Hatchitt, who had taken no more time to transform himself into a hound than Penken-

ton had taken to change into a deer, and who was chasing the
doctor, baying for his blood, scenting the hide of the beast,
discovering his weaknesses and seeing through his ruses, hollowing out short cuts and tunnels through the foliage, passing
between the trees like a sylph—and, when necessary, passing
between the bark and the tree. Lord Hotairwell followed the
hunt at the high speed of a thoroughbred horse, Archibold at
the refined trot of a fine Irish pony, and I, Burton the managing director, being extremely fat, made progress as best I
could, already completely out of breath, less reminiscent of a
hunter than a canon running to catch up with his procession.

How long did that go on? I cannot say—but it was not
the weariness of the quarry or the hunters that put an end to
the furious chase; it was the lack of terrain. A wall of rock
barred their route: the surrounding wall of the cavern, at the
foot of which the human footprints stopped. Had the fugitive
run on before that wall had closed in? Or were they lying,
trapped and crushed, within its thickness. All suppositions
were as possible as they were futile. The tracks had been the
last that the antediluvian family had left on this ground before
finding salvation or death beyond it.

The doctor had understood that; in a despair impossible
to describe, he addressed objurgations and prayers to that implacable wall. Then his excitement seemed to calm down.
Breathless and harassed by fatigue, he sat down, took off his
shoe and set his bare foot on an imprint of the human foot
profoundly molded in the clay. Seeing that it fitted exactly, his
face became paler and he shivered vertiginously. As Lord Hotairwell came to help him, he fell into his arms, and cried: "Oh
yes! It was really him! It was her...." And he burst into sobs.

That inconsiderate chase might have got us irredeemably
lost had fortune not permitted that, although covering a large
distance, we had not achieved a considerable displacement—
as was evidenced by the lighthouse left at the crossroads, shining like the pole star in the subterranean sky. Confident in that
safeguard, we continued on our way. Before we had taken 100
strides, however, we were stopped by a mass of trees: a gigan-

tic thicket forming the rim of a sort of circus, the stages of an arena in the middle of which the victorious athlete that had produced all the debris was on parade. It was a mammoth: the colossus of the ancient world; the elephant-boar whose enormous skeletons, found in various places, were taken for a long time to be the bone of titans or demigods. This one, which measured five meters in height, solidly wedged on its stout curved legs, its hair bristling and its eyes bulging from their orbits, brandishing its trumpet-shaped tusks, seemed to be sounding the charge against the forest that it had attacked and cut into pieces, the debris of which was strewn on the ground, encircling it like a rampart.

"There's nothing extraordinary in the conservation of this animal," said Lord Hotairwell, seeing my astonishment. "It's probably due to the special quality of the air and terrain of this cavern. One finds monks conserved in the same fashion in the crypts of Bonn in Germany."

"Yes," observed Hatchitt, "but the monks are only 200 years old, while that animal…."

"Is much older—but what does that matter? In the present century, have not dogs drunk the blood and eaten the flesh of animals that lived before the Deluge. Joseph de Maistre found the remains of mammoths dead for centuries, with their eyes still bloodshot and their ears covered in hair."[45]

"Conserved in the ice of the Neva," Hatchitt put in.

"Cold isn't necessary," said Archibold. "In Mexico I've seen a horse asphyxiated a long time ago in a layer of borax, which remained fresh at a temperature of 45 degrees."

"This mammoth must also have been asphyxiated," said Lord Hotairwell, "and I think I understand the origin of the carbon dioxide that invaded us; it was the last breath of this forest, buried alive. Before dying, it respired in this darkness

---

[45] Joseph de Maistre (1753-1821) was a Savoyard lawyer who was appointed as the King of Sardinia's envoy to the Tsar of Russia in 1803.

as plants respire during the night—which is to say, by exhaling carbon dioxide through all the stomata of its leaves."

Having rounded this obstacle, we found ourselves back on the path that we had followed initially—traced, as we now saw, by the mammoth itself, also fleeing before the cataclysm; one avalanche pursued by another. The path led straight to the crossroads, so we angled left, toward a clearing that stood out vaguely in the darkness in the light of our lanterns.

In that direction the walls of the cavern, drawing closer and gaining in height like the apse of a temple—thus raising their vault—was buttressed here and there by colonettes of coarse stone, interspersed with branches through which, awakened by the light, facets of granite and bright mica-schists sparkled. There was a little order in this portion of the chaos. This corner of the forest had proved more resistant to the catastrophe; one might have thought that the trees, bent over into a cupola and braided into palisades, had banded together to defend themselves and to defend any guests that had taken refuge in their shelter—for, as we advanced further into the clearing, strange protuberances emerged from the darkness, lying on the ground, projecting from the wall or suspended from the vault: panoplies of bones, comprising entire skeletons; phantoms clothed in the attitudes of life in the semi-darkness.

The cataclysm that had engulfed this land had assembled these fleeing and maddened animals, guided by instinct toward an oasis where they had saved, if not their lives, at least their mortal remains, caught in the poses in which death had taken them—standing, for the most part, with their necks extended and their legs apart to embrace the ground, as contemporary animals do during earthquakes.

On this dislocated terrain, fractured by its fall into an abyss, miniature abysses had opened up that had swallowed prey according to their measure. The antlers of an Irish elk, *Megaceros hibernicus*, protruded from one of these fissures, curved and flattened like the branches of a cactus. Further away, another bodiless ramose head was exhumed, so intricately enlaced with lianas that one could scarcely distinguish the animal's horns from the forest branches. Lord Hotairwell, however, recognized a Sivatherium, a giant among the Tertiary animals, only the heads of which have been discovered: a fatality reproduced one more time.

A stout Batrachian, a relative of the one that Andreas Scheutzer[46] had mistaken for a human and Cuvier for a lizard, was slumbering in the middle of the clearing, enveloped in its scaly coat like a knight in armor: a cold-blooded creature, so little excited by the great catastrophe that death had scarcely taken away its appetite. Its thick lips were sucking in a prey that it had not had time to swallow, or which it had found foul-tasting: a bird, a dodo (*walgvogel*, meaning "disgusting bird"), a cube-shaped creature endowed with wings too short for flight, feet too gross for running, and a repulsive odor. This unfortunate creature, heaped with so many disgraces, to which a horrible death had added the final straw, wore on its face the melancholy expression observed by the naturalist Herbert on a member of its family still living in the 17th century.[47]

---

[46] This reference is garbled. The fossil skeleton in question was discovered in 1726 by Johann Scheuchzer in a quarry in Oeningen; mistaking it for a human child he gave the species the name *Homo diluvi testis* [deluge-witnessing man]—a label that Penkenton has already quoted. Georges Cuvier subsequently recognized it as the skeleton of a giant salamander and renamed it *Salamandra scheuchzeri*, but it was reclassified in 1831 as *Andrias Scheuchzeri* (*andrias* meaning "man-like"). The fossil was acquired by a Museum in Haarlem in the Netherlands in 1802 and is still displayed there. The species acquired much greater fame in the context of scientific romance when Karel Capek wrote a satirical account of the discovery of living specimens in the novel translated as *War with the Newts* (1936).

[47] The English historian and traveler Thomas Herbert (1606-82) described the dodo in 1627.

Around a fruit-tree—an apple-tree with a rounded crown and deeply wrinkled bark, a serpent was coiled by half its body-length, with its furious head turned toward the wall where its tail rested: an image from Dracontian temples, Lord Hotairwell remarked, constructed in the image of serpents attached by the midriff, opening their extremities like limbs, representing in Celtic religion the Father, the Son and Eternity.[48]

On the fateful day that had seen these fugitives assemble under the impulse of the same fear, even the birds, mistrusting the sky, had sought refuge in the trees, around the feet of which their cadavers were strewn. A monkey, which had chosen a similar retreat, hung despairingly from the vault, caught by the waist in its thickness, like a swimmer caught by a suddenly-congealed wave.

Captivated by this marvelous scene, a sanctuary and treasure of all the paleontologies of nature, we were contemplating it ecstatically when a terrible scream froze the blood in our veins.

Who had made that scream? What human could survive here? A primitive man, *Homo speleus*,[49] awakened by the noise of the invasion of his forest and his cavern? And if that were the case, how would the distant representatives of the two extremes of the human species see one another, on finding themselves suddenly face to face? What joy of recognition might burst forth on either side, or what ferocious combat

---

[48] Lord Hotairwell might be slightly confused, although he might also be practicing a kind of mythological syncretism common in his day, conflating the serpentine imagery of the Dracontian temples of ancient Greece with the Welsh imagery that sometimes associated dragons with trees and showed them wound around their trunks.

[49] *Homo speleus* [cave-man] was one of several subsequently-abandoned subdivisions of the genus *Homo* suggested by 19th century paleontologists.

might be engaged between an antediluvian man and four English geologists, avid to capture and collect him?

At any rate, we advanced resolutely. After going around a clump of trees, we found Dr. Penkenton lying face down on the ground, no longer showing any sign of life. The doctor had only fainted, though. At the sound of footsteps and anxious words, he came round, rapidly hid an object in his breast and, putting one forefinger to his lips to command silence, he used the other to point to a part of the clearing as yet unseen.

On the threshold of a cave, the overhanging roof of which was sustained by the branches of a beech-tree like the awning of a cradle, lay two human bodies. I say *bodies*, and not cadavers or skeletons: the bodies of a man and a woman, preserved by death and dressed with its strange beauty.

They lay at the entrance of the cave, which must have been their dwelling, to which they had returned, weary of flight, and to which the collapse had pursued them—and would have annihilated their remains had that tree not made a protective arch, in the shelter of which these deceased persons of an ancient era had awaited in peace the resurrection that had been slow to come. The man was lying in a sitting position, in the usual attitude of the Stone Age dead, with the upper part of his body propped up by an outcrop of rock; his eyes were open, staring at his unexpected visitors. Still anxious and defensive, he was ready to pick up the axe that had slipped from his fingers: the weapon that he had brandished at the first alert, but had dropped on recognizing the enemy, on seeing that it was nature, more ferocious than a bear and stronger than a mammoth, that was attacking him. Hope had faded in his heart, the axe had fallen from his hand, and with the meek fatal resignation of primitive tribes, he had propped himself up on his elbow to await eternal rest.

Immobile and mute as the funerary statues that carry torches around a tomb, we remained there, fascinated by this spectacle: a reality superior to the dream; an Edenic scene; a landscape of ancient days, similar to those Biblical images that depict Adam and Eve in the midst of the boscage of the terrestrial paradise, innocent and happy, surrounded by all of the Creation that renders homage to them, while the serpent uncoils in the branches of the tree of knowledge, watching its prey and awaiting its moment.

The light of electric lanterns, penetrating the cavern walls, was reflected in 1000 gleams from quartz prisms, embroidering a scintillating spangle of diamante granite and enamel-plated micas: a magnificent mortuary tapestry, with stalactites hanging down from the vault and stalagmites surging from the ground, sustaining milky or transparent crystals in their arms. One might have thought that nature, to make excuses to its victims and to offer them expiatory funeral rites in that fiery chapel, was only waiting for witnesses who had finally arrived, and who were now there, with heavy hearts and breathless breasts, deeply plunged in thought or prayer, like sons kneeling around a father who had just expired—for none of us would have dared to say whether these dead people had ceased to live an hour ago or centuries ago.

Struck down by asphyxia, which suspends life without breaking its mechanisms, which banishes the dweller without destroying the dwelling, they were slumbering in the grace of youth, the splendor of their native beauty and the majesty of humankind, the issue of God: primitive parcels of the clay that He modeled with His hands, in His image; clay signed with the imprint of his seal; a creation as superior to reproductions of human manufacture as a statue sculpted by an artist is to the casts taken from molds by an artisan.

Next to the man, at his feet, lay his companion, respectful and submissive until death to her spouse, the king of nature, suddenly dethroned like so many kings to come, by a caprice of his subject. Woman! The Creator's most accomplished work. She was there, chaste and faithful, sharing the long sleep of her husband: a daughter or grand-daughter of the first woman, retaining intact the treasure of beauties and virtues whose heritage would be divided by her descendants; a vase still full of perfumes about to expand.

Reverting by a facile flight to the ages when humanity was born; reawakening these dead people, this fauna, this land, it seemed to us that we that we saw her—that young woman, that young queen—advancing on the morning of the seventh day, to the discovery of her empire, adorned, by way of a royal mantle, by the sculptural splendors of her pure beauty! The Earth had been preparing to welcome her for a long time, ornamenting itself like a temple awaiting its deity. Pliocene nature, intoxicated with youth and vitality, besotted with its charming mistress, squandered its luxuries heedlessly to please her, to win a smile from her, to keep her captive in its flowers and lianas. Concerting its harmonies and forces, it sang to this radiant spouse the most marvelous canticle of canticles, speaking to her of its love by means of all the Aeolian voices of its breezes, all the cries of its fauna, all the graces of its flora—all the flowers and the birds to which it gave birth for her, enveloping her with their perfumes and celebrating her in their songs....

Meanwhile, the old beech-trees, the maples and the elms, already centuries-old, tranquil patriarchs in the midst of that mad nature, extended their mantle of foliage over their sovereign and protected her with their vast shade against the ardors of the Sun, which was equally eager to know and serve her....

As it became brighter, the marvelous scene came to life even more, revealing, beyond its foreground, its secret depths and most obscure retreats. Like a morning Sun, the electric light played among the branches, refracted from the rocks in dazzling cascades, bringing life and movement to an entire world, which the fires of that dawn were doubtless about to awaken....

An illusion broken as soon as it was dreamed! It was an insane hope, to see that life reborn while definitive destruction went to work, before the eyes and beneath the hands of the violators of that sepulcher, by means of the atmospheric air they had introduced, which was killing those dead people and dissolving them with an invincible force. Already, this vegetation and these creatures were swiftly being deprived of their attitudes and their shapes, and the glimpsed Eden vanished like one of those spectral projections that disappear without one being able to mark the stages of their flight. The pure lines of those Adamic bodies were lost in the collapse of death; the statues became cadavers, and had to do no more, to become skeletons, than shake off the remainder of their carnal dust.

Likewise the fauna; likewise the enormous batrachian, which flaked into dust, and the serpent, whose body, librated from the wall by its rupture, strewed the ground with its dismantled coils; likewise the flora, and those powerful trees suddenly worm-eaten, making sinister cracking sounds, ready to detach themselves from the vault that they had stayed for such a long time.

From all these bodies in active decomposition there escaped clouds of brown, fluffy dust: a shroud enveloping that world, which was about to perish anew, inhuming that already-extinct Pompeii beneath its own ashes. It was necessary to get away; the angel of death, urgent in his work, chased the visitors from the terrestrial paradise. Destruction, long held in check in that oasis escaped from its law, resumed its empire; it returned more terrible, promulgating itself with alacrity, executing its task pitilessly, and at the first sign of it, the dust in revolt had returned to dust: *pulvis in pulverem reversus*.

Chapter Eight
A Review

The news of the discovery of this marvelous cavern spread with lightning rapidity through the scientific world, and from the following day onwards, the advance scouts of an army of geologists and paleontologists invested the borders of the geothermal well and mounted an assault thereon—but in vain. The place was defended by a geologist of primal strength and great stature, lying in ambush behind the redoubt, armed with a staff and ready to break the heads of anyone who dared peep over the rim. Prayers and adjurations, invective and wheedling, force and cunning remained impotent. That incorruptible guardian replied, once and for all, that while he lived, no one would enter that grotto and not a single item of debris would be removed—and he threatened criminal proceedings against anyone violating the sepulcher or invading the fossil cemetery.

It was a delicate enterprise to pass over the body of such a man. To attack him from the front would have required good troops and cannon, difficult to direct at a well; no more could they go around Dr. Penkenton to take him from the rear, since he had none, or had it to the central fire. The army of scientists fell back.

When he was left in peace, Penkenton went down and shut himself up in the cavern, where, for several days, sobs and prayers were heard, along with religious songs of an extremely ancient rhythm, and various sounds of rearrangement and piling up. The doctor was evidently conducting funeral rites in the sepulcher of the dead people, and putting their dwelling in order. When he had finished, he had stones and mortar brought, and personally walled up the entrance to the grotto, on which he put seals by means of his cane, with the tip of which he inscribed in the cement the symbols ב א that were engraved on its handle. That done, he retired to Penkenton

House and donned mourning-dress for three months—the duration of a nephew's mourning, Lord Hotairwell remarked.

On the following June 22, in the afternoon, the committee was in session when, happening to cast a glance at the tetroscopic mirror, I uttered an exclamation that brought my colleague running. Anyone who had observed their faces would have had the pleasure in following the ascending scale of astonishment, amazement and fear that their physiognomies expressed, by means of the orbicular, masseter and zygomatic muscles commanded by their facial and trifacial nerves.

A drama was being played out in the tetroscope's mirror: a tragedy in miniature, whose actors and scenery could have been held in the palm of one's hand, but which, several kilometers below ground, was being performed on its natural scale and in reality.

At the bottom of the well, in the midst of suspended tasks and discarded tools, Hatchitt could seen, tied up but gesticulating nevertheless, menacing and furious, with a recumbent white bear beside him and a troop of negroes dancing a bamboula around him, cadenced by their howling. If our eyes could hardly be believed, it was also necessary to doubt our ears—and the telephones, which were beginning to pour out cries and curses through their funnels, along with laughter and all sorts of heterogeneous and cacophonous sounds, which deafened the audience.

"Great God, what's this!" the board-members cried, with one voice. "Another strike? A revolt? A party thrown by Hatchitt for his negroes?"

"That," said Penkenton, after having looked attentively, "I can tell you, thanks to the information I have gleaned in my travels regarding the customs of various tribes, is the dance of savages who are about to eat a prisoner."

"Are they going to eat Hatchitt, then? What about that bear?"

"I am similarly able to tell you," Penkenton continued, "that it's a bear."

"I can see that perfectly well," said Lord Hotairwell, "but how did such a bear get into our well?"

"That I don't know," replied the doctor, "but I don't think it originated there; it doesn't have the appearance of a Tertiary bear that is not on its own geological terrain here. It appears to be enjoying, moreover, a state of health and freshness rare in a fossil."

"I'm going to telephone Hatchitt," said Lord Hotairwell, without paying any heed to this chatter.

The dispatched phonogram remained without response, and had no other effect visible in the tetroscope than to annoy Hatchitt, who began waving his arms and legs about madly and uttering epileptic screeches. A second dispatch appeared to exasperate him even further. He bounded with the agility of a marionette on a string, for such a distance and so high that the negroes interrupted their own dance to look at him.

"Do you really think that they're going to eat William Hatchitt?" asked Lord Hotairwell.

"I have no doubt about it," Penkenton replied, "and I think they're about to eat him immediately. If they stop dancing, it's to start the meal."

"But why is Mr. Hatchitt dancing too, with such zest?" I asked.

"Yes, why is Hatchitt so content to be eaten?" asked Archibold.

"Hatchitt is such a bizarre character!" the doctor replied. "But let's not give them the time." Armed with his cane, he headed for the well with his longest stride.

We followed him in all haste.

"All right!" said Archibold, when we were all seated in the skips. The train let itself down into the abyss at top speed.

When it reached the bottom, the situation was still the same, but was approaching its fatal conclusion. In the meantime, the victim, in spite of the bonds that were shackling him, had engaged in a desperate fight with the savages, and was brandishing a frizzy scalp torn from the head one of his enemies in his hand.

"Bravo, Mr. Hatchitt!" cried the doctor, who, thanks to his long legs, had set foot on the ground 18 seconds before the rest of us. "Bravo! Alone against 50 savages, you're the one who's scalping them! Now we are two!" And Penkenton, launching himself forward with his head lowered and his cane raised, began thrashing about so terribly that nothing could any longer be heard but the hail of his blows falling sonorously upon skulls, dully upon shoulders and with a clicking sound upon shins, opening gaps and clearings in the whirlwind of revolt with the ease of a dog mowing down a set of skittles with the tip of his tail.

The rebels, breathless and decimated, fled toward the walls, less terrified by the blows than the ferocious aspect of their deliverer. The latter, deeming them sufficiently reprimanded, distributed a few extra thrusts for the sake of prudence; then, with the bonhomie of those modern Hercules who dress like everyone else and no longer carry their clubs on their shoulders, he replaced his cane under his arm. The insurrection was defeated, and order reigned at the bottom of the well.

"But what's happened to you, Mr. Hatchitt?" cried Archibold and Lord Hotairwell, as they finished untying the electrical wires that circled the little engineer like a Ruhmkorff coil. "And what on Earth is going on?"

"This," said Hatchitt, whose anger took flight as his limbs were liberated, "was the prelude to a feast in which I was to have the place of honor, in the capacity of the main course."

"Really! My dear Mr. Hatchitt!" said Archibold, almost emotional.

"That surprises you?" Hatchitt continued, bitterly. "You, who have engaged this crew of cannibals—whom you could at least have nourished sufficiently, instead of leaving them to the advice of their hunger."

"Do you really think that they were about to eat you?" the chief engineer hazarded.

"Do you think that it was me who was about to eat them?" the other retorted, angrily.

"Why did you take such an active part in their dance, then?"

"Because they'd tied me up with these electrical wires, and your telegrams, which I received in my body, gave me atrocious shocks that made me leap about involuntarily. It's to that bear that I owe all this; that's what spoiled everything, and I'm astonished that they sent us ice from Greenland so inappropriate as to enclose a bear—for that one came mixed in with the ice." The engineer looked hard at Archibold and concluded: "That part of the external service leaves much to be desired; I'd have preferred an elephant."

"There are no elephants in Greenland," Archibold replied, dryly, "but there are polar bears, which explains how it got mixed in with the ice. Every week for six years I've received three million pounds of ice, which is 936 million in total, in which we've found, for the first time, 800 or 900 pounds of polar bear, which gives a proportion of 900 divided by 936 million, or 96 hundred-millionths, of polar bear—which does not merit the reproach that Mr. Hatchitt has permitted himself to address to his head of service."

"I repeat that I would have preferred an African elephant. These savages would have recognized it for one of their own, and would have welcomed it warmly, whereas, at the sight of the polar bear, they abandoned work, uttering screams, and tied me up—but not without my defending myself." Hatchitt brandished the enemy scalp, angrily. "Oh, my God!" he exclaimed, on seeing some unexpected items fall out of that tuft: a small comb, a shaving-mirror, a pair of spectacles, some wax-polish, pieces of paper, quills and even a few postage-stamps.

"You've scalped a wig!" said Archibold, ironically.

"That savage had everything necessary for writing concealed in his head!" murmured Hatchitt, flabbergasted.

"But in that case," I said, "these savages aren't savages!"

"And this bear isn't a bear!" roared Penkenton, who had been studying the animal for some minutes with kicks and thrusts of his cane.

"And this well isn't a well!" cried Lord Hotairell, in a thunderous voice. "It's a casern!"[50]

"A cavern!" I whispered obligingly to Lord Hotairwell, thinking that he had made a slip of the tongue.

"I said a casern, Mr. Burton, and I meant what I said," the latter replied, angrily running his eyes over the papers that had slipped out of the wing.

"No, it's not a bear," Penkenton repeated, turning the animal over with one last thrust of his foot, "unless it's a stuffed bear."

"Treat that beast with more respect," said Lord Hotairwell. "Even a stuffed bear of such provenance is more redoubtable than a bear from Greenland."

"All the more so since it's alive," said Archibold, who was examining the animal in his turn."

"That's impossible," said the doctor.

"Its heart is beating," replied the engineer. "Hold its head while I ausculate it."

The engineer applied his ear to the bear's breast, listened attentively, and then palpated its entire body. "This bear has no heart!" Archibold said, very gravely. "It has a clock—and its belly is full of sausages."

"Christmas gifts that their wives have sent these savages!" I exclaimed, reassured.

"Your gaiety is inappropriate," Archibold replied, who was splitting the bear's seams. "This animal is filled with sticks of dynamite,[51] whose explosion was to be determined by the clockwork taking the place of a heart. It's a miracle that Penkenton, didn't set them off by hitting the beast all over."

---

[50] I have transcribed *caserne* directly into English in order to preserve the wordplay, although the term is more-or-less obsolete; it refers to a sentry-box or a barrack-room on a rampart.

[51] Dynamite was invented in 1866 and patented in 1867.

After drawing the clock from the animal's body, he added: "Take the bear in your arms, doctor, balance it on your head, and load it into the skip, avoiding friction. Gentlemen, I've tamed the bear—the rest is up to you!"

"Very good!" said Lord Hotairwell, immediately turning to the troop of negroes. "*Achtung! Sich aufzustelen! Starr!*" he commanded, effortlessly resuming the tone and bearing of an officer in the Horse-Guards—meaning "On guard! Close ranks! Stand to attention!"

Immediately, with admirable precision and celerity, the disorderly crowd arranged itself into two rows, facing forwards in the direction of the commandant, with their eyes fixed, elbows by their sides, their arms straight and there fingers seeking reference-points on their trouserless thighs. King Pot'alo, placed on the edge of the formation, verified the alignment of faces and torsos.

"Wigs off!" commanded Lord Hotairwell.

Although not included in normal maneuvers, this command was nevertheless understood, and 102 arms, seizing their heads, removed their hairpieces—beneath which their red or blond hair appeared—and stood up straight again, like ears of wheat bent before the sirocco.

"Present arms!" commanded the commandant. "Face left! On the double, forward march!"

The army corps set off and, taking the circular wall of the well as its base of operations, began to march past at a good clip.

Lord Hotairwell, happy to have resumed his army career, had taken up a position on an eminence, and was following the maneuver very attentively. Penkenton, forming his general staff, stood by his side, his cane raised; both exchanged their impressions as to the fine bearing and alacrity of the troops. James Archibold and I, flanking this principal group, stood with our hands behind our backs, in the awkward and embarrassed manner of civilians watching a review. The poodle Mirk, sitting behind us and presenting arms with his paw, formed the escort and represented the cavalry—and William

Hatchitt, incapable of standing still, all the more excited because he had never seen a review, mobilized himself in every direction, in order not to miss a thing.

Absorbed in this spectacle and in his military thoughts, the general had allowed his troops—already emaciated and out of breath, but spurred on by the terrible gaze of Aide-de-Camp Penkenton—to continue their march for a long time when, suddenly emerging from his reverie, he ordered: "Dismount!"

On hearing this, King Pot'alo seemed stupefied, and attempted to communicate by sign languages the difficulty, for infantrymen, of carrying out such an order—but the warrior had already take account of the situation with single glance. "Halt! Stand at ease!" he commanded, generously. Then, placing himself in front of the troops, and in his loudest voice, he said: "Men, I'm content with you! You have..." Suddenly, however, the orator fell silent, his brows furrowing under the constraint of a painful thought. Waking with a start from his dream, he said to the savages' chief: "Come here, sir. Who are you?"

When the question went unanswered, he added: "I'll tell you." He unfolded the document that had fallen out of the wig and read: *German headquarters, Berlin, June 7. Order to Major Schako and 50 men attached to his command to abduct, during their journey, the negroes purchased by the Central Fire Company, and to introduce themselves in their stead into the well of Industria City.*" And from another piece, a simple railway receipt: "*Sent today, from Berlin, destination Industria City, Ireland: one bear.*" Lord Hotairwell then demanded: "Are you Major Shako?"

"Yes, Milord," the officer replied. "I'm the leader of the mission sent to the bottom of the well, and these men are my attachés."

"Military attachés, evidently?"

"They belong, as I do, to the third regiment of the Prussian Engineering Corps."

"That's the Prussian Engineering Corps all over! The city isn't yet built, the well isn't yet dug, and already the Prussians have introduced a mission to it! What was your purpose?"

"Now that I've been thwarted, I can tell you," the major replied. "I had orders to dig this well, and then destroy it."

"Why dig it?"

"To study its excavation, under the direction of the century's two greatest engineers." The officer bowed profoundly to James Archibold and William Hatchitt.

"And why destroy it?"

"In order that Prussia, which is digging on its own behalf, secretly, can take possession of the central fire before you."

"That was the purpose of the explosive bear?"

"Yes, Milord."

"And it's today that you were to blow up the well?"

"Yes, Milord—at 2 p.m."

"I stopped the bear's heart four minutes before it chimed," Archibold remarked.

"You would have perished in the catastrophe yourselves," Lord Hotairwell continued. "Why then did your men seem so joyful?"

"Because the arrival of the bear was the signal for their departure, the culmination of their labor. The explosion being due to be triggered by the clock mechanism, we should have had time to flee, talking the engineer Herr Hatchitt with us. Unfortunately, I had omitted to block off one of the tetroscopes, and you saw our preparations."

"One last question, sir. How were you, men of the north, able to withstand labor so hard, in such heat?"

"By virtue of discipline, Milord."

"And to live, nourished like savages?"

"By virtue of obedience," the officer replied.

"And what have you done with our savages—the real savages, that is?" asked Archibold.

"They're in Berlin, Herr Chief Engineer, where they're being kept in a hothouse until the German well is hot enough for them to be introduced into it."

111

"Gentlemen," said Lord Hotairwell, "these exceedingly grave circumstances demand urgent deliberation by the board. In consequence, I convene you; we are in conference; the session is open."

"Gentlemen," Archibold began, with the same promptness, "these men merit an exemplary repression, and I would gladly see it applied to them—but they're hewers, and they're acclimatized; they're in the well; let them remain there—for their punishment and our profit!"

"No!" cried Hatchitt, who still bore the marks of the treatment he had received in his heart and on his body. "Or, if you keep these men, you can take charge of their supervision."

"Allow me to explain," the chief engineer replied. "I propose to keep them in quite different conditions, no longer engaging them in our service as savages, but as Prussians."

"What's the difference?" Hatchitt retorted.

"There's a nuance I think I can grasp," said Lord Hotairwell. "Mr. Archibold is proposing to engage these men as free laborers, receiving a salary and associated benefits, which will attach them to our cause."

"The only means of attaching them is the one that they used on me—metal wires or ropes."

"That would prevent them from working," objected Archibold.

"Attach them some other way, if you wish," Hatchitt riposted. "With iron collars, for example, at the end of electrical cables controlling their movements. While I was tied up in almost the same fashion myself and receiving your telephone calls, which moved my limbs involuntarily, I reflected on the advantages of applying the system to others, and the use that an engineer might make of it in guiding his workmen, or a king his subjects—but the idea requires philosophical, psychological and electrical developments in which I don't know whether I ought to get involved."

"Go on!" cried Lord Hotairwell, ever-ready to open his door to striking ideas and already casting aside his soldierly pose to take up that of the philosopher and physiologist.

"My system would be very simple," Hatchitt began, "and would consist, quite straightforwardly in the case under consideration, of linking my cranial battery and cerebral coils to the coils and batteries of my workmen, by appropriate conductive wires."

"Your cerebral battery, your cranial coil?" I exclaimed.

"My battery or yours, Mr. Burton, it hardly matters. Why so bewildered? Are you unaware, perchance, that your brain is an electrical battery of which your skull is the container, your organic debris the elements, your grey and white matter the necessary heterogeneities, your cerebrospinal fluid the hydrochloric acid, and your ventricles numbers one, two and three the reservoirs of fluid that empty, in the middle of your cerebellum, into ventricle number four, in order to produce your movements via currents transmitted through your nerves?"

During this discourse I experienced something akin to the malaise of a person dissected alive, mingled with the astonishment of making electricity, as Monsieur Jourdain spoke prose, without knowing it.

"I'll stop there," Hatchitt continued, "because it's quite unnecessary to demonstrate, after Swedenborg, Van Helmont, Lépine and Charpignon,[52] that the human brain—Mr. Burton's excepted—is the most powerful, most manageable and most costly of electrical batteries, and that the slightest pressure of a switch at a sensitive point can produce idiocy or genius at will."

---

[52] This is a slightly puzzling list. Emanuel Swedenborg (1688-1772) published an important account of the anatomy of the brain in 1732, before he turned to mysticism, but the pioneering chemist Jan van Helmont (1580-1644) has no real relevance to the issue; it is unclear who "Lépine" is, although the reference might be to the French physiologist Raphael Lépine (1840-1919); Louis Charpignon (1815-1886) was a minor practitioner of "animal magnetism."

"Or madness," I added, appositely, thanks to a deft impulse of my battery.

"Genius, madness—my God, Mr. Burton, let's not quibble over words! Genius and madness, hatred, anger and love are manifestations of intelligence, different in form but fundamentally identical, products of the same lympathic vessels: different tastes originating from the same well—like tannin and caffeine, which, although chemically similar, don't have the same aroma. What is anger? An ephemeral eruptive inflammation of the portion of the encephalum situated at the inferior angle of the parietal lobe. And hatred? An induration of anger, the eruption having flowed back and become a cold humor. One treats anger by compresses of ice-water; hatred is only cured at length. And what, then, is love? A slight fever in the brain: a coryza in the cerebellum, to which individuals whose occiput is considerably splayed from one ear to the other are more liable. Love finds its source in the violence of ventricle number four, which releases its fluids into the coils of terminal nerves of which the fingers and the lips are the superficial pulp. When the current arrives at the extremity of the lips, and encounters there an affluent of the opposite polarity, the fluids are wedded, and assume the name of kisses."

"Oh, this is too much!" I cried, sensing everything of the ideal that the soul of a businessman can contain seething within me. "Yes, it's too much!"

"What is too much, Mr. Burton? Did you think that I wanted to devalue your kisses? I'm merely indicating their source, without denting their charm, or their vigor—which must be enormous, to judge by the breadth of distance between your ears, by way of your occiput."

""You're a little too materialistic, Mr. Hatchitt," Lord Hotairwell put in, "And platonic affection..."

"Platonic affection, Milord, is a static electricity, a force that does not act, a stagnant fluid or a feeble current, which arrives neither at the fingertips nor the lips, and which turns back on itself, like any fluid sent forth and not dispensed."

"That's what you say, Mr. Hatchitt!" I cried, unable to contain myself.

"It me who says it, but it's Swedenborg who thinks it, or very nearly—I'm merely completing it. Swedenborg was no madman, I suppose."

"No," said Penkenton, "he was a man of genius, which is the same thing, chemically—as you've just demonstrated."

"Yes," Hatchitt went on, "he was a man of immense genius, but which I surpass, for Swedenborg's brain only worked at ground level, under normal atmospheric pressure. He never knew the overheating of the depths, and he remained vague and mystical, an audacious but indecisive theoretician. Personally, I shall concretize his abstractions; I shall bring about the purification of his dreams and the synthesis of his atoms; I shall draw up the plans—in cross-section and elevation—of his celestial Jerusalem, for the further I descend into the subterranean regions, the more I sense my cerebral power increase and expand in marvelous creations."

"Isn't it rather the heat that's going to his head?" I asked my neighbor.

"I'll give you an example within your scope," Hatchitt went on, striking the pose of a stage magician. "I take the first telegraph operator that I happen upon, who is unprepared. By a very simple means—by speech—I make the telegram that I want to send enter into him. He receives my ideas in his cranial battery, transmits them, via his cerebrospinal fluid, to the coils of his fingers, linked to a Ruhmkorff coil, into which his animal fluid runs, amplifying and guiding their impulses. The operator at the receiving station puts his hand to the conductive wire, receives my message in his fingers in the same way, and resorbs it via his spinal cord into his cerebellum, which discharges it to my correspondent. Economy of apparatus: suppression of Morse receivers, Hugues keyes, autographic registers, pantelegraphics and pantographics! Direct trajectory of thought, without ambiguity or baggage! Head-to-head at any distance! Immeasurable progress!" Hatchitt clicked his fingers, like a conjuror when his trick is finished and the little ball has disappeared, and added: "And which is no more difficult than *that*."

"Your project, Mr. Hatchitt," said Lord Hotairwell, "consists, if I understand rightly, of marrying the electrical fluid and the animal fluid, in order to extend the one in the other and make them ride in the same wire."

"Exactly, Milord."

"But what about the junction—the suture of the two fluids—how do you achieve that? How do you connect your metal wires to your nerve-threads? That seems to me to be a delicate job, welding together dissimilar materials."

"It's nothing at all," relied Hatchitt. "For making an ordinary weld, I address myself to a zinc-worker or a plumber; for this special welding I sent for a physiologist and an electrician. To inject an idea verbally into one skull, withdraw it mechanically therefrom, and precipitate it chemically in another—child's and physicist's play! The road-haulage of ideas! Transport from the brain along a wire is as easy as rolling a wagon along a rail. I propose to do better, and to infuse, not merely ideas but genius in the most obtuse heads—to give a dog the intelligence of a man, and a man that of a god."

Hatchitt resumed his charlatan's pose, and continued. "I take a cretin—a complete cretin—and, by the animal tension that I excite in his apparatus, I make him a man of genius: a genius so sublime that men not electrified as he is will be unable to understand him, and he will not be able to explain himself, because his thoughts will be too great to be expressed in words, and his words by his mouth. Such a flow, if bottled, runs through the neck with difficulty. It's for that reason that greatest men are those who neither speak not act, their genius lacking expression, and that the masterpieces executed by Michelangelo are merely the sketches of those he dreamed! Does that mean that all those that all those who say and do nothing, like paralytics, deaf-mutes and the blind are necessarily the last word in genius? I cannot affirm it, but there is reason to believe it."

"In my opinion," Penkenton put in, "they are only the penultimate word, for the deaf, the mute and the blind are only different from other men in that their senses are turned inwards; the blind can look into themselves, the deaf can hear themselves and the mute can understand themselves—which is the mark of a weak mind. I would place before them those who, being unable to express themselves, can no more succeed in understanding themselves; who cannot even conceive their ideas, because they are so arduous, or attain their thoughts, because they are so elevated. I think that those men are the last word in genius, as I conceive it, without understanding it and without being able to explain it."

"Returning to the immediate object of this discussion," said Hatchitt, seeing himself surpassed, "I propose to apply to apply my electro-cerebral method to the direction of our workers. It consists, as I have indicated, of establishing a current of ideas between my brain and those of these men, connecting their animal induction coils with mine and permitting me to influence their actions at source—which is to say, in the cerebellum."

"Do you think that's the surest means?" asked the chairman of the board. "I'm apprehensive of accidents: a breakdown in the apparatus, an inversion of the current, the receptive brains of your workmen profiting from the disorder and hardening themselves to the point of imposing their ideas on you; those ideas irrupting into your skull, disturbing in your own, chasing them away and taking their place. These negroes, for example—if they were negroes—might substitute their conceptions for yours, their stupidity for your intelligence, their anthropophagy for your frugality, their memories, their loves and their visions of their homeland: in sum, their personality and their identity for yours."

"That's impossible!" cried the two engineers, Archibold and Hatchitt, at the same time miraculously finding themselves in accord. "The cerebral coil of an engineer will always be more powerful than the coils of other men."

117

"Besides," Hatchitt added, "there's an even better means of directing these Germans."

"What's that, Mr. Hatchitt?"

"That of extracting the brain—an operation that Flourens has carried out 100 times on chickens, and which has always succeeded.[53] It consists of removing the frontal lobes and cerebellum from the skull of the individual submitted to this beautiful experiment. The individual loses his intellectual faculties in consequence; he ceases to perceive, to sense, to desire, but his health remains good—he may even get fatter—and he conserves his physical aptitudes, on condition one puts them to work. He moves when he is pushed, does what one wishes, repeats what one says, eats bead or stones without preference, and no longer distinguishes between hot and cold. He retains his arms and legs, and his organs, but no more perception: an organism made into a machine! A machine that has become a body! A body purged of its soul! A marvelous worker, and excellent well-digger, and incomparable elector...!"

"No politics!" the chairman of the board put in, severely.

"Although I'm not a physiologist," Dr. Penkenton said then, "I dare say that the intellectual and perceptive faculties are indeed resident in the cerebrum, but the general direction of movement is centralized and coordinated in the cerebellum—and I have reason to dread, Mr. Hatchitt, that if you suppress both, your men will be unable to coordinate their actions, and their four limbs will go in their own separate directions."

"Have you not understood," Hatchitt riposted, "that it's me who will take charge of organizing their movements, by

---

[53] The French physiologist Jean-Pierre Flourens (1794-1867) was the great pioneer of electrical brain science, far more relevant to Hatchitt's fanciful argument than the four names cited earlier; his classic paper on the subject was submitted to the Académie des Science in 1822. Most of his experiments were, however, carried out on rabbits and pigeons.

means of the connection established between their cerebellums and mine?"

"But since they will no longer have cerebellums...." Penkenton replied.

"They'll no longer have cerebellums, that's true—and I didn't think of that—but I'm quite confident that my impulsion swill be even more efficacious. I shall act directly upon their spinal cords, animating my fluid in their quadrigeminal nerves, and, like dead machines awakening their commanding pulleys with a start, these marionettes will move, suspended from my brain by nervous threads. I shall be the head of their bodies and the brain of their heads; I shall think for them, and they will act for me, suffering when I'm ill and writhing with laughter when I'm cheerful."

"A cephalopod engineer with 1000 feet!" sniggered Dr. Penkenton. "Pardon me, Mr. Hatchitt, but I think you're making a mistake: it's you who'll suffer when your marionettes feel ill, and who will get drunk when they drink, since it's you'll who'll be the brain, the seat of perceptions and sensations."

"That's possible," said Hatchitt, annoyed and having no reply, "but it's my business, and I insist that my project be tried out experimentally."

There was a pause, of which everyone took advantage to retreat into himself and deliberate.

As a simple businessman, who had joined the Central Fire Company to occupy myself specifically with financial and commercial aspects, I was rather vexed by having to come to a decision on a question so alien to my expertise. Quite perplexed, I weighed my voting options, and the German heads grouped anxiously around the board, with my gaze. "I've never seen Mr. Hatchitt so excited," I said to my neighbor, to distract myself, while waiting to form an opinion.

"The cause of that is simple," Archibold relied. "This is the first board meeting we've held underground, at a depth and under an atmospheric pressure which, according to Hatchitt's own explanations, develops and dynamizes his brain."

119

"What will happen to his head when we get even further down?" I asked.

"Like a steam-boiler, his skull might be guaranteed for a certain number of atmospheres and support their pressure," Archibold replied, "but if Hatchitt descends too far and surpasses his measure, he'll certainly explode."

Meanwhile, Lord Hotairwell, with his vast forehead clutched in his palm, seemed to be reflecting profoundly. So accessible to all progressive ideas, he felt seduced by Mr. Hatchitt's and inclined to let it be tried—but he had one objection. "Shouldn't we have some scruples about removing these Germans' brains?" he asked.

"Why?" said the engineer.

"Perhaps we should try something else first," he persisted, scanning the troop of savages—who, in response to an order given by Penkenton, had resumed their circular course. Breathing hoarsely, they were following it with their tongues hanging out and their hips moving madly, exhausted by fatigue but excited by the doctor, who was clicking his tongue and his whip like a circus ringmaster.

"Halt!" commanded Lord Hotairwell, disapproving of a maneuver that he had not initiated.

"That, Mr. Hatchitt," said the doctor, stopping breathlessly, "is how one directs a crew of workmen."

"Soldiers," said Lord Hotairwell to the men, "at ease!"

"*Danke! Gut!*" (Thanks very much.)

"You may also speak."

"*Ei! Ei! Tausend Teufels!*" (A thousand devils!)

"Do you want to return to your own country?"

"No," said 50 voices, as one.

"Do you prefer this well to the skies of Germany?"

"Yes, certainly," relied the same chorus.

"So you want to work here freely? On what conditions?"

"Well paid and well nourished!"

"You will be."

"Beer and sauerkraut?"

"Yes."

"Hard-boiled eggs, lard and cooked meats?"

"You shall have them?"

"So you're bribing them with sausages!" said Hatchitt, shrugging his shoulders.

The bargain was enthusiastically concluded, and the workers, cheering Lord Hotairwell, would have carried him in triumph if a forceful gesture from Penkenton had not subsumed enthusiasm within respect. "Look," he said. "They seem to be regretting their bargain already."

Indeed, the intoxicated men, so delighted a moment before, but now gathered in conference, had the appearance of deliberating conspirators. After a few moments, one of them came forward, very embarrassed, twisting his helmet-wig between his fingers. "Milord," said the large blond fellow, spitting forcefully, peasant-fashion, in order to maintain his composure, "if we undertake to finish the work, we'll be here for a long time; it's a sort of colony that we'll be founding beneath Ireland." He blushed beneath his negro disguise, and added: "We'd like to send for our wives, in order to colonize."

"It's not customary to colonize at the bottom of a well," Lord Hotairwell replied, generously, "but I authorize you to send for your wives in order to colonize at the surface." Addressing himself to Major Schako, he said: "You're free. You may go. It will be up to the Queen's government to obtain the reparations that are due to us."

The promises made on that decisive day were scrupulously kept on both sides, and the engineer William Hatchitt had nothing but praise from then on for the work and the conduct of his white Prussian negroes.

Chapter Nine
In which the Project of Destroying the Earth,
Proposed by Dr. Penkenton,
is Postponed for Want of a Majority

One day, Lord Hotairwell went into the boardroom with a furrowed brow, bearing under his arm the envelope of an official dispatch, as large as a minister's portfolio, secured by a red wax seal as large as a plate.

"Gentlemen," he said, as soon as the meeting was opened, "His Excellency the Earl of Greenwich, Secretary of State for the Ministry of Foreign Affairs, has forwarded to me a dispatch from the cabinet in Berlin, which I have to make known to you:

"To His Excellency the Earl of Greenwich, Secretary of State for the Ministry of Foreign Affairs.

"My Lord,

"The attention of the government of His Imperial Majesty has been called, in recent times, to the actions of an industrial society of extreme importance, by virtue of the sum of its capital, the talent of its directors, and the goal it is pursuing. The General Company for Lighting and Heating by the Central Terrestrial Fire proposes, in fact, as its name indicates, to utilize the Earth's central fire by means of a well presently being dug in Ireland. At the same time, by means of patents taken out in all the other countries of the globe, it seems intent on claiming a monopoly on such exploitation.

"Without prejudging the chances of such an enterprise, the advisers of His Majesty the Emperor cannot view without regret the potential appropriation of such a considerable estate as the terrestrial core to the profit of a single owner. They deem, by his permission, that the cordial relationship of our two countries might be altered on this account, and they recommend the following observations to Your Excellency's urgent attention.

"The central fire, My Lord, is, by nature and by destiny, a patrimony indivisible between humankind: a fire of common interest, which cannot fall prey to the first occupant, because it is already occupied. It is, in fact, a matter of law, in the absence of contrary clauses, that property above ground entails property below ground, in the same way that the possession of the face of a medal invariably implies possession of the reverse side; that the owner of the surface is also the owner of the depths, and has, in consequence, the right of use and abuse (*uti et abuti*). But this right is limited by the parallel right of his neighbor, and does not imply the right of perpendicular descent to the antipode, nor lateral descent into the subsoil of others, either to extract its resources or to emerge into any other heritage by means of a hole drilled from beneath.

"These principles of land-registry are of a primordial order; if they were contested, the regionalization of the Earth would not longer be guaranteed; property in land and agriculture would be fundamentally undermined on the day when their exploitations, already severely tested on the surface, were threatened with invasion from below, and the possibility of the ground and its grass being cut away underfoot..

"Nature itself seems to have taken care to formulate the right of everyone to the subterranean region and to the fire lit in that subterranean region, by placing the central fire in the center, within equal reach of all the inhabitants of the Earth, situated at the limit of the same radius: an indisputable geometric proof, offering no exceptions but the poles, which are closer to the center by virtue of their flattening, and the equator, which is more distant by virtue of its swelling—exceptions confirming the rule, the maternal care of nature having put the poles, which are cold, closest to the fire, and moved away the equator, already too warm.

"These premises having been established, the consequence follows that the exploitation of the central fire cannot be the monopoly of any company, any kingdom or any continent; that it can only be legitimately attempted by common accord between those having the right, after an inquiry *de*

123

commodo et incommodo, following an international conference of specialists, which, to clarify the enlightenment acquired by the work already done, should meet in Ireland, either at the orifice or at the bottom of the commenced well. These delegates of all nations will each claim a share in the fire, determining the mode of its deployment, fixing the dispensable quota according to the extent of its territories and also share out the suboceanic regions, in proportion to the continents.

"It is a scientific notoriety of which you are not unaware, My Lord, that the terrestrial globe, inhabited with so much distinction by Your Excellency, was a sun before it was a planet, gaseous before being solid, and that, being in that era 14 times larger than it is today, it extended as far as the Moon. You also know that it will be reduced, contracted and shriveled at a later date, to the point that the Earth of our day will no longer occupy much more space on that day's Earth than Your Excellency occupies on the present Earth, that result being due to its cooling in space, without humankind having cooperated therein.

"That cooling, measured with exactitude by Fourier[54] and Saussure, is no less than one degree per 57,000 centuries, corresponding to an annual contraction of 1/100th of a millimeter of the Earth's diameter, or a reduction in volume of five cubic kilometers and a diminution of the duration of a day of 1/300th of a second per 2000 years.

"What a progression these already-considerable figures will acquire on the day when, emerging from passivity and opening the floodgates of the central fire, humankind will deliver the remainder of the original flame to all uses and all abuses! On that day, My Lord, it will no longer be in terms of 57,000 centuries that the perishing of the globe will be estimated; it will be in centuries, years, and soon in weeks that its heat will diminish by one degree, its diameter by a ten-

---

[54] Joseph Fourier (1768-1830) published his *Théorie analytique de la chaleur* in 1822.

thousandth. It is by cubic myriameters that its tonnage will be reduced, and precise calculations will be able to identify the day when, the Earth having been reduced to the size of the dome of St. Paul's, hectares having become square millimeters, rivers trickles of water and seas ponds, human beings will be huddled together, climbing on one another's shoulders or devouring one another to make room for themselves: passengers bewildered by the sight of their ship shrinking in transit to the dimensions of a canoe.

"The importance of these considerations cannot escape Your Excellency. The inhabitants of this world have an interest in not shrinking it. The 1,455,933,500 human beings scattered over the 130 million square kilometers of surface area (oceans excluded), which is 8.9290 hectares per head, cannot want to diminish that extent, which is scarcely sufficient to support them. They have a right and a duty to oppose, to the extent of their ability, the decadence of their planet, to maintain in a habitable state that former sun excessively disposed to become a moon, to refrain from squandering it, to enjoy it as good family men, and to transmit intact to human generations yet to be born the heritage that our generation and that of your Excellency have received from their ancestors.

"In sum, My Lord, if the central fire exists…."

"It exists," Dr. Penkenton put in. "I have said so."

"And if it didn't exist," added Hatchitt, angrily, "who would venture to prevent us from exploiting it?"

"It would be very regrettable if it didn't exist," I murmured.

"Why is that, Mr. Burton?"

"Because then we'd be exploiting something that didn't exist."

"What would that matter?" Hatchitt replied. "If there were no central fire, there'd be something else in its place, which we'd exploit."

"But what if there weren't anything in place of the central fire?" I objected.

"There wouldn't be anything but a circumference," opined James Archibold.

"What's that supposed to mean?" asked Hatchitt.

"What it means is that if the center of the Earth is empty, if the Earth is just a ball as hollow a nutshell, and we were to pierce the shell, we'd fall into the void instead of falling into the fire."

"Oh, in that case, what a fine business we'd have!" cried William Hatchitt. "What luck! If the center of the Earth were hollow and we took possession of that void! What an extension of territory for England! What docks for her commerce, situated at the exact center of her business, with exits in both hemispheres, for the little effort required to dig through to the antipodes! A route to Australia as straight as a plumb-line! A route to India less expensive than the Suez canal—which would become worthless and could be sold back to its founders."

"Could Australian coal be brought to England by that route?" I asked, interestedly, entranced by the hypothesis that I had put forward.

"Easily," replied the engineer.

"Would the transport costs still be high?"

"It wouldn't cost anything…."

"But how would coal be raised from Australia to England?"

"In buckets or baskets, coming and going, as in a well."

"But what about the motive force to hoist the baskets?"

"No motive force, Mr. Burton—no electricity, no steam, nor any effort of animals or men. No motor, but motion of its own accord: ideal motion; perpetual motion!"

"I thought that perpetual motion only existed in the imagination of a few clockmakers," I said.

"That's a mistake; it really exists. Just ask Mr. Archibold."

"It does, indeed, exist in the case you're dealing with," replied James Archibold.

"That's obvious, and I'll prove it to you in a few words. Let's suppose, Mr. Burton, that the Earth has been pierced from one side to the other by the well we're constructing, and I throw you into the well; what would you do?"

"I honestly don't know," I replied, "having not yet had the time to formulate a plan."

"You don't understand, Mr. Burton. I mean, how would you behave in the situation that I've described? In accordance with the principles of decorum, no doubt, but more important-ly, in accordance with the law of gravity—for, once projected, you would begin to descend, constantly accelerating your progress toward the center of the Earth, where you would ar-rive promptly and at a speed that is easy to calculate."

"Very easy," said Archibold, who did not even take out his pencil for so simple a calculation. "The radius of the Earth being 6,366,000 meters, we have: Burton's speed equals the square root of 2g times 6,366,000, which equals the square root of 19.618 times 6,360,000, or the square root of 124,888,188, which is 11,430 meters per second, or 41,148 kilometers per hour, or 686 times the speed of an express train. The journey will only have lasted the square root of 2 times 6,366,000 divided by 9 seconds, which equals 1,139 seconds, or one second less than 19 minutes."

"Exactly," Hatchitt continued. "Mr. Burton will be ani-mated, on arriving at the center of the Earth, by a velocity equal to 309 times that of a person falling from the tower of Notre-Dame, the momentum of which will assist him to con-tinue his route, but this time slowing down by virtue of gravi-ty, like a rifle-bullet fired vertically into the air. That second part of his trajectory being equal to the first, Mr. Burton would attain the antipode at the nadir with the same null velocity that preceded his departure from the antipode at the zenith, and from then on, nothing would oppose the continuity of his com-ings and goings. Gravity would carry Mr. Burton back at great velocity to the center, and from the center to the summit at decreasing velocity, indefinitely, without expense, with no loss of time or fatigue, and without anything preventing him

127

from loading up, by turns, with commissions from England to Australia, and from Australia to England."

"On condition," Archibold observed, "that the Earth is immobile, and excluding air resistance, Mr. Burton would be able to move through empty space."

"Exactly," said Hatchitt.

"Since you're in agreement," the chairman of the board put in, who thought it his duty to bring the discussion back to the order of the day, "I'll close the item and resume reading the ministerial dispatch:

"...Therefore, My Lord, the government of His Imperial Majesty, without attempting to resolve by diplomatic means whether the central fire exists or no, deems that its exploitation can only be attempted by unanimous consent, and once an enquiry has demonstrated that the health, the solidity and the very existence of the terrestrial globe will be neither compromised nor destroyed as a result of the exploitation in question."

"Destroy the Earth?" cried Dr. Penkenton, whose eyes were gleaming ferociously. "Would that be possible?"

"Everything is possible to science," said Archibold, authoritatively.

"Easy, even," Hatchitt approved. "The world will be ended by science, as Edenic humankind perished. All religions have predicted it."

"Science must have limits?" I objected, in order to reassure myself.

"Science has no limits," Archibold replied. "Science is progress—a forward march, with no pause, and no terminus. Its law, the law of mind, is to accelerate, just as the law of bodies is to accelerate as they fall, increasing their speed in proportion to the square of the distance. It's only 200 years since man began to conquest of science; he's still stammering its elements, trying his first steps—but he will take his course, and his speed will be multiplied by the square of centuries. We would go mad if it were given to us to see where man has arrived, 1000 years hence, progressing at such a pace, and yet it is we ourselves who will have made that road. For humankind, Pascal says, is but one man 'who always subsists and who learns incessantly;'[55] who will know, one day, the ultimate limits of things; for whom his world will have no more secrets, and who, disdaining even the puerile work of destroying it, will kick it away like a cadaver worn out by the scalpel, and will pursue his studies on a better planet, on golden Vulcan, or even in a sun."

"All that's a long way off," said Penkenton, taking advantage of Archibold's breathlessness, at the end of a rather long sentence, to get a word in, "and my ambition as an elementary man would be satisfied simply by destroying my planet. Like Mr. Hatchitt, I believe that would be easy; the Earth is in a poor state; deluges and eruptions have alternately drowned and desiccated it, set it on fire and muddied it. The recent Lisbon earthquake dislocated it over a twelfth of its continental surface;[56] a dozen similar quakes could put an end to it."

Dr. Penkenton struck the ground with his cane, as if to pulverize that clod of earth.

"It's a terracotta," said Hatchitt in his turn, "a bit of pottery that is cracking, crumbling, coming apart and falling into pieces, a molehill that could be scattered in space by an appropriately vigorous kick: a sick Earth, indecent and unhealthy, which will become less habitable as railways, steamboats, fire-wells and factories multiply, combining volcanoes and human chests more actively to exhale carbon monoxide and carbon dioxide, which cleared forests will no longer absorb. The terrestrial atmosphere will become as obscure as a London fog, and the human species, groping around, will perish,

---

[55] I have translated the famous quote from Blaise Pascal directly; the author's substitution of *survit* for *subsiste*, repeated below, presumably results from misremembrance.
[56] The great Lisbon earthquake of 1755—whose epicenter was beneath the Atlantic, some distance from the shore—was the most destructive on record.

asphyxiated by the fumes—or, worse, still, won't perish, but will be etiolated by consumption, cachexia and fever. The mind will survive the body in that decadence, and man will enter into a phase of retrograde evolution, of a return to the ape, and from the ape to inferior animals, without the end-point of that regression being foreseeable; for humankind—which is, as Pascal and Archibold say, is only one man who 'always subsists and forgets incessantly'—will arrive at an imbecility of which our present stupidity gives us no idea."

"If that's what's going to happen," said James Archibold, annoyed at seeing his quotation made into a turncoat, "it would be better to finish it right away, by destroying the Earth."

"That's what I always say!" cried Dr. Penkenton.

"Unless it can be repaired," Archibold continued. "The first thing to do would be to rectify its axis, in order to equalize the seasons. Fourier[57] envisaged the project, but he neglected to indicate the means."

"Milton asserts that after Adam's fall, an angel was stationed on the north pole, in order to tilt it and disturb the climate,"[58] said Lord Hotairwell, "so the displacement was made a long time ago. The best we can hope to do is sustain the situation, so that the Earth doesn't end up rotating on its poles."

"It's not a question of repairing it," Penkenton put in, "but of destroying it, if there's a means."

"There are 1000 means," said Hatchitt, "and I declare that, in consideration of a price to be determined, according to plans and estimates to be drawn up, I wouldn't mind taking on the contract, in collaboration with Monsieur de Lesseps—who is used to projects of this sort, and who, by cutting isthmuses

---

[57] This reference is to the Utopian writer Charles Fourier (1772-1837), not Joseph Fourier, to whom an earlier reference was made.

[58] Actually, Milton only asserts that "Some say he bid his Angels turn askance/The poles of Earth twice ten degrees and more/From the Sun's axle" (*Paradise Lost* X: 668-70).

to make the continents lose their equilibrium, has made our task much easier and has certainly envisaged our aim."

"Let's draw up the estimates, then," said Penkenton, taking out a pencil and a piece of paper, which he handed to the engineer—for he, with his large antique handwriting, would only have been able to establish such important plans and estimates on an acre of paper, on a scale of actual size.

"The choice of means ought perhaps to precede the drawing up of estimates," observed Archibold, with his invariable competence.

"That's quite true," said Hatchitt, interrupting the figures that he had begun to sketch. "Let's choose the means, then; there's no shortage of them. A few mine-shafts drilled to suitable dimensions, filled with a few million tons of dynamite—would that suit you?"

"There's a possibility that it wouldn't be sufficient," said Archibold. "The fragments of Earth, momentarily disjointed by the explosion, would come together again by virtue of gravitational attraction. The result would be incomplete. In any case, that means has several aspects."

"Four aspects," said Hatchitt.

"I can only see three," said the chief engineer, dryly, annoyed to be one aspect short.

"The means that I propose," Hatchitt continued, "has the sanction of experiment in is favor; it has already succeeded."

"It has succeeded?" I said, anxiously.

"Yes, for what can all the astral debris that you find in the way when you go from Mars to Jupiter be—the broken ring of the asteroids, in more than 100 pieces—if not the remains of an Earth whose humans have blown it up, and whose fragments have drawn apart in spite of gravitation, in such a way as to render its destruction complete?"

"Incomplete," Archibold put in, "since each fragment has remained a petty Earth which orbits the Sun as its mother planet did, and which is probably inhabited."

"Planets for one person or for a family," Hatchitt sneered, "as large as Hyde Park; which their inhabitants can

131

end if they wish. Perhaps they're busy doing so! That's their business. Let's stick to destroying ourselves. If you don't like the idea of blowing up the globe, would it suit you to set it on fire? It could be done. By igniting the remnants of forests, coal and petrol, launching potassium fire-ships on to the seas, decomposing the seas themselves into their elementary gases, and releasing the central fire, one could, I think, obtain a magnificent blaze—in the wake of which nothing would remain but a heap of easily-dispersible ashes."

"One might, perhaps," said Archibold, "make the world explode at a lower cost by closing the mouths of volcanoes. The cubic kilometer of scoria that they vomit forth every year, and he gases seething from the surface, having no more exits, would blow off the lid."

"Would it really be less costly to seal the volcanoes?" Hatchitt reflected. "There are 300 of them."

"Sealing 300 volcanoes wouldn't finish it!" cried Penkenton, bad-temperedly.

"Would you like to proceed more rapidly?" asked Hatchitt. "It's quite easy; put a stop to the Earth's rotation; its movement would be converted into sufficient heat to set fire to it."

"That would satisfy me," said Penkenton, "but how do you intend to stop the Earth's rotation, Mr. Hatchitt?"

"Just as I'd stop a carriage—by putting a stone in front of the wheel. The Earth, colliding with the object with the momentum that animates it…"

"109,800 kilometers an hour," James Archibold specified.

"109,800 kilometers an hour," I repeated, in order to appreciate it better.

"1,373 times as fast as the London-to-Dover train," said Archibold, helpfully.

"How long," I asked, "would it take a train like that to go from London to Dover?"

"Three minutes 47 seconds," Archibold calculated.

"It would arrive almost as soon as it left," I remarked, sagaciously.

"Very nearly, Mr. Burton; and by going a little faster, it wouldn't even have to arrive or depart; it would no longer be moving. Arriving incessantly and always departing, located everywhere and nowhere, equivalent to staying where it is; infinite velocity is equal to immobility."

"We're wasting time," Penkenton put in. "What obstacle, Mr. Hatchitt, would you place in front of the Earth to stop it?"

"Anything at all—the Moon, if you wish."

"The Moon!" cried the doctor, angrily, thinking that he was being made fun of. "With what would you grip the Moon? And how would you place it in front of your wheel?"

"I wouldn't place it in front of my wheel; I'd direct my carriage at the Moon instead, and by means of the collision of the two bodies, the conversion of their motion into heat, I'd give birth to enough flames to set fire to them, to remake suns with those old Earths, to bring them back to the era and state of their creation.."

"On condition," Archibold said, "that the Earth and the Moon collided on encountering one another."

"They would collide," said Hatchitt, "with a violence guaranteed by their velocity of motion."

"That's not certain," the chief engineer insisted. "The Moon, which has no atmosphere, is a hard body, appropriate to receive and land a solid blow, but the Earth, enveloped by air, is an elastic ball. That envelope might make a mattress, deadening the shock and causing the impact to misfire."

"In any event," Hatchitt relied "that mattress, flattened under their weight, would warm up enough to set them on fire; that would still happen."

"I'm inclined to think," Lord Hotairwell put in, "that Hatchitt is on the right track in wanting to destroy the Earth by fire. His ideas conform to those of Saint Peter, who predicted that the elements would be dissolved by fire,[59] to the beliefs of the Egyptians, who expected a deluge of flame during which the Earth would go up in smoke, and to the books of the Vedas, which show Vishnu armed with a sword as bright as a comet, followed by Kali's torrid breath and the serpent Secha, which vomits worlds on which Shiva, wearing Brahma's flaming heads in a necklace, dances a final bamboula."

"The motion of the Earth," said Hatchitt, "is consonant with all that is necessary for the fulfillment of these prophecies."

"If it can be stopped," added Penkenton, "everything is there."

"As I said, I'll stop it by launching the Earth at the Moon."

"But how can it be launched?—everything still rests on that."

"It's quite simple. I'll take my measures, and I'll make the Earth deviate from its ecliptic. Nothing easier, since it already deviates, and deviates every day, since men have destroyed its equilibrium. Do you know of a ship whose stability can resist the displacement of its ballast? The Earth is that ship, which is de-ballasted at a furious rate by the withdrawal from its hold, on an annual basis, of a billion quintals of coal, without bothering to replace them with anything, without thinking that its center of gravity is being displaced, its axis of evolution disturbed. Yes, at the present moment, the Earth is deviating from its route; it's running to its doom."

"That can't be called running," said Penkenton.

"One could let it go," Hatchitt went on, "but one can also help it on its way."

"Great news!" cried the doctor. "My full co-operation is guaranteed—how can I help it?"

---

[59] 2 *Peter* 3:12 refers to "the day of God, wherein the Heavens being on fire shall be dissolved, and the elements shall melt with fervent heat."

"By making a good fire and burning a lot of coal," William Hatchitt replied.

Penkenton shrugged his shoulders.

"But if you want to finish it right away," said Hatchitt, "there's a better means—which is to continue the well as far as the central nucleus, and to release its flames and vapors at full tilt, the pressure of which will launch us through space like a crazy spinning-top, jostling and terrifying the worlds. We shall have created a first-rate aeolipile,[60] which would delight the spirit of Heron of Alexandria."

"All this requires reflection," opined James Archibold. "Without denying the value of the means proposed by Mr. Hatchitt, I think that it wouldn't be superfluous for us to combine them all together. Perhaps, in a question of this importance, which concerns our entire solar system, it would be appropriate to seek the collaboration of other planets—those, at least, which resemble us most closely, by virtue of their age, their size, their constitution and their position in the system, and might share our views: Venus, for example, which is only 27,000,000 leagues away, or Mars, the Earth's twin—to the extent that, if we were transported to its surface, we might think that we were still here."

"I'd prefer to ask for the help of Jupiter," said Hatchitt. "It's the largest planet, and the people who inhabit it must be very strong, since they're 15 feet tall."

"Fifteen feet!" I said, admiringly, being only five feet tall myself.

---

[60] An aeolipile is a device that feeds steam from a boiler into one or more bent tubes attached to a wheel, the emission of which causes the wheel to rotate; the development of such a device by Hero, or Heron, of Alexandria (c.10-70 A.D.) is frequently cited as his entitlement to be considered the inventor of the first steam engine.

135

"It's Christian Wolf[61] who has measured them. That height, in any case, is nothing astonishing; it results from the poor lighting of the planet. The Sun's light is weak on Jupiter, and weak light dilates the pupil of the eye. The largeness of the eye implies the largeness of the body and the inhabitants of Jupiter have large bodies because they have large eyes."

"But elephants and whales have small eyes and large bodies," I observed.

"That's an exception that probably confirms the rule," Hatchitt replied, surprised by the objection.

"In that case," I asked, "can I become a few feet taller by keeping to the shadows or dim light?"

"I don't know," said the irritated Hatchitt. "Ask Christian Wolf."

"The inhabitants of Jupiter," said Archibold, "would be no more useful to us for being 15 feet tall. The destruction of the Earth is more a question of science than muscles. Huygens assures us that, of all the planetary humans, the inhabitants of Mercury are the most knowledgeable, especially in astronomy, because of their proximity to the Sun, which permits them to follow the circulation of the planets more easily. Huygens has almost glimpsed their instruments of observation, and almost conjectured that they were made of wood and zinc.[62] The people of Mercury would be useful allies."

"I think so too," said the doctor, "and like Mr. Archibold, I reckon that this great project requires associates."

"It's a little humiliating," objected Hatchitt, "to confess our impotence to the engineers of other planets."

---

[61] Christian Wolff (1679-1754), whose surname was sometimes shorn of its second f, was the most prestigious German philosopher between Leibniz and Kant; he had a similar appetite for cosmological speculation.

[62] The speculations of Christiaan Huygens (1629-1695) regarding the population of the various planets in the solar system were posthumously published in *Cosmotheoros* (1698).

"That consideration is entirely secondary," retorted Penkenton.

"Everyone has his self-respect," said the engineer.

"No stupid self-respect! The important thing is to succeed. Yes, let's get together with the other worlds. Let's create an international and intercosmic company to destroy... to destroy!" Penkenton bit into the repeated world as if it were prey between the teeth of a tiger. "Destroy everything: worlds, suns, space itself, and time! Annihilate everything, engendering nothingness! What an achievement—greater than creating being! And what a god man will be when he has achieved that creation! But one man, one company, or one world isn't sufficient to the task; we need for associates the 115 planets that surround us and the 38 million suns that flame at the end of our telescopes. So let's get on with it, without wasting a moment, and reach an understanding with our allies."

Penkenton rose to his feet as if to leave, but remained uncertain as to which way he ought to go.

Lord Hotairwell understood his difficulty, and said, with his habitual benevolence: "Perhaps it will be possible for me to facilitate your entry into relationships with the other worlds. I'm correcting the final proofs of a book that will furnish you with useful information to that end.[63] There I document the daily attempts made by the Sun and the planets in our neighborhood to communicate with us, thus far unfruitful by reason of the insouciance of the inhabitants of Earth. But I have no-

---

[63] The author inserts a reference here to "Lord Hotairwell, *Treatise on Intercosmic Telegraphy*, two handsome volumes, London: Watbled." Charles Cros had published *Etude sur les moyens de communication avec les planètes* [A Study of the Means of Communication with Other Planets] (Gauthier-Villars, 1869) before the author of *Ignis* wrote to him requesting a meeting, and this passage seems to be a satirical reference to it; it includes reference to evanescent lights glimpsed by astronomers, suggesting that they might be attempts made by the inhabitants of other planets to communicate with us.

ticed and understood their signals and I am able to say that so-called sunspots, black and changing, are lighthouses with rotating beams; that comets are rockets, gas-balloons without envelopes launched by the Sun to attract our attention; that aeroliths are stones that Venus hurls at us easily, from the heights of mountains four times as high as our own. Mars also addresses specimens of its nature and the character of its inhabitants to us. Like us, they have animals and plants, since they exhale carbon; they warm themselves, for they have peat; they are metallurgists, since they launch metals; and they have pencils, since they throw us graphite."

Lord Hotairwell lowered his voice. "I know even more," he added. "I've discovered that these various materials are not launched at hazard and that each of them represents the letter of an alphabet that I'm deciphering, of which I only have a few letters left to learn, formed by metals unknown here." He added, proudly: "But what I'm already sure of is that English is the language of the heavens."

Lord Hotairwell fell silent, although he obviously knew more.

"I'll read your work with great interest," said Dr. Penkenton, "And my colleagues will thank you, Milord, as I do, for lending us, today as always, the support of your knowledge and your extensive connections. I must nevertheless insist on proceeding, without delay, to the preliminary studies for the destruction project."

"But at the end of the day," said the chairman of the board, "what is the purpose of this destruction?"

"The purpose of destruction," replied Penkenton. "That's sufficient, I think."

"It's not sufficient, if it's not useful for anything," replied Lord Hotairwell, "and what use would it be?"

"To die, or at least to get out of this world."

"To go where?"

"That's not important. The basis of a journey is the departure. Once that condition is fulfilled, one always arrives."

"For myself," said Lord Hotairwell, "however interesting, or even profitable, the results of the enterprise you're proposing might be, I fear exposing myself to reproaches if we were to divert the employment of our capital and the efforts of our engineers to that end, without authorization."

"Reproaches from whom, once the thing is done?" asked Penkenton.

"And as Managing Director of the Company," I said, drawing eloquence from my probity and the anxiety that the project caused me, "I oppose this abuse of its funds." In order not to be so abrupt, I added: "At least, not until the shareholders have been consulted."

"Until all the inhabitants of the Earth have been consulted," Lord Hotairwell agreed.

"And they have calculated the benefits and the risks," I added, supportively.

"What, in fact, will the benefits be?" asked the chairman.

"Yes, what will the benefits be? And if there are any, who will receive them? I proposed that the matter be postponed."

"And I oppose the postponement!" cried Penkenton, violently. "We've discussed it; we should vote on it. I demand that, by virtue of the rules of procedure."

"I shall indeed be forced to take a vote, if it's demanded," the chairman said, impartially.

"I ask to speak on the wording of the question," Archibold put in.

"The question is already posed," replied the doctor. "Are we or are we not going to destroy the Earth?"

"Can't we postpone it until tomorrow?" said Archibold, who had scruples. "It's very late."

"I shall demand a night session, if necessary," the doctor said, implacably, "and I shall sit permanently."

"We'll vote, then," said Lord Hotairwell, submissive to the rules.

The usher passed the urn, and a frisson ran through the members of the board, even the most resolute. Never, in fact,

139

had such a grave question—graver than all the destinies of empires—been submitted to the deliberations of a committee and the hazards of a ballot.

Dr. Samuel Penkenton, as anxious, nervous and feverish as an executioner about to seize his victim, voted first, ostentatiously, with the aim of influencing his colleagues. Never having had to deal with such a proposition during 40 years in business, crushed under the weight of the responsibility that I had to take, although resolute in my duty, I had a headache that got steadily worse as the urn approached. The engineers James Archibold and William Hatchitt did not let their resolutions show in their faces.

After a few minutes, Lord Hotairwell revealed the votes.

Number of voters: four.

In favor of the destruction of the Earth: two.

Against the destruction: two.

There was a tie; Archibold had abstained; and without the chairman's casting vote, it was necessary to hold another ballot.

"We haven't yet done anything today," said Lord Hotairwell, when the excitement had died down. "We haven't even discussed the reply to the Berlin cabinet."

"I reply thus," said Hatchitt, sketching a well-known gesture with his ten fingers aligned in front of his nose."

"It will be difficult to insert that gesture into a letter," objected the chairman of the board.

"Can't we translate it? It seems to me that there's a word in the French language that expresses it," said Hatchitt, searching his memory.

"It's the word *zut!*" said Lord Hotairwell, whose knowledge of the language was deep. "But will the word be understood by Berlin cabinet?"

"Since the word is French, and French is the language of diplomacy, it will certainly be understood," James Archibold observed, accurately.

"I'll draft the response in conformity with your indications," said Lord Hotairwell. "Now, I propose to pass with no further delay to the agenda and Company business."

"It's 7 p.m.," said Hatchitt, who was dining that evening at Penkenton's. "I propose we put it off until tomorrow."

"Company business, tomorrow!" cried the administrative committee, as soon as the usher had distributed the certificates of attendance.

Chapter Ten
The Well Falls into the Water

At the end of 1869 the excavation had descended to 9190 meters and the thermometer had risen to 276 degrees, surpassing the warmest summers of Africa or Australia by 200 degrees. The ultimate means had been brought into effect to sustain the lives of humans in a climate mortal for salamanders. The shipments of ice from Greenland had tripled in frequency, and the Pictet apparatus was fabricating veritable glaciers of solid oxygen without relaxation. Blocks of ice and blocks of air were thrown pell-mell into the well: a frightening spectacle for the men working at the bottom, but devoid of danger, for the rubble of air and water dissolved during its trajectory through that burning atmosphere; the ice arrived melted and the oxygen gaseous.

Overheating himself in that hand-to-hand struggle with the thermometer, the chief engineer attempted to vary and increase the sources of refreshment, to sustain the courage of the workers and relieve the boredom as well as their lassitude by any means possible—notably, by creating perfectly-simulated atmospheric perturbations in every section of the well's interior: tempests, whirlwinds, avalanches of snow, showers of rain, sleet and hail. The last-named generated an authentic cold, but they were costly. One hailstone, according to the estimates of the eminent engineer, worked out at a *sou*, and a complete hailstorm at 12,000 francs.

The release of compressed air similarly procured the workers violent refrigeration, at a lower cost. Sixty taps, disposed like the jets of a hydrotherapeutic bath-house, breathed air currents upon these naked men that were capable of giving them chills—a unimportant inconvenience for the men of which the Company had made its sacrifice. Gin and brandy laced with nitroglycerine were the only aliments that could still be digested by stomachs that were being digested themselves and cooked by that boiling atmosphere. These hot drinks maintained them in equilibrium with the ambient warmth.

The working day was 20 minutes, after which each workman was carried by ambulance to ledge number 2, into a relatively cool temperature of 75 degrees centigrade; taking him any higher, or letting him out, would have exposed him to the temptation of not going back in, and to the unhealthy change of environment that a traveler suddenly transported from the equator to the pole would experience.

In spite of these measures, and although no one dared acknowledge the fact, it became doubtful that they could get through the last 500 meters in the same way that they had employed thus far, or in any other. The means of excavation at a distance—long-range tools, dredgers and drills—that they would have been able to establish on one of the upper ledges, would have encountered insurmountable obstacles, given the nature of the terrain. Nevertheless, Hatchitt was holding up well, and had made no other concession to the heat than to get into his shirtsleeves and to don a sponge-helmet or an ice-mould according to the weather laid on by Archibold. Anxiety was brooding, though, and a grave incident that occurred at this time excited it further.

You will recall the explanations given regarding the method of excavation and the insertion of the steel lining: at the orifice, a crane overhanging the well and furnishing it, as it absorbs them, with sections of tubing that are immediately bolted to the adjacent section; at the bottom, the workmen digging in spirals from the center to the circumference, with the result that the last blows of the pick delivered beneath the lining determine its descent to the level of the cleared plain. The heavy cylinder, already impelled by its mass, is thus additionally drawn by the void excavated beneath its base, and the descent of the lining gives an exact measure of the progress of the excavation, which advances at an average of four meters every 24 hours.

Before noon on January 16, however, in seven hours of work, it had already progressed by five meters.

"How ardently Hatchitt is working this morning," said the astonished Archibold. "Five sections of tube already added today!"

"That tube is sinking like a heavy knife through butter!" said Lord Hotairwell. "Might the interior of the Earth be soft at that depth, and the central fire closer than was thought?"

At that moment, a violent shock imparted from the base sent repercussions to the summit of the lining, which undulated like a blade made supple by its length, and sank down by almost a meter in a single lurch.

What terrible accident was about to happen?

Lord Hotairwell had raced to the tetroscope, but the broken apparatus no longer reflected anything and the telephone remained mute and deaf. Feverishly, Chief Engineer Archibold commanded the maneuvers to connect new sections to the tube, and Penkenton gripped the top in his arms, as one holds up the head of a drowning man to sustain him.

The situation was critical in the extreme, for if the tube were to sink so rapidly that it could no longer be furnished with extensions, the lining and its well, escaping their constructors, would collapse in the same upheaval.

"It's still going down," said Archibold, who was very pale.

"Mirk!" called Lord Hotairwell. He gave the dog a message scrawled in haste, and pointed at the well.

The animal sniffed the edge, and expressed his reluctance with a gesture of his paw, but his master was insistent. The poodle looked at him long and hard, sadly wagged his tail, and launched himself into the gulf as if committing suicide.

The cylinder stated shaking again, having resumed the perpendicular, and continued to descend, making terrible noises caused by the friction of its periphery.

"This is quite inexplicable!" exclaimed Archibold. "There's no underground digger, including Hatchitt, capable of doing as much work. Fifty men working at this rate for eight hours would go clean through Mont Blanc and clear it out into the Savoy. Then again, what can Hatchitt be doing with the rubble, since it's no longer arriving in the skips? One can only dig a hole by creating a void; he's digging furiously and not throwing anything out!"

Meanwhile, the gulf began to exhale vapors: hot and humid fumes, the mingled emanations of a smoking chimney and an oozing swamp; marshy clouds streaked with will-o'-the-wisps and flashes, stagnant and heavy, swirling and light, playful atmospheric phenomena rising in cumulus clouds into aerial volcanoes and thunderous Sinais.

From the middle of one of these clouds Hatchitt suddenly emerged: not the man the reader is used to seeing, young and alert, springing forth from his tube as from a trapdoor, as if undergoing an apotheosis, but an aged Hatchitt, extinct and bewildered, paler than a pantomime Pierrot and dirtier than a sewer-worker. His back was laden with parcels like a colporteur, because he had come up from the well via the braid of ladders, so exhausted on arrival at the rim that he would have fallen back into the gulf if Penkenton had not grabbed hold of his luggage.

"What a state you're in, my dear Mr. Hatchitt!" cried Lord Hotairwell, excitedly. "And why take that route to come up from the bottom of the well?"

"The well no longer has a bottom...the bottom no longer has a well...." Hatchitt croaked. "The well has fallen into the water...the water has caught fire..."

"He's delirious," said Dr. Penkenton.

"I'm not delirious!" Hatchitt retorted, violently, brought back to life by anger. "All is lost, I tell you!"

"Why," said Lord Hotairwell, taking note of the luggage weighing the traveler down, "have you burdened yourself with all that?"

"Because it's all over, and I'm moving house."

"He's moving house—that's obvious," said Penkenton.

"What about your workmen?"

"Fallen into the fire, or the central water—I don't know."

"And Mirk, whom I sent to you on an errand?"

"We crossed paths, but he didn't see me. He was running flat out. I thought that he was looking for me but, seeing him in such a hurry, I didn't want to hold him back."

"All that doesn't tell us what's happened to you," James Archibold put in.

"What's happened, Mr. Chief Engineer, is that, since this morning, I've been digging a well in dirty hot water, mud that ends in a filthy volcano, or in the central fire, if that fire is water. The workers were discontented, and would have gone on strike if they'd been able to stop work. The lining descended of its own accord into the marsh. Suddenly, it fell away with such a noise that I thought the Earth was coming down in my head...but it was under my feet that it collapsed. The bottom of the well visibly sank, and the lining too; the workers had disappeared beneath the mud; the telegraphs were broken, the service tubes drowned; my office remained suspended by a thread...I climbed up that thread, and here I am."

"The unfortunates!" I groaned, thinking of the tragic end of the workers.

"It's not just the men, Mr. Burton," said Lord Hotairwell, bitterly. "Mirk was a dog."

"And the men were no longer any use," Hatchitt added. "They'd done all they could."

"In any case," Archibold concluded, "they can't complain; the entire loss falls to us, who bought them. They no longer owned anything, so they're no losing anything by dying."

"Perhaps they're even gaining," opined Penkenton. "Perhaps those simple Germans and that quaternary dog will one day be curious fossils disinterred by geologists who have advanced further than us beneath the terrestrial crust, who will reconstruct their skeletons and will confidently recognize Mirk as a little human and the Prussians as giant crocodiles. Unless other geologists, Hotairwells to come, based on the proximity of the central fire, identify the bones as those of solar and gaseous humans who imprudently emerged from their fire and accidentally solidified. Unless there are anteprehistoric geologists, aborigines of the central fire, who, in attempting an excursion toward the surface, discover these condensed solar fellow citizens. Unless, finally…"

Penkenton, observing that no one was listening, shut up. The doctor, who always had trouble making others listen, had not even succeeded on this occasion in making himself heard, in the midst of such urgent preoccupations, which were further aggravated with every passing moment by new symptoms. The fumes and vapors were gushing out more intensely, accompanied by terrible explosions and hails of erupting debris: the scourges of the heavens and the abyss combined; deluges of fire and hails of stones raining upwards from below.

The idea that we had encountered a volcanic vein was the one that seemed most plausible, given all these indications.

"To run aground on a volcano!" murmured Lord Hotairwell, despairingly. "To put so much effort into uncorking a crater! What excuse can we give the shareholders, and the public, for such a mistake? I'm sure that it wouldn't be very difficult to pass off a volcano as a well, for the shareholders, but how can we make such a well the source of a civilization and the center of a city? Even Naples, so proud of its Vesuvius, keeps it at a distance and doesn't want it in its streets."

Whether it was going into a volcano or a lake, into water or fire, mud or lava, the lining was descending at a steady pace. All the workshops, combined into one, united their efforts with the same aim: to elongate the tube to an extent equal to the depth of its sinking; to furnish new bodily sections to the monster that was devouring itself. Until then, the required level had been maintained, but the majority of the stored cylinders had been used. Would the order sent with the utmost urgency to the foundries of Killybegs be delivered in time? They could not count on it.

"If the descent of the tube continues at the same rate," Archibold calculated, "the extensions will run out tomorrow evening, and the well will be lost in the abyss."

"I shall follow it," said Lord Hotairwell.

"Where to?" asked the engineer.

"Wherever it stops."

"There's no reason for it to stop."

"It could go all the way to the central nucleus," added Penkenton.

"Past it!" opined Hatchitt.

"Across the other hemisphere!"

"To emerge at the antipode!"

"To continue into the antipodal atmosphere!"

"To carry on into space!"

"To land on another planet!"

"To put a spoke in the cosmic gears!"

"How long a spoke?" James Archibold attempted to calculate.

"More than a spoke!" said Hatchitt. "A driving-shaft grafted to a sun, with command-wires to its satellites! Rotation to rent and for sale, motive force for old moons and planets!"

"Will the foundry at Killybegs be able to construct that drive-shaft?" asked Penkenton.

"All the foundries on Earth wouldn't be able to do it, if they used all its metal—which would reduce the globe to a little ball.

"To a little ball," said Hatchitt, "which, at the end of that long tube, would be reminiscent of the ball in a cup-and-ball game, swallowed by its cup, or of an animal having nothing for a body but a tail—the tail of a lion with the hips of a flea."

This flood of incoherent speech testified to a general alarm by which I was all the more struck because I felt myself to be in full possession of my lucidity, and even more securely seated in my reason than usual. I therefore judged it my duty to intervene, while conducting myself with the deference and in the humble manner required of any man who is not an engineer. "It seems to me," I said, "that there's a simpler means of warding off the catastrophe that threatens us, or at least of gaining time and tube."

At this opening, the physiognomies of my listeners became so admiring that I suspected that I had said something stupid; overcoming that temporary sensation, however, I continued: "That means consists quite simply of attaching the lining to the crane, which will hold it suspended during the time necessary to…." I was, however, obliged to stop my developing argument by the badly-stifled laughter of my colleagues—especially Penkenton, whose elementary education, as you know, left so much to be desired! "I'm awaiting an objection," I contented myself with adding, coldly.

"Here it is," Chief Engineer Archibold replied, immediately. "The crane can support 20,000 kilograms. The lining weighs 1,200,000 tonnes. Your idea, Mr. Burton, has a deficit of 1,199,980 tonnes."

"If only we had adopted my plan to begin with," Hatchitt said, then. "If, instead of making a lining with a single body and a single base, supported from above, we had divided up the length, multiplied the supports and supported the sections underneath, the lining would not have been at risk of being swallowed up in its totality, and we'd be in less difficulty."

"We'd be in much more," retorted the chief engineer, "for, thanks to the system I put in place, we can still retain the tube at the head by elongating it. I'd like to see you shoring up and bolting on sections in the present circumstances, at the bottom of this volcano!"

The hours went by, and the cylinder continued to descend, like the trunk of a gigantic tree growing in the wrong direction. A whose day passed thus; the last two sections of the tube, brought to the worksite, were about to be set in place, soon to be swallowed up, and those men of indomitable will were attempting in vain to prolong the struggle; their powerful hands vainly embraced the lining that the well, as it sank, was about to buried beneath the shovelful of earth that covers everyone who has lived in this world.

During those long hours Lord Hotairwell, the Napoleon of science, stood on his column in order to be buried with it, leaning over the edge with his hands extended, pleading with the abyss, staring unrelentingly into its depths, drinking in its noises, its gleams, its unknown scents. With an avid gaze, he watched over its mysterious confines: the door, opened by a crack, that might yet open wide to give passage to truths of Genesis, prehistoric secrets, and to the central humans themselves: the solar ancestors; the ideal fossil on which the hand of a geologist might chance to fall. An astronomer in reverse, aiming his telescope into the terrestrial depths, at the old nebula that had become the central fire, what magnificent discoveries, recompense or punishment awaited that audacious investigator?

When one opens the flue of a kiln, the flames near the threshold overflow in brilliant sheaves, and the other flames continue, in the depths, to girdle the coving of their moving arches; when one releases the valve of a high-pressure furnace where ore is being smelted, torrents of incandescent liquid and blazing metal pour out; what flames, what torrents and what sparkling spectacle were about to gush from this well, this flue opened over the central fire, this furnace enclosed beneath its vault of clay? Floods of virginal and pure light, as if from drawn from the heart of the Sun! Flames liquefied by the pressure of their envelope! Sunlight atrophied in darkness or as bright as on the first day! A golden cloud, still radiant and young! A drop of fecund light, populated, like a drop of water, with its infusoria, its inhabitants....

"The lining's stopped!" cried William Hatchitt, at that moment, his voice trembling with emotion.

"Ah!" said Lord Hotairwell, dolorously, awakened with a start by these words, as if by a shock.

"In the nick of time!" I cried, joyfully.

"No, not in the nick of time, strictly speaking," Archibold objected. "The tube could still go down another three meters, since we still have a section of that length, which swill go to waste."

Ten minutes, half an hour, half a day went by; the lining, no longer oscillating, seemed to be fixed on solid ground. The eruptions of scoria and vapor had eased; the evaporation of the subterranean lake had concluded and the well was sitting on its bed, having completed its excavation by itself and given its shareholders, *proprio motu*,[64] a considerable profit in depth and calories.

Dr. Penkenton, with his Herculean conceit, had taken that cylinder, three and a half leagues long, by the neck and attempted to shake it, as one does a stake to test its resistance. Lord Hotairwell, equally childishly, scolded him for touching it, as if the poor dwarf of a colossus had the strength to disturb that authentic giant.

The excavation of the geothermal well had lasted 12 years and 10 days. James Archibold, exhausted by such a long effort, collapsed rather than sat down on the rim; William Hatchitt buttoned up his fur coat, in order not to get cold—and the two engineers mopped their brows, for the first time in 10 days and 12 years.[65]

---

[64] *Proprio motu* [by its own motive force] is here being used literally, although the phrase was far more familiar as the technical description of a signed document issued by the Pope on his own initiative.

[65] The story's internal chronology has become rather confusing; at the beginning of this chapter, we were at the end of 1869, and it seemed natural for the reader to assume that the January 16 mentioned thereafter was that of 1870. The note at the beginning of the next chapter, however, implies that it must actually have been 1872. We were told earlier that January 1867 was some six years after the commencement of the well, so there still seems to be a slight discrepancy.

Chapter Eleven
A Grand Dinner

Industria City, July 6, 1872.
Lord Hotairwell and the Central Fire Company invite
Mr.... to do them the honor of dining with them on
August 12 at 2 p.m.

Lord Hotairwell having judged it useful to the Company's interests to crown its work with a solemnity befitting its achievement and success, 2,000 invitations similar to the one you have just read were sent to the political, economic, scientific, literary and industrial notabilities of all the civilized nations. They were accepted with such alacrity that, on the appointed day, some 3,500 guests, conveyed by special trains organized at the ports of Cork, Belfast and Bantry, and then combined into a single train on the Great Central Irish Railway, presented themselves at the gates of Industria City.

The Chairman of the Company, flanked by the Managing Director, Mr. Burton, was waiting for them on the threshold, and greeted them with his habitual affability. Then, after an exchange of cordial speeches, dinner not being ready as yet, the guests spread out in the well. The engineers, James Archibold and William Hatchitt, had prepared their work with minute care for the examination to which it was about to be subjected.

The geothermal well, brightly lit throughout the three leagues of its depth, was invaded by this enthusiastic cosmopolitan and polyglot crowd, eager to touch and to see, unleashing bucket-elevators, hanging from ladders like bunches of grapes, accumulating in pipes, emerging from conduits, grouped on the ledges, arguing tumultuously like a mob at a crossroads. The well was less reminiscent of a well than a sparkling Avenue de l'Opéra or Passage des Panoramas in the evening, with its busy crowd and its atmosphere of human effluvia and cooking odors mounting from ventilators but making themselves sensible here. The ovens of Hotairwell House being insufficient for a dinner of this importance, they had been constrained to install the kitchens on the ninth ledge of the well, where the dishes cooked without ovens, in the ambient temperature.

William Hatchitt, with his usual zest, had taken responsibility for—to use his own expression—"the central stewpot" for the day, and for organizing the service, facilitated by a dumb-waiter circulating from the kitchens to the dining-room situated 15,000 meters above. By 1:45 p.m., the cooking odors became so intense that no one could doubt that Mr. Hatchitt would be prompt in his service, and everyone emerged from the gulf into the hall, which presented a marvelous scene at that moment.

The circular walls of the immense room, decorated with excellent taste, presented all the machinery of the completed excavation suspended from their walls, as shiny as jewelry: the coarser tools and the most delicate instruments, those that were plied by robust arms and those animated by thought; homage to brains and muscles, panoplies of labor and trophies of science. Before them were arranged, in neat order, the larger machines, the powerful motors, the blowers with enormous cylinders, the drills with menacing bits: industrial furniture appropriate to the style of the dining-room; dressers made to measure for its silverware.

Next came the concentric series of circular tables, whose diameter diminished toward the center; the rim of the well was enveloped by the circles, like a drive-shaft and its gear-wheels. Over the orifice, a floor—rapidly set in place after the emergence of the visitors—bore a table at which 80 selected guests took their places, proud of the honor but very anxious to be sitting on top of such a gulf. That table of honor was round, like the others, but narrower, and bordered with place-settings only on its interior circumference, so that the guests were facing the public—which, in feasts as in fairs, loves to see phenomena.

153

The phenomenon in question merited being seen, for, on weighing the intellectual value of these 80 individuals selected from an entirely eminent crowd, one might have thought that the quintessence of human genius was momentarily condensed in that location: that beings of a superior species, gods of a sort, had come to sit down at a human banquet. On the other hand, though, on considering the extraordinary ugliness of these scientists, one might have thought oneself seated at a banquet of apes, and might have said to oneself that if the floor were to give way and precipitate them into the abyss, the geothermal well would become, simultaneously, a well of knowledge and a museum of faces surpassing in horror the finest specimens in Madame Tussaud's.

Is the ugliness of scientists a law of nature? Does their genius only flourish to the detriment of their bodies, like the tulip at the expense of the bulb? Or is it for lack of culture that the physique becomes deformed and withered? The body of a scientist lives poorly, sad and abandoned, malnourished and badly dressed, without pleasures and without perfumes, celibate or ill-married, viewed askance by its soul, which scorns it and considers itself akin to a treasure in an old cellar. Perhaps it is necessarily so; a soul so fine in the body of Apollo, would be vain, while scientists, being physically ugly, are modest.

At that moment, the band of the Horse-Guards, kindly lent by Her Majesty, took its place in the hall, and Mr. Hatchitt, completing the setting of the tables, crowned the edifice with three mounted dishes that were composite masterpieces of cuisine and engineering.

One was a volcano: Cotopaxi, the summit of the Cordilleras, particularly appropriate to imitation by a sugary dish by reason of its sugar-loaf form. This volcano, in full activity, measured 80 centimeters from its base to its crater, whose convulsive and ardent lips were vomiting forth, with perfectly controlled fury, torrents of comestible lava and sulfurous vapors of green custard, which projected their lightning-streaked plumes to the Heavens.

The second was a coal-mine, similarly active and made of sugar, moved by an ingenious but inconstant mechanism, which sometimes let the coal and tits baskets fall noisily, and sometimes hurled its workers and produce into the air. As a result, Dr. Penkenton, who was seated in the vicinity of this eruptive mine, received several lumps of licorice coal and a cardboard miner on his plate, whose provenance he was unable to understand, and the ungluing of which gave him infinite trouble.

Finally, the principal dessert dish, which William Hatchitt placed personally in front of the chairman, was a terrestrial globe, with a circumference reduced by a factor of 40,000,000, opened up from one pole to another like a melon deprived of a slice. Within this cleft, stratified in their order of genesis, all the geological strata were visible: the diluvium at the surface, with its flora and fauna, then the crag, the shell-marl and the gypsum—in which the excavation had halted, but in the bosom of which the confectioner had continued his course, passing through the secondary, transitional and primitive terrains, penetrating to the liquid nucleus represented by a central syrup boiling beneath the crust and oozing eruptive trickles through fissures. Samuel Penkenton, who had furnished the plans of this geological gateau, served himself, when it was passed to him, with a thick slice of Cretaceous terrain mingled with plastic clay, which he seemed to find excellent.

As they had sat down to table at 2 p.m., it transpired that, by 6 p.m., the guests were in a state of plethora in which hunger and thirst were threatening to fail if the stomach were not relieved by a little mental exercise. The "loving cup," full of spiced wine, had been circulating for some time, everyone passing it from hand to hand and holding the lid open while his neighbor drank.

The time for toasts had come; the President of the Central Fire Company rose to his feet. "My Lords and Gentlemen," he said, "I assume that I shall obtain your votes straight away by proposing this first toast to one of the greatest bene-

155

factresses of modern humanity, who, at this moment when she is about to die, merits receiving the testimony of our respectful gratitude and our sympathetic condolences. My Lords and Gentlemen, I propose that we drink to coal!"

(*Yes! Yes! Bravo! Hurrah for coal!*)

"To coal, the bread of industry! The philosopher's stone that transmutes itself into gold! The black diamond with rough facets, from which spring, under the picks of our miners, light, heat and power! The power which, at sea, mocks tempests, and which, on land, has succeeded the Titans!"

(*Very good! Very good! Bravo!*)

"Personally, I hold that black diamond in higher esteem than all the jewels of Visapour and Golconda, incombustible carbon that I rate less valuable than a pound of good coal.

(*Various movements; occasional denials.*)

"Yes," Lord Hotairwell continued, firmly, "I rate a single pound of coal more highly, but if that opinion seems exaggerated to a few individuals, I will consent to interrupt my speech..."

(*No! No! Go on!*)

"Yes, I shall immediately interrupt this discourse, and ask my knowledgeable friend, Mr. Archibold the engineer, if he would care to specify, with the great precision of his speech, the value of a pound of good coal."

Archibold, thus called upon, did not appear to have heard, but he lowered his eyelids in order to concentrate his interior light on his cerebral storehouses, and having found the necessary documents therein, after brief research, he re-raised his shutters, rose to his feet and said: "One pound of good Newcastle coal is worth a fifth of a penny, while a pound of diamonds is worth 55,150,000 pence—but only a few pounds of diamonds exist, while the entire world possesses, in exploitation or in its subterrestrial storehouses, 69,000 billion pounds of coal; these 69,000 billion pounds of coal represent a force of 6250 million horse-power, the equivalent of 19,750 natural horses, or 131.5 billion men; the population of the world being 1.5 billion, each inhabitant of the planet has at his service 4.17 horse-power, or 12.5 natural horses, or 87 dynamic men, which 6250 million horse-power, if each were the same size as a natural horse and they were all harnessed together, would form a convoy 1.8 million kilometers long—which is 45 times around the world, the ecliptic of which they could tilt a speed of one two-hundred-and three-thousandth per second—and those 131 billion dynamic men, if their bodies were combined into a single body, and their arms into a single arm, would form a giant of great strength, tall enough for the colossus to stand on tiptoe and take the Moon between his teeth and swallow it like a pill—for such is the value and the power of coal, and such is its force; but if I consider it in terms of light, I remark that a pound of coal yields 3.67 cubic feet of gas, that the 69,000 billion pounds of existing coal would furnish 253,230 billion cubic feet of gas, capable of supplying 50,650 billion jets for an hour, or one single jet for 56 million centuries; and I remark, finally, that if these 253,230 billion cubic feet of gas were to escape simultaneously, they would envelop the Earth with an unbreathable atmosphere half an inch thick, noxious and so inflammable that it would catch fire at the slightest imprudence, and that the globe, once set alight, would burn for an hour with a heat equal to that of 110,600 square kilometers of Sun and with the brightness of 5140 billion Carcel- or moderator-lamps…"[66]

Having spoken thus, James Archibold suspended his final phrase and held council with himself to determine whether he ought to go on; then he sat down, reckoning these data sufficient, and satisfied at having brought to a good conclusion, without losing his breath or fainting, a sentence measuring no

---

[66] The particular type of oil lamp invented by Bernard Carcel (1750-1818) was adopted as a reference-point for measuring the intensity of light, the "Carcel" becoming a standard unit for some years thereafter.

less than 3 meters 36 centimeters in length, as one can easily ascertain.[67]

"I believe," Lord Hotairwell went on, "that in the wake of such explanations, you will be more willing to endorse my esteem for coal"—

(*Yes! Yes! Hurrah for coal!*)

—"and also for hydrogen gas, about which my savant friend has spoken so exactly—

(*Yes! Yes! Hurrah for hydrogen gas!*)

—"for the gas that gives us its brilliant light and which, replacing hot air in aerostats and inflating the sails of those light vessels, permits the Christopher Columbuses of the atmosphere to navigate the open seas of the fluid ocean and land on cloudy aerial continents, setting a course for the stars and elevating, not merely science but the scientists themselves and their laboratories to heights that, until now, have only been permitted to the wings of poets and birds."

(*Bravo! Hip, hip, hurrah for balloons!*)

"Are these all of the benefits of coal and gas? No, for coal engenders the coke that warms us; the ammoniac salts that fertilize; the tar from which aniline dyes are born, richer in colors than the solar spectrum; the quinoline that cures fever; the picric acid that soothes wounds; the carbolic acid that cures all ills; the nacreously-layered napthaline from which benzene trickles; the benzene which, combined with nitric acid, is ennobled, taking the perfumed name of Essence of Mirbane[68] and transforming itself further, becomes comesti-

---

[67] The author is exaggerating somewhat; in the printed text, the sentence in question only measures a little over 1.57 meters in length. It might, of course, have been considerably longer in manuscript, but the reader would hardly be in a position to ascertain that, any more than I am presently in a position to ascertain the eventual length of the sentence in the printed version of my translation.

[68] Nitrobenzene was christened "essence of mirbane" by French perfumers; English chemists were more prone to de-

ble; do we not eat amyl acetate in stewed pears, amylisovaleriate in stewed apples, and butyric ether in pineapple sorbets?

"In truth My Lords and Gentlemen, although I have contrived to name a few of the virtues of coal, it is in vain that I search for expressions worthy of addressing a eulogy to it, and it is necessary that my illustrious friend Professor Samuel Penkenton will permit me to gather, in the fields of his domain, one of those marvelous allegories with which the ancients loved to clothe the truth.: to compare coal to the first woman of the Greek Genesis, Pandora, modeled by Vulcan, animated by the breath of Minerva, and endowed with a gift by each of the gods."

(*Bravo! Bravo! Hip, hip, hurrah for Pandora and Hotairwell!*)

"And yet, despite her virtues and before having exhausted her riches, coal is about to retire to her profound retreats, and the miner, replacing his pick on his shoulder, will kick her back into the gulf, because her heat and her light will seem lukewarm and pale by comparison with those of the central fire, whose flame we have illuminated and whose radiance we have harvested! My Lords and Gentlemen, I drink to coal!"

When the applause that followed this speech had faded away into silence, Dr. Penkenton was seen to be on his feet, his great height having surged from the tumult like an eruptive island suddenly appearing to astonished mariners during a tempest. As a sign that he wanted to speak, the doctor extended his hand, as long and slender as Neptune's trident, toward the swell of the assembly—and when the waves were calm, his jaws opened, as large and rectangular as the two halves of a folio volume.

---

scribe it as "artificial oil of bitter almonds" (although even that sounds better than "the reek of cyanide"). It was used as a base in the manufacture of dyes and explosives, but not normally of foodstuffs, although all the derivatives of early organic chemistry cited in the remainder of the sentence were employed in that way (and still are).

"As you have said, My Lord, coal is the bread of industry: black bread steeped in blood and the tears of a million English workers who live in it and die in it, stifled by carbon dioxide, inflammable dust and firedamp—other products of coal that you have not named. Similarly, you have omitted the fuchsine that falsifies wine; the potassium picrate that kills more effectively than gunpowder; and petroleum, that liquid coal which also changes itself into gold, and which, more subtly, penetrates even higher spheres and even becomes a divinity..."

(Various movements and murmurs.)

"Do you not know, then," Penkenton continued, quite insensible to the disapproval of his listeners, "that at the time of their religious festivals, the inhabitants of Baku set fire to the Caspian Sea and prostrate themselves on its banks? I have seen these conflagrations, which are very beautiful.

"I intend to complete the eulogies that my savant friend has given to coal, but I cannot share the opinion, to which he has given voice, that this form of carbon is a modern benefit. I am sure that the noble lord is in error on this point, given that I myself, traveling in Greece with one of my friends, Theophrastus,[69] 2000 years ago, visited a deposit of coal on the road to Olympus, of which the smiths of that era were making use. Vulcan, the best-known among them, who burned wood in his subsidiary establishments in Lipara and Lemnos, employed lignite coal in his workshops on Mount Etna..."

These exorbitant announcements, which the doctor was accustomed to making—savant flourishes that no longer astonished his friends—had the effect of annoying William Hatchitt, who could not resist the temptation to interrupt.

---

[69] The peripatetic philosopher Theophrastus (c.371-287 B.C.) was a successor of Aristotle who attempted to carry forward the latter's encyclopedic work on natural history; his surviving writings include a treatise "On Stones," which mentions the mining of coal and its use by metal-workers.

"You've met Vulcan, Doctor?" he said, in his most acid-ic voice.

Penkenton looked at the interrupter as an obelisk questioned by an insect might have done.

"Yes, sir, I've met him," he replied, dryly—and, as a shadow of doubt remained in the engineer's expression, he added: "Yes, Mr. Hatchitt, I've met him, and I've had the honor several times…" But Penkenton stopped short, and bit his lip to bar the passage of the words he was about to pronounce—which must have been of great importance, for the doctor went pale, like a man who has narrowly avoided a great peril. "Suffice it to say that I've met him," he concluded, in a tone that permitted no reply. "No," he continued, "the men of that era had not invented coal, and more than the men of any era. The inventor of coal was the central fire, while it still burned in proximity to the surface. It fertilized the primary humus with it, gave birth to and nourished with carbon the plants that have become coal. It is the subterrestrial sun, which, while your miners exhume that coal, and while your chemist strip her of her wrapping, is now reappearing. It is the solar specter that is emerging from its tomb, relighting its rays and resuming its colors, called fuschsine, azaleine and rose-ine [70] because they are the sisters of the fuschia, the azalea and the rose, which similarly color the Sun of our day.

"My Lords and Gentlemen, I propose to you to drink to the Central Fire, the inventor of coal, and to Vulcan, the great metallurgist, who was the first to utilize it!"

(Laughter and murmurs.)

"And finally," the orator continued, "since my noble friend has thought it his duty to count aerial navigation among the inventions issued from coal, I shall seize this agreeable opportunity to drink to the men who inaugurated that naviga-

---

[70] In English, the second of these dyes—all of which are fuschsine derivatives—is known as magenta, but I have anglicized the French name in order to conserve the reference to the relevant flower.

tion: to the aeronaut Dedalus and his son Icarus, an eminent engineer who understood the necessity of being heavier than air in order to master it, and who, by means of a memorable fall, demonstrated personally, long before Newton and Kepler, the law of gravitation and the efficacy of his weight."

(More laughter.)

"This inappropriate laughter," Penkenton went on, severely, "does not attain the height of those aeronauts, who had the advantage over their present-day colleagues of flying by means of their own wings rather than owing their uplift to hydrogen gas, of not being baggage tied to a goatskin, in a basket, inferior to children's toys, to gold-leaf elephants, incapable of being inflated and rising up like them by virtue of their light specific gravity…"

The assembly, as we have seen, had little sympathy for this orator, who seemed to have taken it upon himself to obfuscate common sense, deprecate his century and compliment, to no purpose, men a long time dead. William Hatchitt, especially, became epileptic on hearing such things, and, losing the reserve appropriate to a dwarf in proximity to a giant, burst into laughter and ironic exclamation, calling Dedalus, Vulcan and Icarus fabulous and ridiculous fossils, drowned in the night of time.

The doctor, previously deaf to the utterances of his colleague, could not contain himself before these words, and, judging that the pygmy had exceeded his ration, he placed his heavy hand on the engineer's head—who, thus thrust back, was plastered to his chair, in the furious impotence of a half-crushed insect. Then, as if to complete this necessary repression, Penkenton let fall upon his adversary these three axioms:

"They are not fabulous individuals, Mr. Hatchitt; the night of time is not dark; and time does not exist. The existence of these men, which you call fabulous, is, on the contrary, more certain than your own; for if your work has great renown, that of Vulcan and Hercules has even more, and they lived more notoriously and with greater intensity than you do. Will there be, in 50 centuries, as many people who remember

162

your passage through this world, as there are today who still talk about Hercules? Will you be hailed, as he was, as a demigod? I don't know—but until that day, your existence does not present me with the same elements of certainty.

"I know that you will cite, in your favor, the testimony of your contemporaries: eye-witness who will affirm that you are sitting to this banquet, and that I am talking to you and can see you myself..."

And the doctor did indeed try, but in vain, to contemplate his contradictor—who, submerged by this flood of words, had taken fight into the well like a mouse into a hole. Penkenton, however, having no need of an interlocutor in order to speak, or even of an audience, continued without anxiety:

"These witnesses, sir, I do not dispute, but I challenge them, having convinced myself, during my long career that eye-witnesses are the termites of truth, who eat it away, mutilate it and disfigure it in the image of their prejudices and enthusiasms, and report nothing but tattered shreds turned into lies. Yes, everything attested by these people that see you must, in my view, be put in doubt; and when I see men believing in the existence of Napoleon I, because a few people survive who might have met him, I accuse those persons of thoughtlessness, and warn them that, in order to decide the question of whether that emperor actually lived or whether he is a poetic synthesis—as has been said of Homer—it is necessary to let the residue of these witnesses perish.

"Hercules, Vulcan and Icarus have escaped these uncertainties, and they appear, not as in darkness, but in the consecration of time, for time is neither a night, nor a distance, nor a shadow; time does not run like a river; it is as stagnant as a lake, or, even more aptly, no more than a word; the pure idea rejects the division of chronological space into fractions, and sees nothing under the same sky but horizons that are equally distant, but differently lit. The present, the past and the future are fictions for the usage of man, who is petty and myopic, who diminishes things to his own dimensions, who fragments distance into leagues, the horizon into planes and duration into

163

days, whereas there is only one space, one day and one Sun, which never rises and never sets."

Penkenton's voice sank to a murmur, as if he were talking to himself. "In order to so see these things, however, it is necessary to be very large and long-lived—as God and I are. And after all, you poor fellows, these mirages are useful to you; the fog that plays the part of distance tames the light for your eyes, and behind its curtain, the truth can strip naked without dazzling you.

"My Lords and Gentlemen, I drink to Vulcan, to Icarus and to William Hatchitt, whose existence I am pleased, if not to recognize, at least to welcome sincerely…"

The doctor, having become entirely amiable, emphasized these gracious words with the hippopotamus-like yawn that served him as a smile. Then he continued:

"My Lords and Gentlemen, before concluding, it will be agreeable to me to drink, with my savant friend, to one of the great discoveries, a benefactress of humankind, and the most perfect of all "—

(movement of attention)

—"to an invention so complete that all your modern science has been unable to improve it and to an inventor so ancient that even I, who knew him well, have forgotten his name: to the inventor of the wheel!"

"Of the wheel!" exclaimed Hatchitt, who was emerging from underground, coming back from his kitchen.

"Yes, sir, of the wheel! Of the circumference, the circle, the disk, of everything rounded about a center, of everything that moves at the same distance from an axis! To the inventor of the wheel, to that man of genius who, gazing at the worlds rotating about their axle in the pathways of the ether, rounded a disk on that sublime model and set on its axis the heavy dray of our earliest ancestors!

"Centuries have passed without any other geometrical conception daring to substitute itself for that circumference. Do we owe the wheel and the cart to Erichthonius of Athens, who had need of it, being lame and in ill-health. To Triptolemus, who constructed them for his agricultural contests with Ceres?[71] To Pallas or to Neptune? The recognition of peoples is divided between these names; but ingenious Greece has placed its goddess Fortuna on that wheel, which does indeed bear the fortunes of the world, on which reposes all dynamic power, all locomotion, on land and on water!"

At that moment, a considerable tumult obliged Penkenton to interrupt himself. A fight, excitedly conducted between two guests, captured the attention of a part of the audience and provoked wagers. It was in the bosom of the loving-cup that discord had been generated between two neighbors, one of whom, plunged shoulder-deep in the urn, had seemed determine to drink it to the dregs, while the other had apparently decided to pull him out of it. Two stewards of greater strength having joined the combatants and separated them, the audience returned its attention to the orator, but no longer found him. Penkenton had taken advantage of the exchange of blows, which took the place of the plaudits he had not received, to sit down.

Lord Hotairwell got up again. "My Lords and Gentlemen," he said, "my knowledgeable friend Dr. Penkenton having drunk, in such eloquent terms, to the central fire, the inventor of coal, the duty remains with me to propose a toast to an inventor even more fecund and ancient, the inventor of the central fire itself: to the Sun! To the Sun, the father of our planet, of the nebula expelled from its bosom in flames, extinguished and cooled in the frost of the ether, on which humankind, arriving one day naked and poor, without clothing or shelter, shivered, catching a bad chill. Humans set fire to trees, and comforted themselves with the flames; they unearthed coal, which armed them more effectively; and petroleum, which they discovered next, seemed even better. Today, it is the central fire, the solar flame, the nebula surviving in the entrails of the globe, which we have succeeded in relighting.

---

[71] Erichthonius was a mythical early ruler of Athens; Triptolemus was a "primordial man" associated with Demeter/Ceres.

"Yes, while other peoples, wretched and bent over the ground, are belatedly gleaning coal therefrom, begging for that dead wood; while America stupefies itself in the heavy intoxication of oil, Old England has descended into geological limbo to raise the tombstone under which the soul of the sleeping Earth was at rest, and has come back, carrying the Sun as a torch!"

(*Bravo! Bravo! Hurrah for Old England!*)

"A conqueror more audacious than Caesar and Alexander, who crossed the Rubicon and the Indus, England has crossed the Styx, the flaming Acheron and its tributary, the Phlegethon. Guided by her engineers more surely than Aeneas or Dante by Virgil, she has entered alive into the infernal regions, the mysterious lands of Tartarus and Erebus, where the wisdom of the ancients anticipated the Kingdom of Fire.

"My Lords and Gentlemen, the Central Fire Company, which has been the instrument of this marvelous enterprise, which has completed this great work in spite of the resistance on nature and men, in spite of the conspiracies of certain individuals"—

(*Bravo! Bravo!*)

—"the Central Fire Company takes possession of these empires today in England's name, and crowns with the triple diadem of the goddess Hecate the head of our gracious sovereign, the Queen of Great Britain, Empress of India, whom we salute as Queen of the Inferno! My Lords and Gentlemen, I drink to the Queen!" When everyone had risen for that toast, the orator continued in a vibrant voice: "My Lords and Gentlemen, *God save the Queen, Empress of India, Sovereign of the Infernal Regions!*"

At these words, the enthusiasm knew no bounds, or surpassed them all. The guests, whose thirst seemed quite staunched, as if one more drop would have caused the vase to overflow, regained courage for that glorious toast. The most excited, or those most confident in their equilibrium, stood on their chairs, howling hurrahs and reciting in chorus the new words of the national anthem: "*God save the Sovereign of the*

166

Infernal Regions!" For that addition proved definitive, and the news, which was transmitted to the Stock Exchange by agile reporters, caused a three-penny rise in the Company's shares.

The tumult suddenly died down, however, and faded away completely, as the croaking of frogs ceases. A noise louder than all of theirs imposed silence upon them, a *basso profundo* voice rising out of the well, as enormous and strident as a thunderclap: the voice of the abyss, the voice of the Infernal Regions themselves, saluting their Sovereign.

The hall vibrated as if it were about to collapse; the ground trembled under the pressure of that subterranean whirlwind; the audience listened, open-mouthed; and the artist of that concert savored his triumph, riding on the cylinder of a blowing machine like a mahout on an elephant's back. It was the engineer Hatchitt, who, by means of intelligent couplings in the well's system of pipes, had employed them as a vast organ alimented with breath and sound by the combination of all the ventilators.

The intelligence of crowds is keen, especially that of elite crowds; they soon understood, and then the admiration was such that applause burst forth, so loudly that Lord Hotairwell gave the order to open the windows to let the noise out—and Hatchitt, seized by 1000 hands, would have been torn into pieces is order to be carried aloft in triumph if he had not climbed in all haste to the summit of his machine.

Having recovered from their surprise, the guests resumed their libations and their toasts, while the musicians of the Horse-Guards' band played the patriotic song again, with the full force of their trombones, drawing ardor from the barrel of gin that served them as a loving-cup. The saxhorns and bugles launched forth torrents of arpeggios from their wind-inflated paunches; the ophicleides roared like wild beasts, like those Mexican whirlwinds that simulate the voice of a lion to the point of causing the frightened traveler to pause, rifle shouldered and finger on the trigger, while seeing nothing coming at him but a funnel of wind. The little flutes and fifes writhed beneath their conductor's baton, whistling more furiously than

167

the hair of the Eumenides when they comb their serpentine diadems to make themselves beautiful. The cymbals, utterly intoxicated, forgetting the rhythm and losing any semblance of measure, clapped their deafening disks like applauding hands, as if to break; and the big drum struck the sonorous sides of his instrument with mighty kicks—seconded by the Chinese bells, who thrashed his tinklers.

Everything grows weary, however, especially enthusiasm, and there came a time when the musicians stopped, out of breath, and the guests, out of thirst, when nothing remained on the deserted horizon of the hall but the huge silhouette of Dr. Samuel Penkenton, looming ever higher as the collapsing crowd isolated him, as a rock grows to its full height on the strand as the tide retreats.

In that man, restored to himself, abstracted from the gaze of other men, a metamorphosis had just been completed. Movement and sentiment—all the symptoms of thought and life—had been effaced from his face like theatrical maker-up, or fallen away like a mask. That 50-year-old man was *old*: an ancient burdened with centuries; a cadaver separated from the tomb. Never had the geologist Samuel Penkenton collected, in his excavations, a more fossilized relic. Under what burden of time might that body have been slumped, at this point? What remorse had hollowed out such wrinkles? Into what memories had that soul absented itself, so far from its domain?

Samuel ב א Penkenton remained there, motionless, lifeless and immense, supported by his enormous staff, like a ruin propped up by a tree—like those pyramids in Memphis which, from the heights of their 40 centuries, gaze sightlessly at our ephemeral era, which agitates at their base without distracting them from their great memories.

PART TWO

Chapter One
A New Human Species

"Life is merely one of the forms of the activity of matter that has attained the final phase of its evolution. It is matter that, in evolving, has given life to the Catharinian monkey,[72] and which has grafted on to that elder branch of the monkeys of the Old World, the branch that calls itself Man.

"These successive creations of the activity of matter are attested by scientists and by the monkeys, whose evolution continues before our eyes. For, if the more agile Catharinian monkeys arrived first, the orangs, chimpanzees and others followed them, in urgent pursuit of the same goal—and one would have to be blind not to see with what activity, laboring their matter, they are making progress toward human form.

"Their eyes fixed on man, they study his mores, attempt his gestures, imitate his physiognomy and adopt his stance. They pluck themselves in order to cease being hairy, shave themselves or only sport sideburns. They flatten the hair on their head, smoothing it or dressing it with wigs and forelocks, kneading their skulls to redress the facial angle, knowing that the head and the tail are their weak points and trying to refuse their examination. Some among them have attained our height, and almost our bearing. Their torso has the same number of nodes; among some of them, the tail has disappeared, or, if it remains, they ennoble that appendage by making it a fifth hand. Ardent and patient studies, which humans, whom they have posed as models, naively call monkey grimaces!

---

[72] I have transcribed the author's *Catharinien* directly into English, although the term—used by early paleontologists to describe a branch of primate evolution—never caught on in England and soon became obsolete in France.

"If they continue thus, time will reward their efforts sooner or later, according to their aptitudes. Some, such as the African cynocephalus monkeys, which are negroes, and the oustitis, which are dwarfs, will never be distinguished men—on the other hand, however, the chimpanzees, orangs and gorillas are nearing that goal. In 400 or 500 years, these supernumeraries of humanity will receive their investiture; they will be humans detached from the branch of the orangs and the mandrills, which were still quadrumanes in the 19th century; and as matter, incessantly involving, always progresses, they will be more accomplished humans than we are. It is, therefore, not without reason that the professors of the Hindu University of Benares have set at the first rank of their hopes that of one day being elevated to the level of the monkey.

"Matter, by virtue of its potential activity, has created the monkey; that substance set out to create humans; humankind is, for the moment, the superior phase of these evolutions. Our scientists have understood that and, seizing the general direction of nature with a firm hand, have set about furthering evolution, playing with molecules as nimbly as astronomers play with stars.

"The chemist who, by mixing potassium carbonate and sulfuric acid, kills those two entities and creates two others, will soon have also created blood, muscles, cerebral fluid and cerebrine—which is to say, the soul, the intelligence of human matter. Yes, the chemist will one day combine from constituent parts humans similar to and superior to us; the human species obtained in his laboratories by science, and the method that nature cannot contrive, will be chemically purer and physically more beautiful, more refined of the Catharinian blood that still visibly affects present-day humankind.

"That will, for science, only be the first step; chemistry will go further. Separating the intermediate elements that obstruct its alembics, it will extract matter from its pure source; it will capture the ultimate atom whose vibration engenders the forms of objects: the irreducible atom glimpsed by Epicurus and contemplated by Graham;[73] the indivisible fraction beyond which nothingness commences. It will cause that atom to vibrate, anatomize that cosmic larva, pass that puerperal dust through a sieve; and the principle of entities, the embryo of geneses, the fetus of stars and unripe planets, put to the question, will confess its secrets!

"Magnificent summits! Sinaic peaks reddened with lightning, from the heights of which science will hand down the laws of nature!

"And yet, chemistry will go further still. In a supreme leap, it will jump over the ultimate and fall into nothingness. It will penetrate the void, grasp the impalpable, dissect the indivisible and grapple with the intangible. It will raise up its horns and will plant its banner on the mysterious terrain that no creation has stained, where uncreated matter does not exist, nameless and devoid of mass and volume, where the past-less present is still to come: that virginal but about-to-be-fecund terrain, where rivers are born without sources, children without fathers, generations without ancestors; where effects have no causes, consequences no premises; where the squaring of the circles resolves of its own accord, by virtue of the identity of the angle and the circumference; where perpetual motion flourishes in its free flight, without motive force, without mechanisms, without any of those organs that produce fiction and wastage.

"Perhaps chemistry will go further still—but I advise chemists to climb those slopes slowly, in order to avoid breathlessness and vertigo, and to accustom their brains to the overheating of their genius. Who can imagine the consequences of madness overtaking such powerful heads? I advise them to attempt creations more modest and intermediate, but useful and easily realizable, as soon as the central fire is conquered.

---

[73] The English chemist Thomas Graham (1805-1869), an early convert to John Dalton's revised atomic theory.

"Humans, having mastered that immense motive force, should construct machines according to its measure, bodies great enough for that soul; we should create a race of mechanical animals strong enough to serve us, and stupid enough to love us: a sort of automated humankind, endowed with a severely circumscribed initiative, activated by cerebral mechanisms analogous to those of Papuan negroes. Any servant that surpasses that limit has the ambition to be a master.

"The other organs of these creatures should receive all the improvements that the present state of science permits. I can imagine them, rather like divers clad in diving-suits: their large heads, with circumvolutions of platinum through which electricity runs, have the form of helmets, and project beams of light from their copper orbits that trace their path; their muscles are made of steel, their hearts of bronze; their enormous bellies are ballooned by the gas accumulated at high pressure in their entrails.

"Marvelous slaves, indefatigable and faithful, devoted servants, modest fellow citizens, Englishmen of the future, I baptize you: *Enginemen*, human-machines![74]

---

[74] The author inserts a long footnote here, attributed to the fictitious text from which he is quoting: "The name *Enginemen* seems much better suited to the new human race that England will engender because *Englishmen* and *Enginemen* are two linguistically-identical words. Any philologist can demonstrate this. *Eng-land* signifying England, *Eng-men* signifies Englishmen, primitive strong-men. The two syllables (*Eng-men*) being dry, however, the articulation has been lubricated by a euphonic syllable, which has produced *Eng(lish)men*. Furthermore, although physical strength was the primordial quality of the race, its aptitude for the mechanical arts has become the distinctive characteristic of the British nation. To substitute *Enginemen* for *Englishmen* is, therefore, no linguistic deviation; it is a blossoming of the idiom, parallel to the progress of the original vocation of the English, who are excellent technologists. Not only does their genius reveal it-

"This initial effort being accomplished, humankind will rest, freed of labor by his creatures, the proletariat being rendered extinct and social problems being resolved by universal wealth and happiness established on so large a scale that the whole of society will belong to the first echelon: wealth and happiness as inexhaustible as their source, the central fire: a submissive force serving us most humbly; the slave of our whims; the Hebe of our intoxications; the enchantress of life, safeguard against death—for death will be modified or postponed by absolute well-being, ideal hygiene, the suppression of labor and pain, sweat and tears; by the good maintenance of the roads of life, without the jolts that break springs, without the friction that wears away strength and which, in biology as in mechanics, is the only obstacle to perpetuity.

"Yes, one day, in this marvelous civilization that my mind envisages, but whose glare my eyes cannot sustain, every country and every people, having dug their wells and made alliance with the central fire, will receive their wealth, their happiness and the government therefrom. Kings and scepters, parliaments and constitutions, will be succeeded by a steam-tap and a manometer; these simple items of apparatus will suffice the humankind to come, distributing force, heat and light thereto, maintaining the life of its slave-machines, regulating seasons and climates—for the Earth, liberated from its servitude, lighting and warming itself, will march before the face of the Sun to the light of its own rays…"

These pages, so admirable and so prophetic, so passionate with terrestrial chauvinism and planetary patriotism, could only have been written by the very inventor of the cen-

---

self, from this viewpoint, in their work, but also—I say this with pride—in their physical and intellectual bearing, in their attitude, their gait, as chronometric as a pendulum, and even in their gestures, which have the forcefulness and stiffness of a connecting-rod fitted to a piston." (Lord Hotairwell, *Treatise on the Generation of Words*, 10 quarto vols. London: Watbled & Sons.)

173

tral fire, His Honor Lord Hotairwell. They are extracted from his fine book *Man Before the Earth* (volume X, p.307ff.), which has already been mentioned.[75]

In the era that we have now reached, the founders of the Central Fire Company have perfected their work. For some years, the city whose first stones thy laid at the same time as they made the first pick-axe blows of the excavation—the city that was confidently mapped out around the rim of the geothermal well, Industria—has flourished in a prosperity exceeding all hopes.

Not only has the Central Fire kept its word and delivered to its shareholders their daily million horse-power, but the force and the heat have unexpectedly exceeded that quota—a circumstance doubtless brought about by some internal lesion opening up a more direct access to the heat, augmenting the heating surface, which initially made the engineers anxious but without anything justifying their fears. The functioning of the well, having become more intense, became regular and merely provided a surfeit of riches that permitted the distribution of the shareholders of a greater dividend of well-being.

For the traveler arriving from the east across the cold fields and desolate vegetation of that part of Ulster, it was a marvelous spectacle when the panorama of Industria City unfurled before his gaze: an immense plain adorned with all sorts of flowers, limited by a circle of hills planted with woods and vineyards, which enveloped the territory with a mantle of green foliage and vines.

At the center is an Oriental city deposited in Ireland along with its sky, its climate, its palaces in lacy stone: a city of scattered villas, white and shady, mounted like daisies in a

---

[75] The author here gives a reference to "Lord Hotairwell, *Man Before the Earth and the Earth Before Genesis*, 40 fine quarto volumes, with plates. London: Watbled & Sons, Publishers." The title may be an ironic echo of Louis Figuier's *La Terre avant le deluge* (1863), about which I shall have something to say in the afterword.

lawn, open to all the breezes of the air and all the perfumes of the fields. On the far side of the plain, beyond the city, the girdle of hills opens to give access to the sea, where a life-sized image of this prosperity is reflected, on a sea with gently blue waves, which come, shaking their foamy manes to present their mirror to the Venus of the shore.

The approaches to Industria's port are defended by electric eels, motionless living torpedoes hidden in the sand, which reveal two gleams, two semi-extinct eyes like dull lanterns; guardians chained to the shore by the wires transmitting their signals. The power of these fish—already great enough to kill horses, as Humboldt has observed—has been further developed by means of Ruhmkorff coils wrapped around them. They cannot sink ships, but their discharges into iron hulls reach the crews, paralyzing them or killing them.

Ships swarm in the harbor; carriage-boats, improved chariots of Amphitrite, whose disks skim the water, and, like halcyons, only dip the tips of their wings into the sea; which cross the Atlantic in 24 minutes, without paying any more heed to storms than a cart pays to potholes—for, properly speaking, there are no more ships and what people call navigation no longer differs from journeys overland. From Ireland to India, from one antipode to the other, journeys are made without changing carriages, without the voyager noticing whether he is moving over land or sea. The wagons descend to the shore by means of a ramp, their wheels boxed in drums which float like barges and turn like wheels; a locomotive, carried by these paddle-wheels, is detached from the shore and harnessed to a train that takes to the open sea and draws away, whistling. If the weather is good, the voyagers go up on to the imperial and savor the marvelous skating with their gaze; if it is bad, they close the windows and the express train, sweeping aside the little waves and hollowing tunnels through the big ones, pursues its course more rapidly than the wind and more furiously that the tempest.[76]

For the transport of goods, at low speed, a few bad habits of the old systems have been preserved; even so, the boats no longer go over the water but under it, 15 or 30 meters deep in the tranquil zone that begins beneath the pellicle of the waves. One can get an idea of ships of this type by imagining large swans with two necks, only allowing these necks to emerge, like the piers of a bridge, sustaining a gangway above the wa-

---

[76] The author inserts a long footnote here: "A few items of practical information will be useful to readers who might be called upon to take one of these express trains. On terrestrial railways, the longest journeys extend for a few 100 leagues; stops are frequent, bends numerous and inclines considerable. This combination of causes restricts speeds to puerile proportions of 80 to 100 kilometers per hour. It is only on the sea that serious speeds can be obtained. Straight lines are almost infinite there: no bends, no slopes, the spherical surface of the globe being level everywhere; no obligatory stops between one continent and another. From the port of Industria to New York is 4000 kilometers in a straight, flat line. What a magnificent racecourse! What a prey for those hungry for space!"

"Now, it is a scientific notoriety that speed suppresses weight; that a wheel—a disk as well as a planet, animated by a rapid velocity, is freed from gravity to the extent of losing a large part, if not the whole, of its weight. It is for that reason that a locomotive in motion weighs on the rails less than a locomotive at rest; in going faster, it weighs even less, and at the extreme limit of speed no longer weighs anything at all. As speed increases, weight diminishes; as weight diminishes, speed increases, without one being able to determine any other limit than the insufficiency of space. Long distances are indispensable, and the 4000 kilometers that separate Ireland and America are scarcely sufficient for maritime trains to be able to launch themselves to the limit and stop time. They would arrive sooner if they had further to go."

ter where passengers stand. Giant ferries, these steamboats! Enormous Saint Christophers marching on the sea-bed, bearing their passengers in their extended arms! Marine monsters as large as islands, frightening to see emerging within view of a port. When they dive to depart, one might thing that a portion of the coast is sinking.

The Protean manifestations of the great source of fire and force can be seen spreading out into the distance and beyond the sea as easily as they do in the plain of Industria City, where hot air and steam, channeled as in a drainage system, warm the soil, excite its vitality, activate organic decompositions and impregnate the atmosphere with a fecundating mist. Thus organized, the countryside is a veritable hothouse! A hothouse in the open air, without any other shelter than the ring of hills, provided that that the thermosiphons are powerful enough to vanquish the Irish weather and to create a tropical climate.

Following the admiration caused by the aspect of the landscape and its flora, a new astonishment takes hold of the visitor, at the sight of the creatures that cultivate these fields, of those country-folk of an unknown species, triple crosses of humans, animals and machines—a fauna unclassified and unclassifiable, as strange as the most peculiar animals of antediluvian nature.

Here, in a field that is being prepared for sowing, is a biped whose enormous breast roars and shakes like a pressure-cooker. Like the angel of the Apocalypse, the legs supporting the trunk are two columns that march stiffly and heavily. It is dragging a ploughshare attached to its waist, which is so heavy that the beast's entire body sweats an oily and rancid mist. No human being guides this laborer, which, from time to time, unhitches itself and goes to a spring, from which it drinks long draughts. Thus refreshed, it resumes its work.

Another worker follows, in the same furrow. Long and flat, it resembles a crocodile whose jaw has been made into a rake; its teeth rake and harrow the soil, completing the work of the plough, and when it has passed, the earth is ready for seed-

177

ing. Then the sewer advances, launching cascades of grain from its open mouth, like the nymph of a fountain, which spread out all around: Ceres, thin and bronzed, a farmer's daughter rather than his wife; a Ceres of iron, forged by Vulcan. A second crocodile follows in the footsteps of the sewer and buries the seeds with its rake.

In the neighboring fields, where the harvest is under way, there is no less activity. Snakes with steel teeth hiss as they undulate through the fallows and bite the bases of the ears of corn, which lean over and fall into the ties extended to them by others in charge of the gathering. Reapers are shaving one field, and there are haymakers that one might take for lunatics, so agitated are their long thin arms, hurling the hay to ridiculous heights, which falls back and settles over them.

These creatures, or people, fill the countryside with their activities, as diverse as their forms, enveloped like phantoms in the clouds of steam they exude. One might imagine that one was seeing a swarm of insects: scarabs with bronze wing-cases and prothoraxes dleaming like suits of armor—but insects promoted to the size of pachyderms.

You will already have recognized the pseudo-human race conceived by Lord Hotairwell and brought into the world by his skillful engineers: the *Enginemen*, or, rather, the *Atmophytes*, for the latter appellation has prevailed; the rural Atmophytes, bloated peasants, as inferior to their colleagues in the city as a farmhand who grooms horses is to a valet who grooms human beings. Only the latter merit the name of Atomphytes—steam-men[77]—for one cannot call facsimiles of

---

[77] The logic of this decoding is dubious. The Greek *atmos* means "vapor," and as the French word for steam is *vapeur*, the first part of the synthesized term can easily be held to signify "steam," but the Greek *phyton*, which gives rise to the English and French suffix –phyte, means "plant," and not, by any stretch of the etymological imagination, "man." I shall endeavor to explain this odd terminology, at least conjecturally, in the afterword.

humans so closely resembling their creators "animals" or "machines". They are men of iron and copper, similar to diving-suits or knights in armor; bodies in which steam has been substituted for blood, in which electricity animates mechanisms so refined, so subtle and so steeped in human genius that they immaterialize themselves by the virtuosity of their matter, and their gestures are less reminiscent of products of force than manifestations of life.

They are creatures perfect enough to disquiet their creators with the possibility that these strange beings should one day cross, by means of their acquired speed, the narrow frontier within which intelligence confines instinct, trying in their turn to scale the heavens, to stifle their bewildered masters against breasts of bronze, and to render into their native dust the human clay that they once took for gods!

Chapter Two
A Comfortable City

It is to the outskirts of the city, to the bosom of the active anthill of the suburbs, that one must go to see this population of automata eagerly about the work that is entrusted to them: the express porters and the steam messengers; the compressed-air warehousemen, heavy-treading iron Hercules carrying mountains of goods on their shoulders; the high-speed tax-icabs, retained with difficulty by their mechanical drivers who sting the metal plebs with lashes of their electric whips to urge them on, making them howl as they receive the discharges and leap forward; the phonographs that transmit orders and news, reading in loud voices the newspapers with which their bellies are filed; the microphones with keen ears, indiscreet jeering street-urchins who pass on everything they hear, crying out the secrets they have discovered, roaring like bulls in deaf ears and adding the excess of their joyful capers to the busy tumult of the populous streets.

These innumerable servants are animated by love of their masters unknown to the domestics of old, and would kill themselves in their service if death were able to claim such solid bodies. They come and go in every direction, their paths interweaving at top speed, skillfully avoiding collisions that would be terrible between such vigorous individuals; they anticipate one another, and converse between themselves by means of a guttural croaking, of which the talking machine at the Paris Exposition[78] might give you some idea. These ardent

---

[78] There had been two *expositions universelles* in Paris when the novel was first published, in 1855 and 1878; it is the second to which the author is referring. No explicit indication is given in the text of how many years has passed since the concluding chapter of Part One, but the one indirect reference (which suggests an interval of only four years) is hardly credi-

workers only pause on the orders of their manometers, in order to drink at the public fountains that fill them up with compressed air, electricity or steam—which is to say, with strength and life!

As one crosses the exterior boulevards, the proletarian tumult suddenly falls silent, this population being swallowed up by the subterranean streets designed for them—for the city is built, in its entirety, over a cellar; it covers a crypt as vast as itself, dedicated to the residence and labors of Atmophytes. It is there that the factories, storehouses, laboratories and steelyards are located, from which ships emerged fully-armed and houses fully-built.

Beneath this vault is a labyrinthine network of sewers and channels, telegraphic and telephonic wires. Tramways suspended from the vault are in motion there, atmospheric tubes unroll there: enormous serpents which swallow and vomit unrelentingly; long culverins which load up travelers at the breech which they fire to their destinations. Rails, tubes, wires, countless engines, to which this civilization is appended, unroll at the foot of their city like the roots at the foot of a tree that enable the flowers to grow in the crown: a city organized like those well-designed modern dwellings which hide the kitchens, the pantry, the servants' quarters and the servants themselves underground, only revealing the glorious face of the master and the façade of the château; a residence of happiness, perfect happiness without deficit and without plethora, without the satiety of an excessively blue sky nor the regret of fog and rain, since the engineers create their own rain and fog when needed.

The houses of Industria, with no shutters other than their blinds of climbing plants, and no defenses other than their masters' probity (that of Atmophytes is beyond question) are far enough apart to leave frontiers of foliage between them,

---

ble and the probability is that this sequence is futuristic rather than belonging—like the events so far described—to an alternative history.

but close enough to one another to defy solitude: family life and public life at the same time; salubrious life in a climate maintained at 15 degrees centigrade—the lukewarm temperature of orange-groves and marriage, propitious for the nurturing of durable sentiments, which evaporate like liquids when one brings them to boiling point.

Most of the habitations are fabricated from blocks of translucent glass, rendered unbreakable by the Bastie process[79] and furnished at a low price by the glassworks of Industria, where the sands of the sea-bed, the central fire and the handiwork of Atmophytes cost nothing.

One of the most curious specimens of this architecture is an edifice in polished crystal, as dull and fleecy as frozen snow, whose first story rests on a heap of little icebergs and which is coiffed, by way of a roof, by an ice-floe surmounted by a polar bear. This construction, which exhales the mists and frosts of the pole, is the head office of the General Company for Perpetual Breakage,[80] whose offices had to be transferred from the north pole by virtue of their growth.

The importance of this enterprise merits its introduction to the reader. Struck by the inconvenience of the variety of seasons, which subjects humans to the elements and whirls them around like leaves in a tornado, without respect and without prophylactic transitions, the engineers of Industria, inspired by Lord Hotairwell, have undertaken to obviate it.[81] It

---

[79] Tempered glass was invented by François Royer de La Bastie in 1874.

[80] I have modified the translation of *Compagnie générale de la Débâcle universelle* that the author provides in the text ("Perpetual Crack General Company") in the interests of euphony and clarity, although it might be argued that "crack-up" would be a more apt translation of *débâcle* than the relatively modest "breakage."

[81] The author inserts another reference here: "*The Domestication of Climates* by Lord Hotairwell, 10 volumes, London: Watbled & Sons, Publishers."

is well-known that on one part of the European continent, the atmospheric variations depend on the fracturing of ice-sheets that break off from time to time from the belt of circumpolar ice. When winter is harsh at the pole, the thicker ice is less easily dislocated; the break-up is slower and, as the rains remain crystallized in their sources, spring is cold and summer rainy.

The General Company for Perpetual Breakage was proposed, as its name indicates, to produce the breakage of the polar ice itself, and to break the ice wherever need dictates, managing the progress of the thaw in the best interests of the countries whose climate it had taken over. Its means of action consisted of cracking the polar ice with the aid of enormous torpedoes submerged in the sea subjacent to holes drilled in the ice; the internal tempests resulting from the explosions disaggregated the ice into floating blocks, which a marine current conducted to Newfoundland, where their melting determined the desired meteorological effects.

The benefits of the enterprise consisted: firstly, in royalties paid to the countries subscribing to the breakage; secondly, in sales of ice, dispatched loose, as complete icebergs; thirdly, in toll-charges to be levied on the polar passage, as soon as the Company has finished breaking the ice and freeing up that passage; and fourthly, in polar bears surprised by the explosion of ice-floes, drifting with the to Europe and sold for acclimatization or for their fur.

Like everything else in this world, the General Company for Perpetual Breakage had suffered a few setbacks. Its most recent exercise had gone awry; the administrators having pushed the breakage too far, and sent the ice-floes in the wrong direction, an avalanche of icebergs had descended upon England. Greenland had blockaded Great Britain. That year, the polar sea was free, but the Channel was blocked; whole populations perished from colds and chills. Only the inhabitants of Industria, huddled by the side of their central fire, had observed no lowering of the thermometer or variation in the condition of the air.

The Company had paid substantial indemnities—but such accidents are merely the sacrifices necessary to avert the caprices of fortune, and besides, important as the principal element of its wealth was, the Company has other sources of prosperity; it has many other stocks of the same sort in its portfolio, and other projects of the same value—which puts the future on a safe footing, and demonstrates that the architecture of the abode of the General Company for Perpetual Breakage is perfectly appropriate to the enterprises that are perpetuated there—that chaos surmounted by a bear really is its emblem and its sign, so eloquent that passers-by, especially shareholders, cannot look at that head office, nor sit down there, without experiencing a shiver.

It is, however, impossible to give a complete description of the marvelous enterprises born around the geothermal well; one would heap up volumes in listing the names of these exploits of industry and science which, to the gaze of a stranger, seem to be prodigies, but which, to the inhabitants of Industria, are merely vulgar manifestations of its power over all the realm of nature: over the flora redesigned, recolored and remade by incomparable chemists; over the fauna manipulated by hybridizations so bold and grafts so strange that some of the resultant beasts no longer resemble the animals of the Creation. Adam would not have recognized them, and Noah would have chased them out of the Ark as paradoxical animal creations, travestied with the manifest aim of annoying nature: furry birds and feathered serpents; white blackbirds rendered yellow by infusions of bile; canaries turned blue by nourishment based on pepper. Even men, or at least their wives, took part in these masquerades, grafting coiffures of living hummingbirds on to their heads, hanging Cleopatra necklaces of sea anemones in aspic around their necks, or even—in imitation of squids, which owe their whiteness to their blue blood—turning their blood blue to whiten their skin, risking their lives by substituting dialyzed Pravais copper for the dialyzed Bravais iron that is the basis of good blood—a dangerous counter-feit.[82]

Let us hasten to add that these excesses are exceptional, and that the science of breeder-chemists is ordinarily applied to more elevated problems, as evidenced by the magisterial creation of the beautiful species of Horse-Dogs, saddle-dogs and equine pointers, incomparable for riding out and hunting.

The habitations of Industria, almost all in glass, are mostly more prepossessing in form and color than that of the General Company for Perpetual Breakage. Violet glass, recognized as extremely tonic, as favorable to human health as to that of plants, is employed for hospitals, which are, in any case, few in number in a city where public health is excellent. Madhouses, which are much more numerous, are constructed on the model of the one run by the celebrated physician who treated mental illness by the homeopathy of colors, *homeochromopathy*.[83]

These houses are in glass of different shades, according to the madness in question. Furious madmen generally obtain benefit from a sojourn in authentically unbreakable bright red

---

[82] The author is going overboard hear for the sake of wordplay; the Bravais to whom he refers is presumably the crystallographer Auguste Bravais (1811-1863), whose relevance to the iron-containing hemoglobin in blood is rather slight; it is unclear who "Pravais" is supposed to be, although the author presumably has the color of copper sulphate in mind in imagining a copper-based substitute for haemoglobin. It was not widely recognized at the time, in spite of the proverbial familiarity people had with the backs of their hands, that venous blood is blue, only turning red when oxygenated. The suggestion that squids and other cephalopods "owe" their white coloring to any kind of pigmentation is, of course, calculatedly absurd.

[83] Homeopathy and chromopathy were both fashionable therapies in 19th century France, but this fictitious combination is fanciful.

double-glazing. Hypochondriacs recover their cheerfulness in padded cells of polished black glass. Overexcited poets calm down when imprisoned in sky-blue glass. Sluggish or anemic intelligences, dotards or idiots, come on miraculously when placed in sunlight, with their eyes wide open, beneath melon-shaped bells—a method imitated by nature, which has made the eye in the form of a globe or a lens, in order that the solar rays are concentrated there, activating the maturation of the brain. Few patients resist these treatments; a few, however, although fully cured, leave the establishment afflicted with Daltonism,[84] having lost the notion of colors, and even that if ideas.

The most elegant private dwellings are Oriental in style, in muslin-glass that is transparent or opaque, according to the owner's mood. When the solar spectrum impregnates these translucent walls, as iridescent as soap-bubbles, one might think them fragments of a rainbow. This is charming by day, but the nights are enchanted in that city, illuminated by all its houses, which light up like lamps within their globes.

In addition to electrical apparatus, a superior system is available for lighting, which consists of storing sunlight by means of a substance called *heliovore*. Every ray of sunlight that falls on a surface coated with heliovoracious glue is captured like a bird in a trap, and the entire city, its inhabitants, their nightclothes and their winter clothing are coated with sunlight by this means, rendered bright and warm. That kind of lighting would supplant all others if it were not necessary to take account of the collection time, in view of which the old Gramme apparatus and Jablokoff moderator lamps are conserved for emergencies.[85]

---

[84] Strictly speaking, Daltonism—named after the atomic theorist John Dalton, who suffered from it—is red/green color-blindness, although the author appears to be using the term as if it applied to general color-blindness.

[85] Zénobe Gramme (1826-1901) patented a direct current generator in 1870, which was used in some early electric lighting

The lighting of the countryside is obtained, without expense, with the collaboration of local glow-worms, the careful selection and skilful cross-breeding of which have increased their size and develop the photogenic aptitude, and to which other luminous insects imported from tropical climates have been added. South-American Elaters, whose vivid gleam permits travelers to read by their light, mark out the roads by night, flamboyant road-workers illuminates on the verges, and millions of Italian Lampyra are distributed in the fields like minuscule lighthouses, emitting their intermittent flashes at regular intervals, along with Pyrophores, secreting droplets of oil that sparkle as they oxidize, and Lucioles, perched like lamps at the tops of blades of grass, their abdomens extended and rounded like opaline globes, constellating the verdure and illuminating the foliage.[86]

You can imagine what decisive elements of success are achieved by nocturnal fêtes with such a provision of lights of all the colors of the prism, and others recently invented, and what a décor in provided by those fields inundated with fires, that city sweating sunlight and those streets parqueted with radiance, populated with sparkling crowds wearing resplendent clothes, in which every passer-by is a gleam, a glare, a scintillation, a flame of joy, an animalcule of phosphorescence!

---

systems. Jablokoff is a once-common rendering of the name of the Russian Pavel Yablochkov (1847-1894), who developed a kind of electrical arc-lamp, known as the Yablochkov candle, in 1876.

[86] The names of these various bioluminescent insects seem to be confused by accidental redundancy; the members of the family of *Elateridae* (click beetles) possessed of this property belong to the genus *Pyrophorus*, while "lucioles" is an alternative term for members of the beetle genus Lampyridae, whose most familiar member is *Lampyris noctiluca*, the common "glow-worm" or "firefly."

These beautiful soirées are prolonged until dawn, until the exhaustion of strength, until ophthalmia takes possession of eyes overloaded by such glare. Then, saturated with pleasure and fleeing the heat, everyone goes home and opens fountains at the summits of their roofs, which shroud the houses with their cascades. If anyone desires sleep and silence, blinds like vast wings are deployed over the dwellings and the houses, as brilliant as beacons a moment before, disappear into semi-darkness—and a spectator in the sky would take those dim lights lurking beneath the foliage for a colony of sleeping glow-worms. If anyone is sad, and has need of noise and daylight, the night that gives birth to dreams is dissipated as easily as it is created; the blinds are removed, the windows are opened, and one is refreshed by the borrowed happiness of neighbors; everyone can see everyone else while remaining at home, separated and united in wire-netting enclosures in the same aviary, taking part, to the extent of their desire, in the same concert of bird-song and colored plumage.

Chapter Three
Yet More Happiness

The inhabitants of Industria are so happy at home that they hardly ever go out, although they are able to stay where they are and go out at the same time. Absence, that sickness of tender souls, has been eliminated. Everyone is ubiquitous, simultaneously at home and elsewhere—a result obtained by perfecting a means formerly proposed for sending telegrams without wires, without any other conductor than the ambient medium: a means abandoned because the first telegrams delivered by their own instinct went astray, the fickle electricity accepting too many conductors and delivering itself to any and all electrodes, but then restudied and made workable by the engineers of Industria, who have succeeded in domesticating the fluid, creating affinities—not to say affections—for it, which render it faithful to a single conductor and a single pole. Electricity is thus animalized and domesticated, only having to be put in contact with its master once, to smell and touch him, for that veritably canine magnetic current to come to heel or recover his trail.[87]

The telechromophotophonotetroscope,[88] invented at the same time, by the same physicists, eliminates absence in an even more radical fashion. The telechromophotophonotetroscope is, as everyone knows, an almost synoptic succession of instantaneous photographic prints, which reproduces electrically the face, speech and gestures of an absent person with a verity equivalent to presence, and which constitutes not so

---

[87] The author's *"veritable chien courant magnétique"* unfortunately loses its pivotal pun on translation.

[88] It is not surprising that this scrupulously-compounded and unintentionally prophetic description of an instrument akin to, but more advanced than, a modern mobile phone never actually caught on as a label.

much an image as an apparition, a duplication of the absent individual.

This very simple apparatus consists of a chromophotograph that provides color prints, a megagraph that magnifies them, a stenophonograph that receives and transcribes the subject's speech, aided by a microphone that amplifies it, enclosed in a telephone conjoined with a tetroscope, to propagate the image and the sound. The different parts of the instrument add their efforts together and emit the product into a recipient commonly called a phenakistiscope—an acoustic and visual instrument by means of which one can see and hear. It works in such a way that, by modifying the operation of the system as required, one can make the absent individual appear, or appear in ones turn to him, at will.

The creation of the various parts of this apparatus go back some years, but the honor of contriving the synthesis and the physical combination is due to the scientists of Industria. You can imagine all the benefits of such an instrument and all the vitality that it lends to relationships. No more isolation or solitude; whether one likes it or not, one receives spectral visits from absent friends, provincial relatives or idle neighbors at all hours, arriving unceremoniously to spend and hour or a few days in your home. What a unification of all the inhabitants of the country, linked into a single family by threads so tight that one could not sever a limb without making the entire body cry out, nor pull out a single hair without tearing off the entire scalp!

The invention just described was also applicable to performances, to which no one went, since everyone could procure their charms at home—so theaters were, in spite of their magnificence, merely music-boxes, drama-factories whose produce was carried into domiciles by the telechromophotophonotetroscope, and whose overflow, escaping through the diaphonic cupola with which every room is provided, expanded into the atmosphere and impregnated it with harmony.

Music was also brought within everyone's range by a method that is not without analogy with that of Messieurs

Cailletet and Pictet for the solidification of gases, and which consists of compressing the sonorous vibrations without extinguishing them, as one compresses a spring without breaking it, and of concentrating them to the point that an operetta can be held in a liter, and a drinking-song in a wine-glass. One of the greatest pleasures of the table was to uncork a brindisi, a polka or a waltz during the dessert, whose notes, as sparkling as Champagne wine, would burst forth from the neck. Sometimes, young Atmophytes would amuse themselves by giving microphones and phonographs the mingled dregs of these harmonic bottles to drink, which would then go out in a drunken state to dribble the discordant concert in the streets.

Although absence, as we have seen, had been averted, material distance had been no less happily vanquished by the most advanced means of transport. In addition to tramways and express tubes, it is appropriate to mention the aeroscaphs—the aerial boats that await use moored to windows like birds, attached by their beaks, constructed in aluminum, that weightless metal, and powered by compressed air—15 pounds of which, reduced to a volume of 100 liters by a pressure of 200 atmospheres, is sufficient to fuel a six-hour journey. Navigation is delightful when, opening one's window and leaping into one's boat as evening approaches, one sets off into the sky, when the enslaved breeze cries the gondola and inflates the sail with perfumed effluvia! Humans become sylphs and sail in a dream, landing on a cloud or skimming the terrestrial soil, protected from ruts and potholes.

But the roads of this region have neither potholes nor ruts, and the wide circular boulevards of the city can, like rivers, be called "moving roads." They do move, their causeways roll on moving cylinders installed in the crypt, dividing into equal sections the quarters inscribed between their borders. Without taking a step, one can make a tour of the city on foot, on these roads that travel, rotate and return, tranquil and majestic. Thus this city and this civilization rotate around their axis and their soul: the Central Fire, whose palace, the center

191

of all these circles and the focal point of all these sectors, appears from all directions in the place of honor that is its due.

The edifice dedicated to the Central Terrestrial Fire, to the god Power, whose name is inscribed in Greek on its fronton, is both a temple and a town hall. The order of its architecture is naturalist, something like the Parthenon reconstructed on the plan of an *assommoir* by Monsieur Zola, architect.[89]

One of the most fortunate inspirations of its constructor has been to give this temple the form of a gigantic locomotive, 900 feet long and 300 wide, surmounted by a copper cupola forming its steam-funnel. The body of the boiler, or the nave, is in sheet steel rendered un-oxydizable by steam-annealing, which preserves all of theimetal's shine. Thus, when the Sun lights this cylinder with the copper-girded flanks, it is difficult to bear the sight. That metallic surface becomes a reflector that returns the Sun's rays blow for blow, and one cannot fix one's gaze upon it without falling into hypnotic ecstasy—a circumstance permitting the impregnation of crowds with the sentiments of mysterious attraction and dread that make the fortune of Sibylline temples.

You must not think, however, that any mysteries are accomplished in this temple and in the religion of a new humankind, promoted by its genius from the rank of creature to that of Creator: a race of Promethean conquerors, having finally discovered the secret of life, having broken its chains, overturned its rock and recovered its entrails from the vulture in order to take its seat at the banquet of the gods.

The interior of the temple is pragmatically adapted with a view to various uses. In the apse, at the rear of the actuary, is the God: the well of the Central Fire, linked by gross nozzles to the dome in which the great flux of the mounting waves of

---

[89] The word *assommoir*, which provides the title of one of Emile Zola's most famous "naturalist" novels, published in 1877, is not usually translated when that novel is rendered into English, so I have preserved it here; it refers to a drinking den where cheap liquor is sold.

hot air is accumulated. That dome, whose superior hemisphere floats above the edifice like a huge copper aerostat, penetrates into the apse to the full extent of the other half of its sphere, which it deploys like a cup.

A colossal statue serves that cup as a pedestal: the statue of the goddess Antrakia,[90] coal: the daughter of the Central Fire, born of its endeavors in the first ages of the world, when its heat, still close to the surface, caused the growth and distillation of vegetation. Now, the goddess Antrakia, vanquished, chained in the pose of Michelangelo's captives, lifts the arms of a black slave above her head to support the sphere that envelops the bristling braids of her hair like flames.

Around the Central Fire are grouped the emblems of its power, the objects of its usage and the tools of its labors: all the forms that the iron, copper and bronze softened by its flame and molded by man can acquire, as manifestations of its force: stout shiny tubes in which steam respires, oppressed and hoarse; guiding-rods and driving-rods which move back and forth like a carpenter's arms; valves and alarm-whistles, and the manometers that their tension causes to quiver; pipes that creep, interlacing and coiling, brazen serpents with monstrous taps for heads; piston-pumps that plunge into cylinders as deep as wells and return spilling out rivers; condensers, reminiscent of huge organs, into which steam surges noisily, then murmurs a sad song that grows ever-fainter. An Apotheosis of boiler-making!

To the right of the Central Fire, in the place of honor that a decorous god offers his colleague, stands the statue of a mysterious deity—a *Deae ignotae*, still almost unknown, so reticently does it reveal itself—hiding away from mortals, not in the shadows but in the blinding glare of its radiance. I have named this god Electros, electricity, a close relative of the Central Fire, its equal, perhaps its superior—a benevolent and terrible god, who alternately fulfils his worshipper' wishes

---

[90] This name is improvised from the Greek term for a type of coal, which also gives rise to the term "anthracite."

humbly or strikes them down carelessly; the soul of matter, matter impalpable as soul, similarly endowed with love and hate, attraction and repulsion, at the whim of his two poles, his two sexes, which hate the similar and seize the contrary.

Formed of metals that this divinity has chosen as his servitors, the statue of Electos rests, isolated from the ground, on a rock of crystal; seated before a spinning-wheel, he moves a glass disk, and his spindles unwind electrical wires; one might imagine him to be the Fate Lachesis spinning the lives of humans—but this terrible spinning-wheel engenders thunder, and those wires impregnated with human thought wind around the terrestrial globe like a neural network within a body.

At the feet of the god are scattered the souvenirs of his infancy, the emblems of his works: the zinc and copper that coupled to give him birth and nourish him by devouring one another; the piles and the Leyden jars, the statuettes and galvanoplastic medallions that Electros has taught human beings to sculpt.

So much for the lay-out of the apse.

The nave is fitted out as a legislative hall; it is here that the Assembly is held on solemn days. In the ordinary course of parliamentary life, the sessions are held in a cupboard that holds 200 telephone receivers, linked to those of the 200 delegates, who can attend the sessions and take part in the debates by that means, without leaving home. Positioned on a table at the center of these items of apparatus, a presidential Phonograph records the discussion and issues rulings.

These kinds of meetings are usually peaceful; sometimes, however, storms burst out in the cupboard, which might then be mistaken, so loud is the racket, for a drum filled with enraged drummers. On such days, people gathered outside the cupboard, as fond as anyone else of seeing the political wheels in motion, amuse themselves by collecting the crumbs of noise that escape through the cracks.

In any case, thanks to the telephone network, all the citizens can attend the sessions from a distance, like the delegates; in emergencies, they can also invade the hall telephonically, mount the podium, expel the phonograph and overthrow the government, without any physical displacement or loss of time, without fatigue and without absenting themselves from their customary occupations.

The remainder of Industria's form of government is pantopantarchic, which means the rule of all over all. Every citizen, at birth, finds a crown in his cradle, and, on reaching the age at which he can wield a scepter, exercises absolute power, without any limit other than the absolute power of his neighbor. The necessary authority and the even-more-precious liberty are thus exactly balanced.

This mode of government has been denigrated by people who do not understand that, although a similar kind of crozier could not have sufficed the kings of old, pastors of poor, suffering flocks inclined to revolt, it does, by contrast, suit a population of contented millionaires, happy enough and rich enough to satisfy the most avid, in a social estate arrived at true equality: an equality obtained without lowering summits or scything down tall stems; a lofty equality, by virtue of the accession of all stems to the light, consisting entirely of crowned heads, by virtue of the elevation of an entire people to a throne solid enough and large enough to seat them all.

What simplicity there is in the workings of that society and its government: no universal suffrage, no elections and no electors, all elected! Nevertheless, as sages have observed, every good rule needs confirmation by exceptions that violate it, and there is no embarrassment in saying that Industria possesses a Parliament, an administrative council elected in by the best possible method, since it is nature, more impartial than man, that elects—or, rather, selects—it.

The intelligence of an individual is, as everyone knows, proportional to his encephalic mass, just as his appetite corresponds to the dimensions of his stomach, so every candidate for the legislature, having passed a preliminary examination by Dr. Mosso's plethysmograph[91]—which measures the intensity of the blood-flow to the head—is then submitted to the measurement of the cubic capacity of his cranial cavity: the depressions and protrusions, the slightest phrenological circumstances, are measured by a jury of strong minds, who are hardly ever mistaken about the quantity of cerebral labor and intellectual sap that the subject can furnish.

Every brain weighing less than two pounds is excluded from the management of affairs. It is not that exceptional intelligences are taken—monstrous brains like that of Pascal, which weighed 1,784 grams, or Cuvier's, which attained 1,829 grams.[92] On the contrary, they are wary of these anomalies, which are, in any case, rare among men who, under the influence of the climate they have created, have become luxurious Orientals whose health is superb health but whose minds and facial angles are rather obtuse. Their souls have not swollen in proportion to their abdomens. The legislators, therefore, exclude geniuses of excessive magnitude from affairs of state, by necessity and also by reason; recognizing the inconvenience of uniting disparate intelligences is a single assembly, the most luminous of which would seek to extinguish the rest, as would occur in a room simultaneously lit by electricity, gas, oil and smoky candles—either the electric light oppresses the lesser

---

[91] The Italian physiologist Angelo Mosso (1846-1910) did not actually invent the first plethysmograph (that was probably Francis Franke), but he was the first person to report (in 1878) on extensive experiments carried out with one. He subsequently invented a sphygmomanometer for measuring arterial blood pressure.

[92] The author inserts a footnote here: "It is well-known that, from the viewpoint of encephalic development, humans, canaries and robins are best-favored by fortune, the mass of the brain proportional to that of the body being, for a human, 1/35th, and for a canary, 1/32nd. The latter creature, long assumed to be stupid, is thus, in realty, better endowed than a man.

lights, which represents despotism, or a general fog is produced which symbolizes anarchy.

There is nothing similar in this parliament, where all brains are identical in weight and think as one, except for the brains of Lord Hotairwell, estimated at 3,800 grams (nearly four pounds heavier than Cuvier's) and Dr. Penkenton, which, by contrary excess, only attains the minimum for admission. That emptiness in such a large head, combined with a collection of phrenological protuberances better suited to the skull of a wolf than that of a geologist, had left the jury somewhat nonplussed, as well as exciting the mockery of its chairman, William Hatchitt, and Penkenton had only been admitted by virtue of a favorable weighting.

Apart from these two exceptions, there is not ten grams of difference between the cerebral engines of the 200 delegates, which are all stamped by the same pressure, presenting identical heating surfaces, the same length of travel, and delivering an equal number of piston-strokes within the cylinder. Thus, arguments are rare between these colleagues, who are all seated on the right, all conservatives, not only because they are mostly over 60, but more especially because they have attained the extreme limits of well-being and progress.

There is no more agreeable and serene spectacle than that assembly: that family of 200 brothers exchanging conciliatory ideas and emitting exactly similar opinions without passion; those beautifully-formed ivory skulls, so similar that they seem to be united, oscillating in signs of assent and benevolence for the orator who expresses, from the podium, the opinion that is their own.

Such is the usual state of these parliamentary debates, but there are exceptions, as we have said, and the present session, which commenced yesterday and whose end is not yet in sight, will go down as the longest and most exciting page in Industria's history.

Chapter Four
A Stormy Session

Since 3 p.m., Lord Hotairwell has been presiding, not over an assembly, but a tempest, without his tranquility and impartiality failing for an instant. He is like a pilot at the helm, lashed to the presidential armchair, which the waves submerge, the currents drag away and the crazed crew cover with dribble and foam; he is thrown into the sea ten times over but rises to the surface and fight the storm with broad sweeps of the tiller, still steering even though the ship is sinking, holding its course even underwater, anxious to damp down the wreck on the deep strand where sailors and ships sleep, to wait in the shelter of the winds, beneath the vault of the waters, until he can set sail again.

James Archibold, William Hatchitt and Edward Burton, clinging to the ministerial bench, where the tempest is also unleashed, support the valiant commodore as best they can. Dr. Samuel Penkenton is absent on leave, as often happens since he has unexpectedly launched himself into commerce, against all probability and in spite of his aptitudes, and has become a ship-owner. At least, he has taken delivery, a few days before, of two fully-laden ships, which he piloted personally into a safe harbor, with 1000 precautions, as if their cargo were particularly fragile or mystery were indispensable to the success of his speculation.

A storm as violent as it is unexpected is, therefore, raging in the assembly. Parties whose existence was previously unsuspected have suddenly surged forth. For several hours, the parliamentary body has had a right and a left, center-rights, center-lefts and center-centers, groups and sub-groups, which deliberate, shout, fuse or break up, choking in an excess of wrath or strangling in furious alliance. It is a hydra with 200 heads; a maddened octopus tangled up in its own tentacles, fighting itself fiercely; a mêlée of opinions that collide with

198

one another, raise bruises and howl in pain; a confusion of arms that vote, torsos and legs that rear up and kick beneath the president's whip, which no longer draws any distinction between its right and its left, its friends and its adversaries, distributing the stings of its discipline aimlessly.

A calm materializes, by virtue of hazard or lassitude, and Lord Hotairwell hastens to take advantage of it. "Gentlemen," he says, "for the tenth time I give the floor to the honorable Sir William Barnett, who has not yet succeeded in taking it. The floor is yours, sir."

"Gentlemen," said Sir William Barnett, "I come to appeal for the solicitude of the honorable gentlemen who sit with so much luster in the councils of State, on matters of the utmost gravity, perils all the more redoubtable because these gentlemen are showing themselves indifferent, to the extent that you can see them sleeping, lying full length on their benches, in the naïve quietude habitual to all governments."

(*Hear hear!*)

"Symptoms of revolt have appeared among the Atmophytes. These machines have proffered seditious squeaks; these slaves have insulted citizens; and several among them, emerging from the subterranean region to which our constitution restricts them, have taken the air in the street. These fits are the result of the excessive development that you have allowed the Atmophytes' organs to acquire—unconsidered improvements by which you have given them not merely instincts, but souls and the power of thought.

"Yes by a deplorable effort of the genius of your engineers, you have raised to the level of human intelligence these coarse organisms"—(*murmurs*)—"whose inept brains, maladapted to so much light, have been dazzled and crazed in seeing themselves become as intelligent, or even more intelligent, than you!"

(*Urgent denials on a large number of benches.*)

"They are dreaming now of replacing you and destroying you, or perhaps letting you live, to make *you* into *their* Atmophytes."

199

(Protestations and ironic laughter.)

"Gentlemen, if there is a Hercules among you capable of taming a hydra with the size and strength of two million horsepower, let him rise to his feet and take up his club!"

(Prolonged sensation.)

"Personally, I demand exemplary punishments for these criminals; I demand the immediate destruction of any Atmophyte whose cerebral equipment surpasses in perfection the quantity useful to a good domestic."

On descending from the podium, the speaker receives the congratulations of a great many of his friends.

"The floor is give to the honorable Mr. Greatboy, who has asked for it," says the president.

"Gentlemen," says Greatboy, "as I lent a saddened ear to the discourse to which you have just been subjected, that envenomed accusation leveled against the progress and well-being of Atmophytes, I asked myself whether, by a curious coincidence, my eminent opponent might not have lost precisely the quantity of intelligence that he reproaches these poor individuals for having found."

"Your language is not parliamentary," a member to the right puts in.

(Cries of Order! Order!)

"I invite Mr. Greatboy to explain his words," says the president.

"Out of respect for Mr. President's authority," says Greatboy, "I shall explain my meaning, even though it is sufficiently clear; and I shall say that the intelligence of my eminent friend seems to me to have fallen beneath that of a brute."

(Loud protests. Censure! Censure!*)*

"The speaker having explained his words," says the president, "these protests are pointless."

"But in explaining them," says Mr. Powell, "he has aggravated them!"

"You do not have the floor, Mr. Powell," says the president, "and the president believes that he knows the rules as well as you do. Now, the rule demands that the speaker explain any regrettable words that have escaped him. Mr. Great-boy has explained his, and I call the interrupters to order. The matter is closed."

"I demand to speak against the closure," says Powell.

"What closure?"

"The closure of the matter."

"No," says the president, "you can't reopen a matter that I've closed."

"Gentlemen," says Powell, "The interpretation that Mr. President…"

"You're reopening the matter…."

"By breaking the closure," put in Lord Calhamborough.

(Laughter.)

"I withdraw the floor from you," says the president.

(Protests from the center-right and the center-center. The president is abused. Discordant cries are heard, and the disorder threatens to mount.)

"If I can identify those responsible for these cries, I shall not hesitate to reprimand them."

(All of us! All of us!)

"I call the chamber to order."

"There's no justice anymore!" says Powell.

"Who said that?" says the president.

"You're presiding with a disgusting partiality," Powell retorts.

"Who said that?" repeats the president.

(All of us! All of us!)

"I invite the persons who say that I'm presiding with disgusting impartiality to come to the podium to explain themselves."

The Assembly rises to its feet in order to mount the podium; Mr. Powell, arriving first, takes the floor.

"Gentlemen," says Powell, "It is only my profound respect for the President's authority that has drawn me to the podium, since I have nothing to say."

"Then why have you mounted the podium?" asked the president.

201

"Because you invited me to, along with everyone else—but since you oblige me to, I'll speak, in spite of the fact that I have nothing to say, and I hope that, silence being the last of our liberties, you will leave it to us. I shall, therefore, speak…"

"No, don't speak!" several members put in.

"You have a right to shut up—use it," says William Barnett.

"Don't speak," other voices advise. "Get down from the podium!"

Powell quits the podium and receives the congratulations of his friends.

"The speaker having refused to explain himself," says the president, "the matter is closed, and I give the floor to Mr. Greatboy for the continuation of his speech."

"As I was saying, Gentlemen…" Greatboy begins.

"You weren't saying anything," says Mr. Stopman, "and since you're preventing our orators from speaking, you shan't say anything."

"Besides, there are more of us," says William Barnett.

"One is still sufficiently numerous to speak, and I shall speak," says Greatboy.

(*No! No! Yes! Yes!*)

At this juncture, the right descends to the floor and heads for the bar.

"Yes," Greatboy continues, "I shall speak, if only to condemn the scandalous exit of a part of this Chamber, a seditious manifestation that I denounce to the severity of the rules and the judgment of the nation."

All the members who left come back in and take their seats again.

"Yes, I qualify as seditious…"

"There was no sedition," says William Barnett, "just some people going to the bar."

(*Incredulous murmurs and smiles.*)

"It is physiologically implausible," says Greatboy, "that all of you had the same need at the same moment. The nation shall be the judge! The truth is that you were obeying an order."

(*No! No!*)

"We went out because the president of our group offered to buy a round," says William Barnett.

"I don't care," says Greatboy. "I protest, and I say that a parliament in which…"

"Whoever speaks, lies," put in Lord Calhamborough.[93]

(Laughter.)

"That pun isn't parliamentary," says the president.

"I don't claim that the orator who is speaking is lying." *(Laughter.)* "On the contrary, he says excellent things; and I cannot, when people speak to me on the subject, keep quiet."[94]

(Laughter.)

"I was saying," Greatboy resumed, "that a parliament in which such mores become established, in which every opinion prompts a need to walk out in order not to listen to the opposing opinion, will sooner or later be dissolved. I've said it, and I repeat it, because I'm right; such actions are unintelligible, seditious and indecent, so far as the country is concerned."

(Cries of Order!*)*

The right gets up and heads for the bar again, but the president, strongly supported by the secretaries, lands such blows with his hand-bell on the heads of the column emerging on to the floor that they stop, indecisively.

Mr. Greatboy hastens to take advantage of the pause. "I resume, Gentlemen, and I shall be brief…the honorable Sir William Barnett demands severe punishment for the childish behavior of a few Atmophytes, but I say to you: do nothing! Don't force springs that are already too taut; don't squeeze steam that is roaring and water that is boiling into narrower

---

[93] This old joke does not translate; the French *parlement* [parliament] can be separated into *parle* [speaks] and *ment* [lies].

[94] Again, the pun (*quand on m'en parle, m'en taire*), this time on *parlementaire* [parliamentarian] does not translate.

dikes, for their pressure, rendered uncontainable, will bring down their prison walls on their jailers."

(Prolonged sensation.)

"Does that mean, however," Greatboy continues, "that there is nothing to be done—that there is no crisis, or that there is no remedy for the crisis? If there is a crisis and there is a remedy, it is necessary to apply it quickly, but above all: don't punish severely, forgive! Don't tear apart, cure! Improve, instruct, elevate these Atmophytes, your creatures, your children, to the dignity of men! Lose slaves and win friends! I ask the Government to give its opinion."

This speech is followed by a long agitation. The session is suspended *de facto*. James Archibold, Edward Burton and William Hatchitt, the only ministers present at the session, hold a hasty conference on the floor, and decide to delegate William Hatchitt, in whose supple and insinuating ways render him more likely to find the juncture between two pinions and penetrate their interstices without bursting them asunder. After an interruption of a quarter of an hour, the session resumes.

"Mr. William Hatchitt has the floor," says the president.

"Gentlemen," says Hatchitt, "to the honorable gentleman who asks our opinion on the opinions successively expressed at this podium, it will suffice for me to reply that the Government has gathered those opinions carefully, that it shares them, and that it will regulate its conduct accordingly."

(Hear hear!)

"The Government thinks, with the honorable Mr. Barnett, that the maintenance of order is the primordial interest to which all others must be sacrificed—to a certain extent, of course. The Government is convinced, like the honorable Mr. Barnett, that it is appropriate to oppose violence forcefully, and to reduce by pitiless repression any rebellion devoid of excuse."

(Hear hear!)

"But it agrees with Mr. Greatboy in the firm resolution only to employ force united with gentleness."

(Hear hear!)

"Such are our rules of conduct, immutable but ready to bend to the will of the advice of our friends seated on this side of the Chamber, and in the direction of the indications of our adversaries seated on the other side. For, Gentlemen, if we are the Government, you are the Opposition; if we are the strength, you are the light; if we are the power, you are another. We steer the cart, we are the coachmen, but it is you who choose the route. Sitting on the seat, we hold the reins and crack the whip, but from the depths of the carriage you are the guides."

(Denials and murmurs.)

"Gentlemen, when it pleases you to climb upon the seat, we shall hasten to get down therefrom, to replace you in the carriage, or, preferably, to go on foot. But while awaiting the day you have appointed for discharging us of the burden of power"—*(further denials)*—"trust that we shall apply ourselves with even greater zeal, not only to the satisfaction of your demands but to anticipate the development of your desires, and to give you all the satisfactions that a government is happy to offer to its friends, because it loves them, and to its adversaries, because it fears them."

Loud protests are heard in the ranks of the opposition, and Mr. Greatboy, its leader, heads for the podium, very pale and emotional.

"Mr. Greatboy has the floor," says the president.

"Gentlemen," says Greatboy, "the protests against the Minister's words that are still resounding, have already paid that man his wages." (*Order! Order!*) "I shall therefore not delay in taking seriously his requests for advice and his offers of alliance. I shall content myself with asking him two questions, to which I shall provide my own replies. You have, Mr. Minister, just promised us satisfactions. Is your promise sincere? No, you say? Then it is despicable."

"I didn't say anything," says Hatchitt.

"Don't interrupt," says the president.

"I shall continue your interrogation," says Greatboy, "and I say again: is your promise sincere? Yes, you reply, this time. Oh! Then it's redoubtable and subversive, prejudicial to the constitution and the very foundations of parliamentary rule." (*Hear hear!*) "You don't know, you say?"

"I say nothing," says Hatchitt.

"Your interruption is nonsensical, since I've warned you that I shall provide the questions and answers myself. So you say—a childish excuse—that you don't know! So, under your reign, in my country, the primary instruction has come to the point of superior ignorance, and it is incumbent on me to inform you that the primordial law of parliamentary rule excludes any transaction and any truce between the ruling power and the opposition. And you, Minister, a crank violator of this dogma, have just offered us alliances and to permit us satisfactions! Ah, in truth, it is as smooth as it is perfidious, this Calino-Machiavellian[95] politics, consisting of curing famine by plethora, of giving everything to prevent anything being taken, of keeping our mouths full in order to shut us up, tying our hands by embracing us in your arms."

(*Hear hear!*)

"No, Mr. Minister. 'Never strike a woman, even with a flower,' says the poet Saadi;[96] never enchain a people even with benefits!" (*Cheers and applause.*) "To each his task, and no misalliance. You are the Government! We are the Opposition! Our job is to attack you, to undermine your bases, to saw through your roots, to break your branches and gather your fruits."

"Your job, Minister, is to defend yourself. If we knock you down, get up again; if we chase you away, come back; if we break your ministerial bench, sit down on it more forceful-

---

[95] The first part of this portmanteau term is presumably derived from the French verb *caliner*, meaning to coax or wheedle.

[96] Saadi was the familiar signature of the Persian poet Abu Muslih bin Abdallah Shirazi (1184-1283), whose principal works were *Bustan* [The Orchard] (1257) and *Gulistan* [The Rose Garden] (1258). The quotation is probably apocryphal.

ly; and know that it is only by the observance of these principles that you render your profession of Government almost blameless.

"I think I have painted a portrait of Government as everyone knows it"—(*Yes! Yes!*)—"and which he alone contrives not to understand—which proves that he's none too strong. Now, what we want is a strong Government, a Government that can be attacked without crumbling, can been doused without drowning, knocked down without breaking—that can, finally, be undermined generally with the patriotic certainty that it will not collapse as a result!" (*Cheers, and a salvo of applause.*) "But if you capitulate at the first critical word and demand mercy at the slightest blow, how can we undermine you? If we can't undermine you, who, then, should we undermine? And if we don't undermine anyone, how do you expect us to be crushed?" (*Hear hear! That's right.*) "Our job, thank God, is neither to be governors, nor governed, nor governable!

"Such is the conclusion of the non-welcome that we oppose to the Minister's offers; and in truth, this paints a..."

"Oh," says Lord Calhamborough, "you shouldn't say that..."

"I don't understand the meaning of that interruption," says Greatboy.

"You said: *This fellow...*"[97]

"What!"

"You don't use the word *fellow* in talking about a Minister."

"Indeed," says the president. "I must ask the speaker to make use of another expression."

Greatboy tried again. "I said that this paints a..."

"Precisely," observed Lord Calhamborough.

"I didn't say *this fellow*; I said *this paints a*...but if the words offend you, I withdraw them."

"Yes," says Calhamborough, "withdraw the fellow."

---

[97] Yet another bad pun. Greatboy said "*Cela peint la...*"; Calhamborough construes it as "*Ce lapin-là...*"

"With respect to the verb *to paint*," says Greatboy, "I shall select another tense…"

"That's right," says Calhamborough. "Pick better weather."[98]

"I shall therefore say that what the Minister has painted…"[99]

"Point of order!" cries Calhamborough.

"What point of order?" asks Greatboy.

"You said Scapin the Minister—you called the Minister Scapin."

"I didn't say *Scapin the Minister*; I said that *what the Minister has painted*…but I'll change the construction yet again, and say that, in a word, the Minister would paint."[100]

"What! The Minister, that dauber! You call the Minister a dauber! Withdraw that word."

"Since that's the way it is," says Greatboy, "I'll withdraw my entire speech and come down from the podium."

"Yes," says Calhamborough, "withdraw yourself, as well as your speech."

"Anyway, I've accomplished my task—I've notified the Government of our wishes."

"Your desires," says Mr. Stopman.

"No, our wishes," Greatboy insists, "for the majority has the right to wish, and we're the majority."

"But you're only four in 200," Stopman objects.

"That may be," says Greatboy, "but we're the majority in the country."

(Protests.)

---

[98] *Temps* means both "tense" (in the grammatical sense) and "weather" in French.

[99] *Ce qu'a peint le Ministre*—inviting Calhambrough, inevitably, to misconstrue the phrase as *Scapin le Ministre*, recalling the protagonist of Moliére's farce *Fourberies de Scapin* (1671), a knavish servant.

[100] *Sera peint*, misconstruable as *ce rapin*, if the silliness is to be extrapolated to its ultimate limit.

"If the members who are interrupting me were more knowledgeable in history," Greatboy continues, "they would know that in all times and all countries, in the bosoms of the most respectable of the oldest Parliaments, it has always been the custom for the minority in the Chamber to say that it is the majority in the country; besides, it's true."

(No! No! Yes! Yes!)

"Yes, it's true, because the minority is the opposition, and opposition is natural, while Government is merely a fiction brought forth by the people, as imperfect as its creators: an artificial creation, more often than not deformed—a sort of monster!"

(Loud protests from the Ministerial bench.)

"For the fourth time, I shall sum up, and resume my speech at the point where I left off, in order to talk about something else. I sum up our position, in demanding, for our slaves, the right to daylight. I demand that their working hours be reduced and that they be allowed, when their work is done, to go out to take the air and mingle a little oxygen with the carbon dioxide that corrodes their lungs in their workplaces. And with the aim of hastening the hour of justice when they will be admitted to sit within these walls"—*(loud protests from a large number of benches)*—"I demand for the Atmophytes the means of self-education. I demand the creation, for the most advanced among these machines, of a College of Applied Mechanics, to which our eminent engineers will surely be proud to lend their collaboration, in order that these poor people may learn to know themselves, and also to reproduce themselves and to love one another."

(Cheers.)

"On the subject of rumors of alleged revolt, I would be glad if someone would procure me a few moments' conversation with the insurrectionists, taking the responsibility upon myself of immediately resolving any difficulties that they will have the honor of submitting to me."

(Approving laughter and applause.)

At this moment, Mr. Stopman, coming in from outside, climbs up to the armchair and exchanges a few words with the President.

"Gentlemen," says Lord Hotairwell, "I have learned from a source, which is the very mouth of our honorable colleague, Mr. Stopman, that the revolt of the Atmophytes is assuming the gravest proportions." (*Laughter on several benches.*) "They have quit the workshops in large numbers and are running tumultuously through the city."

"That's a false report, intended to influence the vote," says Greatboy.

(*Yes! Yes! That's what it is!*)

"I call you to order, sir," says the president.

"You'd do better to call the Atmophytes to order."

(*Laughter.*)

The president continues: "In view of this grave news…"

"Alarming!" says another voice.

(*Laughter.*)

"Frightful!" says another.

(*Laughter.*)

"Grotesque!" says Greatboy.

(*Laughter.*)

"In view of this news," the president insists, "I propose that a special committee, representative of various sections of the Assembly, should go immediately to the top of the dome, from where it will be easy to establish the essence of the situation at a glance."

(*All of us! Let's all go!*)

The session is interrupted, and the Assembly heads for the staircase of the dome.

Chapter Five
A Mechanical Mob [101]

In a matter of moments, the Assembly arrived on the balcony, where a terrifying spectacle was offered to their eyes.

Like geotrupe insects extracting themselves from the dirt, discarding their pupal husks and spreading their wings, that catachthonic population was exhuming itself from its limbo, escaping from its jail through every possible issue from the crypt: through ventilators and drain-openings, crevices and fissures, swarming, innumerable and terrible. The Atmophytes were in open revolt—and in their wake, machines of an inferior order, less intelligent and more sedentary, which ought to have been retained by their weight or difficulties in mobility, were quitting their workshops and invading the city.

As they approach, following custom, shopkeepers close their shutters to protect themselves from the mob, but leave their doors ajar in order to enjoy the sight of its passing.

Barricades are already obstructing several avenues, and the mechanical coachmen of steam-cabs and omnibuses, exhibiting a human intelligence, are overturning their vehicles across the streets. Behind these advance positions, still hesitating to cross them, an unspeakable confusion of vagabond automata is swarming: riotous machines and Atmophytes attained by furious atmomania, [102] staggering around, drunk on the electricity they have consumed to excess—for the majority of these wretches are less ardent for insurrection than intoxication, and the fountains of hot air and steam, along with the electrical reservoirs, are the primary objects of their covetousness.

---

[101] In the first edition this chapter was entitled "A Mechanical Revolution."
[102] The author inserts a footnote to define *atmomania* as "steam madness."

Menacing gangs besiege the fountains, howling. The earliest arrivals and the most dunk, squatting on the outlets, deaf to their manometers, open their enormous valves and aspire torrents. Others, more sensual, thirsty for more acrid liqueurs, have invaded the telegraphs and are drinking from the acid-baths, plunging into them and emerging streaming with sparks. They are trying to operate the apparatus, peppering one another with enormous discharges—intense voluptuous sensations which shake and sting them, provoking outbursts of sardonic laughter that conclude in screams.

While these odious scenes are being played out on the upper stages, other insurgents, which have descended into the cellars, re-emerge carrying baskets full of Leyden jars. They break them open and drink gluttonously. Their platinum brains turn red, madness advertising itself therein. They are flaming lunatics that set alight everything they touch, carelessly propagating fires that make them laugh, into which they hurl themselves to cause explosions.

It is necessary to see such things to believe them, and yet the spectacle has actors more hideous still: the women, the Furies and Bacchantes of the mob, its most ferocious bit-part players, the most ardent to wallow in the cup of the public orgy. They rise at the dawn of every bloody day in history, marching in the front rank of violent revolution, and are not lacking in this one.

Here are sewing-machines, good working-girls a short while before, dedicated to their tasks, which, now furious by virtue of irrational contagion, are gnashing teeth as fine as vipers' tongues. Their needle-bearing jaws move in empty space, with a silent and crazy velocity, like people so overwhelmed by anger that word quiver on their obstructed lips without emitting any sound. And here are other female machines, coarser still, vomiting monstrous utterances: obscene emissions of all the filth that the belly of a mechanical charwoman in a state of drunkenness can contain.

From all of this rise the unspeakable gusts of an indecent, noisy, fetid racket: the reek of the crowd, the clink of metal sweating rage, grease and oil. The conflagration spreads, everything bursts into flame on contact the incendiaries. To see these demons in this sea of flame, one might think that Hell has overflowed, that the geothermal well had broken through its floodgates, unleashing its steam-horses,[103] which have taken the bit in their teeth, foaming at the mouth, whinnying, rearing up and kicking their coachmen in the face.

Night, which descends over these horrible scenes, does not seem likely to put an end to them; on the contrary, the fire spreads, the destruction extends as far as the port, where the two ships so carefully towed in by Dr. Penkenton suddenly sink and disappear, as if a mysterious hand has just pierced their hulls.

There are symptoms more frightful still: through the semi-darkness, rallying in the suburbs, the mob's reserves are glimpsed, and the prudent machines only desirous of rebellion if success is guaranteed. Further away, beyond the city limits, the Atmophytes of the countryside, in tumultuous disorder, are filling the roads and hastening toward the city: rural populations, gentle and hard-working, broadly-built, with smug faces; lions concealed beneath the pelts of oxen, which study the horizon with an oblique gaze as they work, and which, when the clouds gather and the storm bursts and endures, cast their disguises aside and expose their manes; good people who do not sew revolt, but which, when it is ripe, lend a hand to the harvest.

Already, with a marvelous instinct, mechanical reapers have beaten their blades into swords and pikes. The harvesters are sharpening their scythes. The haymakers, who have quit work at the first indications from emissaries, come running, hampered by their wigs of hay, and the plows follow them, taking the middle of the road and tracing their furrow in that turf with their plowshares.

---

[103] The French measure normally translatable as "horse-power" is *chevaux-vapeur* [steam-horses]; I have used the literal translation here to comply with the wordplay.

The darkening night renders this spectacle even more fantastic. All these monsters have lit up their eyes, but their bodies, steeped in darkness, only reveal themselves by the gleam of their gazes, which project and intersect like flamboyant *épées* in the hands of invisible fencers.

Could so much aptitude to imagine evil action, and so much skill in committing it, be spontaneous, even among the most advanced Atmophytes? Was it necessary to believe, with William Barnett, that the engineers had imprudently exaggerated the provision of instinct in these machines and inadvertently inoculated their brains with a little of the human virus? Was it, in fact, among the Atmophytes that the insurrection had found its organizer and its leader? For it had a leader, there was no doubt about it. The king of the mob could be glimpsed, here and there, in the great clearings that the flames cut out of the darkness; he could be followed by the track of the popular acclaim that greeted him as he moved from quarter to quarter, inspecting his barricades, stimulating his insurgents, sewing along his route a trail of more devouring fire, more frenzied intoxication.

Lord Hotairwell, leaning on the rail of the balcony, silently watched his work destroying itself, crushed by his impotence to hold his creations in check. What could oppose such assailants? Neither force nor persuasion. One cannot reason with a runaway locomotive; one cannot employ force against a cannonball.

As I looked at him, similarly downcast, without saying anything, but seeking to penetrate his thoughts, he said: "Mr. Burton, the work that is being carried out surpasses the range of the most intelligent of our Atmophytes; they are the perfect instruments, but a human hand and a human mind are directing them. That hand…"

Lord Hotairwell was unable to finish. A more intense clamor, of cries of joy, signaled a more ferocious and decisive attack enveloping the temple like a whirlwind, from the bosom of which an enormous monster advanced—pulled, pushed and carried in triumph.

It was the god of this apotheosis: a sort of elephant armed with a club sheathed in its trunk, something like a living anvil brandishing its own hammer. It was a pile-driver weighing 200,000 kilograms, which the insurgents, with prodigious strength and skill, had extracted from the crypt and were setting up before the gate as a battering-ram.

At the same time, having rendered themselves masters of the entire network of wires and tubes centralized at the town hall, they had tangled the tubes in the wires to the point of rendering transmissions unintelligible and dangerous; they were sending electrical discharges through the conductors, enormous lightning-bolts, impregnating the walls of the edifice so that no one could any longer touch them without receiving a shock. The atmosphere of the hall was saturated with it; a handshake led to an exchange of sparks between the electrified bodies, shaken like frogs by the Voltaic arc—less reminiscent of men than electrical vibrators, automata, Atmophytes with no authority over their limbs, incapable of maintaining the dignified attitude required at such a moment.

All the transmitters, thus transformed into malevolent agents and instruments of revolt, were vomiting, according to their aptitude, hails of projectiles or torrents of insults, which the microphones took care to amplify and the phonographs recorded and repeated with mechanical obstinacy, mingling their shrill voices with the thunderous blows of the pile-driver. Telephones became cacophonic and phonographs cacographic: a confusion of tongues embroiled in skeins of steel wire. Atmospheric tubes were transformed into artillery pieces which the barbarians loaded with peaceful citizens, launching themselves with such violence that, departing as cannonballs, they arrived as grapeshot—a grapeshot of human shreds.

It was thus that we had the incomparable pain of seeing the return of the disfigured remains of the engineer William Hatchitt, who, with his obliging nature and habitual devotion, proud of his great familiarity with underground travel, had undertaken a reconnaissance mission in a tube, in order to

215

obtain a better appreciation of the revolt and to attempt, by taking it by the tail, to hold it in respect.

Industria's final hour had sounded. The doors of the temple yielded to the redoubled blows of the hammer. Through the gap came ferocious stares, whistling blasts of air, claws that attached themselves to fissures in order to enlarge them, scythes and sickles attempting, with professional skill, to mow down men like ears of corn.

The Assembly had resumed sitting. Its members, having become calm in the face of the supreme anger, was no longer thinking of anything but dying well, when James Archibold, having consulted his watch and asked for the president's authorization, headed for the apse at a rapid pace. As soon as he arrived he closed the tap that distributed the motive force emerging from the well to the Atmophytes of the city and the countryside.

A thunder of applause saluted the execution of such a simple idea, which cut off the fuel, and the very life, of the insurgents, ensuring a spectacular victory, and a decisive repression. A second salvo of cheers welcomed Archibold when he returned to his place, having saved Industria with that small expenditure of common sense…or, at least, would have saved it if he had acted sooner. Unfortunately, at that extreme hour, would not the work of the insurrection be completed by virtue of acquired momentum, before the motive force drained from the channels had ceased to fuel the Atmophytes?

Every effort of the pile-driver made a more prominent dent in the doors. The encouraged assailants were increasing their pressure, scaling the walls and crowning the edifice, which was crushed beneath the crowd like a tree collapsing under the weight of its own fruit.

Inside, no one any longer had any fear of death; they desired it, and would have called out to it if there had been any chance that it might hear in the midst of such a tumult. Lord Hotairwell stood up at the armchair, and put his hat on in order to receive the mob, while Archibold attentively followed the flea-jumps of the second hand on his watch.

Suddenly, under the effort of a more formidable shove, the doors gave way and fell, opening to the gaze of the besieged the indescribable spectacle of the battlefield and its combatants: an undisciplined and frenzied mass of furious machines and ferocious scrap metal, into the hands of which the disarmed masters were finally about to fall....

Against all expectation, however, it was not a cry of triumph that went up from the bosom of that crowd, but a death-rattle. The clamors, oaths and threats were frozen in their throats, or died like plaints on platinum lips—and the pile-driver, its fist lifted, remained stuck in that attitude.

Paralysis struck the Atmophytes as the power flowing to the fountains ran out and drained away. Stupefied by the transition from plethora to dearth, from the paroxysm of strength to overwhelming inertia, they tottered, fighting for life—but their eyes were extinguished in their orbits and their limbs fell limply beside their bodies, which collapsed like empty suits of armor. Progressively, by rapid contagion, as the wells dried up, holes were cut through the crowd from the threshold of the temple to the extreme suburbs, as if a haphazard harvest had commenced.

Industria was saved.

The 400 hands of the 200 members of the Legislative Body joined together in a cordial handshake, and extended toward those of Mr. Archibold, who was busy replacing his watch in his waistcoat pocket.

"Gentlemen," said the chief engineer to his colleagues, who surrounded him, "our slaves leave something to be desired, but our other machines are excellent. I calculated that the insurrection would cease 12 seconds after the closure of the conduit distributing compressed air to the fountains, where the first ranks of the insurgents were refueling themselves, [104]

---

[104] The first edition text differs from this point on. The comma was there replaced by a full stop and the next sentenced began: "That conduit, 50 centimeters in diameter and 2000 meters long, then contained 310 cubic meters of compressed air,

but my chronometer has shown me that 11-1/2 seconds were sufficient. The compressed air has therefore taken action, watch in hand, in conformity with my calculations—and if it had been three-quarters of a second out, the hinges of the door would have bust asunder and the insurgents would have invaded this refuge. Yes, the character of the Atmophytes needs to be retouched, but our other apparatus is excellent!"

Concluding thus, Archibold, in a fit of extreme satisfaction, forgot himself so far as to rub his hands together, without taking account of the expenditure of energy and frictional losses that the gesture would occasion.

---

whose release might have furnished 6,510,000 kilogrammeters and ought to have concluded at the end of 12 seconds, including the delay of four per cent caused in the debit by the elbows, but my chronometer has shown me that eleven and a quarter seconds sufficed to stop the mob short. In addition, Gentlemen, admire the precision with which the pile-driver has been struck. It has opened a breach in the three-inch thick steel plates that formed the battens of the doors which I have just measured and is 750 square decimeters, requiring a force of 110,000 kilogrammeters per decimeter, which is 825,500,000 kilogrammeters for the entire breach. Now, the conduit furnishing, at a speed of 400 meters per second, a force of 11,625,000 kilogrammeters, the completion of that breach should only have required seven seconds—but in reality, it lasted nine seconds and three-quarters, as I have observed. The difference is due to the passive resistance of the mechanism, which, for that exceptional labor, had exceeded the ordinary proportion of 25%, without taking account of the futile kicks and negligible punches applied by the atmophytes against the doors. It is therefore evident, Gentlemen, that the compressed air…" The text then continues as in the fourth edition, except that the figure given there as three quarters of a second is misrendered as "two seconds."

Chapter Six
And Then the Key to the Abyss was Given to Them...[105]

"Gentlemen," said Lord Hotairwell, after having rung his presidential hand-bell to re-establish silence, "We have just gained a great victory—a dolorous victory, too dearly bought by the tragic death of William Hatchitt, our eminent colleague and friend: a man of science and devotion, whose life could not find a worthier end than his death."

(General assent.)

"At least William Hatchitt has been avenged, for the Atmophytes too have perished, as any creature ought to perish that threatens its creator! Gentlemen, if no one requests the floor, I shall conclude this painful session, as a sign of mourning."

"I request the floor," cried a voice from the apse, as hollow as the well from which it seemed to emerge.

"The floor is yours," said Lord Hotairwell, surprised.

"My Lords and Gentlemen...." the voice began.

"To the podium, to the podium!" cried the Assembly.

"No," the speaker retorted. "I shall speak from where I am."

As obedient as a frightened child, the Assembly turned toward the apse.

"Gentlemen," he continued, "at this late hour, I shall not make a speech; I only wish to add my personal approval to the President's words: 'Perish the creature that defies its creator!' And the Atmophytes have perished; that was justice. But you too, Gentlemen, shall perish, and that will be justice, because

---

[105] The author adds a reference here to Chapter 9 of *Revelation*, but the quotation from the first verse does not correspond to the version familiar to English readers in the King James Bible, which reads: "I saw a star fall from Heaven unto the Earth; and to him was given the key of the bottomless pit."

you have defied your creator, because you have made your-selves creators and gods—and I am the one the Lord has cho-sen to carry out his noble work, to be your executioner."

As he pronounced these words, the mysterious orator had stood up like a specter, profiling his enormous and indecisive silhouette on the wall of the apse.

You can imagine what a state of physical debility and moral depression that assembly was in, having been in session for two days, weighed down by various emotions, like a field over which the dozen children of Aeolus had poured out their winds in turn. The appearance of this fatal orator, fulminating like a god in the darkness of his sanctuary, had brought that enervation to a head, and more than one listener among those men of positivistic conviction, was inclined to see something supernatural and diabolical therein. Who knows, they asked themselves, whether the Central Fire Company might not have been temeritous in taking no account of the kings of the infer-nal regions whose existence the ancients had affirmed? Who knows whether the fracture that had recently occurred in the well, considered as accidental, might not have been the work of one of these subterranean kings, disturbed in his empire?

It might be Osiris, the great judge, the jealous king of Amenthes, who travels its 75 zones relentlessly while watch-ing over his 42 assessors at the center: Osiris, the incarnation of fire, the Central Fire himself, furious at the invasion of his zones and come to protest against the violators. It might be Hel, daughter of Loki, whose breast nurtured seven rivers of serpents; or Yama, the implacable king who governed Tamissa and Borava, the lands of darkness and tears, the foul abode Pontimithrica, Asipahanava the forest of swords and Redjicha, the stove on which the wicked fry.

Others, by reason of the phantom's great stature, guessed that they were dealing with the giant Kaifi, king of Zazzarra-gouan; the ferocious metallurgist Pluto, the mastiff of Vulcan, who forges the souls of the Mariannais—whose refinement is entrusted to him—in his furnace; yet others thought of Zagara, reduced to ashes for having offended his divinity by penetrating into the entrails of the Earth.[106]

"Who are you?" came the cry from every side. "Who are you?"

The orator came out of the shadows then, threatening and brandishing an enormous club, ready to become the instrument of divine vengeance.

"Who am I?" he said. "You shall know, for the hour is propitious and the time has come."

Samuel Penkenton—for it was him—advanced to the threshold of the apse, into the full glare of the statue of Electros, and there, as indifferent to the silence as to the murmurs, he remained immobile, with his arm extended and his eyes fixed upon an object visible only to him. His angry face, now bathed in tears, became more serene as his gaze pierced the darkness more fully, as if he glimpsed in the distance of his ecstasy, at the very end of a long stretch of centuries, an enchanting spectacle—which, contrary to the rules of perspective, became more distinct as it retreated from the foreground.

"Who am I?" he repeated. And, pointing his finger at the fascinating vision: "Out there, out there! On that oriental slope that faced the Genesis and the first dawns, in the plain of Chaldea, watered by the river with four sources, I lived when I was young, innocent and happy, in the midst of a population formed by my brothers and my sisters, beneath the scepter of my father, who was a king...."

"Then, one fateful day, I saw my father draw near a tree whose branches were serpents, which awoke and offered him their fruits. And those fruits were death, hatred, the rivalry of races, the dispersal of peoples, and the confusion of tongues...."

---

[106] Some of the mythological references in this passage are rather esoteric; I cannot identify Kaifi or Zagara, although the latter term is widely used in Greek myth to represent the scent of citrus-flowers and is also the name of a stream. The references are probably literary rather than mythological.

"And after a short time, those fruits had borne fruits of their own…

"And in the land of Shinar where Babylon would rise, the tribes, daughters of the sons of Noah, no longer able to understand one another, drew apart…

"Ready to say a final farewell, they constructed a tower so high that those who have seen its ruins thought that the Titans had built it with heaped-up mountains…

"And on the ruins of that tower, I saw the enormous temple of Belus[107] rise up, and on the ruins of Belus, the palace of Nimrod, more gigantic still. And thus the Earth was populated by colossi.

"And during my long life, I have visited all these colossi.

"In the land of Anahuac, which you call Mexico, I have seen the pyramid of Cholula, higher than that of Cheops, built on the plan of Babel, as the Toltecs—distant predecessors of the Chichimecs and the Aztecs—attest. And not far from that pyramid, I have seen temples dedicated to the Sun and the Moon, and I have seen mountains carved into the forms of gigantic animals by a sculptor people who have left no record of their name.

"In China, I have seen the temple of the 1000 Lamas, populated by stone beasts, which watch over other monsters born from the same granite, ferocious worshippers that cause their god to tremble.

"In Egypt, I have seen a statue of Ramses made of a single block of stone weighing two million pounds, and I have dragged that block from Syene to Thebes, hitched to it with 3000 Hebrews, my brothers, breaking my back, bloodying my shoulders, strapped like a beast into my crude harness made of tresses of aloes.

"Finally, after 5000 years, I have seen Babel reborn from its ashes, and an audacious people construct in an abyss a tower so high as to surpass the first Babel by several million

---

[107] Belus is one of the many names of the Mesopotamian deity most commonly known nowadays as Bel-Marduk.

cubits. And from the bosom of that profound tower, I have seen a great fire rise up, with fumes and strange creatures named Atmophytes, which I recognized for the scourge that was shown to St. John of the Apocalypse, when the seventh seal was broken:

" 'And then,' says John, 'the key of the abyss was given to them, and they opened it, and he showed them the smoke of a great furnace in the well… And from that furnace he brought locusts, and these locusts resembled horses armed for combat… And their faces were like the faces of men, and they had breastplates of fire, and the sound of their wings was like a sound of chariots… And their power was to harm men.' [108]

"The Lord," Samuel Penkenton continued, in a terrible tone, "punishes prideful creatures according to his pleasure; he drowns them in a deluge, in the flames of the Dead Sea; or, more severely, he forgets them; he allows time to bury them beneath the grass, the centuries to wear away their memories,

---

[108] In the King James Bible, Chapter 9 continues: "And he opened the bottomless pit; and there arose a smoke out of the pit, as the smoke of a great furnace; and the Sun and the air were darkened by reason of the smoke of the pit. And there came out of the smoke locusts upon the Earth; and unto them was given power, as the scorpions of the Earth have power… And the shapes of the locusts were like unto horses prepared unto battle; and on their heads were as it were crowns of gold, and their faces were like the faces of men… And they had breastplates, as it were breastplates of iron; and the sound of their wings was as the sound of chariots of many horses running into battle. And they had tails like unto scorpions, and there were stings in their tails: and their power was to hurt men five months….And they had a king over them, which is the angel of the bottomless pit, whose name in the Hebrew tongue is Abbadon, but in the Greek tongue hath his name Apollyon." I have quoted more of the text than Penkenton does because its relevance to the text seems to extent further than his brief excerpt.

and scientists to sieve their dust without gleaning a name or a fragment of debris therefrom."

The orator became more exalted still, letting the lightning of his gaze and the thunder of his voice off the bridle. "Sometimes, again," he continued, "when a people descends to the level of beasts, as you have done in becoming the slaves of your machines, the Lord changes them into beasts, as he did with Nebuchadnezzar, or he destroys them and chooses, among the guilty, an avenger who obtains his grace in becoming an executioner—who is named, according to the century, Samson or Samuel Penkenton, who brings down the temple, kills the Philistines and perishes with them in the ruins."

This time combining action and threat, Samuel Penkenton assailed the defenseless statue of Anthrakia with his cane—and that of Electros, an irascible god whose body, inflamed with anger and bristling with sparks, tried in vain to strike down the sacrilege.

Intoxicated by his task, the demented Iconoclast multiplied his ravages, sparing nothing in the sanctuary—neither reigning gods, nor fallen gods, nor the Central Fire itself, whose apparatus he smashed, pulverizing the manometers, wringing cries of distress from the safety-valves and alarm-whistles, which he silenced with deadly blows. This massacre of objects was only a prelude; for from the heart of the tumult, compounded from the exclamations of the spectators, the laughter of the turncoat and the squealing of metal, an even more terrible noise rose up, and even the madman halted in alarm.

The Assembly had understood the infernal deed that he had just accomplished and, transfixed by anguish, cowering in terror, had fallen silent, listening to the deafening roar of the cataract falling into the abyss: the sound of the lake in communication with the geothermal well pouring into the well with all the velocity of its vertical fall, over the entire breadth of the sluice-gates that Samuel Penkenton had just broken in a fit of range.

As the sea irrupted through a subterranean fault into a crater near the shore, its waves, its waves vaporized and their volume, centupled 17 times over, acquired a pressure that dislocated the ground and projected the debris into the air. Had any such phenomenon had ever been manifest before, given that its cause had only just been created, by assembling the elements and hurling a lake into a volcanic well, into the central fire, father of all volcanoes? Not merely the city of Industria but the Earth itself might be compromised by such a redoubtable means of destruction.

Such a grave situation required extremely powerful measures—but what measures could be sufficiently powerful against the elements allied with a madman, having gone as mad as him?

Lord Hotairwell, Archibold and I had launched ourselves forward, but Samuel Penkenton was on his guard and prevented us from getting near him by lashing out in every direction with his staff, so that the slightest contact would have smashed our skulls like fragile cups and strewn their contents around. Then again, what was one more risk in the midst of so many perils? The waters precipitated into the gulf were already rising up in clouds, and the dome, no longer relieving its pressure since Archibold had closed the flap-valve, had attained such a powerful tension that compressed air was hissing out through the pores of the metal.

Meanwhile, the indefatigable organizer of these disasters, intent on carrying them through and drunk with success, was repeating these words: "*Hinneh haratson Jehovah! Hinneh haratson Jehovah!*"

"What does it mean?" I asked.

"*Hinneh, hallephets Jehovah,*" Lord Hotairwell replied, so much the polyglot that, without being aware of it, he was explaining the Hebrew in Coptic—but he started over, saying: "It means: God wills it."

Suddenly, the earth shook in rapid jolts. One might have imagined that the Earth was trampling itself down. Then an enormous oscillation occurred; the ship of the temple, surprised by this pitching, reared up from apse to vestibule as if bitten in the bow by the waves, and the dome burst with a terrible bang.

Had the Earth gone off the rails of its ecliptic and turned over in space? Or were those subterranean noises merely an echo of the explosion of the dome?

The terrestrial globe continued to oscillate, as if Charlemagne were shaking it in his hand. The darkness was profound, compounded from steam, smoke, dust and the debris floating in the atmosphere. The Assembly tried to flee, but death was guarding all the exits. Lord Hotairwell, Archibold and I remained motionless, no longer able to distinguish between life and death in the midst of the universal devastation, the explosions and the collapses.

When the light returned, after a period of time that I cannot specify, it found us in the same attitude, like actors who hold the poses in which the denouement has left them while the curtain is falling once the play is over; all three of us were safe and sound. Samuel Penkenton had disappeared into space or into the abyss, the expiatory victim of his own crime.

All around us was desolation and death, the walls of the temple convulsively reduced to twisted tatters of metal. The corpses of men and Atmophytes were everywhere, the latter having achieved the equality for which they had fought: the molecular equality of the grave, which brings cadavers and debris to the same level.

In the distance, as close by, destruction was triumphant; there were ruins in the process of crumbling and others already heaped up, ready to receive their fated shroud: moss and oblivion.

Chapter Seven
Intercosmic England

The orifice of the shattered geothermal well, increased in size and flared by the vibration, formed a funnel whose rim opened at our feet. Lord Hotairell went a little way down the slope, but scarcely had he looked into it than he uttered a cry and stood there, frozen in amazement, with his arm extended and his eyes staring into the abyss.

"The Earth!" he cried. "The Earth!"

Archibold and I had drawn nearer. If there is anyone who had found himself in a similar situation, let him take my pen and try to describe what he has experienced.

The well no longer had a bottom! It was now no more than a tunnel, a tubular vertical valley, at the end of which appeared the Earth, already distant but distinct.

It was, therefore, not merely the dome and the temple that had been blown up by the influence of masses of vaporized water, but also a portion of the terrestrial globe—and we ourselves were among the shrapnel of that explosion, the scoria of that eruption, doomed to the scalpels of selenite or solar scientists, who were already watching us through their telescopes, in order to capture us in their orbit.

Seated on the rim of that Valley of Death, Lord Hotairell and I remained silent, unable to find words or thoughts at the height of such a disaster. Nearby, leaning over the gulf, with his eyes glued to his opera-glasses, Archibold was sounding the bottomless pit.

"Oh," he said, after a little while. "Oh!" He wiped the lenses of his binoculars in order that he might see more clearly. "That's better!" Then he aimed the instrument again, and concluded: "All right!"

"What is it?" said Lord Hotairell, surprised by this exuberance of exclamations without sequels and words without meanings. "What can you see that can possibly surprise you, after what we've seen?"

"I see a glimmer of hope."

"Hope of returning to Earth?" I asked.

"No, Mr. Burton, but a hope of staying there."

"How can we stay there, since we've already departed?"

"Have we departed, Mr. Burton?"

"Do you doubt it?" asked Lord Hotairwell.

"I neither believe not doubt; I'm asking myself the question, and I haven't got an answer yet."

"What doubt can you have, when we can see the Earth, at that distance, beneath our feet?"

"We can see the Earth beneath our feet, that's true," replied Archibold, "but we can also see Industria upon that Earth, in its usual place, its town hall, its houses and its inhabitants."

Lord Hotairwell took the opera-glasses, looked through them for some time, gave them back to Archibold and then took them back again, unable to decide whether to believe his eyes.

I looked in my turn and was astonished, to the point of turning the glasses around in order to assure myself that the things I was seeing had not been set inside them.

"Well, what did you see?" asked Archibold.

"I saw Industria in its place," replied Lord Hotairwell, "its temple standing, and little black dots on the balcony of the temple that one might take for people, and other black dots moving in the streets. In sum, reduced to infinitesimal proportions by the distance, I saw things as they were at the moment of the explosion."

"I saw exactly the same thing," I said.

"And both of you saw it clearly," Archibold confirmed.

"But in that case," I exclaimed, "Industria hasn't been destroyed! We haven't left the Earth! This catastrophe is nothing but a dream!"

"No, a reality," the engineer put in, his face having darkened again. "Forgive me for the illusion that I've caused you to share."

228

"Are you reverting to the belief that we've been blown up?" I asked, anxiously.

Without replying, Archibold pointed at the surrounding ruins, and made me touch the walls of the demolished town hall with my fingers.

Lord Hotairwell remained mute, but I, racked by horrible doubts, cried out wildly: "This is all insane! I don't understand you, Mr. Archibold! Either we've departed, or we haven't."

"Why is that, Mr. Burton?"

"Because, although I'm no scientist, I know that we can't be both on the Earth and not on it."

"Prove that, I beg you," the engineer replied.

"I prove it by saying that, if it's the case, it's absurd, and if it's absurd, it isn't the case."

"And I say that we're on the Earth, and we're not on it. It's not absurd. On the contrary, it's so simple that I'm ashamed to have been delayed by hypotheses instead of grasping the truth. Yes we're here *and* there. That's obvious, and simply proves that our explosion was so violent, and our initial speed so rapid, that we've traveled faster than light."

"And what if we have traveled faster than light?" I asked. "What effect does that have?"

"The effect that we have preceded into space the news of the events of which we are victims—that we have traveled faster than our own image, which is only transmitted at the speed of light, was able to follow us; it is running after us like a dog that has lost its master, or a shadow that has lost its man. Do you understand?"

"Not in the slightest."

"It is, however, a matter of elementary physics; and, not wishing to offend you, the least intelligent of the inhabitants of the Sun understands that, when he looks at the Earth. You know that visual information and a ray of light travel at the same speed, the one carrying the other. Now, since sunlight takes eight minutes 13 seconds to travel to the Earth, and as long to return, carrying the image of events that are happening there, an event occurring at noon on our globe is not known on the Sun until eight minutes 13 seconds past noon. The more distant worlds receive the news with an even greater delay. Some stars are learning the first things about our ancient history at this moment; others, more distant, are only up to the Deluge; others perceive the Earth before its creation, or, to put it a better way, cannot see it yet. On the other hand, if it were destroyed, those same stars would continue to see it.

"If, therefore, Industria appears to us to be still flourishing, it's because the solar rays that show us its image have left the Earth before the catastrophe, while other rays, bearers of the news, have not reached our present altitude. Which proves, Mr. Burton, that we are going extraordinarily quickly, that we've already attained a very great height, and, in consequence, that we've departed. But it also proves that we're slowing down, since the solar rays are catching us up."

Archibold continued as if he were talking to himself. "What frightful explosive force did it need, though, to launch this terrestrial debris with a velocity superior to that of light? More than 19 million kilometers a minute, 800 times as fast a cannonball.[109] Is that possible? No, it's not possible! It's only the first step that's costly, of course; weight diminishes the higher one rises, and once beyond Earth's gravitational attraction, it's only a matter of free fall. But the departure—the initial force! What force did it require!"

Archibold leaned on a rock and, taking out his notebook, set about writing figures—but he stopped. "Mr. Burton," he said, "at how many meters do you estimate the depth of this hole?"

"About 100 meters," I replied, having looked into the precipice. "Poor William Hatchitt could have told you better than me."

---

[109] These figures make no sense, but I have left them as they are on the assumption that their nonsensicality is deliberate. I have done the same for all of the following figures, in spite of several blatant inconsistencies.

"Poor William Hatchitt!" said Lord Hotairwell. "He would already have descended into the gulf. What a pity to have left him behind!"

"We haven't left William Hatchitt behind," Archibold replied. "We've left him ahead, since he's already dead and we haven't yet succeeded in doing as much. William Hatchitt is at his post, in the advance guard, as usual. Doubtless he's already digging in a better world than this miserable asteroid on which I'm wasting my time, and where his activity would only have to continue."

"He would have given us good advice," replied Lord Hotairwell, who could not accept the loss of his friends so stoically, "and I'm sure he would have found a way of getting away from this debris."

"It's necessary to love one's friends for themselves," replied Archibold, whose firm reason never compromised, "And I'm quite content that William Hatchitt is dead, since he's better off that way."

"But is it quite certain that he's dead," I asked, "and how he died? For, in truth, it was difficult to recognize him in his fragmentary remains."

"He's dead," said Archibold. "That's quite certain, and will do him no good for us to find out how he died, even if we could carry out an autopsy."

"Can an autopsy of a man tell us whether, when he was alive, he was an engineer or a man like any other?" I asked.

Archibold shrugged his shoulders without answering, and picked up the thread of his calculations. "You said just now, Mr. Burton, that the gulf is 100 meters deep. Let's go for 100 meters. Now, what length and breadth would you attribute to our planetary fragment?"

"Why make these measurements?" I asked.

"To find out whether we've departed."

"What! You're still in doubt?"

"I don't doubt it; I don't know anything."

"But just now, science in hand, you convinced us of it."

"Science, Mr. Burton, serves to create various convictions on the same subject, that's all. What dimensions, Milord would you attribute to our spheroid?"

"It's quite impossible for me to make an estimate," Lord Hotairwell replied.

"But I need these measurements. How else can I calculate the volume?"

"Perhaps there's a means to obtain them without displacement," said Lord Hotairwell, pointing to a portion of the town hall that was still standing. "The telephone and telegraph office seems to be almost intact. If the wires are still there, and the employees at the end of the wires survive, let's appeal for their collaboration. I propose that we send three phonograms to three station-masters on the Circum-Industria railway. Their response or silence will give us an approximate idea of our periphery."

Archibold having approved the plan, we immediately headed for the telephone and telegraph office.

The disorder was considerable; the compasses, commutators and galvanometers, precipitated from their shelves, were lying pell-mell amid inverted hand-sets, along with batteries and broken receivers. By making a selection from the debris, however, and reconnecting the wires, we quickly reconstituted an adequate apparatus, and I immediately telephoned the following message, whose brevity seemed to me most appropriate, after the terrible events of the night:

Edward Burton, Esq. to the Station-master, Cumnoch.
Have you had a good night?
                    E. Burton.

Five minutes later, the bell rang and the autophone receiver recited, in a voice that was still sleepy, punctuated by the yawns of the sender, the following reply:

Station-master, Cumnoch, to the very honorable Edward Burton, Esq.
Have had good night, thanks. Have you? Slightly disturbed at about 5 a.m., don't know why. Don't understand, either, why

trains no longer passing through. Going back to bed. Good
night.

Edward Henshaw.

"There's a chap who sleeps very soundly," said Lord Hotairwell, astonished. "But he sleeps, so he's alive; so our world extends, in that direction, as far as him."

A second message was immediately sent.
Edward Burton, Esq. to the Station-master, Grantley.
Have you had a good night?

E. Burton.

The response was slightly slower, but it arrived nevertheless.
Deputy station-master, Grantley, to the very honorable Burton, Esq.
Had bad night. Station-master imprudently leaned over edge fragment terrestrial globe, fell into Atlantic. Very anxious regarding his fate. Eminent chief, loss painful. Am adequate replacement.

Deputy station-master, Grantley.
Z. Appleton.

There, the catastrophe had been perceived, and in addition, the terrible accident that had befallen the station-master demonstrated that Grantley station was, in that direction, the extreme frontier of the asteroid.

A final phonogram was sent.
Edward Burton, Esq. to the Station-master, Galoshiels.[110]
Have you had a good night?

E. Burton.

I had scarcely finished telephoning when the reply reached me, as rapid as the lightning that carried it.

---

[110] I have left the name Galoshiels as the author renders it; he cannot mean Galashiels, which is in Scotland.

Station-master Galoshiels to Burton.

........!

> *Station-master, Galoshiels,*
> *Kembrown.*

This official's response was so laconic, excessive and scarcely adequate that in other circumstances, it would have got its author the sack by return of fluid, but it was necessary to take account of the confusion thrown into minds and the services by such events; then again, the message, though scarcely appropriate, was nonetheless conclusive.

"Let's content ourselves with these data," said Archibold,[111] who set about aligning an interminable series of figures in his notebook.

"It would have needed more than 1400 quatrillions for us to have departed!" he exclaimed, after a few moments.

"As much as that!" I said, in order to give myself the appearance of understanding.

"Yes," the engineer continued, "the asteroid that is carrying us, which I have just weighed, according to the measurements that you have furnished, represents 800,000 tonnes. An 800,000-tonne cannonball, in order to be launched by its cannon to a height of only ten kilometers, requires a charge of powder of 200,000 tonnes, corresponding to an explosive force of 1,436 quatrillion calories. In order to be launched to the same height by its volcano, and asteroid needs the same

---

[111] It is at this point in the text that the most substantial substitution takes place between the first and fourth edition—the one that accounts for the two-page difference in their page counts; Archibold's calculation is given in much greater detail and complexity in the first edition, the fourth edition version being drastically (and mercifully) abridged and the figures amended. The near-identity of the text is resumed on the following page, with the paragraph beginning: "While holding this discussion..." But the figures subsequently given are altered to tally with the amended calculation

explosive force. Now, the river vaporized in the well could only have produced 42.5 billion calories, when it required 1,436 quatrillions. Therefore, we have a deficit of 1,435,999,957,500,000,000 calories. Therefore, our explosion is implausible, our departure impossible and we have not departed. I say so, I have proved it, and I shall not remain a moment longer under an illusion unworthy of serious men."

Having spoken thus, Archibold wiped his forehead and breathed in forcefully, in order to restore the pressure in his lungs—for one cannot engender such a sequence of logical deductions without fatigue, especially on an empty stomach and in a rarefied atmosphere. Then he put his pencil in his notebook and his notebook in his pocket, and buttoned up his frock-coat.

While holding this discussion, we had returned to the edge of the precipice, at the bottom of which the Earth was still visible, but more indistinct.

"What other proof is necessary?" said Lord Hotairwell, drawing the engineer's attention to this spectacle. "Isn't the truth that leaps to our eyes sufficiently persuasive?"

"Eyes, Milord," replied Archibold, annoyed at seeing a discussion he had closed reopened, "can be myopic or presbyopic, weak and variable. Figures have no such infirmities."

"Figures, Mr. Archibold, cannot contend against evidence."

"Evidence!" cried the engineer, to whom the word seemed to be a joke, to the extent that we thought he—a man who had laughed less often than Rosinante[112] had galloped—was about to burst out laughing. "What is evidence?"

"Evidence," replied Lord Hotairwell, "is the very foundation of certainty. It's a truth so firmly united with its proof that one can neither distinguish nor separate them: a light so dazzling that one can scarcely bear to look at it and cannot analyze it."

---

[112] Rosinante was Don Quixote's horse.

"So that one cannot see or comprehend it," sneered Archibold. "In the matter of certainty, Milord, I only know mathematical certainty, and I only admit facts that can be expressed in numerical terms."

"Nevertheless, Mr. Archibold, Aristotle, Descartes, Jacobs, Fichte and Kant—all great minds—have informed us that it is necessary to admit certain evidence."[113]

"I am a dwarf by comparison with those intellectual giants, who must have been very clever if they understood one another—but in my opinion, evidence is only a conclusion without premises, an affirmation without a basis, a statue without a pedestal, which imposes itself on the sight but vanishes to the touch. I'm only a poor mathematician, a humble geometer-surveyor, who earns his certainty by the sweat of his brow, who counts his proofs, weighs them, calculates their volume and measures them according to heir density. And, as evidence has no proof—as you admit—I hold as false everything that is evident. I therefore do not yield to the supposed evidence of our explosion; I shall take no account of it until someone proves to me that a paltry force of 42 billion calories could hurl an 800,000,000-tonne cannonball millions of kilometers."

Art that moment, however, Archibold was interrupted by an item of evidence that, although devoid of proof, nevertheless presented certain characteristics of certainty. It was darkness—an instantaneous and opaque night which, without the slightest crepuscular prelude, had just obscured the little planet as suddenly as a sunlit room whose shutters have been closed.

"Night already!" said the astonished engineer. "I looked at the time only a few moments ago. It's only 6 a.m."

---

[113] The odd man out in Hotairwell's list is Christian Jacobs (1764-1847), a German classical scholar of no great distinction. The others all made significant contributions to the philosophy of knowledge, although the citation of Kant's disciple Johann Ficthe is out of chronological sequence.

"I see this phenomenon as a further proof of our severance from the Earth and the autonomy of our asteroid," said Lord Hotairwell.

"I see nothing at all," replied Archibold, forcefully—who could, indeed, see nothing at all in the darkness.

"We shall see how long the night lasts," I said, "but, according to my watch, the day that has just finished lasted no more than a quarter of an hour."

"Which proves," Lord Hotairwell continued, "that we're on an asteroid that is rotating independently, proportioning its days to its velocity and its small volume."

"I don't believe that," Archibold replied.

"Would you admit it momentarily as a hypothesis?" asked Lord Hotairwell.

"Hypothesis is the first step toward belief; I cannot admit it hypothetically, but I shall admit it out of kindness."

"Admitting, then, momentarily, that an explosion has projected us out of the sphere of terrestrial attraction," Lord Hotairwell continued, "would our situation be desperate?"

"I would fear so," said Archibold.

"I don't think so," Lord Hotairwell wet on, "and I suggest that we would have in our hands a means of salvation as powerful as the impulsion that projected us. It would be that impulsion itself, which would be at our disposal."

"We would be able to dispose of that impulsion to much the same extent as man disposes of the rotation and velocity of the Earth; he profits from it, but it is not at his disposal."

"As you say Mr. Archibold—but let's try to control the force that's bearing us away; that's where salvation lies."

After a short while, daylight returned as suddenly as it had gone.

"The nights on this world are 15 minutes long, like the days," said Archibold. "We've fallen into the equinox."

"Admitting, therefore," Lord Hotairwell continued, "that this fragment of Earth has bee launched into space, what else can we do but influence its course, either by changing its direction so that it will take us back to Earth or by guiding it into a cosmic region that will suit us better?"

"And the means of execution, Milord?" Archibold queried.

"We have them. We have the impulsion, the motive force. We're heavier than the ether, and, in consequence, dirigible. We're a ship under pressure and in motion, but which is sailing aimlessly because it lacks a rudder."

Lord Hotairwell continued more ardently, passing from reasoning to lyricism, as the idea, brooding in the ashes, revived and lit its flame: "Let's construct that rudder, and regulate the course of the ship. Let's run the colors of the fatherland of the mainmast! Let's rally the crew dispersed by the tempest! Let's lift up these stones and scour these ruins, in order to exhume the sailors!

"You, Mr. Archibold, take the helm; Mr. Burton, the forward watch. I'll climb up on the maintop to give you the course! We shall sail upon the long waves of the ether—blue waves without storms; oceans without shores, strewn with enormous islands, which we call planets and suns, where navigators can travel for billions of leagues without running into a world or a star. Pilots of the intercosmic navigation that will one day be established, an aerial colony of England, we shall sing her glory to the stars and populate the solitudes of space in her name.

"Yes, at the very moment when our old England is about to disappear forever, let us swear an oath to maintain, no matter how distant she might become, our obedience and our faith. Let us accomplish the duty of faithful subjects in dedicating these new regions to Her Majesty the Queen of Great Britain, Empress of India, whom I proclaim today the Queen of Space. Gentlemen, the Queen!"

Lord Hotairwell had taken off his hat, and, with his hand extended over the abyss, took it as witness to his oath.

The Earth was still apparent in the depths, but even more distant and vague in the midst of a milky atmosphere, blurred at one point by an accumulation of little wisps of black vapor, like smoke escaping through a 1000 cracks from a rustic furnace in which foresters are concerting wood into charcoal.

Our gazes, without common agreement, and our hearts, without anything being said, locked on to these clouds, to their moving spirals, their ground-skimming flight, so far from the heavens. And soon, with our eyes filled with tears, kneeling on the ground, we bid farewell for the last time to the supreme vision of the fatherland—for that smoky sky, that dome of fluid coal, was London; it was the sky of the nation.

Chapter Eight
In which Mr. Burton melts,
while Dr. Penkenton evaporates

Twenty minutes had gone by since the last sunrise. The new day had already surpassed the duration of the previous one by a quarter. Archibold, who had a horror of inexactitude, however it might arise, had made the observation bitterly.

"This little planet, if it were one, would be ridiculous," he said. "There is no other world in the heavens so negligent, lengthening and diminishing its days at hazard without any astronomical motive."

"That's true," I agreed. "Not to mention that such a rapid rotation goes to my head and stifles me."

"Having departed like a cannon-shot, however," said Lord Hotairwell, "we can't complain about spinning like a shell. Then again, it's necessary to be indulgent toward a little world that has just been born and is attempting to rotate; a child not yet weaned rolls his hoop awkwardly."

"That may be," Archibold replied, "But in England, the director of Greenwich Observatory would not have tolerated a day elongated by half."

The heat was increasing by the minute, and the Sun was shooting rays as sharp as darts through the excessively thin atmosphere.

"Do you really think," Archibold went on, sponging his brow, "that it will be possible to set to work in such a temperature, on a world with such inconstant days?"

"It is, indeed, quite warm, and the days are short," relied Lord Hotairwell, whose oppressed respiration punctuated his speech, "but one result of that brevity is a more frequent alternation between work and rest, which could be salutary—in the long term, that is, for I confess that, for the moment, the changing climate is making me ill."

The heat was frightful. Archibold and I—I even more so, because of my obesity—were steaming with sweat, which enveloped us in fog as it evaporated. Lord Hotairwell, being thin and anhydrous, furnishing little in the way of evaporation, suffered even more, and was desiccated. The overheated blood expanding in our veins distended our bodies, augmenting their volume and diminishing their weight—and, aided by the slight gravity of the little world, we felt as if we were about to be take off into space by virtue of its rapid rotation. There was not a moment to lose before retreating—but where could we go?

"Isn't that opening in the rock," said Lord Hotairwell, pointing at a spot in the side wall of the gulf, "the entrance to the cavern enclosing the fossils?"

"Assuredly," replied Archibold, "and that cavern will make an excellent shelter for us; I think we can reach it without too much trouble."

Indeed, prudently descending the abrupt, near-vertical pathways on the side wall of he cone, we arrived at the entrance to the grotto and immediately went in.

I cannot say that it was cool beneath that vault, already fully impregnated with sunlight, but in an oven, even when it is hot, one is in the shade. Tracked by the light, we precipitated ourselves delightedly into the darkness, and we soon reached the part of the cavern that narrowed and curved into an arch, on the threshold of the crypt where we had once exhumed marvelous paleontological discoveries, and where the human remains were still buried.

Archibold, who was in the lead, suddenly came to a halt.

The crypt was illuminated, and an enormous human shadow, moving back and forth along the wall, repeated the gestures of its invisible body.

We advanced in silence.

What a revolution there had been in that Eden since the day when it had appeared to us in its glory! What further destruction had heaped its produce upon its ruins! On the terrain that had once been populated by the cadavers of its inhabitants, its animals and its plants, there was nothing now but a layer of dull brown dust, like a monk's robe!

A ray of sunlight, insinuating itself like a lizard through a crack in the wall, fell from the vault like a stalactite of light, discolored by its subterranean trajectory: a flickering ray that framed the great shadow, and then broke up, in a seed-bed of flickering flames, on a long and broad slab like a double sarcophagus: on the tomb of the dead people found in the crypt and buried by Samuel Penkenton.

Next to that slab there was a newly-dug open grave, whose dusty debris was still trickling down its sides, and at the head of the double sepulcher stood a tombstone, without a cross. A crown was hanging upon it—just one, but big enough to ring two foreheads, and the inscription, in enormous and tremulous handwriting, bore these words, which Lord Hotairwell read in amazement:

PENKENTON FAMILY
TO THE MEMORY OF MY GOOD RELATIVES
S. ב א PENKENTON EREXI.

A man, shaken by sobs, was kneeling on this tomb, so absorbed in his dolor that he had not heard the visitors. It was Dr. Samuel Penkenton.

Samuel Penkenton, son or brother of these fossils! Could madness—even that of a geologist—extend so far?

Retracing a path through my memories, I recalled the fit of dementia that had taken hold of the doctor in this very place: his hectic race; his fainting fit; the object furtively hidden in his breast; his jealous insistence on maintaining a vigil over the bodies of these fossils until he had walled up the cavern.

We were about to withdraw—for, once the initial surprise had passed, the sight of the man was odious to us—but he, having heard us, turned round, so angrily that his gaze was streaked with a red gleam. It was merely a flash, though; abruptly reconciling himself to being disturbed, he put a smile on his lips, like a host resigned to the arrival of unwelcome guests.

"Welcome, my friends…Gentlemen," he said, on seeing our stern faces. "Welcome to my cavern, and permit me to do the honors."

The complacency of that wretch, in front of his victims, surpassed all measure. As indignation took possession of us again, I made ready to pour out reproaches, Lord Hotairwell turned away scornfully, and the ever-pragmatic Archibold drew his revolver.

Lord Hotairwell restrained him, though. "This man is mad," he said. "One doesn't avenge oneself on a madman; one puts him in a safe place—if one can."

"My intention is precisely that—to put him in a safe place, conclusively," replied the engineer, aiming his pistol.

"What good would it do?" Lord Hotairwell persisted. "Has the man not finished his work? Is there any crime left for him to commit?"

"Gentlemen," continued Penkenton, who did not appear to have taken any heed of this discussion, "you've doubtless come here in search of coolness, and I'm very sorry to have so little to offer you, but I assure you that I shall make every to render your stay bearable…."

Lord Hotairwell and Archibold, however, immediately turned away, left the grotto and, at the risk of sudden death, sat down at the entrance. I wanted to follow my colleagues but, slowed down by my weight and suffocated by the heat, I was constrained to sit down for a moment.

The doctor had accompanied the others as far as the threshold, multiplying his effusions of politeness and his attempts to retain them. Having been left behind by them, he hurriedly came back to me, the sole interlocutor remaining to him.

"Those gentlemen are committing an extreme imprudence," Penkenton told me. "An imprudence that might easily shorten their lives by an hour or two. I burned my hand just now, while presenting my pocket thermometer to the Sun. It marked 110 degrees centigrade, but here, in the shade, it's only 84—still a considerable figure, Mr. Burton, even for humans, who are the most able of all animals to support changes in climate and thermal variations. No, in truth, even in my travels in Australia with Henry Russell-Killough,[114] I never experienced such heat; we only observed 70 degrees in the Sun and 49 in the shade—and already, public health was damaged, the mortality great; birds let themselves be taken in hand, and came to drink from teapots.

"I know that this temperature would be mere trifle for the rotifers and tardigrades that let themselves dry out at 100 degrees and gaily come back to life as soon as they're thrown into water, but your constitution, Mr. Burton, differs from that of rotifers. And then, we have overly abrupt changes on this little world; its nights are as cold as its days are hot; its excessively thin atmosphere serves us neither as a screen nor as a blanket—circumstances irreconcilable with good prophylaxy.

"You might say, Mr. Burton, that at the point we've reached, questions of hygiene are of little importance. I agree with you, and I shall even complete your thought with a few considerations."

I had not breathed a word, and physical force alone prevented me from strangling the chatterbox.

"Mind you," Penkenton continued, "I'm surprised that the heat isn't even more intense, and that, having been traveling toward the Sun for two days—two 15-minute days, admittedly—we haven't yet arrived. I would rather have talked about that to Mr. Archibold than you, Mr. Burton, who under-

---

[114] Henry Russell-Killough (1834-1909), most famous for his exploits as a Pyrenean mountaineer, undertook a long voyage to the East, including a sojourn in Australia, in 1859-61; his published account of it, *Seize mille lieues à travers l'Asie et l'Océanie* [Sixteen Thousand Leagues Across Asia and Oceania] (1864) was said to have inspired Jules Verne to write *Le Tour du monde en quatre-vingt jours*. (Russell-Killough wrote in French because that was his mother's native tongue; his father was Irish.)

stand nothing, but the devilish fellow was in so much of a hurry!"

The doctor felt his cheeks, which were as flat and brown as dried pears. "I recognize, however," he continued, "that the temperature has increased considerably. I'm visibly desiccating. There's a real progression, and if the night doesn't arrive unexpectedly to cool us down, we can expect an imminent cremation. Our little planet won't long survive us; like us, it will catch fire, and in that state, might worthily fuse with the Sun.

"Can we hope to witness that fusion? No, sine we'll have melted ourselves. Let us therefore enjoy it in advance, in the imagination. Can you form a precise idea of our incandescent individuality, liquefied or gaseous? One has difficulty in doing so, at first, but one can get used to everything. As for me, I declare to you, Mr. Burton, that that transformation of your matter will not change my sentiments, and that, gaseous or liquid, I will be happy to continue my friendly relationship with you."

Completing this amiable speech with a gracious gesture, Penkenton took my hands in his own burning hands, causing me as much pain as if red-hot pincers had gripped me.

"Such are, Mr. Burton, the observations that I desire to submit to you, and to which you have the faculty of replying, provided that you do it immediately—for time is running out, and we can't have long to live: a little more, or a little less, according to temperament. I, for example, have only a moment; I'm almost cooked; my flesh is roasting, my blood and lymph are evaporating; my synovial fluid is so dry that my bones are ridiculously loose in my joints. Just now, when I went out into the Sun, I heard the song of liquid that is about to boil in my veins, and I don't consider it impossible than an abrupt rise in temperature might cause me to explode.

"To you, Mr. Burton, who are extremely fat, it seems at first that hot climates would be inimical, and yet I think that you'll survive me. Oh, by a few minutes, nothing much—I'm not jealous. God knows how impatient I am to die! But your

245

fat gives you an aptitude for transpiration, precious in this instance, for transpiration is produced by the raised temperature of the body; a sweating man is a living porous jug. Maintain your sweat, therefore, Mr. Burton—and in order to do that, drink a lot. Science informs you that by drinking unrelentingly you can lower your internal temperature to a third of the ambient heat. No doubt, by drinking even more, you could succeed in bringing yourself down below zero.

"Believe that, and drink water, if there is any to be found on this little globe—which I doubt, for it's too thin for a well to be dug here, and at our present altitude, in any case, it would be a well of boiling water. At sea level, water boils at a 100 degrees; at the summit of Mont Blanc, it boils at 84—and at the summit of 84 Mont Blancs, it would boil below zero. That would be boiling ice, on which nothing would prevent you from skating.

"Fortunate Mr. Burton! You'll be able to witness our death, and our new molecular state, for longer and at closer range than me—provided, however, that your mental faculties, which seem feeble, permit it, and that obesity, on which I congratulated you a little while ago, does not present, on reflection, the danger that your oils and fats melt too rapidly and catch fire prematurely. Pork fat, for example—which, solely from a chemical viewpoint, is identical to yours—melts at a low temperature.

"I call your attention to this point, Mr. Burton, for you might finish sooner than I thought, and catch fire of you leave my cavern—so stay here, in order to prolong your existence, although I'm neither advising you to do that nor wishing it upon you, for, when Death is here, kindly extending his scythe to draw us to him, it's better not to make him wait.

"Death, Mr. Burton—the disembarrassment of life! What a dream! What compensation for the petty annoyances we suffer! I hope that, in spite of the evident weakness of your intelligence, you retain enough of its to enjoy your last moments, but you'll never enjoy them as much as me—that's impossible, and I'll tell you why, if there's still enough time and I don't have other more important things to tell you."

After a pause, employed in drawing the most cavernous of his intonations from his larynx, the doctor exclaimed: "Mr. Burton! Since, all things considered, it's likely that you'll survive me by a small margin, I shall settle my choice on you, in order to confide my last thoughts to you and establish you as my heir upon this asteroid—for I find myself unable to leave you the wealth I left down below."

The he howled, in a voice so piercing that it ran through my nervous system like an electrical discharge, and forcibly awoke my attention: "Mr. Burton!! I have, in addition, my confession to make to you, and your mercy to implore—but it is appropriate, for that, that I embrace your knees."

With these words, that huge body, disarticulated by its cooking, sank down at my feet, causing its joints to groan and expanding around it the heat of a smelting furnace.

"Edward Burton!" said the doctor, solemnly, "Managing Director of the Association of the Central Fire, currently in liquidation, I address myself in your person to all the administrators, all the shareholders, all my friends—if I have any, which I don't know—and I beg their pardon for having deceived them. For I am neither Samuel, nor Penkenton, nor a professor, nor a geologist; I am not myself; no one knows me, and it would be necessary to dig into the deepest dust of the ages to recover the bones of the woman and the man who engendered me." Penkenton paused, then added: "These are my intials," pointing to the symbols sculpted on his staff.

As he saw that I was stupefied, incapable of understanding, he went on: "Do you remember, Mr. Burton, those two human corpses found lying here, near to whom I shall soon lie, in the grave that I've prepared for myself? Do you recall their features?"

"Yes," I said, "I remember them perfectly."

"Then, do you recognize this portrait?"

As he spoke, Penkenton handed me a fragment of reindeer antler, on which the face of a young man was

247

represented: a design of naïve craftsmanship, but very clear in its contours, and bearing a striking resemblance to one of the dead people discovered in the cave; a work of prehistoric art, analogous to those found in Tertiary caves.

"It's the portrait of the fossil man," I said, immediately. Then, fixing my gaze, still imprinted with that image, upon Samuel Penkenton, I exclaimed: "And it's also your portrait!"

Samuel Penkenton had placed himself in the ray of light that descended from the ceiling, in order to outline his profile and demonstrate his perfect resemblance to the carving.

"That image, Mr. Burton, is indeed mine, and if it resembles, as you affirm, the fossil man found here, the reason is simple: the fossil man is my nephew, his wife is my niece. I had just taken it out of their hands at the moment when you found me fainted having succumbed to emotion. This family picture, the priceless portrait of a geological fossil, I give as a legacy to you, Mr. Burton!"

As the doctor pronounced these last words, an intense fog streaked with fantastic hallucinations invaded my brain. Was it the darkness mingled with glimmers that envelops the soul as the end of one's life? Was it Death, who had arrived clandestinely while I thought I was still alive, and had delivered me the Inferno and to the expiatory tortures that this loquacious and insane devil was inflicting upon me? These uncertainties were frightful, and the need to extract myself from them gave me the strength to address a few words to my torturer:

"Sir, am I still in this world or some other? Will you please tell me, unless you prefer to shut up, which would be even better—for it seems to me beyond doubt that you don't know what you're saying, any more than I understand what I'm hearing—how these antediluvian cadavers can be your kindred? How can you, who are still alive at the present time, or seem to be, be the uncle of a nephew and a niece who died thousands of years ago?"

"I can affirm," the doctor replied, simply, "that these fossils are my nephew and niece, and I can prove it by the resemblance that you have observed for yourself."

Penkenton was right: the authenticity of the engraving was indisputable; his argument was incontrovertible.

"Well," I continued, "if these fossils are your kindred, you must know their names; introduce me to them—and yourself. Who are you? I beg, you at this supreme hour, to tell me."

"You'll know in time," replied the doctor.

"In the Sun, then?"

"No, in the second volume."

"But will the author of this book write a second volume?" I asked, anxious, and thinking myself mad because the absurdity of such a question no longer shocked me.

The doctor remained mute this time, doubtless because he had been asked to speak, and as I prepared to persist, I searched for him with my gaze, in vain. Samuel Penkenton had disappeared, without my being able to understand how. Had he evaporated sooner than he expected? Had he succumbed to a lightning-fast combustion? I could not say, for neither in the air or on the ground, no matter how hard I looked, could I see a bubble of vapor or a pinch of ashes that seemed to resemble the mortal remains of Dr. Samuel Penkenton.

Chapter Nine
Lord Hotairwell's Last Dream

This painful conversation, terminated by that fantastic disappearance, had delivered my brain to a tempest of vague and mad ideas that seemed to me to be gushing out like jets of stream through all the cracks in my red-hot skull—but the very acuity of my suffering gave me strength; I made a supreme effort and I got to my feet to flee that cavern, in order to go to die with my friends, and to see once again the Earth and the beautiful Sun that was killing us.

The radiant executioner had drawn closer, embracing us more ardently with its arms of flame, and its red lidless eye, applied to the orifice of the cone, burned us with its end-bringing gaze.

And yet, there was a man there who did not lower his eyes before that terrible stare, who was conversing with the giant. Lord Hotairwell, radiant himself—as if he had borrowed a little of the Sun's halo—was contemplating it face-to-face, aspiring its burning waves with delight, intoxicating himself in its effluvia. His feet no longer seemed to be touching the ground, nor his body the wall of the gulf; he was detached, like a caryatid taking flight and floating above the abyss, his hands reaching out toward the star, in the same fashion as the glorious bodies of saints who, lighter than the angels, having no need of wings, rise into the pure ether because they are purer still.

Archibold also seemed extremely absorbed, but in a diametrically inverse ecstasy. Lying prone on the ground and leaning over the rim, having taken all possible measures to avoid falling, he was staring into the depths of the precipice at the Earth, which was now no more than a vague and distant mist. I dared not ask him about the subject of his reverie, but I conjectured that such a strong mind must be busy with appeasement, making the necessary concessions to the evidence.

"Oh! Come here, Mr. Burton!" cried Lord Hotairwell, on perceiving me. "Come and enjoy this beautiful sunlight before it absorbs us into itself. On Earth, an impure atmosphere surrounds us and falsifies or view. Light, like truth, reaches us obliquely and diffusely; it deceives us with its protean refractions and by its mirages, which simulate shade and springs in the arid plain. But here, at this magnificent altitude, the air is pure, the light true, and sight limitless; we are penetrating the secrets of space, entering the region of eternal genesis, and the cosmogonic dogmas will expand before our eyes like the spotless suns of these infinite expanses.

"Already, we can recognize that the Sun is inhabited—or, rather, that it is nothing but an aggregate of inhabitants, a swarming cluster of luminous beings. Can you see, Mr. Burton, those corpuscles, so brilliant that my eyes cannot rest upon them, changing, ungraspable, almost incorporeal forms that one might imagine to be souls incompletely divested of their bodies? At times, their forms become more distinct, and I recognize some of them. I've seen them on Earth, but they're not men: they're ideas, of which the Sun is perhaps the native country, the generative hearth.

"Yes, these billions of corpuscles are ideas: the ideas that have come, or will come, to all planets, in all times, in all countries; which, from the birth of worlds onwards, provoke the labors of all humankinds. It's from the Sun that they're born, and it's there that they return when they have completed their careers in bodies or in extinct worlds.

"And can you see those arriving over there, all dusty from the road, impregnated still with material contacts and terrestrial soiling? So they remain in quarantine on the surface, until they merit advancement toward the center. It is, undoubtedly, those impure ideas which form the sunspots that our astronomers have observed....

"Yes, as the waves of the Ocean mingle at the whim of the heat that penetrates them, and as the winds intersect and exchange, along their regular routes, the rigors of the pole for the effluvia of the tropics, thus movement reigns in the star

251

that I'm contemplating: the incessant exchange of an atomic population that rises to the periphery or precipitates itself therefrom; an immense swarm of bees filling that sphere with the sequined sound of their wings and the sparkle of their activity."

Lord Hotairwell fell silent for a few moments while his gaze, ardently mirroring that hearth of light, attempted to penetrate it more deeply still. Then he continued:

"As my eyes become accustomed to the spectacle, I understand its order and its actors better; I can distinguish more clearly the atoms that are returning from cosmic depths, slow and heavy, like weary voyagers and fall to the solar surface like Earthly snowflakes, while others, preparing for departure, brilliant with illusions and youth, freed of weight by a purer immateriality, take flight lightly toward all the poles of space....

"No, my eyes haven't deceived me in showing me, in this crowd of human resemblances, incorporeal forms that the eye can scarcely grasp, shades that survive their vanished bodies. I've seen them, among these corpuscles, which advance majestically and modestly, like the ideas of economists and academicians. Their faces are austere and their skulls have the form of the cupola of the Institut...

"Look, there are warrior ideas, with masculine attitudes; political ideas confused with crazy ideas and false ideas; they march in a disorderly manner, as loudly as the clinking of swords or the tinkling of bells. There are old and banal ideas, rounded like pebbles; and further away, young ideas, poetic ideas, which float in the ether like the Virgin's tresses. And there are others, younger still, which have not even lived and return before time, ashamed, like convicts hiding their stigmata...oh, don't veil yourselves thus, poor little things! I've seen through you, I know who you are; on Earth, from which you've come, as I have, I knew and loved you. You're my sisters and my daughters, chimerical ideas, new ideas, certified ideas, and you bear the mark S.G.D.G.,[115] which men, in their scorn, have imprinted on your shoulders. But here, you shall be pardoned, because you have labored and suffered. Go in peace, my sisters, and beware of the black ideas and unhealthy ideas that you follow, ever-ready to offer alliance to such wretches."

Lord Hotairwell raised his hand to his forehead, like someone chasing away a fly, or who has received a shock. "Oh! Oh, look, Mr. Burton, within that crowd of ideas there's one that has a body, for one of them, as it flew, collided with my forehead. It was like a hailstone shining with prismatic fire; perhaps it was coming back, still frozen, from a wintry mission in the cold climates of Uranus or Saturn…"

He put a finger to his lips. "But listen! Can you hear that humming noise, which reflects, like an echo, without the mouth that pronounces it being visible, the impalpable shocks of the words and gestures of all times and all places? It's so slight that it scarcely troubles the silence, and I can't tell whether those immaterial interlocutors are really exchanging words, or whether their language only consists of their colors, their attitudes and their multiform, infinite, chameleon evolutions.

"Ah! How regrettable it is that our excessively coarse human senses can't perceive these subtle creatures more clearly! My gaze is dazzled by these brilliant visions, and I find myself as frustrated as a body trying to see its soul with its carnal eyes. And yet, although the details of this world and its intense life escape me, like the movements of a crowd seen from afar, I can clearly distinguish a marvelous phenomenon, which is that, in the midst of that apparent confusion, absolute order reigns and harmony is triumphant.

---

[115] S.G.D.G. stands for *sans garantie du government*; it was a legal formula absolving the French State from any responsibility for the non-functionality of patented goods, used routinely from the 1840s until the 1960s.

"They reign by virtue of Newton's law, the law of universal gravitation, which commands that ideal empire as well as the material worlds: the law of attraction, the pure essence of force, powerful enough to hold the worlds in their vertiginous courses; the law of love, the law creative of all harmony, promulgated at the commencement of the ages by the word given to men and to worlds: 'Love one another.' It is by virtue of that word that the worlds are launched into space, that planets besotted with their suns have espoused its course; that suns, guiding their planetary processions, set themselves to pursue unknown stars that hide their fire in the infinity of the ether. It is in the name of that law that drops of water unite into oceans, that pollen courts flowers, that a magnet or magnetized needle maintains its incomparable fidelity to the mysterious spouse that awaits it near the pole: testimonies of obedience as magnificent as the ungraspable marriages of the atom as in the gigantic amours of planetary satellites for their suzerain suns.

"It is by virtue of this compact of love that I can see the ideas that inhabit the Sun, dissolving their activities and tendencies into a single movement from the periphery toward the center, which draws them to itself by the attraction of its light and its pure beauty. For it's at the center of the solar globe, in the heart of all those luminous inhabitants, that the supreme clarity is resplendent, compared with which the lights that surround us are merely darkness; the ideal light in the radiance of which all others pale, bowing down and twisting into fiery spirals, amorous meanders, consuming themselves like incense. That light of lights is the central fire of the Sun, the virginal idea, the uncorrupted and fecund idea—the purest thing that God has created, after the soul, to which He has donated it for a servant and a companion.

O Sun, fatherland of ideas! Their cradle and their tomb! Home port from which they sail on new missions, to which they return when their cycle is complete! O Sun, here is the greatest idea of its time, the conquest of the central terrestrial fire, returning, ahead of time, to renew itself in you! Here is one which, by a favor due to its merit and your clemency, is traversing space, borne in triumph by a portion of the Earth that it has fecundated, guided to your bosom by the men in whom it was incarnate! O Sun, welcome this world favorably; accord to this idea, to its apostles and its martyrs, a sepulcher within your light, and aureole of your radiance. Give them…"

An enormous mocking laugh—which, growing as it progressed with an influx of sonorous echoes, seemed to be the laughter of an entire crowd—interrupted Lord Hotairwell at this point. From where did that indecorous laughter come? From the base of the cone or the summit? From the Earth or the Sun? I was trying to work it out when the same voice continued:

"Flies! Files, Milord! They're flies, not ideas. Look harder, and you'll distinguish the swarm of insects that is flying around you. These poor creatures have also come to take refuge in this current of air, and the Sun is making them shine like sparks. Oh, my God! There's no shame in mistaking flies for ideas. The scientists of Earth have made similar mistakes! I can name one among them who, in warm weather like today's, harvested from the field of his telescope a flight of insects that he mistook for a rain of bolides.

Lord Hotairwell had not even honored his interrupter with a shrug of the shoulders. Perhaps he had not heard him. His strength exhausted, he had collapsed on a rock, still gazing but no longer speaking.

As for me, when, after having gathered all my strength, I had succeeded in raising my head toward the point from which the voice seemed to me to have descended, I was no only blinded the Sun but lost what little was left of my reason as I saw Dr. Samuel Penkenton standing on the summit of the precipice, looking at me and smiling.

The doctor's huge stature stood out clearly on this pedestal made to his measure, and his nudity showed off his athletic build—for Penkenton had nothing on but a short animal-pelt wrapped around his loins. Dressed, like Adam, in the wild animal skin that the first man had hastily donned in the wake

255

of his sin, he was imposing in his majesty. At the same time, one could imagine that an astronomer, on finding this giant, thus clad, standing on his spheroid, in the field of his telescope, might have taken him for an interplanetary acrobat rolling his ball through the heavens.

Samuel Penkenton was still smiling, visibly enjoying my surprise. Then, helping himself with his staff like a shepherd with his crook, he set about descending the steep path of the gulf, and when he was no more than a few steps away, he said: "Mr. Burton, I've come to ask you for the honor of a further conversation."

Chapter Ten
Samuel ב א Penkenton

The prospect of a second conversation with that man caused me such fright that I was would have hastened to flee had I not been cornered by the void. The doctor perceived that, but persisted in his design.

"Mr. Burton," he said, when he reached me, "has my costume changed me so much that you no longer recognize me? Take a good look at me, I beg you."

"I recognize you," I relied, coldly, "and I ask you what new fit of madness has led you to adopt this scarcely seemly disguise?"

"It's not a disguise," the doctor replied. "It's my true costume, which I've put on again—the costume of my parents, the goatskin that I've kept for 6000 years, waiting for the day of my death to put it on again. That fine day has arrived, and I've put on my party clothes, resuming my true personality and my name, not wanting to hide myself in order to die as I have hidden myself in order to live."

"Who are you, then?" I interrupted, dryly.

Samuel Penkenton lowered his head without answering.

"You're the Wandering Jew!" I exclaimed, enlightened by a sudden intuition.

The doctor smiled bitterly. "I knew Isaac Lak-Edem,"[116] he said. "We often ran into one another in society. Compared

---

[116] I have preserved the author's particular rendering of Isaac Laquedem, one of the many names attributed to the Wandering Jew—most famously, in 19th century French literature, by Alexandre Dumas. I have, however, substituted a C for the K he subsequently uses in citing Penkenton's true name, in conformity with common English usage. It is conceivable that the author chose the two symbols representative of Penkenton's

with me, though, Lak-Edem is only an infant; he attempted his first steps when I had been walking for 4000 years. He'll catch me up, though, for he has a long road still to travel before the end of time, and I've arrived. God has pardoned me, since he's letting me die. May you forgive me too, Mr. Burton, in the name of all those I've offended, in the name of my parents, whom I drove to despair, in the name of my brother, whom I murdered…"

The doctor's voice trembled so much on these words that it faded away without being able to complete the sentence, and he held put his hand so me, so humbly and so beseechingly, that I had to make an effort not to pres it in my own.

"Before anything else," I said, "I need to know who you are."

"You shall be satisfied," murmured the unfortunate, whose trembling lips opened and closed by turns on the passage of the confession that he wanted to make. Then, in a thunderous voice, as if to stifle his secret with sound, he cried: "I am Cain! Cain, elder son of the first man, brother of the unfortunate Abel. This staff of gopherwood[117] is the instrument of the first murder, and I am the first murderer!"

After a pause, punctuated by sobs, he added: "You must have heard mention of my crime, Mr. Burton. It was in 128, in the month of May. Abel and I had just immolated a few ewes on our altars, and my brother's smoke, more agreeable to God, climbed straight into the sky, while my smoke fell back upon me. I was suffocated, jealous, and resolved to avenge myself. The next day, when Abel went to the fields, I rose up before him, and struck him down at my feet with a solid blow from this cane."

---

initials because of their vague resemblance to an A lying on its side and a curly K.

[117] Gopherwood is mentioned once in *Genesis*, as the material from which Noah built his Ark; the reference is mysterious.

As he said this, Cain held out the time with which he had committed his crime—his staff—which I pushed away in horror; but the letters engraved n its bark attracted my attention.

"What do those symbols mean?" I asked.

"They're my initials, א ב—Cain-Adam—in Syrian, the language that we spoke in the terrestrial paradise.

"Appalled by my crime, I tried to flee, but a voice called out to me: 'What have you done to your brother?' I recognized the voice and I wanted to deny it—impossible! God had seen me. 'Cain, the Lord said to me, 'I have condemned your parents, who have sinned, to death, but you, who have killed, I condemn to live: I make you immortal, to wander over the Earth, with no name and no fatherland, *eris in terra Nad*: [118] that wooden staff the instrument of your crime, will remain attached to your side like your shadow, and in that shadow you shall march eternally. Go!' And I fled."

Cain's tall figure folded up under the weight of these memories. His dry and suntanned hands were trembling like dead leaves, and rivulets of sweat were running through the ravines of his face.

"*Eris in terra Nad!*" he repeated, with a start, as if the terrible voice had just repeated those words. "You are familiar, Mr. Burton, with the dissertations written on that word *Nad*, and you understand that the savants who have not translated it as *wandering* are mistaken, as are those who say that I was killed by my nephew Lamech—a calumny without any excuse, my relationship with Lamech having always been excellent, as with Tubal-Cain, his son, to whom I gave my name, and whom I pushed into metallurgy, in which he made his fortune, since Tubal-Cain and Vul-Cain are the same person under different names. Might I add, Mr. Burton, that that is

---

[118] I have reproduced this phrase as the author renders it, although it appears to be an awkward hybrid of Hebrew and Latin. The King James version of the relevant phrase is "a fugitive and a vagabond shalt thou be in the Earth" (*Genesis* 4:12).

said by way of rectification? The macrobiography of a man born in the ninth month of year 1, and still living today, aged 5880 years,[119] 73 times an octogenarian, would require several 1000 volumes.

"Having departed, as I just told you, I marched without pause, as if the Earth had an end and my journey a goal, seeing no living soul, since the greater part of the globe was still un-inhabited. Having returned to Armenia after 15 centuries of absence, I found myself an orphan, my father and mother having been dead for 700 years. Noah was the head of the family, which, having had only had a few members at the time of my departure, had increased by hundreds of thousands and was beginning to spread out.

"Keasair,[120] the wife of my cousin Canaan, and my niece in the British fashion, was about to leave for the north to found a colony. I went to find her, and I told her about our close kinship, and put my experience as a traveler at her disposal. I succeeded in vanquishing the scruples that my bad ancestry inspired in her, and in the month of July 1628 my niece, her husband, their 24 children, their servants, their camels and I set off for Ireland.

---

[119] If one takes Archbishop Ussher's calculation of the date of creation as definitive, it implies that this scene is taking place in the year 1876 or 1877; as this seems unlikely in terms of the story's internal chronology, one is tempted to infer instead that the passage might have been initially drafted in that year. Jules Verne's *Hector Servadac*—in which a fragment of the Earth is carried into space by a comet and the characters make careful measurements of the resultant anomalous phenomena—was initially published in book form in 1877.

[120] Queen Keasair is named in the 11th century collection of Irish legends, *Lebor Gabála Érenn* [The Book of Conquests] as the first settler of Ireland; the linkage between her and Noah's grandson, Canaan, is improvised for the purposes of the story.

"The Earth, in that era, had reached its Tertiary maturity, and almost had the face with which you're familiar. There existed seas, however, that the continents have since expelled, just as parts of continents have descended beneath the waters—but ancient geography was familiar to me, and as my niece feared the sea, I planned the route in such a way that our caravan arrived in Ireland without leaving *terra firma*.

"Along the shores of the Mediterranean, from Asia Minor to the lagoons of Gabes, we reached the Pillars of Hercules—or, rather, their future location, for Hercules had not yet separated Africa and Europe: a childish whim of the giant, who thought that by opening a strait he could empty the Mediterranean into the Ocean. From the point of view of our journey we could only be grateful that Hercules and Monsieur de Lesseps had not yet cut Africa loose, each of them at his own end, and we passed into Europe on foot, leaving Atlantis, which had just come into view, on our left.

"The journey through Spain was easy, that through France less easy. From Angers to Châlons and Clermont to Valenciennes, as can be seen on my Tertiary maps, and in the entire Paris basin, since abandoned by the waters, the country was nothing but a marsh crannied with arms of the sea and natural channels. We had to make a long detour to the east.

"The caves of Bruniquel in Tarn-et-Garonne, those of Hérault, the caves and bones of Vergisson in Saône-et-Loire, and Arcy-sur-Cure and Saint-Remy in the Meurthe, were the principal stations of our route; the broken marrow-bones, flint-knives and needles and the wooden depictions of reindeer that have been found there are merely the traces of our passage, the remains of our meals, our household objects and my nephew Canaan's carvings.

"Our final stop in France was near Abbeville, at Moulin-Quignon, where our camel-driver Eleazer died, carried off in a matter of hours by the malaria endemic in the region. In this respect, Mr. Burton, you will remember the controversy aroused by the discovery of the jaw of an antediluvian man at Moulin-Quignon by my colleague Boucher de Perthes—but

261

you cannot imagine how much these debates amused me, who knew the truth for certain: that Boucher de Perthes was right and that the jaw was as antediluvian as me. But can you believe that, when I tried to intervene and settle the question in a decisive manner, offering to reveal the name of that fossil man, his age, his profession and even the circumstances of his final illness, Boucher de Perthes himself, whom I supported, mocked me, and the entire clan of geologists, with one voice, claimed that I was mad. It was, however, quite simple, and I knew that jaw as well as I know yours, since it was that of our camel-driver Eleazer—who had died, as I have had the honor of telling you, during our passage through Moulin-Quignon."

Cain paused, then added, bitterly: "Moreover, it was the same every time I tried to give people the advantage of my exceptional experience; they took me for a madman. They did not know, and I could not say, how much of my geological knowledge was due to my childhood memories; they would have ceased to see me if they had known.

"It was via a fordable passage between Calais and Boulogne—where the present sea is still not very deep—that we arrived in England, and in Ireland some time afterwards. Our journey, accomplished with a rapidity exceptional for the period, had lasted 20 years.

"It was here, at the place where I am now speaking, that our caravan made a conclusive halt in September 1648, and that my nephew Canaan and my niece Keasair—both of whom were intelligent, learned, active and still quite young, since they had only 500 years between them—established the site of Keasair, Canaan, Cain & Co.—for I joined in. I can say that our metallurgical products lost nothing by comparison with those of my other nephew Vul-Cain, established on Etna, when the fatal year of 1656 arrived, and the catastrophe with which you are familiar."

Cain caught sight of signs of boredom in my face. "But I'll cut my story short," he said, "by passing on to the Deluge, since it's precisely that great event that was about to occur.[121]

"For 150 days, as Moses has described, in excellent terms, the cataracts of the sky were united into a single Ocean; the mountains sank, hollowing out abysses which vomited flames—for the central fire had been unleashed—and it was under the force of all these scourges, of which Ireland still bears the scars, that this part of it territory was swallowed up,

---

[121] The author adds a footnote here: "This story completes and confirms the *Précis de l'histoire d'Angleterre, d'Ecosse et d'Irlande* by Mme P. Rolland, in which it is stated that the first colony that populated Ireland arrived there a short time after the Deluge, led by Keasair, the niece of Noah and grand-niece of Cain. Four hundred years after the Deluge, Bartho-lam, a descendant of Japhet, returned to populate the land and, in the time of Jacob, other travelers of the same provenance settled here. It is not without reason that the Irish say that they are the most ancient people of Europe."

Le Précis de l'histoire d'Angleterre, d'Ecosse et d'Irlande [A Summary of the History of England, Scotland and Ireland] was a reprint of a book originally entitled *Histoire d'Angeletrre depuis les temps les plus reculés jusqu'à nos jours* [A History of England from the Remotest Times to Our Own Days] (1838), which did bear the signature "Mme. P. Rolland," although the writer—a noted pioneering femin-ist—is more usually known as Pauline Roland (1805-52). The name "Bartholam" is presumable taken from Rolland's book; it refers to the Partholón of the *Book of Conquests*, whose des-cent from the Biblical Japheth is traced therein. Another early text, usually known as the *Annals of the Four Masters*, gives the date of Partholón's arrival in Ireland, as the second colo-nizer following the extinction of Keasar's people, as 2,600 B.C—guesswork presumably based on the account of Noah's descendants given in *Genesis*.

along with its inhabitants, along with my nephew and my niece, punished thus for their generosity to me.

"It was here, Mr. Burton, that that catastrophe stole them away from my love, and it is in this cave that I found them again, on the ground where they lived, beneath the trees that I planted. Do you understand, now, why I was so emotional on the day when they appeared to me?"

The doctor tottered, and his huge body was shaken by such sobbing that he would have rolled into the abyss if I had not immediately held him back. After a brief pause, he went on:

"In the pain of losing people so dear to me, and in the rage of having survived them, I rebelled against my condemnation to life and attempted every means of suicide. I hurled myself into the mouths of volcanoes, which received me gently in their elastic lava and vomited me out without violence; I hurled myself against rocks in order to shatter my skull, but my skull shattered the rocks; in vain I struck myself with this staff, and in vain I attempted to drown myself; the sea closed its abysses to me; its waves, suddenly congealing, braced themselves beneath my like crystal cradles.

"And when the rains of heaven were leveled with the oceans; when the waters covered the entire surface of a shoreless sphere, from one pole to the other, there were only two black floating dots to be seen. One was me: the huge figure of Cain, swimming in spite of himself, tossed about by the waves like an erratic rock, so hard and so high that the waves that displaced it could neither shatter nor swallow it. The other was the Ark of my relative Noah! How many times, during that 50 days, I saw it pass by without daring to hail it, because I was accursed! It bore forgiveness, hope, the future. The breath of God inflated its sail, the waves calmed before its hull, and the patriarch, manning the helm, lifted his eyes to the zenith to follow the rainbow that displayed its dawn and pointed its curvature toward Mount Ararat.

"What do you say now, Mr. Burton? I have seen humankind born and grow old, following my vagabond course at hazard, but always returning to the charming shores of the Mediterranean. That sea is, for me, the lake in Hyde Park on whose bank the stroller pauses and watches children launch their flotillas. Thus I toured the Mediterranean. Having nothing to do, having centuries to waste, I watched the games and combats of those infant peoples; I tried to interest myself in their revolutions, which they thought very terrible, and in their migrations, which they judged very distant as they ran around the world from Pont-Euxin to the pillars of Hercules. Greeks, Tyrians, Carthaginians, Romans, troupes of nomadic actors, paraded before me in the costumes and scenery of the times: a varied spectacle, so mobile that men and things sometimes renewed themselves before I had completed a tour of the lake; I found different combatants on the waves, new colonies on the shores.

"While always keeping myself apart, I sought to make myself useful. How many services, of which they are unaware, all those people owed to my attentive benevolence! How many times I used my staff to refloat their little ships, whose crews, without saying thank you, raised their sails and set out to sea, less afraid of shipwreck than their savior!

"The Trojan War, the time of the fine prowess of adolescent humanity, was one of the best of my life, and the spectacle that attracted my keenest interest. In that year—1270—I was traveling in Eubea, which you now call Negroponte, and stopped one evening on the edge of the Aegean Sea, where, a few years earlier, I had watched the Argonauts' ship disappear into the passes of Propontis. With Delphi at my back, my gaze was savoring those joyful shores and winds, which a silky Oriental fog was enveloping for the night, when a furious clamor, something like the oath of an entire people, made me turn my head toward Greece.

"Menelaus led the racket, in which Mycenae and the neighboring nations soon joined, with the result that, momentarily, there was a general croaking throughout the Peloponnessus of all those petty tribes and their kinglets. Paris, sent by Priam to collect his aunt Hesione, abducted by Hercules, had

265

abducted Helen, and Greece was an amorous chevalier, arming to avenge his lady.

"My nephew Vul-Cain, a friend of the Greeks, was naturally favored by their orders for the furnishing of the weapons the war required, and his forges on Olympus and their subsidiary branches in Lipara, Etna and Lemnos saw an enormous increase in activity.

Suffering from an innate lameness aggravated by a fall, and poorly supported by his wife, Venus, who was solely preoccupied with her beauty and spent the greater part of the year in Paphos, my nephew appealed to his old uncle for help. My experience in metallurgy, my strength and my stature gave me the necessary authority to supervise the cyclops. I took charge of the Etna workshops and his took an active part in the manufacture of Achilles' armor, Agamemon's scepter and many other masterpieces of sculpture, due to the hammers of my best workers: Pyracmon, Acamas and Steropes, eminent cyclops whose names history did well to conserve.

"When these jobs were done and the deliveries had been made, I hastened to quite the furnace and went to sit down at Chalcis, on the bank of the Euripe, facing Aulis, where the Greek fleet was assembled. I watched its departure, and I can still see that magnificent spectacle: the Greek phalanges crowning the summits of Attica all morning, from the forests of Oeta to Laurium, and descending the slopes like rapid torrents. Some of them come from the fertile plains of Orchomenus, from tempestuous Oenispus, Stymphalus, where Alpheus drank; from the highlands of Cyllene, where intrepid men were born. Others leave Sparta and Helos; Menelaus, burdened with responsibility, commands them. I see him crossing the narrow isthmus of Corinth; his soldiers follow him like a furious flock, pressing so close that several of them fall into the water, but they hasten to drink the bitter waves, swim to the shore and resume their places in the ranks.

"Then other warriors arrive: the Acadians, a people of ancient nobility, older than the Moon, who had emerged from the earth like the cicada, their emblem. The Ionians with beardless faces and bodies of marble, surge like living statues from the quarries of Pentelicus, whose paths they descend; they are clad in linen armor, brightly multicolored, and the bees of Hymettus crowd the thresholds of their hives, thinking they see a host of flowers. The Boeotians arrive last, even though they are the nearest neighbors of Aulis; Peneleus and Prothenor, their leaders, are spurring on their heavy soldiers, but their aqueous, enormous bodies are stumbling on the slope, collapsing like rocks, piling up on the shore and rolling as far as the ships, which are broken by their impact—a people whose understanding is obscured by fogs, and which nevertheless produced Hesiod, Pindar, Corinna, Epaminondas and Plutarch.

"Agamemnon, the herdsman of tribes, hurries to the shore, welcomes these human flocks, marks them, counts them and drives them with great thrusts of his scepter into the hulls, which are bloated by the weight of so many warriors—for the ships are there, waiting, chained up with their sails folded down below; there are 1,175 of them—I was the one who gave that figure to Homer.

"The fleet having set sail, I let it get a few years start. Then, leaping from rock to rock and cyclad to cyclad, skimming the water over the sunken mountains that once joined Asia Minor to Eubea, I passed into Asia and arrived outside Troy just as Ulysses was completing the construction of his horse. I volunteered to take my place within the body of that animal, where Menelaus, always in the front rank but much changed by ten years of troubles, had already placed himself. With my legs inserted into the front legs of the horse, my feet in its hooves and my eyes in its orbits, I formed the advance-guard of the citadel, while Ulysses, established in the hind-quarters, watched through the embrasure, and kept an eye on the troops camped in the flanks.

"You know what happened next. The Greeks took Troy. Personally, I took the horse, and added it to my collection. I had a liking for ancient things, already dear to that epoch, all the more rare because the world was younger, and I anticipated the value that the object would one day acquire, like so many others even more ancient, which I was obliged to remove from my display-cases as they turned to dust.

"When the siege of Troy was over, I just had time to run to the Mediterranean, where other spectacles attracted me— but humankind, having reached a mature age, no longer fought over a woman. By this time, mercantile peoples—the Phoenicians, the Tyrians, the Carthaginians, occupy the world stage. The Romans, tragic actors, come on in their turn and stay there for some time. The scenery darkens, the costumes are bloodstained. War is no longer a heroic mêlée, in which insults and lumps of rock are exchanged between men and gods, swords ring on sonorous breastplates and warriors receive mortal wounds, releasing rivers of blood, and then retire peacefully to their tents at the end of the day. The new wars are implacable. People fight for possession; they strike to kill; they die for real, often devoid of glory, poetry and celebration in song— for there are no Homers for such battles.

"So I continued along my interminable road, marching without progressing, growing old without dying, working to forget and derisively choosing—me, the eldest son of the family—the most trivial and brutal tasks, to which my strength and my size render me appropriate: toiler, laborer, fairground giant, studio model. I posed for Chares for the Colossus of Rhodes, which I set in place when it was finished. In ancient Egypt, no one dared move an obelisk without summoning me, and I often lent my arms to God. I have been, obligingly, Goliath, Samson, Gabbara and Teutobochus:[122] coarse labors,

---

[122] Gabbara is the name of one of Rabelais' giants, credited with being the founder of the tradition of drinking toasts. Teutobochus was a legendary king alleged to have flourished in Europe in the second century B.C. The latter enjoyed a second bout of fame in France when some bones said to be those of a 30-foot-tall human giant, exhumed from a quarry in Dauphiné in 1613 and exhibited widely thereafter, were claimed as his,

after which they said I was dead because they recovered my empty garments. It wasn't true alas! I had merely changed clothes.

"The prohibition of death exasperated me more than anything else, and unfortunately drove me to several revolts—in the second century of this era, for example, when I instituted Cainism and proclaimed myself a god of evil, matching one altar with another.[123] My dogmas, borrowed by the cosmogonies of Persia, reinforced the Gnosticism of Chaldea and the ophism necessary to complete the syncretism opposed to the

---

prompting Jean Tissot to write a "biography" explaining how Teutobochus had met his death on that particular spot.

[123] The author inserts a footnote here: "The sect of Cainism did, indeed, appear in the time of Tertullian, proclaiming the existence of an all-powerful principle of evil, considering Cain as the issue of that principal, and superior to Abel, representing good. One branch of the sect took the name of Quintillia, its founder. The Abelians, who followed, extolled the superiority of Abel and assumed a duty to die, like him, without posterity: inoffensive nihilists limiting their destruction to abstinence from creation." Tertullian (160-c.220 A.D.) was one of the earliest Christian polemicists, who railed against various heresies, especially Gnosticism. He does mention a Quintilia, but only as arguing that salvation can be achieved by faith alone, without good works; the Quintillia cited by Cain and the author is fictitious, as are his sects of "Cainism" and Abelism," although the term "Cainism" has flourished since *Ignis* was published, not only being adopted by biologists as a label for sibling murder among birds but also being adopted by a few lifestyle fantasists of a neo-Satanist stripe. The idea of a principle of evil locked in an eternal struggle with a good God is much older—the "Persian cosmologies" to which the author refers include that of the Zoroastrian Magi—and did not become the basis of the Christian Manichaean heresy until after Tertullian was dead (Mani was crucified in 276 A.D.).

knowledge of the faith: the Bible was no more than a series of parables, my crime merely an allegory, and I ceased to be a real murderer.

"My religion, having all the vices for a base, naturally gathered many initiates. My altar was besieged, my temple overflowing with adherents so fervent that I was unable to fulfill their desires. There were malcontents; women, always excited, got involved. Quintillia, one of my serving-girls, wanted to be a priestess. That didn't suit me; she took her leave of me and created the sect of Quintillianists, and heresy made its appearance within my cult.

"The impiety of a few old Gnostics had already roused the Abelians—who worshipped my brothers and practiced virtue—against me. That was an awkward revival of an old quarrel between Abel and me, which transformed a personal quarrel into a theological dispute. The war was so heated and the battle so confused, that in all the tohu-bohu,[124] neither gods nor worshippers were any longer able to distinguish good from evil. The expression *cahin-caha* (as much good as evil), arose from that mess, and is nothing but my name, Cahin, coupled with that of one of my priestesses, Caha.[125]

"Overwhelmed by ennui, unable to do all the evil that I would have wished, the butt of all reproaches and no longer daring to go out of my temple, having God against me and the Devil—jealous of a rival of my strength—even more so, I fled, swearing that no one would ever find me again.

"If you want more detailed information about my sect, Mr. Burton, you will find them in my *Memoirs*, which remain

---

[124] The author inserts a footnote: "There is no surprise in finding these words of pure Hebrew in Cain's mouth; *tohu-bohu*, or *thohou-bohou*, signifies *chaos*."

[125] The author notes: "One observes how mistaken those frivolous etymologists are who claim that *cahin-cha* is derived from the Latin *qua hic, qua hac*." The French use *cahin-caha* much as the English might use "so-so" or "muddling along;" it is, of course, the author who is indulging in frivolity here.

on Earth and which the executors of my will have instructions, in the improbable event of my death, following the example of Talleyrand, not to publish until the era when they are no longer of any interest to anyone. I've deposited them in the Bank of England, enclosed in 77 lead-lined boxes. They've given me a great deal of work in the last few centuries, for, having begun them at a young age and continued them, in conformity with the progress and transformation of languages and writing, the first chapters were engraved on the antlers of reindeer and aurochs in ideographic characters, and the following ones on stone and clay tablets, in phonetic Akkadian; others were written on fish-skins, on sheets of lead and on papyrus, in Egyptian stenography; the most recent in English, on Bristol paper. My editor would never have been able to publish them if I had not courageously dedicated myself, for 200 years, to reproduce them in modern script. Those 77 boxes contain 7777 folio notebooks, entirely in fair copy."

I sketched a fearful gesture.

"Chapter 7 of my *Memoirs* will give you the explanation to the quantity of sevens that surprises you, and will also tell you why the number 7 has the form of an axe and a key. It's entitled *Heptaism; or, the Influence of the Number 7*. It's one of the most curious. Perhaps you'd like to hear a few excerpts."

As he said this, Cain took a manuscript from his loincloth—but my face must have been so beseeching, or so terrible, that he did not insist.

"Don't think, though, Mr. Burton," he went on, changing the subject, "that by reason of my misanthropy I've lived as a savage, a stranger to ongoing events. No, I've been acquainted with all the important men of ancient history, welcomed by them with antique urbanity, but excluded from the intimacy of their families by an instinctive suspicion of the curse that weighed upon me.

"It's in contemporary society that I've penetrated furthest. Welcome there is banal, and hospitality open to all the winds; one doesn't find it comfortable, but one gets in easily.

271

My reputation as a geologist opened the doors of all scientists to me, and I've often laughed at what I heard. I knew them all. I was close to Cuvier, and gave him notes from which he was able to take a great deal, but I could do nothing with Buffon.

"I still have relatives who bear my name, with variations in spelling excusable for a word submitted to the proof of so many alphabets and idioms: the Cains, Kanes, Cohens and so on—most of them in industry, in which our family excels. I don't see them; I've stained the name, and no one likes to re-member that he has a murderer for an ancestor.

"It's also to my status as a geologist that I owe my intro-duction to the Central Fire Company, which immediately in-spired me with the hope of finding death. So I devoted myself to its project, and I think, Mr. Burton, that you will give just recognition to my contribution."

"Yes, Dr. Penkenton," I replied, not yet daring, out of kindness, to call him Cain, "but your contribution concluded with a fit of madness that has cost us dear."

"I have never been mad for a moment," Cain replied.

"I regret that, on your behalf, that being your sole excuse."

"No, I'm not mad, and never have been; I've acted with discernment and premeditation, convinced of being agreeable to God in destroying you. I glimpsed this means of obtaining forgiveness and I marched straight toward it, trampling under-foot the puerile scruples that might have stopped men of your time. And yet, in memory of our past relationship, I would have preferred not to be your executioner myself, and to have left that role to the Atmophytes. To that end, I fomented and organized their revolt; I directed their efforts as best I could...."

"You fomented the revolt of the Atmophytes!" I inter-rupted violently.

"Yes, for, as I've had the honor of telling you, I desired, out of a sense of propriety, not to steep my hands in your blood—but those brutes, having begun their riot so well, lost time breaking down your doors. You cut off their power-source, and I was constrained to enter the line with my reserves. I must, however, give due credit for the remarkable explosive results that I obtained to the engineers, Mr. Hatchitt and Mr. Archibold."

"What!" Archibold put in, his attention having been alerted a few moments before. "Are you claiming me as your accomplice?"

"God forbid, Mr. Archibold," Cain replied. "I am quite determined not to share the merit of my action with anyone; I only mean that, in order to blow up part of the Earth, I utilized the means that you and William Hatchitt had already suggested for its destruction."

"Would it be indiscreet, Mr. Cain, to ask you how you put it into action?"

"Oh, not at all—there's no further need for secrecy. Seeing that the revolt of the Atmophytes might not achieve the end that I had in mind on its own, I had recourse to the latter means."

"Ah!" said Archibold, becoming interested.

"I opened the floodgates of the lake, and I poured a river into the well."

"A mediocre means," said Archibold. "I know about that—let's pass on."

"This river, considerable in volume, gave rise to a gigantic quantity of steam in that enormous furnace."

"Pooh!" Archibold interrupted, his curiosity blunted. "A few 1000 atmospheres! Insufficient to expel us from the Earth's orbit.

"That river," said Cain, "was not a river like any other."

"Ah!" said the engineer.

"It was a prepared river."

"A prepared river?" said Archibold, becoming interested again.

"An explosive river," Cain continued, "since it emerged from a lake in which I had sunk my two ships. Did you see my ships sink?"

"Yes, I saw them sink," I said, "but what does it matter?"

"It matters, Mr. Burton, because, in falling into the lake, the contents of my ships were mingled with it."

"And what was contained in your ships?"

"10,000 tones of nitroglycerine. The result of which was that the river emerging from the lake drew that vast quantity of extremely explosive substance into its waters."

"Wretch!" I cried.

"Calm down for a moment," Archibold said to me, "and let me put a few figures down." The engineer had reopened his notebook at the page already covered by his calculations, and his face lit up in satisfaction as his pencil designed algebraic hieroglyphs.

"Thank you, Mr. Cain," he said, on seeing the result. "It will take time to manipulate all these figures, but, thanks to your information, I can see some hope of explaining our catastrophe and perishing in accordance with the scientific data. So thank you, sir."

Bowing once again to take his leave, Archibold skillfully avoided the hand that Cain held out to him.

"What about you?" the latter said, turning to me. "Will you also refuse me your hand? Do you bear me a grudge for having sacrificed the little time that you had to live, in order to out an end to my own interminable life?"

As he said that, Penkenton was still holding out his hand. Exasperated by such cynicism, however, and unable to control myself, I pushed it away violently.

A cry of fury, followed by a hail of curses and insults, replied to this brutal action, whose consequences I had certainly not calculated.

Chapter Eleven
In which Mr. Burton, already so sorely tried, is subject to further trials, burns his calves, gets drenched, and finds himself back in the bosom of his family.

The giant body of Cain Penkenton, reduced by the baking heat, as dry and light as lint, had weighed no more than an ounce in my hand—which, in pushing his own away, had precipitated him into the abyss.

The unfortunate howled as he rolled down into the gulf, which was taking him to Earth by the most direct route; his hands were scrabbling at the slope, searching for a fissure where his long bony fingers might take hold, or asperities whose points might stick into his flesh and halt his fall. Vain efforts! The crumbling stones were giving way beneath his feet, collapsing on his head, piling up around him the moving materials of his sepulcher. He disappeared into that funereal apotheosis, and from the bosom of that chaotic debris, in which his skull, as white as the rocks, was rolling pell-mell with them, his convulsive head addressed blasphemies and threats to me. He would have thrown stones at me if he could, like a dead man picking a quarrel with his gravedigger, hurling back at him the spadefuls of earth that he receives.

I was still standing on the edge, stupid and bewildered, shocked by my action, gripped in the heart and the throat by regret for my brutality, and remorse at having sent back to Earth, and perhaps to life, the unfortunate who made such a song and dance about dying.

The noise of the fall, Cain's cries, my groans and my desperate pantomime drew Archibold from his calculations momentarily, and Lord Hotairwell from his thoughts. The latter darted a vague glance toward the abyss, sketching a gesture that signified *What does it matter?* and returned to his meditations. Forgetting my anguish for a moment, I paused to look at him.

He was still half-extended on the rock on to which fatigue had thrown him, but his ecstasy had continued more intensely, his vision more lucidly. His gaze was fixed on mirages that had deceived him a short while before and were still deceiving him: that of the transitory sun, the immaculate light, creative and uncreated, a star without stain or shadow, without dusk or dawn, from which emanated the life of worlds, which dispensed bread to human beings and radiance to the stars. Marveling like one of the elect who, on the threshold of a celestial portico, glimpses the eternal verities and the seraphic sensualities, his face was more radiant and his contemplation more avid—and his lips were murmuring, more fervently, Goethe's prayer: "More light, O Lord, more light!"

It was a sublime spectacle: that dying man, consumed, diaphanous, as immaterial as the thought that strove to survive him, and who, on the brink of corporeal extinction, illuminated himself one last time with the most beautiful fires of the sunset! Like a traveler adapting his farewells to the duration of his absence, the soul of that phantom hesitated to flee and extinguish him, revisiting the dwelling in which it had suffered, worked and loved, in order to assure itself one last time, by a final check, that it had not left behind anything immortal, anything of itself, in the husk that was about to perish.

As for Archibold, being somewhat reconciled with Cain by the information given *in extremis*, which gave him hope of establishing, on a sound mathematical basis, the reality of the catastrophe, he had followed his fall with more interest.

"I regret," he said, generously, "that Cain has fallen into that hole before I thought of asking him whether it is true that his father Adam was 123 feet tall, and his mother 118, as Henrion of the Académie Française affirms."[126] Then, after having

---

[126] Abbé Nicolas Henrion (1663-1720) was scholar of Middle Eastern languages and a noted pioneer of numismatics, but his actual achievements were far overshadowed by this allegation, made in a paper read to the Académie des Inscriptions et Belles-Lettres in 1718. He had planned to write a book in sup-

studied the avalanche into the midst of which Cain had disappeared, he added: "But perhaps we have some hope of seeing him again, for Penkenton's accident can be envisaged as having several possible outcomes."

"Really!" I cried, joyfully, as hope was renewed. "List the possibilities, for I can only see one, implacable and irremediable."

"Yes," said the engineer. "Penkenton's fall presents three possibilities. Firstly, Penkenton might fall back to Earth; secondly, Penkenton won't fall back at all; and thirdly, Penkenton will reach an intermediate destination."

Firmly established on the tripod of these three premises, Archibold began his reasoning: "Penkenton will fall to Earth, as will we, if the terrestrial gravitational attraction extending towards us vanquishes the terrifugal force that is bearing us away. We can be certain that it is making every effort to do so, to which I add all my prayers.

"If terrestrial gravitational attraction is not the stronger, and if we escape from its sphere of influence, Penkenton will not fall back, any more than we will; we shall remain together, and he will settle for the voyage to the far side of our asteroid on which he is presently embarked.

"However, if the personal velocity acquired by Penkenton during this voyage becomes sufficient to extract him from the gravitational field of our little globe, he will be separated from us—but the third possible outcome is divided into two subsidiary possibilities.

"Firstly, if he is projected away from this spheroid by the force that he is storing up during his fall, Penkenton, benefiting from the initial impulsion that is common to us, might continue to follow us, provided that his density is similar to ours.

---

port of the claim that human stature had progressively diminished over time, but his estimates of the relative heights of various characters in *Genesis* attracted so much ridicule that he abandoned the project.

"Secondly, if his density is lower, Penkenton might stop before us, like a feather which, launched at the same time and with the same force as a bullet, will neither travel as fast nor as far. We would, in that case, have the regret of losing Penkenton, of leaving him in space, utterly isolated, unable to move, in spite of any efforts he might make to swim, forming his own planet and its inhabitant, until the end of his life—which, it appears, is not bound to end.

"Everything depends on Penkenton's specific gravity; his fate is in his own hands, and it is futile to occupy ourselves with it any longer. In any case, I feel ill, probably on the point of death. Will you therefore permit me, Mr. Burton, to cut this conversation short. Will you also accept, and accept on behalf of the Central Fire Company, my deepest apologies for dying in the difficult circumstances through which it is going, and my profoundest regrets for not having been able, before me death, to confirm the reality of our explosion—for, all things considered, I must have made a mistake. It's evident that our asteroid required 1,436 quatrillion calories for a journey of a mere ten kilometers, and, given that nitroglycerine only produces 16.25 billion per tonne, Cain's 10,000 tonnes only provide 162.5 quatrillions—which is to say, only 2.5 thousandths of the necessary force—and that, in consequence…"

"In consequence?" I asked, avidly.

"We haven't departed."

"Then where are we?" I asked, breathlessly.

"That I don't know," the engineer replied. "Or, rather, I don't know whether I know—for to say that I don't know where we are would be to admit that we're somewhere! Now, are we somewhere, or are we nowhere? I daren't make a judgment…which is embarrassing…very embarrassing. You see, Mr. Burton, what appears to me most true about all this is that it's all false…and yet, if it's all false, what I say can't be true! For, if nothing is true, then there is something true, which is that everything is false…which can't be true, since nothing is. No, it can't be true that it's true that it's all false. But then, it must be true that it isn't true that it must be true that nothing is true, mustn't it? Do you dare to contend that, Mr. Burton? Personally, I don't; and I say quite simply that I don't know whether it's true that it's not true that it's true that it's all false...or more simply, that I don't know whether I don't know whether I don't know...but then, what do I know?"

I listened in bewilderment to this series of irrationalities, indicative of a complete disturbance of the faculties of the engineer—who, having glimpsed my anguished expression, interrupted his psychological equations to say: "You seem discontented, Mr. Burton; is it my dialectic that confuses you? Have I said something obscure? Don't you know that the greatest philosophers reason no differently, nor any better? Pyrrho, Aenisidemus, Montaigne, Schulze,[127] the masters of

---

[127] Pyrrho (c.360-270 B.C.) is reputed to be the first great skeptic, who allegedly contended that, as it was impossible to know anything for certain (he employed an argument against induction similar to the one developed in modern times by David Hume), the only intellectually-respectable attitude was one of *acatalepsia* (indecision) coupled with *ataraxia* (not worrying about it). In the first century A.D. this doctrine was adopted by Aenisidemus as the foundation of a school of Pyrrhonism; its followers included Sextus Empricus, whose *Outline of Pyrrhonism* is the definitive account of the philosophy. Aenisidemus attacked deduction as well as induction, producing a famous tract *Against the Mathematicians*—the eleven-part text wrongly credited by *Ignis*' author to Sextus Empiricus. After the Renaissance, skepticism was revived, albeit in a milder form, by Michel de Montaigne (1533-1592), who made the catch-phrase "Que sais-je?" [What do I know?] famous, thus laying the foundation for later skeptics like Hume and providing the starting-point for René Descartes' *Meditations*. In Germany, the philosophy of knowledge contained in Kant's *Critique of Pure Reason* and supported by Karl Reinhold was attacked by Gottlob Ernst Schulze (1761-1833), who presented his arguments in the form of a classical dialogue en-

skepticism, say nothing different; and I feel that if mathematics had not distracted me from philosophy, I would have equaled them. If you don't believed me, read Pyrrho; he didn't write anything, but Sextus Empiricus wrote for him; read his *Hypoptopes* and his eleven books *Against Mathematics*, which I have refuted in the course of my life. Study that, Mr. Burton, and bring me news of those great skeptics."

The engineer was getting drunk on words. "You're striking a suspicious attitude," he continued. Are you an antiskeptic? Is so, say so! Declare yourself! Enter the arena, gird your loins, oil your torso, fight hand-to-hand with those athletes, brain-to-brain with those psychologists. Ah, that would be a fine bout, and would make some noise in the worlds. On one side, the army of philosophers commanded by Pyrrho; on the other, Edward Burton, former businessman, alone and naked on his asteroid, like Milo on his disk! [128] Burton, director of the Central Fire, in flight, a vagabond of space! A man without a world! A citizen without a country! A lunatic without a padded cell! Ha ha ha!"

And the engineer burst out laughing, with the vigor of a man who, for the 60 years he has been in the world, has been holding himself in, in order to remain serious.

These rambling were so painful to hear that I resolved to cut them short, and spoke in an authoritative tone. "Mr. Archibold," I said, "leave this excessively intellectual discussion there; an excess of science dazzles as an excess of light blinds, and a blind man can no longer distinguish night from day, nor error from the truth."

When I had finished, Archibold looked at me with so much pity and scorn that, thinking that I had said something

---

titled *Aenisidemus* (1792), in which the earlier Pyrrhonist takes the leading part.

[128] This appears to be a compound reference, placing the famous Greek wrestler Milo of Croton on a wheel similar to the one on which the Greek king Ixion was sent spinning through the Heavens by the gods.

stupid, I consequently adopted a similar expression of scorn and pity. That concession did not disarm the engineer, however.

"Mr. Burton!" he cried. "You talk like Sancho Panza, whose appearance you have, and your naïve statements are worthy of being screeched from Prudhomme's cradle. Learn, for your guidance, that neither truth nor error exists, but only divergent points of view; neither light nor darkness, but only different suns: the white Sun that we call day, the black Sun that we call night; stars that are equivalent in value, for I do not know that the black Sun is inferior to the white, the blue to the red, or that nature has instituted any hierarchy of precedence for the colors. Prove the contrary if you can

"You have nothing to say! Thus, these stars are equal; they co-exist like the Frères Lyonnet[129] or Siamese twins, united with one another like the two sides of a medal. Have you ever seen a medal without a reverse side, or a reverse side without a medal? No, for the front implies the back, being implies non-being, the negation of this is the affirmation of that; and existence proves nothing, with the reservation that if nothing exists, it doesn't exist, since, if it existed, it would no longer be nothing…it's as clear as day—or night, as you wish.

"This law of contrasts is incontrovertible; nothing exists outside itself; one cannot, without it, see anything or hear anything, since to see an object is to distinguish it from that which surrounds it; to hear a sound is to distinguish it from another; to perceive silence is to distinguish it from a sound. Always hearing a sound is equivalent to hearing nothing, and have no doubt, Mr. Burton, that if someone sounded a trumpet in your ears all day, you'd end up believing that a profound silence reigned therein.

"Abandon your sophisms, therefore; open your eyes to the light and, seeing that a white Sun exists, conclude that there is a black Sun and bow down with me; let us salute the

---

[129] The Frères Lyonnet were identical twins who made their living in the Parisian theatrical world.

dark star, the shadow-light, queen of space and of suns, which she freezes and embraces in her eternal mourning! 'And one sees it in the utmost depths, when the eye dares to descend there,/Beyond life and breath and sound,/The enormous black Sun that radiates the night.'"[130]

Archibold declaimed these words emphatically, and continued: "Incomparable star! Greater than infinity, since the universe is includes in its poles, and creation entire is nothing but a black sphere flecked with planets and stars, an ebony globe encrusted with rubies. A marvelous spectacle, but offered to few gazes, for in order to contemplate it, one needs to get out of it. Perhaps we'll succeed in doing so, if the impulsion that is propelling us aliments our course sufficiently. Our destiny, already so fine, would then become unparalleled. Can you see us, Mr. Burton, stripped of our being, liberated from the materiality, weight, attraction and gravitation that bow creatures down over the fields of planets—sitting in the void, gazing at the night, seeing creation from its far side, truth from error. Are we already there? I could believe so, given that I feel such physical lightness, and a lucidity of intelligence that you must find striking."

"I think you're completely mad," I said, this time without hesitation.

"Do you think so?" the engineer retorted, having become very pale. "Personally, I don't know anything about it—no, in truth, I don't know, I don't know anything."

"Is that your final word, then?" I said to him.

"Yes!" he replied. "It's the final word of science."

In saying these words, his voice became calm and grave; he murmured them like a sigh, and when, seeing him totter, I seized him with my hand to support him, I clasped the hand of a cadaver. James Archibold no longer existed.

Such powerful characters have no weakness in life, no agony before death—no crepuscular transition for them; they

---

[130] The author inserts a reference for this quotation from Victor Hugo's *Contemplations*.

either are or are not. Archibold, the eve of his life having arrived, his day being done, had at down in order to die comfortably and correctly, without fatigue as without apathy, his head and upper body set against the rock with his hands resting on his thighs, in order to prop up the body and bear the burden of age without flinching, in the exact attitude of the colossi of Luxor, guardians sculpted in stone, which have been on watch for 30 centuries on the threshold of the desert of the Pharaohs.

A comparison, perhaps lacking in propriety, came to mind just then; I remembered having heard the illustrious engineer compared to a steam-engine that could only be, while it existed, all-powerful or utterly inert: the ideal model of the Atmophyes that he had created. Such had been James Archibold, chief engineer of the Central Fire Company; so he passed, without transition, and without any other declaration than a brief philosophical delirium, from full pressure to total inertia. The organs of the machine had stopped dead at the point of death.

Lord Hotairwell and Archibold were no more. Penkenton had disappeared.

"What about me?" I cried, gripped by fear and despair on finding myself left alone, a Robinson Crusoe of the ether, on that islet. "What about me, O Death? Am I not to die? Have I not deserved you? Look at my body, blackened by the solar flame, my cracked hands, my fingers peeling like overly dry cigars! O Death! Close my eyes to that light, which is devouring them, whose ardent fire is mirrored in my brain. I should have perished like my companions; why this delay? Why cause my husk, which is falling into ruin, to survive? My body is worn out; like everyone else, I have a right to get out of it, or at least to exchange it.

"Great God! I think I have it—everything is explained. My crime! Murderer of Cain! Murderer of the murderer! His blood is rising against me. God said that the man who harmed Cain would be punished twice seven times; Cain has demanded his twice seven vengeances against me, and this is the first, so terrible…what will the others be, my Lord?

"Yes, he's contrived that I shall succeed him in his eternal life, that I shall take the consequence of his punishment. That's it, I feel it; I feel his goatskin, which is draping itself about my skeleton, his staff, which is taking my hand. I am Cain, murderer of Cain and Abel, charged with two bloody crimes, twice immortal and twice accursed! He's laughing, the true Cain—I can hear him. I can hear him grinding out his laughter with his enormous jaws; he's laughing because his goatskin is too big for me, his staff too heavy…

"He finds me ridiculous, and he's right, for he at least had a body. Job, the poorest of men, was a property-owner, he had a dung-heap…but as for me, I must live in a fragmented cadaver, on a fragmented earth, and suffer what I'm suffering…"

At that moment, I felt an impression of heat so painful that I uttered a terrible scream…

My valet, Joe, came running in response to that noise; my son Edward, my daughters Mary-Ann, Kitty, Jane and Arabella, and my wife Mrs. Burton, arrive in their turn, precipitately opening my study door, uttering similar exclamations in unison, closing the door again and disappearing, only to come back with lightning speed, armed with pails, buckets, little pumps and all the other apparatus appropriate to extinguish a domestic fire. Under the enlightened direction of Mr. Hatchitt the engineer—who, in spite of the great attention that he is giving to the Channel Tunnel, has come back to the surface to spend Sunday with me—they pour the contents of all these vessels over me…which completes my awakening.

They were just in time, for, without the Sun having anything to do with it, I was about to perish by fire. Already, my burning slippers were charring my feet, spreading the double reek of our juxtaposed hides, and my legs were beginning to redden along with my trousers.

The Sun, the Central Fire, Lord Hotairwell and the engineer James Archibold had, I repeat, nothing to do with the disaster; they were merely phantoms of a nightmare which might have taken hold on anyone, like me, with a little imagination who went to sleep too close to the fire and too soon after dinner, leaving his brain at odds with his stomach.

My burns healed, but the dream is so firmly encrusted in my mind that it is confused there with the truth, and there are days when, no longer distinguishing between them, I take quite seriously the existence of the Central Fire Company, the duties of managing director that I fulfilled within it, and the final catastrophe that bore me away into space.

"The story is not even plausible," one of my friends told me, after I had told it to him. "All the characters are mad!"

"That's exactly what leads me to believe that it's true," I replied, with the common sense of my better days.

Another painful consequence of the dream is the involuntary mistrust inspired in me since that time by my old comrade, Professor Samuel Penkenton. I suspect him, in spite of myself, of having really been one of the fomenters of that drama, and I confess to having been tempted on several occasions to carry out the experiment of calling out *Cain!* unexpectedly, while looking him full in the face. Penkenton did not appear to understand, but he has let me know—indirectly, by means of one of our common acquaintances—that he considers that I have fallen prey to mental illness...

When Chatterton, having been introduced to the Lord Mayor, received from him the advice to abandon the miserable profession of poetry, sterile for him, his fellow citizens and his fatherland, he replied:

"The poet has his task; he seeks among the stars the route that the Lord's finger is pointing out to us."

And we, without raising to the stars contemplations that are only offered to genius, have tried to glimpse, in a dream, among the Lord's aims, a new route for the ship, a new conquest for humankind—but the activity of the century has rendered this role of harbinger difficult. The science of our day has the gaze and wingspan of an eagle; it contemplates spaces without vertigo and crosses them with a wing-beat; it outstrips its prophets, and often, the poet, still asleep, wakes up to the sound of his dream already realized.

Who knows whether, while my pen is tracing an imaginary route into the geological abysses, the pick and the sound, directed toward the same end, are not already trepanning some part of the world's ancient skeleton in order to extract new marrow therefrom?—not, any longer, to steal the fire of Heaven, like Prometheus, but to subjugate the fire of the Earth and capture it in its Plutonian lair.

I think that the future will see that great enterprise realized, that men will conquer that magnificent patrimony, and that the generations that follow ours, chillier in advancing into their 100-times-centenary old age, will come, led by science, to warm themselves by sitting down around that great hearth—unless the Earth's central fire is, itself, only a dream of scientists and poets. *That is the question!*

THE END

Afterword

Ignis has become established as an important work of French proto-science fiction primarily because of its description of the Atmophytes and their revolt, which anticipates the subsequent importance in 20th century science fiction of "robots," and the ambivalent attitudes to them manifest in the genre. Indeed the Atmophytes bear a much closer resemblance to the mechanical robots of American science fiction than they do to the artificial humans featured in the work that coined the term, Karel Capek's *R.U.R.* (1922). It is also the presence of mechanical humans that allies *Ignis* thematically with Villiers de l'Isle-Adam's *L'Eve future*, encouraging the coupling of the two works in Alfred Jarry's brief essay on *romans scientifiques*.

In fact, the idea of "steam men" had been around for some time before the publication of *Ignis*, whose author might well have been aware of the attempt by an American inventor, Zadoc P. Dederick of Newark, New Jersey, to build an actual "steam man," which came close enough to success for a prototype model to take a few steps in 1868—prompting, among other reactions, the production of Edward S. Ellis's dime novel *The Steam Man of the Prairies* (1868). The idea of channeling geothermal power was not new either, although actual projects tended to be much less ambitious than the one planned by the Central Fire Company. The notion of the potential source of such power contained in the story was colored by cosmological theories popularized in France by Pierre Laplace, and supported by Camille Flammarion's early exercises in the popularization of astronomy (of which the author of *Ignis* seems to have been vaguely aware), but was presented in the novel in a fashion that even contemporary readers might have thought excessively flamboyant.

The existence of these precedents does not, of course, detract from the striking imagery of *Ignis*, nor from the fact that it is a highly original text. Even if the final section was in-

287

spired by Jules Verne's *Hector Servadac*, it seems more modern than that its rival in its acceptance of the fact that the notion of a fragment of the Earth flying away into space, bearing passengers who are not much inconvenienced by the consequences of such an accident, is essentially surreal. That section of the novel—which is, in its way, a remarkable *tour de force*—has much closer links with such similarly-premised *avant-garde* fantasies as William Gerhardi's *Jazz and Jasper* (1928) and John Cowper Powys's "Up and Out" (1952) than it has with Verne or with the parody of *Hector Servadac* contained in Albert Robida's *Saturnin Farandoul*.

It is arguable, however, that the most interesting aspect of *Ignis* from a historical point of view is not its employment of themes linked to other works of proto-science fiction, but its ardent embrace of ideas that were subsequently to be rejected and avoided by science and science fiction alike—but which have, by contrast, become intensely controversial in more recent times as Biblical Fundamentalists have mounted a fervent rearguard action against the corrosion of the account of human history offered in *Genesis* by the discoveries of geology, paleontology and evolutionary biology. If, as some of these unbending advocates of Christian faith believe, there is an alternative to orthodox science worthy of the title "creation science," then *Ignis* is surely *the* great classic of "creation-science fiction," for its fundamental purpose, as a satire and as a polemic, is to attack the corrosion of the Biblical account of human origins by contemporary geologists and evolutionists, and to defend *Genesis* by fighting fire with fire.

It tends to be forgotten nowadays that Jules Verne actually produced two versions of *Voyage au centre de la Terre*, revising his initial text because his principal source, Louis Figuier's *La Terre avant le Déluge* (1863; tr. as *The World Before the Deluge*), had been extensively revised in 1867 and Verne wanted to take account of the revision; it is the second edition of *Voyage au centre de la Terre*, likewise produced in 1867, that is now the standard text (and the basis of all its English translations).

In the first edition of his own book, Figuier had adopted a stance very similar to that of the author of *Ignis*, accepting that the story of *Genesis* was true and attempting to adapt recently-discovered geological and paleontological evidence to that account, and the first version of Verne's novel contained nothing contradictory to that thesis. The second edition of Figuier's book, however, reflected his "conversion" to the conviction that *Genesis* could not be true, and must be construed as an allegory, not merely because the world had to be very much older than *Genesis* implied, but that humankind must have undergone a slow evolution from very remote ancestors. Verne took account of this by introducing one of the most memorable episodes of his novel: the striking passage in which Axel, after finding a giant human jawbone, sees (or, perhaps, dreams that he sees) a primitive human of huge proportions tending a herd of mastodons.

Figuier's conversion, and the subsequent transmutation of Verne's novel, was occasioned by a particular event that the author of *Ignis* mentions twice in his text, and clearly considered important: the discovery by Jacques Boucher de Perthes of a human jawbone in a quarry at Moulin-Quignon, near Abbéville, which occurred too late in 1863 for Figuier to have taken account of it in the first edition of his book. Boucher had been arguing fervently for more than 30 years that hand-worked flints he had found in the same area must be evidence of human habitation—which, if geological estimates of the age of the rocks could be trusted, must mean that humankind had existed long before the beginning of the 6000-year chronology suggested by *Genesis*—but he had not yet convinced his opponents.

The Comte de Buffon and Georges Cuvier had already accepted that the history of the world itself must be much more ancient than 6000 years, and that the six "days" of Biblical creation must each have been tens of thousands of years long, at the least, but that was a minimal concession, and many scholars continued to insist long into the 19th century that the findings of geology and paleontology were still compatible with the account of human origins offered in *Genesis*. Such scholars contended that the apparent evidence of hand-working on Boucher' flints must be accidental, and they had backed up this claim by asserting that if the flints really had been hand-worked, then actual human remains should have been found too; the absence of such remains had become a crucial pivot in the argument, so their actual discovery made a tremendous impact on some waverers—including Figuier—who promptly changed sides, while forcing others—including the author of *Ignis*—to shift their ground, insisting instead that the flints themselves could not be as old as the evidence implied, and must be post-diluvian.

The most ironic twist to this story is that the particular jawbone found by Boucher de Perthes was not what it seemed, having been planted as a hoax, much like the famous skull of "Piltdown man." Genuine human remains were to be found subsequently, not merely in Europe, but in distant parts of the world, gradually accumulating into the basis of a highly elaborate story of human evolution and migration extending back for millions of years to a remote "African genesis;" in the 1870s, however, when *Ignis* was probably written, the evidence of that evolution was still slender, and the author's suspicion of the supposedly-crucial Moulin-Quignon jawbone was not entirely unjustified. Figuier's conversion turned out, in the end, to be a step in the right direction, but it was launched from a shaky foundation, and Verne might well have been wise to leave the possibility open in his own story that what Axel saw might have been a hallucination rather than a reality.

Ignis is by no means the only literary work produced in the 19th century that warrants retrospective consideration as a work of "creation-science fiction." The earlier representatives of that phantom genre would include crucial sequences in Humphry Davy's *Consolations in Travel* (1830) and Robert Hunt's *Panthea* (1849)—the latter having been written before Hunt's conversion to evolutionism and subsequent friendship with Charles Darwin—both of which are more explicit visionary fantasies than *Ignis*. The relative lateness of *Ignis* has to be considered a weakness in terms of the history of scientific orthodoxy, because its author had access to much more evidence than Davy or Hunt, but in terms of literary history it permitted the author to take account of some significant developments in narrative technique as well as to draw inspiration from other models—however much or little he owed to Verne in the exact terms of mundane borrowing and satirical opposition, he was certainly aware of Verne's work and reputation, and that awareness was undoubtedly one of the factors shaping the narrative.

Given the circumstances of its production, and its affiliation to a phantom genre of creation-science fiction, it is not inappropriate that the entire narrative of *Ignis* should ultimately turn out to be a dream, experienced by a man who has gone to sleep with his feet too close to the fireplace. The narrative move in question is nowadays considered unusable, by virtue of being worn out, but it was not only acceptable in its day, but virtually compulsory for the literary dramatization of futuristic and cosmological speculations, which then had no other means of plausible narrative access. Indeed, what is surprising about *Ignis* is not so much that the protagonist wakes up at the end, but that he continues to insist thereafter that his dream cannot have been merely a dream, and that it must have some claim to reality, even though that leads inevitably to the suspicion that he is mad. The end of *Hector Servadac* does not feature any explicit awakening, but it does retain an obvious implication—like the crucial scene added to *Voyage au centre de la Terre*—that Servadac's adventure might not actually have happened, strengthened in that instance by the fact that the world seems to be undisturbed by, and its inhabitants ignorant of, events that could not possibly have left such an absence of effect.

Such ambiguity was not unusual in literary works of the time, as evidenced by the various fantasies by Paul Féval that I have translated for Black Coat Press, all of which were published before *Ignis* and all of which struggle with paradox as they reach their final narrative fade to "reality"—but no such work ever struggled quite so dramatically as *Ignis*, whose real battle with its own epistemological status is not the re-awakened Burton's inability to accept that Samuel Penkenton is not really Cain, but the bizarrely rhapsodic argument presented by James Archibold aboard the "asteroid" hurtling toward the Sun. Although it is juxtaposed with Cain's story and Lord Hotairwell's more orthodox rhapsodic vision, both of which have many more literary analogues, the fact that Archibold's rant comes after them, thus providing that fraction of the story with its finale, is significant of its importance. If only Burton were not such a down-to-earth sort of fellow, apparently too dull to experience such visions himself—but only apparently, since Archibold is an artifact of his dream—he would surely have been prepared to take his ultimate stand with Archibold and Pyrrho in asserting that the only thing he could *really* be sure of, as regards his experience, was that he could not be sure of anything, and that the only intellectually-respectable position for him to adopt with respect to his vision of a past that might have been (in more than one sense) was that of *acatalepsia* coupled with *ataraxia*.

We do, of course, need to remember that the account of Archibold's final rhapsody is scathingly sarcastic, and that Burton's creator, being a man of faith, is steadfastly opposed to skepticism, but his very terror of it is revealing, and he is certainly not averse to using skeptical arguments when they suit him. He was not the only Swiftian satirist to emulate his model so wholeheartedly as to end up tacitly cutting the ground from his own feet as well as his opponents', despite his initial commitment to its solidity. At the end of the day, though, Archibold *was* correct, however crazy the conclusion seemed, to conclude that what was happening to him could not be real, because rational consideration proved, beyond a sha-dow of a doubt, that it was not. If the characters in other works of imaginative fiction were capable of such rigor, their pre-tences of actuality might be reckoned a little more honest—but the author of *Ignis* is also correct in contending that the manifest evidence of a story has to be taken seriously, in spite of any impossibility it might contain, and that even if it has, in the end, to be written off as a crazy dream, it can still provide an authentic aliment of thought.

On that basis, because rather than despite its flamboyant absurdity, *Ignis* deserves to be reckoned a fine book. The virtual non-existence of the genre to which it belongs in terms of rational classification only provides further support for its classic status within that genre.

I promised in one of the footnotes to take up consideration of the reasons why the author might have employed the seemingly-inappropriate term Atmophytes (i.e. "steam-plants") for his "steam men." In retrospect, Lord Hotairwell's choice—Enginemen—seems more appropriate, and it might not be obvious to the modern reader why the author of *Ignis* would not endorse that coinage himself. The fact is, however, that—notwithstanding the etymological joke included to demonstrate the synonymity of "Enginemen" and "Englishmen"—"Enginemen" is a hybrid term, the first component being derived from the Latin *ingenium* while the second is Anglo-Saxon. No Classically-educated individual, especially a Frenchman, could find such a hybrid anything other than abhorrent, and it is not surprising that the author of *Ignis* could not bring himself to entertain it for more than a moment, although he is quite willing to attribute it to a character of whose theoretical views he disapproves. As soon as he tried to find a substitute for it, however, problems set in.

Because the author's first recourse, when coining new terms, is always to the Greek, his inevitable instinct is to back-translate "steam" as the prefix *atmo-*, but that has the disadvantage of ending in a vowel, while the Greek term for human being, *anthropos*, begins with one. The "correct" term for a "steam man" would therefore be *atmoanthropos*, which is undeniably awkward and definitely does not trip off the tongue even in the singular; in the plural—and the demands of the story require that the relevant term is almost invariably used in the plural—it becomes a tongue-twisting nightmare. Given his total lack of respect for the female of the species, the author of *Ignis* might have been momentarily tempted to employ the Greek term for "man" in the narrower sense, but that is *andros*, which is no better. A measure of feminist sympathy might have led him to see the advantage of "atmogynes," but he was unable to allocate his "female machines" any other role but those of seamstresses and charwomen, so the opportunity to use the term for the whole gamut of laborers was lost.

At any rate, in order to have a nice ring to it, the second part of the portmanteau term needed to start with a consonant, and it needed to end with a phoneme on to which the letter *s* could conveniently be appended—and that, I believe, is why the author of *Ignis* picked a suffix which, although it is certainly peculiar in terms of its meaning, leaves little to be desired in terms of euphony. He could have used the suffix meaning "animal" rather than the one meaning "plant," thus making "atmozoon" rather than "atmophyte," but any slight advantage is relevance would have been outweighed by an equal disadvantage in euphony.

It might be worth noting, further to this point, that the author of *Ignis* was not the only French writer of scientific romance to run into problems of this sort, and that writers in English have a distinct advantage in simply being able to stick "man" on the end of all sorts of compounds, not only because it begins with a hard consonant but because it forms a convenient plural in "men." Thus, for instance, the English "superman" and the German *übermensch* have an entirely appropriate robust quality that is absent from the French *surhomme*. Admittedly, one of the pioneers of French scientific romance, Han Ryner, did consent to write a novel entitled *Les Surhommes* (1929), but Ryner was a devout pacifist who was wholeheartedly in favor of mildness as a key characteristic of humankind's successors; Alfred Jarry, who was not, titled his own superman novel *Le Surmâle* [The Supermale] (1902).

Pierre Versins, in his encyclopedia, could hardly have avoided including an article entitled "Surhomme," but it is notable that the first literary character he can discover who is explicitly identified by that term, Honoré de Balzac's Louis Lambert (in the eponymous novella of 1832), is even more of a wimp than Ryner's pacifists, and that the first example of the term's use in a title, André Couvreur's *Caresco, surhomme* (1904), is sarcastic, its application being to a mad scientist. The protagonist of George Lebas' *Jean Arlog, le premier surhomme* (1921) certainly does not lack ambition, but there is more than a hint of madness in his aspiration to become a god by means of the power of positive thinking. Hélène Pittard, who wrote as Noëlle Roger, titled her detailed study of the possibility of superhumanity *Le Nouvel Adam* (1924)— although that did, admittedly, fit a pattern in her oeuvre, which also included *Le Nouveau Déluge* and *Le Nouveau Lazare*. Is it permissible, in view of this evidence, to wonder whether the noticeably greater Anglo-American and German literary fascination with supermen and *übermensch* might owe as much to etymological vigor as to national inclination—or even, perhaps, that national inclination might turn on something as trivial as the essential weakness of an aspirate? It is a matter on which, I think, the only intellectually-respectable thing to do, especially for a man who is not arch-bold, is to remain undecided.

IGNIS. — Les Atmophiles, en pleine révolte, envahissant la ville.

BLACK COAT PRESS

Gustave Le Rouge. *The Vampires of Mars*
Jules Lermina. *Panic in Paris*
Gaston Leroux. *Chéri-Bibi*
Gaston Leroux. *The Phantom of the Opera*
Jean-Marc Lofficier. *The Katrina Protocol*
Jean-Marc & Randy Lofficier. *Edgar Allan Poe on Mars*
Jean-Marc & Randy Lofficier. *Robonocchio*
Lofficier. *Tales of the Shadowmen 1: The Modern Babylon*
Lofficier. *Tales of the Shadowmen 2: Gentlemen of the Night*
Lofficier. *Tales of the Shadowmen 3: Danse Macabre*
Lofficier. *Tales of the Shadowmen 4: Lords of Terror*
Lofficier. *Tales of the Shadowmen 5: The Vampires of Paris*
Xavier Mauméjean. *The League of Heroes*
William Patrick Maynard. *The Terror of Fu Manchu*
Frank J. Morlock. *Sherlock Holmes: The Grand Horizontals*
Marie Nizet. *Captain Vampire*
C. Nodier, Beraud & Toussaint-Merle. *Frankenstein*
Charles Nodier. *Lord Ruthven the Vampire*
G. de Pawlowski. *Journey to the Land of the 4th Dimension*
Henri de Parville. *An Inhabitant of the Planet Mars*
John William Polidori. *Lord Ruthven the Vampire*
P.-A. Ponson du Terrail. *The Vampire and the Devil's Son*
Albert Robida. *The Clock of the Centuries*
Eugène Scribe. *Lord Ruthven the Vampire*
Brian Stableford. *The Germans on Venus*
Brian Stableford. *News from the Moon*
Brian Stableford. *The New Faust at the Tragicomique*
Brian Stableford. *The Shadow of Frankenstein*
Brian Stableford. *Sherlock Holmes - The Vampires of Eternity*
Brian Stableford. *The Stones of Camelot*
Brian Stableford. *The Wayward Muse*
Villiers de l'Isle-Adam. *The Scaffold*
Villiers de l'Isle-Adam. *The Vampire Soul*
Philippe Ward. *Artahe: The Legacy of Jules de Grandin*
P. de Wattyne & Y. Walter. *Sherlock Holmes vs. Fantômas*
David White: *Fantômas in America*